JESS

JESS

H. Rider Haggard

HUTCHINSON LIBRARY SERVICES

HUTCHINSON LIBRARY SERVICES LTD
3 Fitzroy Square, London W1

London Melbourne Sydney Auckland
Wellington Johannesburg Cape Town
and agencies throughout the world

First published in 1887
This edition 1972

Printed in Great Britain by litho on antique wove paper
by Anchor Press, and bound by Wm. Brendon,
both of Tiptree, Essex

ISBN 0 09 112480 8

DEDICATION

———✦———

TO MY WIFE

LONDON:

December 31, 1885.

CONTENTS

JESS

CHAPTER I

JOHN HAS AN ADVENTURE

THE day had been very hot even for the Transvaal, where
the days still know how to be hot in the autumn, although
the neck of the summer is broken—especially when the
thunderstorms hold off for a week or two, as they do
occasionally. Even the succulent blue lilies—a variety
of the agapanthus which is so familiar to us in English
greenhouses—hung their long trumpet-shaped flowers
and looked oppressed and miserable, beneath the burning
breath of the hot wind which had been blowing for hours
like the draught from a volcano. The grass, too, near
the wide roadway that stretched in a feeble and indeter-
minate fashion across the veldt, forking, branching, and
reuniting like the veins on a lady's arm, was completely
coated over with a thick layer of red dust. But the hot
wind was going down now, as it always does towards
sunset. Indeed, all that remained of it were a few
strictly local and miniature whirlwinds, which would
suddenly spring up on the road itself, and twist and twirl
fiercely round, raising a mighty column of dust fifty feet
or more into the air, where it hung long after the wind had

passed, and then slowly dissolved as its particles floated to the earth.

Advancing along the road, in the immediate track of one of these desultory and inexplicable whirlwinds, was a man on horseback. The man looked limp and dirty, and the horse limper and dirtier. The hot wind had 'taken all the bones out of them,' as the Kafirs say, which was not very much to be wondered at, seeing that they had been journeying through it for the last four hours without offsaddling. Suddenly the whirlwind, which had been travelling along smartly, halted, and the dust, after revolving a few times in the air like a dying top, slowly began to disperse in the accustomed fashion. The man on the horse halted also, and contemplated it in an absent kind of way.

'It's just like a man's life,' he said aloud to his horse, 'coming from nobody knows where, nobody knows why, and making a little column of dust on the world's highway, then passing away, leaving the dust to fall to the ground again, to be trodden under foot and forgotten.'

The speaker, a stout, well set-up, rather ugly man, apparently on the wrong side of thirty, with pleasant blue eyes and a reddish peaked beard, laughed a little at his own sententious reflection, and then gave his jaded horse a tap with the sjambock in his hand.

'Come on, Blesbok,' he said, 'or we shall never get to old Croft's place to-night. By Jove! I believe that must be the turn,' and he pointed with his whip to a little rutty track that branched from the Wakkerstroom main road and stretched away towards a curious isolated hill with a large flat top, which rose out of the rolling plain some four miles to the right. 'The old Boer said the second turn,' he went on still talking to himself, 'but perhaps he lied. I am told that some of them think it a good joke to send an Englishman a few miles wrong. Let's see, they told me the place was under the lee of a table-topped hill, about half an hour's ride from the main road, and that is a table-topped hill, so I think I will try it. Come on, Blesbok,' and he put the tired nag into a sort of ' tripple ' or ambling canter much affected by South African horses.

' Life is a queer thing,' reflected Captain John Niel to himself as he cantered along slowly. ' Now here am I, at the age of thirty-four, about to begin the world again as assistant to an old Transvaal farmer. It is a pretty end to all one's ambitions, and to fourteen years' work in the army ; but it is what it has come to, my boy, so you had better make the best of it.'

Just then his cogitations were interrupted, for on the farther side of a gentle slope suddenly there appeared an extraordinary sight. Over the crest of the rise of land, now some four or five hundred yards away, a pony with a lady on its back galloped wildly, and after it, with wings spread and outstretched neck, a huge cock ostrich was speeding in pursuit, covering twelve or fifteen feet at every stride of its long legs. The pony was still twenty yards ahead of the bird, and travelling towards John rapidly, but strive as it would it could not distance the swiftest thing on all the earth. Five seconds passed —the great bird was close alongside now—Ah ! and John Niel turned sick and shut his eyes as he rode, for he saw the ostrich's thick leg fly high into the air and then sweep down like a leaded bludgeon !

Thud ! It had missed the lady and struck her horse upon the spine, just behind the saddle, for the moment completely paralysing it so that it fell all of a heap on to the veldt. In a moment the girl on its back was up and running towards him, and after her came the ostrich. Up went the great leg again, but before it could come crashing across her shoulders she had flung herself face downwards on the grass. In an instant the huge bird was on the top of her, kicking at her, rolling over her, and crushing the very life out of her. It was at this juncture that John Niel arrived upon the scene. The moment the ostrich saw him it gave up its attacks upon the lady on the ground and began to waltz towards him with the pompous sort of step that these birds sometimes assume before they give battle. Now Captain Niel was unaccustomed to the pleasant ways of ostriches, and so was his horse, which showed a strong inclination to bolt; as, indeed, under other circumstances, his rider would have been glad to do himself. But he could not abandon beauty in distress, so, finding it impossible to control his horse, he slipped off it, and with the sjambock or hide-whip in his hand valiantly faced the enemy. For a moment or two the great bird stood still, blinking its lustrous round eyes at him and gently swaying its graceful neck to and fro.

Then all of a sudden it spread out its wings and came for him like a thunderbolt. John sprang to one side, and was aware of a rustle of rushing feathers, and of a vision of a thick leg striking downwards past his head. Fortunately it missed him, and the ostrich sped on like a flash. Before he could turn, however, it was back and had landed the full weight of one of its awful forward kicks on the broad of his shoulders, and away he went head-over-heels like a shot rabbit. In a second he was on his legs again, shaken indeed, but not much the worse, and perfectly mad with fury and pain. At him came the ostrich, and at the ostrich went he, catching it a blow across the slim neck with his sjambock that staggered it for a moment. Profiting by the check, he seized the bird by the wing and held on like grim death with both hands. Now they began to gyrate, slowly at first, then quicker, and yet more quick, till at last it seemed to Captain John Niel that time and space and the solid earth were nothing but a revolving vision fixed somewhere in the watches of the night. Above him, like a stationary pivot, towered the tall graceful neck, beneath him spun the top-like legs, and in front of him was a soft black and white mass of feathers.

Thud, and a cloud of stars! He was on his back, and the ostrich, which did not seem to be affected by giddiness, was on *him*, punishing him dreadfully. Luckily an ostrich cannot kick a man very hard when he is flat on the ground. If he could, there would have been an end of John Niel, and his story need never have been written.

Half a minute or so passed, during which the bird worked his sweet will upon his prostrate enemy, and at the end of it the man began to feel very much as though his earthly career was closed. Just as things were growing faint and dim to him, however, he suddenly saw a pair of white arms clasp themselves round the ostrich's legs from behind, and heard a voice cry :

'Break his neck while I hold his legs, or he will kill you.'

This roused him from his torpor, and he staggered to his feet. Meanwhile the ostrich and the young lady had come to the ground, and were rolling about together in a confused heap, over which the elegant neck and open hissing mouth wavered to and fro like a cobra about to strike. With a rush John seized the neck in both his hands, and, putting out all his strength (for he was a strong man), he twisted it till it broke with a snap, and after a few wild and convulsive bounds and struggles the great bird lay dead.

Then he sank down dazed and exhausted, and surveyed the scene. The ostrich was perfectly quiet, and would never kick again, and the lady too was quiet. He wondered vaguely if the brute had killed her—he was as yet too weak to go and see—and then fell to gazing at her face. Her head was pillowed on the body of the dead bird, and its feathery plumes made it a fitting resting-place. Slowly it dawned on him that the face was very beautiful, although it looked so pale just now. Low broad brow, crowned with soft yellow hair, the chin very round and white, the mouth sweet though rather large. The eyes he could not see, because they were closed, for the lady had fainted. For the rest, she was quite young—about twenty, tall and finely formed. Presently he felt a little better, and, creeping towards her (for he was sadly knocked about), took her hand and began to chafe it between his own. It was a well-formed hand, but brown, and showed signs of doing plenty of hard work. Soon she opened her eyes, and he noted with satisfaction that they were very good eyes, blue in colour. Then she sat up and laughed a little.

'Well, I am silly,' she said; 'I believe I fainted.'

'It is not much to be wondered at,' said John Niel politely, and lifting his hand to take off his hat, only to find that it had gone in the fray. 'I hope you are not very much hurt by the bird.'

'I don't know,' she said doubtfully. 'But I am glad that you killed the *skellum* (vicious beast). He got out of the ostrich camp three days ago, and has been lost ever since. He killed a boy last year, and I told uncle he ought to shoot him then, but he would not, because he was such a beauty.'

'Might I ask,' said John Niel, 'are you Miss Croft?'

' Yes, I am—one of them. There are two of us, you know ; and I can guess who you are—you are Captain Niel, whom uncle is expecting to help him with the farm and the ostriches.'

' If all of them are like that,' he said, pointing to the dead bird, ' I don't think that I shall take kindly to ostrich farming.'

She laughed, showing a charming line of teeth. ' Oh no,' she said, ' he was the only bad one—but, Captain Niel, I think you will find it fearfully dull. There are nothing but Boers about here, you know. No English people live nearer than Wakkerstroom.'

' You overlook yourself,' he said, bowing ; for really this daughter of the wilderness had a very charming air about her.

' Oh,' she answered, ' I am only a girl, you know, and besides, I am not clever. Jess, now—that's my sister— Jess has been at school at Capetown, and she *is* clever. I was at Cape Town, too, though I didn't learn much there. But, Captain Niel, both the horses have bolted ; mine has gone home, and I expect yours has followed, and I should like to know how we are going to get up to Mooifontein—beautiful fountain, that's what we call our place, you know. Can you walk ? '

' I don't know,' he answered doubtfully ; ' I'll try. That bird has knocked me about a good deal,' and accordingly he staggered on to his legs, only to collapse with an exclamation of pain. His ankle was sprained, and he was so stiff and bruised that he could hardly stir. ' How far is the house ? ' he asked.

' Only about a mile—just there ; we shall see it from the crest of the rise. Look, I'm all right. It was silly to faint, but he kicked all the breath out of me,' and she got up and danced a little on the grass to show him.

'My word, though, I am sore! You must take my arm, that's all; that is if you don't mind?'

'Oh dear no, indeed, I don't mind,' he said laughing; and so they started, arm affectionately linked in arm.

CHAPTER II

HOW THE SISTERS CAME TO MOOIFONTEIN

'CAPTAIN NIEL,' said Bessie Croft—for she was named
Bessie—when they had painfully limped one hundred
yards or so, 'will you think me rude if I ask you a
question?'

'Not at all.'

'What has induced you to come and bury yourself in
this place?"

'Why do you ask?'

'Because I don't think that you will like it. I don't
think,' she added slowly, 'that it is a fit place for an
English gentleman and an army officer like you. You
will find the Boer ways horrid, and then there will only
be my old uncle and us two for you to associate with.'

John Niel laughed. 'English gentlemen are not so particular nowadays, I can assure you, Miss Croft, especially
when they have to earn a living. Take my case, for
instance, for I may as well tell you exactly how I stand.
I have been in the army fourteen years, and I am now
thirty-four. Well, I have been able to live there because
I had an old aunt who allowed me 120*l.* a year. Six
months ago she died, leaving me the little property she
possessed, for most of her income came from an annuity.
After paying expenses, duty, &c., it amounts to 1,115*l.*
Now, the interest on this is about fifty pounds a year,

and I can't live in the army on that. Just after my aunt's death I came to Durban with my regiment from Mauritius, and now they are ordered home. Well, I liked the country, and I knew that I could not afford to live in England, so I got a year's leave of absence, and made up my mind to have a look round to see if I could not take to farming. Then a gentleman in Durban told me of your uncle, and said that he wanted to dispose of a third interest in his place for a thousand pounds, as he was getting too old to manage it himself. So I entered into correspondence with him, and agreed to come up for a few months to see how I liked it; and accordingly here I am, just in time to save you from being knocked to bits by an ostrich.'

'Yes, indeed,' she answered, laughing; 'you've had a warm welcome at any rate. Well, I hope you *will* like it.'

Just as he finished his story they reached the top of the rise over which the ostrich had pursued Bessie Croft, and saw a Kafir coming towards them, leading the pony with one hand and Captain Niel's horse with the other. About twenty yards behind the horses a lady was walking.

'Ah,' said Bessie, 'they've caught the horses, and here is Jess come to see what is the matter.'

By this time the lady in question was quite close, so that John was able to gather a first impression of her. She was small and rather thin, with quantities of curling brown hair; not by any means a lovely woman, as her sister undoubtedly was, but possessing two very remarkable characteristics—a complexion of extraordinary and uniform pallor, and a pair of the most beautiful dark eyes he had ever looked on. Altogether, though her size was almost insignificant, she was a striking-looking person, with a face few men would easily forget. Before he had time to observe any more the two parties had met.

' What on earth is the matter, Bessie ? ' Jess said, with a quick glance at her sister's companion, and speaking in a low full voice, with just a slight South African accent, that is taking enough in a pretty woman. Thereon Bessie broke out with a history of their adventure, appealing to Captain Niel for confirmation at intervals.

Meanwhile Jess Croft stood quite still and silent, and it struck John that her face was the most singularly impassive one he had ever seen. It never changed, even when her sister told how the ostrich rolled on her and nearly killed her, or how they finally subdued the foe. ' Dear me,' he thought to himself, ' what a very strange woman ! She can't have much heart.' But just as he thought it the girl looked up, and then he saw where the expression lay. It was in those remarkable eyes. Immovable as was her face, the dark eyes were alight with life and a suppressed excitement that made them shine gloriously. The contrast between the shining eyes and the impassive face beneath them struck him as so extraordinary as to be almost uncanny. As a matter of fact, it was doubtless both unusual and remarkable.

' You have had a wonderful escape, but I am sorry for the bird,' she said at last.

' Why ? ' asked John.

' Because we were great friends. I was the only person who could manage him.'

' Yes,' put in Bessie, ' the savage brute would follow her about like a dog. It was just the oddest thing I ever saw. But come on ; we must be getting home, it's growing dark. Mouti '—which, being interpreted, means Medicine—she added, addressing the Kafir in Zulu— ' help Captain Niel on to his horse. Be careful that the saddle does not twist round ; the girths may be loose.'

Thus adjured, John, with the help of the Zulu, clambered into his saddle, an example that the lady quickly followed, and they set off once more through the gathering darkness. Presently he became aware that they were passing up a drive bordered by tall blue gums, and next minute the barking of a large dog, which he afterwards knew by the name of Stomp, and the sudden appearance of lighted windows told him that they had reached the house. At the door—or rather, opposite to it, for there was a verandah in front—they halted and got off their horses. As they dismounted there came a shout of welcome from the house, and presently in the doorway, showing out clearly against the light, appeared a striking and, in its way, a most pleasant figure. He—for it was a man—was very tall, or, rather, he had been very tall. Now he was much bent with age and rheumatism. His long white hair hung low upon his neck, and fell back from a prominent brow. The top of the head was quite bald, like the tonsure of a priest, and shone and glistened in the lamplight, and round this oasis the thin white locks fell down. The face was shrivelled like the surface of a well-kept apple, and, like an apple, rosy red. The features were aquiline and strongly marked; the eyebrows still black and very bushy, and beneath them shone a pair of grey eyes, keen and bright as those of a hawk. But for all its sharpness, there was nothing unpleasant or fierce about the face; on the contrary, it was pervaded by a remarkable air of good-nature and pleasant shrewdness. For the rest, the man was dressed in rough tweed clothes, tall riding-boots, and held a broad-brimmed Boer hunting-hat in his hand. Such, as John Niel first saw him, was the outer person of old Silas Croft, one of the most remarkable men in the Transvaal.

'Is that you, Captain Niel?' roared out the stentorian

voice. 'The natives said you were coming. A welcome to you! I am glad to see you—very glad. Why, what is the matter with you?' he went on as the Zulu Mouti ran to help him off his horse.

'Matter, Mr. Croft?' answered John; 'why, the matter is that your favourite ostrich has nearly killed me and your niece here, and that I have killed your favourite ostrich.'

Then followed explanations from Bessie, during which he was helped off his horse and into the house.

'It serves me right,' said the old man. 'To think of it now, just to think of it! Well, Bessie, my love, thank God that you escaped—ay, and you too, Captain Niel. Here, you boys, take the Scotch cart and a couple of oxen and go and fetch the brute home. We may as well have the feathers off him, at any rate, before the aasvögels (vultures) tear him to bits.'

After he had washed himself and tended his injuries with arnica and water, John managed to limp into the principal sitting-room, where supper was waiting. It was a very pleasant room, furnished in European style, and carpeted with mats made of springbuck skins. In the corner stood a piano, and by it a bookcase, filled with the works of standard authors, the property, as John rightly guessed, of Bessie's sister Jess.

Supper went off pleasantly enough, and after it was over the two girls sang and played whilst the men smoked. And here a fresh surprise awaited him, for after Bessie, who apparently had now almost recovered from her mauling, had played a piece or two creditably enough, Jess, who so far had been nearly silent, sat down at the piano. She did not do this willingly, indeed, for it was not until her patriarchal uncle had insisted in his ringing, cheery voice that she should let Captain Niel hear how she could sing that she consented. But at last she did consent, and then, after letting her fingers stray somewhat aimlessly along the chords, she suddenly broke out into such song as John Niel had never heard before. Her voice, beautiful as it was, was not what is known as a cultivated voice, and it was a German song, therefore he did not understand it, but there was no need of words to translate its burden. Passion, despairing yet hoping through despair, echoed in its every line, and love, unending love, hovered over the glorious notes—nay, possessed them like a spirit, and made them his. Up! up! rang her wild sweet voice, thrilling his nerves till they answered to the music as an Æolian harp answers to the winds. On went the song with a divine sweep, like the sweep of rushing pinions ; higher, yet higher it soared, lifting up the listener's heart far above the world on the trembling wings of sound—ay, even higher, till the music hung at heaven's gate, and falling thence, swiftly as an eagle falls, quivered, and was dead.

John sighed, and, so strongly was he moved, sank back in his chair, feeling almost faint with the revulsion of feeling that ensued when the notes had died away. He looked up, and saw Bessie watching him with an air of curiosity and amusement. Jess was still leaning against the piano, and gently touching the notes, over which her head was bent low, showing the coils of curling hair that were twisted round it like a coronet.

'Well, Captain Niel,' said the old man, waving his pipe in her direction, 'and what do you say to my singing-bird's music, eh? Isn't it enough to draw the heart out of a man, eh, and turn his marrow to water, eh ?'

'I never heard anything quite like it,' he answered simply, 'and I have heard most singers. It is beautiful.

Certainly, I never expected to hear such singing in the Transvaal.'

Jess turned quickly, and he observed that, though her eyes were alight with excitement, her face was as impassive as ever.

'There is no need for you to laugh at me, Captain Niel,' she said quickly, and then, with an abrupt ' Good-night,' she left the room.

The old man smiled, jerked the stem of his pipe over his shoulder after her, and winked in a way that, no doubt, meant unutterable things, but which did not convey much to his astonished guest, who sat still and said nothing. Then Bessie rose and bade him good-night in her pleasant voice, and with housewifely care inquired as to whether his room was to his taste, and how many blankets he liked upon his bed, telling him that if he found the odour of the moonflowers which grew near the verandah too strong, he had better shut the right-hand window and open that on the other side of the room. Then at length, with a piquant little nod of her golden head, she went off, looking, John thought as he watched her retreating figure, about as healthy, graceful, and generally satisfactory a young woman as a man could wish to see.

'Take a glass of grog, Captain Niel,' said the old man, pushing the square bottle towards him, 'you'll need it after the mauling that brute gave you. By the way, I haven't thanked you enough for saving my Bessie! But I do thank you, yes, that I do. I must tell you that Bessie is my favourite niece. Never was there such a girl—never. Moves like a springbuck, and what an eye and form! Work too—she'll do as much work as three. There's no nonsense about Bessie, none at all. She's not a fine lady, for all her fine looks.'

'The two sisters seem very different,' said John.

'Ay, you're right there,' answered the old man. 'You'd never think that the same blood ran in their veins, would you? There's three years between them, that's one thing. Bessie's the youngest, you see—she's just twenty, and Jess is twenty-three. Lord, to think that it is twenty-three years since that girl was born! And theirs is a queer story too.'

'Indeed?' said his listener interrogatively.

'Ay,' Silas went on absently, knocking out his pipe, and refilling it from a big brown jar of coarse-cut Boer tobacco, 'I'll tell it to you if you like: you are going to live in the house, and you may as well know it. I am sure, Captain Niel, that it will go no further. You see I was born in England, yes, and well-born too. I come from Cambridgeshire—from the fat fen-land down round Ely. My father was a clergyman. Well, he wasn't rich, and when I was twenty he gave me his blessing, thirty sovereigns in my pocket, and my passage to the Cape; and I shook his hand, God bless him, and off I came, and here in the old colony and this country I have been for fifty years, for I was seventy yesterday. Well, I'll tell you more about that another time, it's of the girls I'm speaking now. After I left home—some years after —my dear old father married again, a youngish woman with some money, but rather beneath him in life, and by her he had one son, and then died. Well, it was but little I heard of my half-brother, except that he had turned out very badly, married, and taken to drink, till one night some twelve years ago, when a strange thing happened. I was sitting here in this very room, ay, in this very chair—for this part of the house was up then, though the wings weren't built—smoking my pipe, and listening to the lashing of the rain, for it was a very foul night, when suddenly an old pointer dog I had, named Ben, began to bark.

' "Lie down, Ben, it's only the Kafirs," said I.

'Just then I thought I heard a faint sort of rapping at the door, and Ben barked again, so I got up and opened it, and in came two little girls wrapped in old shawls or some such gear. Well, I shut the door, looking first to see if there were any more outside, and then I turned and stared at the two little things with my mouth open. There they stood, hand in hand, the water dripping from both of them ; the elder might have been eleven, and the second about eight years old. They didn't say anything, but the elder turned and took the shawl and hat off the younger—that was Bessie—and there was her sweet little face and her golden hair, and damp enough both of them were, and she put her thumb in her mouth, and stood and looked at me till I began to think that I was dreaming.

' "Please, sir," said the taller at last, "is this Mr. Croft's house—Mr. Croft—South African Republic ? "

' "Yes, little Miss, this is his house, and this is the South African Republic, and I am he. And now who might you be, my dears ? " I answered.

' "If you please, sir, we are your nieces, and we have come to you from England."

' "What ! " I holloaed, startled out of my wits, as well I might be.

' "Oh, sir," says the poor little thing, clasping her thin wet hands, "please don't send us away. Bessie is so wet, and cold and hungry too, she isn't fit to go any farther."

'And she set to work to cry, whereon the little one cried also, from fright and cold and sympathy.

'Well, of course, I took them both to the fire, and

set them on my knees, and called for Hebe, the old
Hottentot woman who did my cooking, and between us
we undressed them, and wrapped them up in some old
clothes, and fed them with soup and wine, so that in half
an hour they were quite happy and not a bit frightened.

'"And now, young ladies," I said, "come and give me
a kiss, both of you, and tell me how you came here."

'This is the tale they told me—completed, of course,
from what I learnt afterwards—and an odd one it is.
It seems that my half-brother married a Norfolk lady—
a sweet young thing—and treated her like a dog. He
was a drunken rascal, was my half-brother, and he
beat his poor wife and shamefully neglected her, and
even ill-used the two little girls, till at last the poor
woman, weak as she was from suffering and ill health,
could bear it no longer, and formed the wild idea of
escaping to this country and of throwing herself upon my
protection. That shows how desperate she must have
been. She scraped together and borrowed some money,
enough to pay for three second-class passages to Natal
and a few pounds over, and one day, when her brute of
a husband was away on the drink and gamble, she
slipped on board a sailing ship in the London Docks, and
before he knew anything about it they were well out to
sea. But it was her last effort, poor dear soul, and the
excitement of it finished her. Before they had been ten
days at sea, she sank and died, and the two little children
were left alone. What they must have suffered, or
rather what poor Jess must have suffered, for she was
old enough to feel, God only knows, but I can tell you
this, she has never got over the shock to this hour. It
has left its mark on her, sir. Still, let people say what
they will, there is a Power who looks after the helpless,
and that Power took those poor, homeless, wandering

children under its wing. The captain of the vessel befriended them, and when at last they reached Durban some of the passengers made a subscription, and paid an old Boer, who was coming up this way with his wife to the Transvaal, to take them under his charge. The Boer and his vrouw treated the children fairly well, but they did not do one thing more than they bargained for. At the turn from the Wakkerstroom road, that you came along to-day, they put the girls down, for they had no luggage with them, and told them that if they went along there they would come to Meinheer Croft's house. That was in the middle of the afternoon, and they were till eight o'clock getting here, poor little dears, for the track was fainter then than it is now, and they wandered off into the veldt, and would have perished there in the wet and cold had they not chanced to see the lights of the house. That was how my nieces came here, Captain Niel, and here they have been ever since, except for a couple of years when I sent them to the Cape for schooling, and a lonely man I was when they were away.'

'And how about the father?' asked John Niel, deeply interested. 'Did you ever hear any more of him?'

'Hear of him, the villain!' almost shouted the old man, jumping up in wrath. 'Ay, d—n him, I heard of him. What do you think? The two chicks had been with me some eighteen months, long enough for me to learn to love them with all my heart, when one fine morning, as I was seeing about the new kraal wall, I saw a fellow come riding up on an old raw-boned grey horse. Up he comes to me, and as he came I looked at him, and said to myself, "You are a drunkard you are, and a rogue, it's written on your face, and, what's more, I

know your face." You see I did not guess that it was
a son of my own father that I was looking at. How
should I?

'"Is your name Croft?" he said.

'"Ay," I answered.

'"So is mine," he went on with a sort of a drunken
leer. "I'm your brother."

'"Are you?" I said, beginning to get my back up, for
I guessed what his game was, "and what may you be
after? I tell you at once, and to your face, that if you
are my brother you are a blackguard, and I don't want to
know you or have anything to do with you; and if you
are not, I beg your pardon for coupling you with such a
scoundrel."

'"Oh, that's your tune, is it?" he said with a sneer.
"Well, now, my dear brother Silas, I want my children.
They have got a little half-brother at home—for I have
married again, Silas—who is anxious to have them to
play with, so if you will be so good as to hand them over,
I'll take them away at once."

'"You'll take them away, will you?" said I, all of a
tremble with rage and fear.

'"Yes, Silas, I will. They are mine by law, and I
am not going to breed children for you to have the
comfort of their society. I've taken advice, Silas, and
that's sound law," and he leered at me again.

'I stood and looked at that man, and thought of how
he had treated those poor children and their young
mother, and my blood boiled, and I grew mad. Without
another word I jumped over the half-finished wall, and
caught him by the leg (for I was a strong man ten years
ago) and jerked him off the horse. As he came down he
dropped the sjambock from his hand, and I laid hold
of it and then and there gave him the soundest hiding a

man ever had. Lord, how he did holloa! When I was tired I let him get up.

'"Now," I said, "be off with you, and if you come back here I'll bid the Kafirs hunt you to Natal with their sticks. This is the South African Republic, and we don't care overmuch about law here." Which we didn't in those days.

'"All right, Silas," he said, "all right, you shall pay for this. I'll have those children, and, for your sake, I'll make their lives a hell—you mark my words—South African Republic or no South African Republic. I've got the law on my side."

'Off he rode, cursing and swearing, and I flung his sjambock after him. This was the first and last time that I saw my brother.'

'What became of him?' asked John Niel.

'I'll tell you, just to show you again that there is a Power which keeps such men in its eye. He rode back to Newcastle that night, and went about the canteen there abusing me, and getting drunker and drunker, till at last the canteen keeper sent for his boys to turn him out. Well, the boys were rough, as Kafirs are apt to be with a drunken white man, and he struggled and fought, and in the middle of it the blood began to run from his mouth, and he dropped down dead of a broken blood-vessel, and there was an end of him. That is the story of the two girls, Captain Niel, and now I am off to bed. To-morrow I'll show you round the farm, and we will have a talk about business. Good-night to you, Captain Niel. Goodnight!'

CHAPTER III

MR. FRANK MULLER

JOHN NIEL woke early the next morning, feeling as sore and stiff as though he had been well beaten and then strapped up tight in horse-girths. He made shift, however, to dress himself, and then, with the help of a stick, limped through the French windows that opened from his room on to the verandah, and surveyed the scene before him. It was a delightful spot. At the back of the stead was the steep boulder-strewn face of the flat-topped hill that curved round on each side, embosoming a great slope of green, in the lap of which the house was placed. It was very solidly built of brown stone, and, with the exception of the waggon-shed and other outbuildings which were roofed with galvanised iron, that shone and glistened in the rays of the morning sun in a way that would have made an eagle blink, was covered with rich brown thatch. All along its front ran a wide verandah, up the trellis-work of which green vines and blooming creepers trailed pleasantly, and beyond was the broad carriage-drive of red soil, bordered with bushy orange-trees laden with odorous flowers and green and golden fruit. On the farther side of the orange-trees were the gardens, fenced in with low walls of rough stone, and the orchard planted with standard fruit-trees, and beyond these again the oxen and ostrich kraals, the latter full of long-necked birds. To the right of the house grew thriving plantations of blue-gum and black wattle, and to the left was a broad stretch of cultivated lands, lying so that they could be irrigated for winter crops by means of water led from the great spring that gushed out of the mountain-side high above the house, and gave its name of Mooifontein to the place.

All these and many more things John Neil saw as he looked out from the verandah at Mooifontein, but for the moment at any rate they were lost in the wild and wonderful beauty of the panorama that rolled away for miles and miles at his feet, till it was bounded by the mighty range of the Drakensberg to the left, tipped here and there with snow, and by the dim and vast horizon of the swelling Transvaal plains to the right and far in front of him. It was a beautiful sight, and one to make the blood run in a man's veins, and his heart beat happily because he was alive to see it. Mile upon mile of grass clothed veldt beneath, bending and rippling like a corn-field in the quick breath of the morning, space upon space of deep-blue sky overhead with ne'er a cloud to dim it, and the swift rush of the wind between. Then to the left there, impressive to look on and conducive to solemn thoughts, the mountains rear their crests against the sky, and, crowned with the gathered snows of the centuries whose monuments they are, from æon to æon gaze majestically out over the wide plains and the ephemeral ant-like races who tread them, and while they endure think themselves the masters of their little world. And over all—mountain, plain, and flashing stream—the glorious light of the African sun and the Spirit of Life moving now as it once moved upon the darkling waters.

John stood and gazed at the untamed beauty of the scene, in his mind comparing it to many cultivated prospects which he had known, and coming to the conclusion that, however desirable the presence of civilised man might be in the world, it could not be said that his operations really add to its beauty. For the old line, 'Nature unadorned adorned the most,' still remains true in more senses than one.

Presently his reflections were interrupted by the step of Silas Croft, which, notwithstanding his age and bent frame, still rang firm enough—and he turned to greet him.

'Well, Captain Niel,' said the old man, 'up already! It looks well if you mean to take to farming. Yes, it's a pretty view, and a pretty place too. Well, I made it. Twenty-five years ago I rode up here and saw this spot. Look, you see that rock there behind the house? I slept under it and woke at sunrise and looked out at this beautiful scene and at the great veldt (it was all alive with game then), and I said to myself, "Silas, for five-and-twenty years have you wandered about this great country, and now you are getting tired of it; you've never seen a fairer spot than this or a healthier; be a wise man and stop here." And so I did. I bought the 3,000 morgen (6,000 acres), more or less, for 10l. down and a case of gin, and I set to work to make this place, and you see I have made it. Ay, it has grown under my hand, every stone and tree of it, and you know what that means in a new country. But one way and another I have done it, and now I have grown too old to manage it, and that's how I came to give out that I wanted a partner, as Mr. Snow told you down in Durban. You see, I told Snow it must be a gentleman; I don't care much about the money, I'll take a thousand for a third share if I can get a gentleman—none of your Boers or mean whites for me. I tell you I have had enough of Boers and their ways; the best day of my life was when old Shepstone ran up

the Union Jack there in Pretoria and I could call myself
an Englishman once more. Lord! and to think that there
are men who are subjects of the Queen and want to be
subjects of a Republic again—Mad! Captain Niel, I tell
you, quite mad! However, there's an end of it all now.
You know what Sir Garnet Wolseley told them in the
name of the Queen up at the Vaal River, that this country
would remain English till the sun stood still in the
heavens and the waters of the Vaal ran backwards.[1]
That's good enough for me, for, as I tell these grumbling
fellows who want the land back now that we have paid
their debts and defeated their enemies, no English
Government is false to its word, or breaks engagements
solemnly entered into by its representatives. We leave
that sort of thing to foreigners. No, no, Captain Niel, I
would not ask you to take a share in this place if I wasn't
sure that it would remain under the British flag. But we
will talk of all this another time, and now come in to
breakfast.'

After breakfast, as John was far too lame to walk about
the farm, the fair Bessie suggested that he should come
and help her to wash a batch of ostrich feathers, and,
accordingly, off he went. The *locus operandi* was in a space
of lawn at the rear of a little clump of 'naatche' orange-
trees, of which the fruit is like that of the Maltese orange,
only larger. Here were placed an ordinary washing-tub
half-filled with warm water, and a tin bath full of cold.
The ostrich feathers, many of which were completely
coated with red dirt, were plunged first into the tub of
warm water, where John Niel scrubbed them with soap,
and then transferred to the tin bath, where Bessie rinsed
them and then laid them on a sheet in the sun to dry.
The morning was very pleasant, and John soon came to

---

[1] A fact.—AUTHOR.

B

the conclusion that there are many more disagreeable occupations in the world than the washing of ostrich feathers with a lovely girl to help you. For there was no doubt but that Bessie was lovely, looking a very type of happy, healthy womanhood as she sat opposite to him on the little stool, her sleeves rolled up almost to the shoulder, showing a pair of arms that would not have disgraced a statue of Venus, and laughed and chatted away as she washed the feathers. Now, John Niel was not a susceptible man: he had gone through the fire years before and burnt his fingers like many another confiding youngster, but, all the same, he did wonder as he knelt there and watched this fair girl, who somehow reminded him of a rich rosebud bursting into bloom, how long it would be possible to live in the same house with her without falling under the spell of her charm and beauty. Then he began to think of Jess, and of what a strange contrast the two were.

' Where is your sister? ' he asked presently.

' Jess? Oh, I think that she has gone to the Lion Kloof, reading or sketching, I don't know which. You see in this establishment I represent labour and Jess represents intellect,' and she nodded her head prettily at him, and added, ' There is a mistake somewhere, she got all the brains.'

' Ah,' said John quietly, and looking up at her, ' I don't think that you are entitled to complain of the way in which Nature has treated you.'

She blushed a little, more at the tone of his voice than the words, and went on hastily, ' Jess is the dearest, best, and cleverest woman in the whole world—there. I believe that she has only one fault, and it is that she thinks too much about me. Uncle said that he had told you how we came here first when I was eight years old. Well, I remember that when we lost our way on the veldt that night, and it rained so and was so cold, Jess took off her own shawl and wrapped it round me over my own. Well, it has been just like that with her always. I am always to have the shawl—everything is to give way to me. But there, that is Jess all over ; she is very cold, cold as a stone I sometimes think, but when she does care for anybody it is enough to frighten one. I don't know a great number of women, but somehow I do not think that there can be many in the world like Jess. She is too good for this wild place; she ought to go away to England and write books and become a famous woman, only——' she added reflectively, ' I am afraid that Jess's books would all be sad ones.'

Just then Bessie stopped talking and suddenly changed colour, the bunch of lank wet feathers she held in her hand dropping from it with a little splash back into the bath. Following her glance, John looked down the avenue of blue-gum trees and perceived a big man with a broad hat and mounted on a splendid black horse, cantering leisurely towards the house.

' Who is that, Miss Croft ? ' he asked.

' It is a man I don't like,' she said with a little stamp of her foot. ' His name is Frank Muller, and he is half a Boer and half an Englishman. He is very rich, and very clever, and owns all the land round this place, so uncle has to be civil to him, though he does not like him either. I wonder what he wants now.'

On came the horse, and John thought that its rider was going to pass without seeing them, when suddenly the movement of Bessie's dress between the ' naatche ' trees caught his eye, and he pulled up and looked round. He was a large and exceedingly handsome man, apparently about forty years old, with clear-cut features, cold, light-blue eyes, and a remarkable golden beard that hung down over his chest. For a Boer he was rather smartly dressed in English-made tweed clothes, and tall riding-boots.

'Ah, Miss Bessie,' he called out in English, 'there you are, with your pretty arms all bare. I'm in luck to be just in time to see them. Shall I come and help you to wash the feathers? Only say the word, now——'

Just then he caught sight of John Niel, checked himself, and added:

'I have come to look for a black ox, branded with a heart and a "W" inside of the heart. Do you know if your uncle has seen it on the place anywhere?'

'No, Meinheer Muller,' replied Bessy, coldly, 'but he is down there,' pointing at a kraal on the plain some half-mile away, 'if you want to go and ask about it.'

'*Mr.* Muller,' said he, by way of correction, and with a curious contraction of the brow. '"Meinheer" is very well for the Boers, but we are all Englishmen now. Well, the ox can wait. With your permission, I'll stop here till "Oom" Croft [Uncle Croft] comes back,' and, without further ado, he jumped off his horse and, slipping the reins over its head as an indication to it to stand still, advanced towards Bessie with outstretched hand. As he came the young lady plunged both her arms up to the elbow in the bath, and it struck John, who was observing the scene closely, that she did this in order to avoid the necessity of shaking hands with her stalwart visitor.

'Sorry my hands are wet,' she said, giving him a cold little nod. 'Let me introduce you, Mr. (with emphasis) Frank Muller—Captain Niel—who has come to help my uncle with the place.'

John stretched out his hand and Muller shook it.

'Captain,' he said interrogatively—'a ship captain, I suppose?'

'No,' said John, 'a Captain of the English Army.'

'Oh, a "rooibaatje" (red jacket). Well, I don't wonder at your taking to farming after the Zulu war.'

'I don't quite understand you,' said John, rather coldly.

'Oh, no offence, Captain, no offence. I only meant that you rooibaatjes did not come very well out of that war. I was there with Piet Uys, and it was a sight, I can tell you. A Zulu had only to show himself at night and one would see your regiments "skreck" [stampede] like a span of oxen when they wind a lion. And then they'd fire—ah, they did fire—anyhow, anywhere, but mostly at the clouds, there was no stopping them; and so, you see, I thought that you would like to turn your sword into a ploughshare, as the Bible says—but no offence, I'm sure—no offence.'

All this while John Niel, being English to his backbone, and cherishing the reputation of his profession almost as dearly as his own honour, was boiling with inward wrath, which was all the fiercer because he knew there was some truth in the Boer's insults. He had the sense, however, to keep his temper—outwardly, at any rate.

'I was not in the Zulu war, Mr. Muller,' he said, and just then old Silas Croft rode up, and the conversation dropped.

Mr. Frank Muller stopped to dinner and far on into the afternoon, for his lost ox seemed to have entirely slipped his memory. There he sat close to the fair Bessie, smoking and drinking gin-and-water, and talking with great volubility in English sprinkled with Boer-Dutch terms that John Niel did not understand, and gazing at the young lady in a manner which John somehow found unpleasant. Of course it was no affair of his, and he had no interest in the matter, but for all that he thought this remarkable-looking Dutchman exceedingly disagreeable. At last, indeed, he could bear it no longer, and hobbled out for a little walk with Jess, who, in her abrupt way, offered to show him the garden.

'You don't like that man?' she said to him, as they went slowly down the slope in front of the house.

'No; do you?'

'I think,' replied Jess, quietly, but with much emphasis, 'that he is the most odious man I ever saw—and the most curious.' Then she relapsed into silence, only broken now and again by an occasional remark about the flowers and trees.

Half an hour afterwards, when they arrived again at the top of the slope, Mr. Muller was just riding off down the avenue of blue gums. By the verandah stood a Hottentot named Jantjé, who had been holding the Dutchman's horse. He was a curious, wizened-up little fellow, dressed in rags, and with hair like the worn tags of a black woollen carpet. His age might have been anything between twenty-five and sixty; it was impossible to form any opinion on the point. Just now, however, his yellow monkey face was convulsed with an expression of intense malignity, and he was standing there in the sunshine cursing rapidly beneath his breath in Dutch, and shaking his fist after the form of the retreating Boer—a very epitome of impotent but overmastering passion.

'What is he doing?' asked John.

Jess laughed, and answered, 'Jantjé does not like Frank Muller any more than I do, but I don't know why. He will never tell me.'

CHAPTER IV

BESSIE IS ASKED IN MARRIAGE

In due course John Niel recovered from his sprained ankle and the other injuries inflicted on him by the infuriated cock ostrich (it is, by the way, a humiliating thing to be knocked out of time by a feathered fowl), and set to work to learn the routine of farm life. He did not find this a disagreeable task, especially when he had so fair an instructress as Bessie, who knew all about it, to show him the way in which he should go. Naturally of an energetic and hard-working temperament, he very soon fell more or less into the swing of the thing, and at the end of six weeks began to talk quite learnedly of cattle and ostriches and sweet and sour veldt. About once a week or so Bessie used to put him through a regular examination as to his progress; also she gave him lessons in Dutch and Zulu, both of which tongues she spoke to perfection; so it will be seen that John did not lack for pleasant and profitable employment. Also, as time went on he grew much attached to Silas Croft. The old gentleman, with his handsome, honest face, his large and varied stock of experience and his sturdy English character, made a great impression on his mind. He had never met a man quite like him before. Nor was this friendship unreciprocated, for his host took a wonderful fancy to John Niel.

'You see, my dear,' he explained to his niece Bessie,
'he is quiet, and he doesn't know much about farming, but he's willing to learn, and such a gentleman.
Now, where one has Kafirs to deal with, as on a place
like this, you must have a *gentleman*. Your mean white
will never get anything out of a Kafir; that's why the
Boers kill them and flog them, because they can't get
anything out of them without. But you see Captain Niel
gets on well enough with the "boys." I think he'll do,
my dear, I think he'll do,' and Bessie quite agreed with
him. And so it came to pass that after this six weeks'
trial the bargain was struck finally, and John paid over
his thousand pounds, becoming the owner of a third
interest in Mooifontein.

Now it is not possible, in a general way, for a man of
John Niel's age to live in the same house with a young
and lovely woman like Bessie Croft without running
more or less risk of entanglement. Especially is this so
where the two people have little or no outside society or
distraction to divert their attention from each other. Not
that there was, at any rate as yet, the slightest hint of
affection between them. Only they liked one another
very much, and found it pleasant to be a good deal
together. In short, they were walking along that easy,
winding road which leads to the mountain paths of love.
It is a very broad road, like another road that runs
elsewhere, and, also like this last, it has a wide gate.
Sometimes, too, it leads to destruction. But for all that
it is a most agreeable one to follow hand-in-hand,
winding as it does through the pleasant meadows of
companionship. The view is rather limited, it is true,
and homelike—full of familiar things. There stand the
kine, knee-deep in grass; there runs the water; and
there grows the corn. Also you can stop if you like

By-and-by it is different.   By-and-by, when the travellers tread the heights of passion, precipices will yawn and torrents rush, lightnings will fall and storms will blind ; and who can know that they shall attain at last to that far-off peak, crowned with the glory of a perfect peace which men call Happiness?   There are those who say it never can be reached, and that the halo which rests upon its slopes is no earthly light, but rather, as it were, a promise and a beacon—a glow reflected whence we know not, and lying on this alien earth as the sun's light lies on the dead bosom of the moon.   Some declare, again, that they have climbed its topmost pinnacle and tasted of the fresh breath of heaven which sweeps around its heights—ay, and heard the quiring of immortal harps and the swan-like sigh of angels' wings ; and then behold ! a mist has fallen upon them, and they have wandered in it, and when it cleared they were on the mountain paths once more, and the peak was far away.   And a few there are who tell us that they live there always, listening to the voice of God ; but these are old and worn with journeying—men and women who have outlived passions and ambitions and the fire heats of love, and who now, girt about with memories, stand face to face with the sphinx Eternity.

But John Niel was no chicken, nor very likely to fall in love with the first pretty face he met.   He had once, years ago, gone through that melancholy stage, and there, he thought, was an end of it.   Moreover, if Bessie attracted him, so did Jess in a different way. Before he had been a week in the house he came to the conclusion that Jess was the strangest woman he had ever met, and in her own fashion one of the most attractive. Her very impassiveness added to her charm ; for who is there in this world who is not eager to learn a secret ?

To him Jess was a riddle of which he did not know the key. That she was clever and well-informed he soon discovered from her rare remarks; that she could sing like an angel he also knew; but what was the main-spring of her mind—round what axis did it revolve—this was the puzzle. Clearly enough it was not like most women's, least of all like that of happy, healthy, plain-sailing Bessie. So curious did he become to fathom these mysteries that he took every opportunity to associate with her, and, when he had time, would even go out with her on her sketching, or rather flower-painting, expeditions. On these occasions she would sometimes begin to talk, but it was always about books, or Eng-land or some intellectual question. She never spoke of herself.

Yet it soon became evident to John that she liked his society, and missed him when he did not come. It never occurred to him what a boon it was to a girl of consider-able intellectual attainments, and still greater intellectual capacities and aspirations, to be thrown for the first time into the society of a cultivated and intelligent gentleman. John Niel was no empty-headed, one-sided individual. He had both read and thought, and even written a little, and in him Jess found a mind which, though of an inferior stamp, was more or less kindred to her own. Although he did not understand her she understood him, and at last, had he but known it, there rose a far-off dawning light upon the twilight of her heart that thrilled and changed it as the first faint rays of morning thrill and change the darkness of the night. What if she should learn to love this man, and teach him to love her? To most women such a thought more or less involves the idea of marriage, and that change of status which for the most part they consider desirable. But Jess did not think much of that: what she did think of was the blessed possibility of being able to lay down her life, as it were, in the life of another—of at last finding somebody who understood her and whom she could understand, who would cut the shackles that bound down the wings of her genius, so that she could rise and bear him with her as, in Bulwer Lytton's beautiful story, Zoe would have borne her lover. Here at length was a man who *understood*, who was something more than an animal, and who possessed the god-like gift of brains, the gift that had been a curse rather than a blessing to her, lifting her above the level of her sex and shutting her off as by iron doors from the comprehension of those around her. Ah! if only this perfect love of which she had read so much would come to him and her, life might perhaps grow worth the living.

It is a curious thing, but in such matters most men never learn wisdom from experience. A man of John Niel's age might have guessed that it is dangerous work playing with explosives, and that the quietest, most harmless-looking substances are sometimes the most explosive. He might have known that to set to work to cultivate the society of a woman with such tell-tale eyes as Jess's was to run the risk of catching the fire from them himself, to say nothing of setting her alight: he might have known that to bring all the weight of his cultivated mind to bear on her mind, to take the deepest interest in her studies, to implore her to let him see the poetry Bessie told him she wrote, but which she would show to no living soul, and to evince the most evident delight in her singing, were one and all hazardous things to do. Yet he did them and thought no harm.

As for Bessie, she was delighted that her sister should have found anybody to whom she cared to talk or who could understand her. It never occurred to her that Jess might fall in love. Jess was the last person in the world to fall in love. Nor did she calculate what the results might be to John. As yet, at any rate, she had no interest in Captain Niel—of course not.

And so things went on pleasantly enough to all concerned in this drama till one fine day when the storm-clouds began to gather. John had been about the farm as usual till dinner time, after which he took his gun and told Jantjé to saddle up his shooting pony. He was standing on the verandah, waiting for the pony to appear, and by him was Bessie, looking particularly attractive in a white dress, when suddenly he caught sight of Frank Muller's great black horse, and upon it that gentleman himself, cantering up the avenue of blue gums.

'Hullo, Miss Bessie,' he said, 'here comes your friend.'

'Bother!' said Bessie, stamping her foot; and then, with a quick look, 'Why do you call him my friend?'

'I imagine that he considers himself so, to judge from the number of times a week he comes to see you,' John answered with a shrug. 'At any rate, he isn't mine, so I am off shooting. Good-bye. I hope that you will enjoy yourself.'

'You are not kind,' she said in a low voice, turning her back upon him.

In another moment he was gone, and Frank Muller had arrived.

'How do you do, Miss Bessie?' he said, jumping from his horse with the rapidity of a man who had been accustomed to rough riding all his life. 'Where is the "rooibaatje" off to?'

'Captain Niel is going out shooting,' she said coldly.

'Ah, so much the better for you and me, Miss Bessie

We can have a pleasant talk. Where is that black monkey Jantjé? Here, Jantjé, take my horse, you ugly devil, and mind you look after him, or I'll cut the liver out of you!'

Jantjé took the horse, with a forced grin of appreciation at the joke, and led him off to the stable.

'I don't think that Jantjé likes you, Meinheer Muller,' said Bessie, spitefully, 'and I do not wonder at it if you talk to him like that. He told me the other day that he had known you for twenty years,' and she looked at him inquiringly.

This casual remark produced a strange effect on her visitor, who turned colour beneath his tanned skin.

'He lies, the black hound,' he said, 'and I'll put a bullet through him if he says it again! What should I know about him, or he about me? Can I keep count of every miserable man-monkey I meet?' and he muttered a string of Dutch oaths into his long beard.

'Really, Meinheer!' said Bessie.

'Why do you always call me "Meinheer"?' he asked, turning so fiercely on her that she started back a step. 'I tell you I am not a Boer. I am an Englishman. My mother was English; and besides, thanks to Lord Carnarvon, we are all English now.'

'I don't see why you should mind being thought a Boer,' she said coolly: 'there are some very good people among the Boers, and besides, you used to be a great "patriot."'

'Used to be—yes; and so the trees used to bend to the north when the wind blew that way, but now they bend to the south, for the wind has turned. By-and-by it may set to the north again—that is another matter—then we shall see.'

Bessie made no answer beyond pursing up her pretty

mouth and slowly picking a leaf from the vine that trailed overhead.

The big Dutchman took off his hat and stroked his beard perplexedly. Evidently he was meditating something that he was afraid to say. Twice he fixed his cold eyes on Bessie's fair face, and twice looked down again. The second time she took alarm.

'Excuse me one minute,' she said, and made as though to enter the house.

'Wacht een beeche' (wait a bit), he ejaculated, breaking into Dutch in his agitation, and even catching hold of her white dress with his big hand.

Drawing the dress from him with a quick twist of her lithe form, she turned and faced him.

'I beg your pardon,' she said, in a tone that could not be called encouraging : 'you were going to say something.'

'Yes—ah, that is—I was going to say——' and he paused.

Bessie stood with a polite look of expectation on her face, and waited.

'I was going to say—that, in short, that I want to marry you!'

'Oh!' exclaimed Bessie, with a start.

'Listen,' he went on hoarsely, his words gathering force as he spoke, as is the way even with uncultured people when they speak from the heart. 'Listen! I love you, Bessie ; I have loved you for three years. Every time I have seen you I have loved you more. Don't say me nay—you don't know how I do love you. I dream of you every night ; sometimes I dream that I hear your dress rustling, then you come and kiss me, and it is like being in heaven.'

Here Bessie made a gesture of disgust.

'There, I have offended you, but don't be angry with me. I am very rich, Bessie; there is the place here, and then I have four farms in Lydenburg and ten thousand morgen up in Waterberg, and a thousand head of cattle, besides sheep and horses and money in the bank. You shall have everything your own way,' he went on, seeing that the inventory of his goods did not appear to impress her—'everything—the house shall be English fashion; I will build a new " sit-kamé " '—(sitting-room)—' and it shall be furnished from Natal. There, I love you, I say. You won't say no, will you?' and he caught her by the hand.

'I am very much obliged to you, Mr. Muller,' answered Bessie, snatching away her hand, ' but—in short, I cannot marry you. No, it is no use, I cannot indeed. There, please say no more—here comes my uncle. Forget all about it, Mr. Muller.'

Her suitor looked up; there was old Silas Croft sure enough, but he was some way off, and walking slowly.

' Do you mean it?' he said beneath his breath.

'Yes, yes, of course I mean it. Why do you force me to repeat it?'

'It is that damned rooibaatje,' he broke out. 'You used not to be like this before. Curse him, the white-livered Englishman! I will be even with him yet; and I tell you what it is, Bessie: you shall marry me, whether you like or no. Look here, do you think I am the sort of man to play with? You go to Wakkerstroom and ask what sort of a man Frank Muller is. See! I want you—I must have you. I could not live if I thought that I should never get you for myself. And I tell you I will do it. I don't care if it costs me my life, and your rooibaatje's too. I'll do it if I have to stir up a revolt against the Government. There, I swear it by God or by the Devil, it's all one to me!' And growing inarticulate with passion, he stood before her clinching and unclinching his great hand, and his lips trembling.

Bessie was very frightened; but she was a brave woman, and rose to the emergency.

'If you go on talking like that,' she said, 'I shall call my uncle. I tell you that I will not marry you, Frank Muller, and that nothing shall ever make me marry you. I am very sorry for you, but I have not encouraged you, and I will never marry you—never!'

He stood for half a minute or so looking at her, and then burst into a savage laugh.

'I think that some day or other I shall find a way to make you,' Muller said, and turning, he went without another word.

A couple of minutes later Bessie heard the sound of a horse galloping, and looking up she saw her wooer's powerful form vanishing down the vista of blue gums. Also she heard somebody crying out as though in pain at the back of the house, and, more to relieve her mind than for any other reason, she went to see what it was. By the stable door she found the Hottentot Jantjé, shrieking, cursing and twisting round and round, his hand pressed to his side, from which the blood was running.

'What is it?' she asked.

'Baas Frank!' he answered—'Baas Frank hit me with his whip!'

'The brute!' said Bessie, the tears starting to her eyes with anger.

'Never mind, missie, never mind,' gasped the Hottentot, his ugly face growing livid with fury, 'it is only one more to me. I cut it on this stick'—and he held up a long thick stick he carried, on which were several notches, including three deep ones at the top just below the knob. 'Let him look out sharp—let him search the grass—let him creep round the bush—let him watch as he will, one day he will find Jantjé, and Jantjé will find him!'

'Why did Frank Muller gallop away like that?' asked her uncle of Bessie when she got back to the verandah.

'We had some words,' she answered shortly, not seeing the use of explaining matters to the old man.

'Ah, indeed, indeed. Well, be careful, my love. It's ill to quarrel with a man like Frank Muller. I've known him for many years, and he has a black heart when he is crossed. You see, my love, you can deal with a Boer and you can deal with an Englishman, but cross-bred dogs are bad to hándle. Take my advice, and make it up with Frank Muller.'

All of which sage advice did not tend to raise Bessie's spirits, that were already sufficiently depressed.

CHAPTER V

DREAMS ARE FOOLISHNESS

WHEN, at the approach of Frank Muller, John Niel left Bessie on the verandah, he had taken his gun, and, having whistled to the pointer dog Pontac, he mounted his shooting pony and started in quest of partridges. On the warm slopes of the hills round Wakkerstroom a large species of partridge is very abundant, especially in the patches of red grass with which the slopes are sometimes clothed. It is a merry sound to hear these birds calling from all directions just after daybreak, and one to make the heart of every true sportsman rejoice exceedingly. On leaving the house John proceeded up the side of the hill behind it—his pony picking its way carefully between the stones, and the dog Pontac ranging about two or three hundred yards off, for in this sort of country it is necessary to have a dog with a wide range. Presently seeing him stop under a mimosa thorn and suddenly stiffen out as if he had been petrified, John made the best of his way towards him. Pontac stood still for a few seconds, and then slowly and deliberately veered his head round as though it worked on a hinge to see if his master was coming. John knew his ways. Three times would that remarkable old dog look round thus, and if the gun had not then arrived he would to a certainty run in and flush the birds. This was a rule that he never broke, for his patience had a fixed limit. On this occasion, however, John arrived before it was reached, and, jumping off his pony, cocked his gun and marched slowly up, full of happy expectation. On drew the dog, his eye cold and fixed, saliva dropping from his mouth, and his head, on which was frozen an extraordinary expression of instinctive ferocity, outstretched to its utmost limit.

Pontac was under the mimosa thorn now and up to his belly in the warm red grass. Where could the birds be? *Whirr*! and a great feathered shell seemed to have burst at his very feet. What a covey! twelve brace if there was a bird, and they had all been lying beak to beak in a space no bigger than a cart wheel. Up went John's gun and off too, a little sooner than it should have done.

'Missed him clean! Now then for the left barrel.' Same result. We will draw a veil over the profanity that ensued. A minute later and it was all over, and John and Pontac were regarding each other with mutual contempt and disgust.

'It was all you, you brute,' said John to Pontac. 'I thought you were going to run in, and you hurried me.'

'Ugh!' said Pontac to John, or at least he looked it. 'Ugh! you disgusting bad shot. What is the good of pointing for you? It's enough to make a dog sick.'

The covey—or rather the collection of old birds, for this kind of partridge sometimes 'packs' just before the breeding season—had scattered all about the place. It was not long before Pontac found some of them, and this time John got one bird—a beautiful great partridge he was too, with yellow legs—and missed another. Again Pontac pointed, and a brace rose. Bang! down goes one; bang with the other barrel. Caught him, by

Jove, just as he topped the stone. Hullo! Pontac is still on the point. Slip in two more cartridges. Oh, a leash this time! bang! bang! and down come a brace of them—two brace of partridges without moving a yard.

Life has joys for all men, but, I verily believe, it has no joy to compare to that of the moderate shot and earnest sportsman when he has just killed half a dozen driven partridges without a miss, or ten rocketing pheasants with eleven cartridges, or, better still, a couple of woodcock right and left. Sweet to the politician are the cheers that announce the triumph of his cause and of himself; sweet to the desponding writer is the unexpected public recognition by reviewers of talents with which previously nobody had been much impressed; sweet to all men are the light of women's eyes and the touch of women's lips. But though he have experienced all these things, to the true sportsman and the *moderate shot*, sweeter far is it to see the arched wings of the driven bird bent like Cupid's bow come flashing fast towards him, to feel the touch of the stock as it fits itself against his shoulder, and the kindly give of the trigger, and then, oh thrilling sight! to perceive the wonderful and yet awful change from life to death, the puff of feathers, and the hurtling passage of the dull mass borne onward by its own force to fall twenty yards from where the pellets struck it. Next session the politician will be hooted down, next year perhaps the reviewers will cut the happy writer to ribbons and decorate their journals with his fragments, next week you will have wearied of those dear smiles, or, more likely still, they will be bestowed elsewhere. Vanity of vanities, my son, each and all of them! But if you are a true sportsman (yes, even though you be but a moderate shot), it will always be a glorious thing to go out shooting, and when you chance to shoot well earth holds no such joy as that which will glow in your honest breast (for all sportsmen are honest), and it remains to be proved if heaven does either. It is a grand sport, though the pity of it is that it should be a cruel one.

Such was the pæan that John sang in his heart as he contemplated those fine partridges before lovingly transferring them to his bag. But his luck to-day was not destined to stop at partridges, for hardly had he ridden over the edge of the boulder-strewn side, and on to the flat table-top of the great hill which covered some five hundred acres of land, before he perceived, emerging from the shelter of a tuft of grass about a hundred and seventy yards away, nothing less than the tall neck and whiskered head of a large ' pauw ' or bustard.

Now it is quite useless to try and ride straight up to a bustard, and this he knew. The only thing to do is to excite his curiosity and fix his attention by moving round and round him in an ever-narrowing circle. Putting his pony to a canter, John proceeded to do this with a heart beating with excitement. Round and round he went; the ' pauw ' had vanished now, he was squatting in the tuft of grass. The last circle brought him to within seventy yards, and he did not dare to ride any nearer, so jumping off his pony he ran in towards the bird as hard as he could go. When he had covered ten paces the ' pauw ' was rising, but they are heavy birds, and he was within forty yards before it was fairly on the wing. Then he pulled up and fired both barrels of No. 4 into it. Down it came, and, incautious man, he rushed forward in triumph without reloading his gun. Already was his hand outstretched to seize the prize, when, behold! the great wings spread themselves out and the bird was flying away. John stood dancing upon the veldt, but observing that it settled within a couple of hundred yards, he ran back, mounted his pony, and pursued it. As he drew near it rose again, and flew this time a hundred yards only, and so it went on till at last he got within gun-shot of the king of birds and killed it.

By this time he was across the mountain-top, and on the brink of the most remarkable chasm he had ever seen. The place was known as Lion's Kloof, or Leeuwen Kloof in Dutch, because three lions had once been penned up by a party of Boers and shot there. This chasm or gorge was between a quarter and half a mile long, about six hundred feet in width, and a hundred and fifty to a hundred and eighty feet deep. Evidently it owed its origin to the action of running water, for at its head, just to the right of where John Niel stood, a little stream welling from hidden springs in the flat mountain-top trickled from stratum to stratum, forming a series of crystal pools and tiny waterfalls, till at last it reached the bottom of the mighty gorge, and pursued its way through it to the plains beyond, half-hidden by the umbrella-topped mimosa and other thorns that were scattered about. Without doubt this little stream was the parent of the ravine it trickled down and through, but, wondered John Niel, how many centuries of patient, never-ceasing flow must have been necessary to the vast result before him? First centuries of saturation of the soil piled on and between the bed rocks that lay beneath it and jutted up through it, then centuries of floods caused by rain and perhaps by melting snows, to carry away the loosened mould; then centuries upon centuries more of flowing and of rainfall to wash the débris clean and complete the colossal work.

I say the rocks that jutted up through the soil, for

the kloof was not clean cut. All along its sides, and here and there in its arena, stood mighty columns or fingers of rock, not solid indeed, but formed by huge boulders piled mason fashion one upon another, as though the Titans of some dead age had employed themselves in building them up, overcoming their tendency to fall by the mere crushing weight above, that kept them steady even when the wild breath of the storms came howling down the gorge and tried its strength against them. About a hundred paces from the near end of the chasm, some ninety or more feet in height, rose the most remarkable of these giant pillars, to which the remains at Stonehenge are but as toys. It was formed of seven huge boulders, the largest, that at the bottom, about the size of a moderate cottage, and the smallest, that at the top, perhaps some eight or ten feet in diameter. These boulders were rounded like a cricket-ball—evidently through the action of water—and yet the hand of Nature had contrived to balance them, each one smaller than that beneath, the one upon the other, and to keep them so. But this was not always the case. For instance, a very similar mass which once stood on the near side of the perfect pillar had fallen, all except its two foundation stones, and the rocks that formed it lay scattered about like monstrous petrified cannon-balls. One of these had split in two, and seated on it, looking very small and far off at the bottom of that vast gulf, John discovered Jess Croft, apparently engaged in sketching.

He dismounted from his shooting pony, and looking about him perceived that it was possible to descend by following the course of the stream and clambering down the natural steps it had cut in its rocky bed. Throwing the reins over the pony's head, and leaving him with the dog Pontac to stand and stare about him as South African shooting ponies are accustomed to do, he laid down his gun and game and proceeded to descend, pausing every now and again to admire the wild beauty of the scene and examine the hundred varieties of moss and ferns, the last mostly of the maiden-hair (*Capillus Veneris*) genus, that clothed every cranny and every rock where they could find roothold and win refreshment from the water or the spray of the cascades. As he drew near the bottom of the gorge he saw that on the borders of the stream, wherever the soil was moist, grew thousands upon thousands of white arums, 'pig lilies' as they call them in Africa, which were now in full bloom. He had noticed these lilies from above, but thence, owing to the distance, they seemed so small that he took them for everlastings or anemones. John could not see Jess now, for she was hidden by a bush that grows on the banks of the streams in South Africa in low-lying land, and which at certain seasons of the year is completely covered with masses of the most gorgeous scarlet bloom. His footsteps fell very softly on the moss and flowers, and when he passed round the glorious-looking bush it was evident that she had not heard him, for she was asleep. Her hat was off, but the bush shaded her, and her head had fallen forward over her sketching block and rested upon her hand. A ray of light that came through the bush played over her curling brown hair, and threw warm shadows on her white face and the whiter wrist and hand by which it was supported.

John stood there and looked at her, and the old curiosity took possession of him to understand this feminine enigma. Many a man before him has been the victim of a like desire, and lived to regret that he did not leave it ungratified. It is not well to try to lift the curtain of the unseen, it is not well to call to heaven to show its glory, or to hell to give us touch and knowledge of its yawning fires. Knowledge comes soon enough; many of us will say that knowledge has come too soon and left us desolate. There is no bitterness like the bitterness of wisdom: so cried the great Koheleth, and so hath cried many a son of man following blindly on his path. Let us be thankful for the dark places of the earth—places where we may find rest and shadow, and the heavy sweetness of the night. Seek not after mysteries, O son of man, be content with the practical and the proved and the broad light of day; peep not, mutter not the words of awakening. Understand her who would be understood and is comprehensible to those that run, and for the others let them be, lest your fate should be as the fate of Eve, and as the fate of Lucifer, Star of the morning. For here and there beats a human heart from which it is not wise to draw the veil—a heart in which many things are dim as half-remembered dreams in the brain of the sleeper. Draw not the veil, whisper not the word of life in the silence where all things sleep, lest in that kindling breath of love and pain pale shapes arise, take form, and fright you!

A minute or so might have passed when suddenly, and with a little start, Jess opened her great eyes, wherein the shadow of darkness lay, and gazed at him.

'Oh!' she said with a little tremor, 'is it you or is it my dream?'

'Don't be afraid,' he answered cheerfully, 'it is I—in the flesh.'

She covered her face with her hand for a moment, then withdrew it, and he noticed that her eyes had changed curiously in that moment. They were still large and beautiful as they always were, but there was a change.　Just now they had seemed as though her soul were looking through them.　Doubtless it was because the pupils had been enlarged by sleep.

'Your dream !　What dream ?' he asked, laughing.

'Never mind,' she answered in a quiet way that excited his curiosity more than ever.　'It was about this Kloof —and you—but " dreams are foolishness." '

CHAPTER VI

THE STORM BREAKS

'Do you know, you are a very odd person, Miss Jess,' John said presently, with a little laugh. 'I don't think you can have a happy mind.'

She looked up. 'A happy mind?' she said. 'Who *can* have a happy mind? Nobody who feels. Supposing,' she went on after a pause—'supposing one puts oneself and one's own little interests and joys and sorrows quite away, how is it possible to be happy, when one feels the breath of human misery beating on one's face, and sees the tide of sorrow and suffering creeping up to one's feet? You may be on a rock yourself and out of the path of it, till the spring floods or the hurricane wave come to sweep you away, or you may be afloat upon it: whichever it is, it is quite impossible, if you have any heart, to be indifferent.'

'Then only the indifferent are happy?'

'Yes, the indifferent and the selfish; but, after all, it is the same thing: indifference is the perfection of selfishness.'

'I am afraid that there must be lots of selfishness in the world, for certainly there is plenty of happiness, all evil things notwithstanding. I should have said that happiness springs from goodness and a sound digestion.'

Jess shook her head as she answered, 'I may be

wrong, but I don't see how anybody who feels can be quite happy in a world of sickness, suffering, slaughter, and death. I saw a Kafir woman die yesterday, and her children crying over her. She was a poor creature and had a rough lot, but she loved her life, and her children loved her. Who can be happy and thank God for his creation when he has just seen such a thing? But there, Captain Niel, my ideas are very crude, and I dare say very wrong, and everybody has thought them before: at any rate, I am not going to inflict them on you. What is the use of it?' and she went on with a laugh: 'what is the use of anything? The same old thoughts passing through the same human minds from year to year and century to century, just as the same clouds float across the same blue sky. The clouds are born in the sky, and the thoughts are born in the brain, and they both end in tears and re-arise in blind, bewildering mist, and this is the beginning and end of thoughts and clouds. They arise out of the blue; they overshadow and break into storms and tears, then they are drawn up into the blue again, and the story begins afresh.'

'So you don't think that one can be happy in this world?' he asked.

'I did not say that—I never said that. I do think that happiness is possible. It is possible if one can love somebody so hard that one can quite forget oneself and everything else except that person, and it is possible if one can sacrifice oneself for others. There is no true happiness outside of love and self-sacrifice, or rather outside of love, for it includes the other. This is gold, and all the rest is gilt.'

'How do you know that?' he asked quickly. 'You have never been in love.'

'No,' she answered, 'I have never been in love like

that, but all the happiness I have had in my life has come
to me from loving.   I believe that love is the secret of
the world : it is like the philosopher's stone they used to
look for, and almost as hard to find, but if you find it
it turns everything to gold.   Perhaps,' she went on with
a little laugh, ' when the angels departed from the earth
they left us love behind, that by it and through it we may
climb up to them again.   It is the one thing that lifts us
above the brutes.   Without love man is a brute, and
nothing but a brute ; with love he draws near to God.
When everything else falls away the love will endure
because it cannot die while there is any life, if it is true
love, for it is immortal.   Only it must be true—you see it
must be true.'

He had penetrated her reserve now ; the ice of her
manner broke up beneath the warmth of her words, and
her face, usually impassive, had caught life and light from
the eyes above, and acquired a certain beauty of its own.
John looked at it, and understood something of the untaught
and ill-regulated intensity and depth of the nature of this
curious girl.   He met her eyes and they moved him
strangely, though he was not an emotional man, and was
too old to experience spasmodic thrills at the chance
glances of a pretty woman.   He moved towards her,
looking at her curiously.

' It would be worth living to be loved like that,' he
said, more to himself than to her.

Jess did not answer, but she let her eyes rest on his.
Indeed, she did more, for she put her soul into them and
gazed and gazed till John Niel felt as though he were
mesmerised.   And as she gazed there rose up in her
breast a knowledge that if she willed it she could gain
this man's heart and hold it against all the world, for her
nature was stronger than his nature, and her mind,

untrained though it might be, encompassed his mind and could pass over it and beat it down as the wind beats down the tossing seas. All this she learnt in a moment, in the twinkling of an eye : she could not tell how she knew it, but she did know it as surely as she knew that the blue sky stretched overhead, and, what is more—for the moment, at any rate—he knew it too. This strange strong certainty came on her as a shock and a revelation, like the tidings of some great joy or grief, and for a moment left her heart empty of all things else.

Jess dropped her eyes suddenly.

' I think,' she said quietly, ' that we have been talking a great deal of nonsense, and that I want to finish my sketch.'

He rose and left her, for he was wanted at home, saying as he went that he thought there was a storm coming up ; the air was so quiet, and the wind had fallen as it does before an African tempest. Presently on looking round she saw him slowly climbing the precipitous ascent to the table-land above the gulf.

It was one of those glorious afternoons that sometimes come in the African spring, although it was so intensely still. Everywhere appeared the proofs and evidences of life. The winter was over, and now, from the sadness and sterility of its withered age, sprang young and lovely summer clad in sunshine, bediamonded with dew, and fragrant with the breath of flowers. Jess lay back and looked up into the infinite depths above. How blue they were, and how measureless ! She could not see the angry clouds that lay like visible omens on the horizon. Look, there, miles above her, was one tiny circling speck. It was a vulture, watching her from his airy heights and descending a little to see if she were dead, or only sleeping.

Involuntarily she shuddered. The bird of death reminded her of Death himself also hanging high up yonder in the blue and waiting his opportunity to fall upon the sleeper. Then her eyes fell upon a bough of the glorious flowering bush under which she rested. It was not more than four feet above her head, but she lay so still and motionless that a jewelled honeysucker came and hovered over the flowers, darting from one to another like a many-coloured flash. Thence her glance travelled to the great column of boulders that towered above her, and that seemed to say, 'I am very old. I have seen many springs and many winters, and have looked down on many sleeping maids, and where are they now? All dead—all dead,' and an old baboon in the rocks with startling suddenness barked out '*all dead*' in answer.

Around her were the blooming lilies and the lustiness of springing life ; the heavy air was sweet with the odour of ferns and the mimosa flowers. The running water splashed and musically fell ; the sunlight shot in golden bars athwart the shade, like the memory of happy days in the grey vista of a life ; away in the cliffs yonder, the rock-doves were preparing to nest by hundreds, and waking the silence with their cooing and the flutter of their wings. Even the grim old eagle perched on the pinnacle of the peak was pruning himself, contentedly happy in the knowledge that his mate had laid an egg in that dark corner of the cliff. All things rejoiced and cried aloud that summer was at hand and that it was time to bloom and love and nest. Soon it would be winter again, when things died, and next summer other things would live under the sun, and these perchance would be forgotten. That was what they seemed to say.

And as Jess lay and heard, her youthful blood, drawn by Nature's magnetic force, as the moon draws the tides,

rose in her veins like the sap in the budding trees, and
stirred her virginal serenity. All the bodily natural part
of her caught the tones of Nature's happy voice that bade
her break her bonds, live and love, and be a woman.
And lo! the spirit within her answered to it, flinging
wide her bosom's doors, and of a sudden, as it were,
something quickened and lived in her heart that was of
her and yet had its own life—a life apart ; something that
sprang from her and another, which would always be
with her now and could never die. She rose pale and
trembling, as a woman trembles at the first stirring of
the child that she shall bear, and clung to the flowery
bough of the beautiful bush above, then sank down again,
feeling that the spirit of her girlhood had departed from
her, and another angel had entered there ; knowing that
she loved with heart and soul and body, and was a very
woman.

She had called to Love as the wretched call to Death,
and Love had come in his strength and possessed her
utterly ; and now for a little while she was afraid to pass
into the shadow of his wings, as the wretched who call to
Death fear him when they feel his icy fingers. But the
fear passed, and the great joy and the new consciousness
of power and of identity that the inspiration of a true
passion gives to some strong deep natures remained, and
after a while Jess prepared to make her way home across
the mountain-top, feeling as though she were another
being. Still she did not go, but lay there with closed eyes
and drank of this new intoxicating wine. So absorbed
was she that she did not notice that the doves had ceased to
call, and that the eagle had fled away for shelter. She
was not aware of the great and solemn hush which had
taken the place of the merry voice of beast and bird and
preceded the breaking of the gathered storm.

At last as she rose to go Jess opened her dark eyes, which, for the most part, had been shut while this great change was passing over her, and with a natural impulse turned to look once more on the place where her happiness had found her, then sank down again with a little exclamation. Where was the light and the glory and all the happiness of the life that moved and grew around her? Gone, and in its place darkness and rising mist and deep and ominous shadows. While she lay and thought, the sun had sunk behind the hill and left the great gulf nearly dark, and, as is common in South Africa, the heavy storm-cloud had crept across the blue sky and sealed the light from above. A drear wind came moaning up the gorge from the plains beyond; the heavy rain-drops began to fall one by one; the lightning flickered fitfully in the belly of the advancing cloud. The storm that John had feared was upon her.

Then came a dreadful hush. Jess had recovered herself by now, and, knowing what to expect, she snatched up her sketching-block and hurried into the shelter of a little cave hollowed by water in the side of the cliff. And now with a rush of ice-cold air the tempest burst. Down came the rain in a sheet; then flash upon flash gleaming fiercely through the vapour-laden air; and roar upon roar echoing along the rocky cavities in volumes of fearful sound. Then another pause and space of utter silence, followed by a blaze of light that dazed and blinded her, and suddenly one of the piled-up columns to her left swayed to and fro like a poplar in a breeze, to fall headlong with a crash which almost mastered the awful crackling of the thunder overhead and the shrieking of the baboons scared from their crannies in the cliff. Down it rushed beneath the stroke of that fiery sword, the brave old pillar that had lasted out so many centuries, sending

C

clouds of dust and fragments high up into the blinding rain, and carrying awe and wonder to the heart of the girl who watched its fall. Away rolled the storm as quickly as it had come, with a sound like the passing of the artillery of an embattled host ; then a grey rain set in, blotting the outlines of everything, like an endless absorbing grief, dulling the edge and temper of a life. Through it Jess, scared and wet to the skin, managed to climb up the natural steps, now made almost impassable by the prevailing gloom and the rush of water from the table-top of the mountain, and on across the sodden plain, down the rocky path on the farther side, past the little walled-in cemetery with the four red gums planted at its corners, in which a stranger who had died at Mooi-fontein lay buried, and so, just as the darkness of the wet night came down like a cloud, home at last. At the back-door stood her old uncle with a lantern.

'Is that you, Jess?' he called out in his stentorian tones. 'Lord! what a sight!' as she emerged, her sodden dress clinging to her slight form, her hands torn with clambering over the rocks, her curling hair which had broken loose hanging down her back and half covering her face.

'Lord! what a sight!' he ejaculated again. 'Why, Jess, where have you been? Captain Niel has gone out to look for you with the Kafirs.'

'I have been sketching in Leeuwen Kloof, and got caught in the storm. There, uncle, let me pass, I want to take these wet things off. It is a bitter night,' and she ran to her room, leaving a long trail of water behind her as she passed. The old man entered the house, shut the door, and blew out the lantern.

'Now, what is it she reminds me of?' he said aloud as he groped his way down the passage to the sitting-room. 'Ah, I know, that night when she first came here out of the rain leading Bessie by the hand. What can the girl have been thinking of, not to see the thunder coming up? She ought to know the signs of the weather here by now. Dreaming, I suppose, dreaming. She's an odd woman, Jess, very.' Perhaps he did not quite know how accurate his guess was, and how true the conclusion he drew from it. Certainly she had been dreaming, and she was an odd woman.

Meanwhile Jess was rapidly changing her clothes and removing the traces of her struggle with the elements. But of that other struggle she had gone through she could not remove the traces. They and the love that arose out of it would endure as long as she endured. It was her former self that had been cast off in it and which now lay behind her, an empty and unmeaning thing like the shapeless heap of garments. It was all very strange. So John had gone to look for her and had not found her. She was glad that he had gone. It made her happy to think of him searching and calling in the wet and the night. She was only a woman, and it was natural that she should feel thus. By-and-by he would come back and find her clothed and in her right mind and ready to greet him. She was glad that he had not seen her wet and dishevelled. A girl looks so unpleasant like that. It might have set him against her. Men like women to look nice and clean and pretty. That gave her an idea. She turned to her glass and, holding the light above her head, studied her own face attentively. She was a woman with as little vanity in her composition as it is possible for a woman to have, and till now she had not given her personal looks much consideration. They had not been of great importance to her in the Wakkerstroom district of the Transvaal. But to-night all of a sudden they became very important; and so she stood and looked at her own wonderful eyes, at the masses of curling brown hair still damp and shining from the rain, at the curious pallid face and clear-cut determined mouth.

'If it were not for my eyes and hair, I should be very ugly,' she said to herself aloud. 'If only I were beautiful like Bessie, now.' The thought of her sister gave her another idea. What if John were to prefer Bessie? Now she remembered that he had been very attentive to Bessie. A feeling of dreadful doubt and jealousy passed through her, for women like Jess know what jealousy is in its bitterness. Supposing that it was in vain, supposing that what she had given to-day—given utterly once and for all, so that she could not take it back—had been given to a man who loved another woman, and that woman her own dear sister! Supposing that the fate of her love was to be like water falling unalteringly on the hard rock that heeds it not and retains it not! True, the water wears the rock away; but could she be satisfied with that? She could master him, she knew; even if things were so, she could win him to herself, she had read it in his eyes that afternoon; but could she, who had promised to her dead mother to cherish and protect her sister, whom till this day she had loved better than anything in the world, and whom she still loved more dearly than her life—could she, if it should happen to be thus, rob that sister of her lover? And if it should be so, what would her life be like? It would be like the great pillar after the lightning had smitten it, a pile of shattered smoking fragments, a very heaped-up débris of a life. She could feel it even now. No wonder, then, that Jess sat there upon the little white bed holding her hand against her heart and feeling terribly afraid.

Just then she heard John's footsteps in the hall.

'I can't find her,' he said in an anxious tone to some one as she rose, taking her candle with her, and left the room. The light of it fell full upon his face and dripping clothes. It was white and anxious, and she was glad to see the anxiety.

'Oh, thank God! here you are!' he said, catching her hand. 'I began to think you were quite lost. I have been right down the Kloof after you, and got a nasty fall over it.'

'It is very good of you,' she said in a low voice, and again their eyes met, and again her glance thrilled him. There was such a wonderful light in Jess's eyes that night.

Half an hour afterwards they sat down as usual to supper. Bessie did not put in an appearance till it was a quarter over, and then sat very silent through it. Jess narrated her adventure in the Kloof, and everybody listened, but nobody said much. There seemed to be a shadow over the house that evening, or perhaps it was that each of the party was thinking of his own affairs. After supper old Silas Croft began talking about the political state of the country, which gave him uneasiness. He said that he believed the Boers really meant to rebel against the Government this time. Frank Muller had told him so, and he always knew what was going on. This announcement did not tend to raise anybody's spirits, and the evening passed as silently as the meal had done. At last Bessie got up, stretched her rounded arms, and said that she was tired and going to bed.

'Come into my room,' she whispered to her sister as she passed. 'I want to speak to you.'

CHAPTER VII

LOVE'S YOUNG DREAM

AFTER waiting a few minutes, Jess said 'Good-night,' and went straight to Bessie's room. Her sister had undressed, and was sitting on her bed, wrapped in a blue dressing-gown that suited her fair complexion admirably, and with a very desponding expression on her beautiful face. Bessie was one of those people who are easily elated and easily cast down.

Jess came up to her and kissed her.

'What is it, love?' she said. And Bessie could never have divined the gnawing anxiety that was eating at her heart as she said it.

'Oh, Jess, I'm so glad that you have come. I do so want you to advise me—that is, to tell me what you think,' and she paused.

'You must tell *me* what it is all about first, Bessie dear,' she said, sitting down opposite to her in such a position that her face was shaded from the light. Bessie tapped her naked foot against the matting with which the little room was carpeted. It was an exceedingly pretty foot.

'Well, dear old girl, it is just this—Frank Muller has been here to ask me to marry him.'

'Oh,' said Jess, with a sigh of relief. So that was all? She felt as though a ton-weight had been lifted from her heart. She had expected this bit of news for some time.

'He wanted me to marry him, and when I said I would not, he behaved like—like——'

'Like a Boer,' suggested Jess.

'Like a *brute*,'. went on Bessie with emphasis.

'So you don't care for Frank Muller?'

'Care for him! I loathe the man. You don't know how I loathe him, with his handsome bad face and his cruel eyes. I always loathed him, and now I hate him too. But I will tell you all about it;' and she did, with many feminine comments and interpolations.

Jess sat quite still, and waited till she had finished.

'Well, dear,' she said at last, 'you are not going to marry him, and so there is an end of it. You can't detest the man more than I do. I have watched him for years,' she went on, with rising anger, 'and I tell you that Frank Muller is a liar and a traitor. That man would betray his own father if he thought it to his interest to do so. He hates uncle—I am sure he does, although he pretends to be so fond of him. I am certain that he has tried often and often to stir up the Boers against him. Old Hans Coetzee told me that he denounced him to the Veld-Cornet as an "uitlander" and a "verdomde Engelsmann" about two years before the annexation, and tried to get him to persuade the Landdrost to report him as a law-breaker to the Raad; while all the time he was pretending to be so friendly. Then in the Sikukuni war it was Frank Muller who caused them to commandeer uncle's two best waggons and spans. He gave none himself, nothing but a couple of bags of meal. He is a wicked fellow, Bessie, and a dangerous fellow; but he has more brains and more power about him than any man in the Transvaal, and you will have to be very careful, or he will do us all a bad turn.'

'Ah!' said Bessie; 'well, he can't do much now that the country is English.'

'I am not so sure of that. I am not so sure that the country is going to stop English. You laugh at me for reading the home papers, but I see things there that make me doubtful. The other party is in power now in England, and one does not know what they may do; you heard what uncle said to-night. They might give us up to the Boers. You must remember that we far-away people are only the counters with which they play their game.'

'Nonsense, Jess,' said Bessie indignantly. 'English-men are not like that. When they say a thing, they stick to it.'

'They used to, you mean,' answered Jess with a shrug, and got up from her chair to go to bed.

Bessie began to fidget her white feet over one another.

'Stop a bit, Jess dear,' she said. 'I want to speak to you about something else.'

Jess sat or rather dropped back into her chair, and her pale face turned paler than ever; but Bessie blushed rosy red and hesitated.

'It is about Captain Niel,' she said at length.

'Oh,' answered Jess with a little laugh, and her voice sounded cold and strange in her own ears. 'Has he been following Frank Muller's example, and proposing to you too?'

'No-o,' said Bessie, 'but'—and here she rose, and, sitting on a stool by her elder sister's chair, rested her forehead against her knee—'but I love him, and I *believe* that he loves me. This morning he told me that I was the prettiest woman he had seen at home or abroad, and

the sweetest too; and do you know,' she said, looking up
and giving a happy little laugh, ' I think he meant it.'

' Are you joking, Bessie, or are you really in earnest ? '

' In earnest! ah, but that I am, and I am not
ashamed to say it. I fell in love with John Niel when
he killed that cock ostrich. He looked so strong and
savage as he fought with it. It is a fine thing to see a
man put out all his strength. And then he is such a
gentleman!—so different from the men we meet round
here. Oh yes, I fell in love with him at once, and I have
got deeper and deeper in love with him ever since, and
if he does not marry me I think that it will break my
heart. There, that's the truth, Jess dear,' and she dropped
her golden head on to her sister's knees and began to cry
softly at the thought.

But the sister sat there on the chair, her hand hanging
idly by her side, her white face set and impassive as that
of an Egyptian Sphinx, and the large eyes gazing far
away through the window, against which the rain was
beating—far away out into the night and the storm. She
heard the surging of the storm, she heard her sister's
weeping, her eyes perceived the dark square of the window
through which they appeared to look, she could feel
Bessie's head upon her knee—yes, she could see and
hear and feel, and yet it seemed to her that she was *dead*.
The lightning had fallen on her soul as it fell on the
pillar of rock, and it was as the pillar is. And it had
fallen so soon! there had been such a little span of
happiness and hope! And so she sat, like a stony Sphinx,
and Bessie wept softly before her, like a beautiful,
breathing, loving human suppliant, and the two formed a
picture and a contrast such as the student of human
nature does not often get the chance of studying.

It was the elder sister who spoke first after all.

'Well, dear,' she said, 'what are you crying about? You love Captain Niel, and you believe that he loves you. Surely there is nothing to cry about.'

'Well, I don't know that there is,' said Bessie, more cheerfully; 'but I was thinking how dreadful it would be if I lost him.'

'I do not think that you need be afraid,' said Jess; 'and now, dear, I really must go to bed, I am so tired. Good-night, my dear; God bless you! I think that you have made a very wise choice. Captain Niel is a man whom any woman might love, and be proud of loving.'

In another minute she was in her room, and there her composure left her, for she was but a loving woman after all. She flung herself upon her bed, and, hiding her face in the pillow, burst into a paroxysm of weeping—a very different thing from Bessie's gentle tears. Her grief absolutely convulsed her, and she pushed the bedclothes against her mouth to prevent the sound of it penetrating the partition wall and reaching John Niel's ears, for his room was next to hers. Even in the midst of her suffering the thought of the irony of the thing forced itself into her mind. There, separated from her only by a few inches of lath and plaster and some four or five feet of space, was the man for whom she mourned thus, and yet he was as ignorant of it as though he were thousands of miles away. Sometimes at such acute crises in our lives the limitations of our physical nature do strike us after this fashion. It is strange to be so near and yet so far, and it brings the absolute and utter loneliness of every created being home to the mind in a manner that is forcible and at times almost terrible. John Niel sinking composedly to sleep, his mind happy with the recollection of those two right and left shots, and Jess, lying on her bed, six feet away, and sobbing out her stormy heart over him, are indeed but types of what is continually happening in this remarkable world. How often do we understand one another's grief? And, when we do, by what standard can we measure it? More especially is comprehension rare, if we chance to be the original cause of the trouble. Do we think of the feelings of the beetles it is our painful duty to crush into nothingness? Not at all. If we have any compunctions, they are quickly absorbed in the pride of our capture. And more often still, as in the present case, we set our foot upon the poor victim by pure accident or venial carelessness.

Presently John was fast asleep, and Jess, her paroxysm past, was walking up and down, down and up, her little room, her bare feet falling noiselessly on the carpeting as she strove to wear out the first bitterness of her woe. Oh that it lay in her power to recall the past few days! Oh that she had never seen his face, which must now be ever before her eyes! But for her there was no such possibility, and she felt it. She knew her own nature well. Her heart had spoken, and the word it said must roll on continually through the spaces of her mind. Who can recall the spoken word, and who can set a limit to its echoes? It is not so with most women, but here and there may be found a nature where it is so. Spirits like this poor girl's are too deep, and partake too much of a divine immutability, to shift and suit themselves to the changing circumstances of a fickle world. They have no middle course; they cannot halt half-way; they set all their fortune on a throw. And when the throw is lost their hearts are broken, and their happiness passes away like a swallow.

For in such a nature love rises like the wind on the quiet breast of some far sea. None can say whence it comes or whither it blows; but there it is, lashing the

waters to a storm, so that they roll in thunder all the long
day through, throwing their white arms on high, as they
clasp at the evasive air, till the darkness that is death
comes down and covers them.

What is the interpretation of it? Why does the great
wind stir the deep waters? It does but ripple the shallow
pool as it passes, for shallowness can but ripple and
throw up shadows. We cannot tell, but this we know—
that deep things only can be deeply moved. It is the
penalty of depth and greatness; it is the price they pay
for the divine privilege of suffering and sympathy. The
shallow pools, the looking-glasses of our little life, know
nought, feel nought. Poor things! they can but ripple
and reflect. But the deep sea, in its torture, may perchance catch some echo of God's voice sounding down
the driven gale; and, as it lifts itself and tosses its waves
in agony, may perceive a glow, flowing from a celestial
sky that is set beyond the horizon that bounds its
being.

Suffering, or rather mental suffering, is a prerogative
of greatness, and even here there lies an exquisite joy at
its core. For everything has its compensations. Nerves
such as these can thrill with a high happiness, that will
sweep unfelt over the mass of men. Thus he who is
stricken with grief at the sight of the world's misery—as
all great and good men must be—is at times lifted up
with joy by catching some faint gleam of the almighty
purpose that underlies it. So it was with the Son of
Man in His darkest hours; the Spirit that enabled Him
to compass out the measure of the world's suffering and
sin enabled Him also, knowing their purposes, to gaze
beyond them; and thus it is, too, with those deep-hearted
children of His race, who partake, however dimly, of
His divinity.

Thus, even in this hour of her darkest bitterness and grief, a gleam of comfort struggled to Jess's breast just as the first ray of dawn was struggling through the stormy night. She would sacrifice herself to her sister— that she had determined on; and hence came that cold gleam of happiness, for there is happiness in self-sacrifice, whatever the cynical may say. At first her woman's nature had risen in rebellion against the thought. Why should she throw her life away? She had as good a right to this man as Bessie, and she knew that by the strength of her own hand she could hold him against Bessie in all her beauty, however far things had gone between them; and she believed, as a jealous woman is prone to do, that they had gone much farther than was the case.

But by-and-by, as she pursued that weary march, her better self rose up, and mastered the promptings of her heart. Bessie loved him, and Bessie was weaker than she, and less suited to bear pain, and she had sworn to her dying mother—for Bessie had been her mother's darling—to promote her happiness, and, come what would, to comfort and protect her by every means in her power. It was a wide oath, and she was only a child when she took it, but it bound her conscience none the less, and surely it covered this. Besides, she dearly loved her—far, far more than she loved herself. No, Bessie should have her lover, and she should never know what it had cost her to give him up; and as for herself, well, she must go away like a wounded buck, and hide till she got well—or died.

She laughed a drear little laugh, and stayed to brush her hair just as the broad lights of the dawn came streaming across the misty veldt. But she did not look at her face again in the glass; she cared no more about

it now. Then she threw herself down to sleep the sleep
of utter exhaustion before it was time to go out again and
face the world and her new sorrow.

Poor Jess! Love's young dream had not overshadowed her for long. It had tarried just three hours.
But it had left other dreams behind.

'Uncle,' said Jess that morning to old Silas Croft as
he stood by the kraal-gate, where he had been counting
out the sheep—an operation requiring much quickness of
eye, and on the accurate performance of which he greatly
prided himself.

'Yes, yes, my dear, I know what you are going to say.
It was very neatly done; it isn't everybody who can
count out six hundred running hungry sheep without a
mistake. But then, I oughtn't to say too much, for you
see I have been at it for fifty years, in the old colony and
here. Now, many a man would get fifty sheep wrong.
There's Niel for instance——'

'Uncle,' said she, wincing a little at the name, as a
horse with a sore back winces at the touch of the saddle,
'it wasn't about the sheep that I was going to speak to
you. I want you to do me a favour.'

'A favour? Why, God bless the girl, how pale you
look!—not but what you are always pale. Well, what is
it now?'

'I want to go up to Pretoria by the post-cart that
leaves Wakkerstroom to-morrow afternoon, and to stop
for a couple of months with my schoolfellow, Jane
Neville. I have often promised to go, and I have never
gone.'

'Well, I never!' said the old man. 'My stay-at-
home Jess wanting to go away, and without Bessie, too!
What is the matter with you?'

'I want a change, uncle—I do indeed. I hope you won't thwart me in this.'

Silas looked at her steadily with his keen grey eyes.

'Humph!' he said; 'you want to go away, and there's an end of it. Best not ask too many questions where a maid is concerned. Very well, my dear, go if you like, though I shall miss you.'

'Thank you, uncle,' she said, and kissed him; then turned and went.

Old Croft took off his broad hat and polished his bald head with a red pocket-handkerchief.

'There's something up with that girl,' he said aloud to a lizard that had crept out of the crevices of the stone wall to bask in the sun. 'I am not such a fool as I look, and I say that there is something wrong with her. She is odder than ever,' and he hit viciously at the lizard with his stick, whereon it promptly bolted into its crack, returning presently to see if the irate 'human' had departed.

'However,' he soliloquised, as he made his way to the house, 'I am glad that it was not Bessie. I couldn't bear, at my time of life, to part with Bessie, even for a couple of months.'

CHAPTER VIII

JESS GOES TO PRETORIA

THAT day, at dinner, Jess suddenly announced that she
was going on the morrow to Pretoria to see Jane
Neville.

'To see Jane Neville!' said Bessie, opening her blue
eyes wide. 'Why, it was only last month you said that
you did not care about Jane Neville now, because she
had grown so vulgar. Don't you remember when she
stopped here on her way down to Natal last year, and
held up her fat hands, and said, "Ah, Jess—Jess is a
genius! It is a privilege to know her"? And then she
asked you to quote Shakespeare to that lump of a brother
of hers, and you told her that if she did not hold
her tongue she would not enjoy the privilege much
longer. And now you want to go and stop with her for
two months! Well, Jess, you are odd. And, what's
more, I think it is very unkind of you to run away for
so long.'

To all of which prattle Jess said nothing, but merely
reiterated her determination to go.

John, too, was astonished and, to tell the truth, not
a little disgusted. Since the previous day, when he had
that talk with her in Lion Kloof, Jess had assumed a
clearer and more definite interest in his eyes. Before
that she was an enigma; now he had guessed enough

about her to make him anxious to know more. Indeed, he had not perhaps realised how strong and definite his interest was till he heard that she was going away for a long period. Suddenly it struck him that the farm would be very dull without this very fascinating woman moving about the place in her silent, resolute way. Bessie was, no doubt, delightful and charming to look on, but she had not her sister's brains and originality; and John Niel was sufficiently above the ordinary run to thoroughly appreciate intellect and originality in a woman, instead of standing aghast at it. She interested him intensely, to say the least of it, and, man-like, he felt exceedingly annoyed, and even sulky, at the idea of her departure. He looked at her in protest, and, with an awkwardness begotten of his irritation, knocked down the vinegar cruet and made a mess upon the table; but she evaded his eyes and took no notice of the vinegar. Then, feeling that he had done all that in him lay, he went to see about the ostriches; first of all hanging about a little in case Jess should come out, which she did not do. Indeed, he saw nothing more of her till supper time. Bessie told him that she said she was busy packing; but, as one can only take twenty pounds weight of luggage in a post-cart, this did not quite convince him that it was so in fact.

At supper Jess was, if possible, even more quiet than she had been at dinner. After it was over, he asked her to sing, but she declined, saying that she had given up singing for the present, and persisting in her statement in spite of the chorus of remonstrance it aroused. The birds only sing whilst they are mating; and it is, by the way, a curious thing, and suggestive of the theory that the same great principles pervade all nature, that now when her trouble had overtaken her, and that she had

lost the love which had suddenly sprung from her heart
—full-grown and clad in power as Athena sprang from
the head of Jove—Jess had no further inclination to
use her divine gift of song.   Probably it was nothing
more than a coincidence, although a strange one.

The arrangement was, that on the morrow Jess was
to be driven in the Cape cart to Martinus-Wesselstroom,
more commonly called Wakkerstroom, there to catch
the post-cart, which was timed to leave the town at midday, though when it would leave was quite another
matter.   Post-carts are not particular to a day or so in
the Transvaal.

Old Silas Croft was to drive her with Bessie, who
wished to do some shopping in Wakkerstroom, as ladies
sometimes will; but at the last moment the old man
felt a premonitory twinge of the rheumatism to which
he was a martyr, and could not go.   So, of course, John
volunteered, and, though Jess raised some difficulties,
Bessie furthered the idea, and in the end his offer was
accepted.

Accordingly, at half-past eight on a beautiful morning
up came the tented cart, with its two massive wheels,
stout stinkwood disselboom, and four spirited young
horses; to the heads of which the Hottentot Jantjé, assisted by the Zulu Mouti, clad in the sweet simplicity of
a moocha, a few feathers in his wool, and a horn snuff-
box stuck through the fleshy part of the ear, hung on
grimly. In they got—John first, then Bessie next to him,
then Jess.   Next Jantjé scrambled up behind; and after
some preliminary backing and plunging, and showing a
disposition to twine themselves affectionately round the
orange-trees, off went the horses at a hand gallop, and
away swung the cart after them, in a fashion that would
have frightened anybody, not accustomed to that mode of

progression, pretty well out of his wits. As it was, John had as much as he could do to keep the four horses together, and to prevent them from bolting, and this alone, to say nothing of the rattling and jolting of the vehicle over the uneven track, was sufficient to put a stop to any attempt at conversation.

Wakkerstroom is about eighteen miles from Mooifontein, a distance that they covered well within the two hours. Here the horses were outspanned at the hotel, and John went into the house whence the post-cart was to start and booked Jess's seat, and then joined the ladies at the 'Kantoor' or store where they were shopping. When their purchases were made, they went back to the inn together and ate some dinner ; by which time the Hottentot driver of the cart began to tune up lustily, but unmelodiously, on a bugle to inform intending passengers that it was time to start Bessie was out of the room at the moment, and, with the exception of a peculiarly dirty-looking coolie waiter, there was nobody about.

' How long are you going to be away, Miss Jess ? ' asked John.

' Two months, more or less, Captain Niel.'

' I am very sorry that you are going,' he said earnestly. ' It will be dull at the farm without you.'

' You will have Bessie to talk to,' she answered, turning her face to the window, and affecting to watch the inspanning of the post-cart in the yard on to which it looked.

' Captain Niel ! ' she said suddenly.

' Yes ? '

' Mind you look after Bessie while I am away. Listen ! I am going to tell you something. You know Frank Muller ? '

'Yes, I know him, and a very disagreeable fellow he is.'

'Well, he threatened Bessie the other day, and he is a man who is quite capable of carrying out a threat. I can't tell you anything more about it, but I want you to promise me to protect Bessie if any occasion for it should arise. I do not know that it will, but it might. Will you promise?'

'Of course I will; I would do a great deal more than that if you asked me to, Jess,' he answered tenderly, for now that she was going away he felt curiously drawn towards her, and was anxious to show it.

'Never mind me,' she said, with an impatient little movement. 'Bessie is sweet enough and lovely enough to be looked after for her own sake, I should think.'

Before he could say any more, in came Bessie herself, saying that the driver was waiting, and they went out to see her sister off.

'Don't forget your promise,' Jess whispered to him, bending down as he helped her into the cart, so low that her lips almost touched him, and her breath rested for a second on his cheek like the ghost of a kiss.

In another moment the sisters had embraced each other, tenderly enough; the driver had sounded once more on his awful bugle, and away went the cart at full gallop, bearing with it Jess, two other passengers, and her Majesty's mails. John and Bessie stood for a moment watching its mad career, as it fled splashing and banging down the straggling street towards the wide plains beyond; then they turned to enter the inn again and prepare for their homeward drive. At that moment, an old Boer, named Hans Coetzee, with whom John was already slightly acquainted, came up, and, extending an enormously big and thick hand, bid them 'Gooden daag,'

Hans Coetzee was a very favourable specimen of the better sort of Boer, and really came more or less up to the ideal picture that is so often drawn of that 'simple pastoral people.' He was a very large, stout man, with a fine open face and a pair of kindly eyes. John, looking at him, guessed that he could not weigh less than seventeen stone, and that estimate was well within the mark.

'How are you, Captain?' he said in English, for he could talk English well, 'and how do you like the Transvaal?—must not call it South African Republic now, you know, for that's treason,' and his eye twinkled merrily.

'I like it very much, Meinheer,' said John.

'Ah, yes, it's a beautiful veldt, especially about here— no horse sickness, no "blue tongue," [1] and a good strong grass for the cattle. And you must find yourself very snug at Oom [Uncle] Croft's there; it's the nicest place in the district, with the ostriches and all. Not that I hold with ostriches in this veldt; they are well enough in the old colony, but they won't breed here—at least, not as they should do. I tried them once and I know; oh, yes, I know.'

'Yes, it's a very fine country, Meinheer. I have been all over the world almost, and I never saw a finer.'

'You don't say so, now! Almighty, what a thing it is to have travelled! Not that I should like to travel myself. I think that the Lord meant us to stop in the place He has made for us. But it is a fine country, and' (dropping his voice) 'I think it is a finer country than it used to be.'

'You mean that the veldt has got "tame," Meinheer?'

'Nay, nay. I mean that the land is English now,' he answered mysteriously, 'and though I dare not say so among my volk, I hope that it will keep English. When

---

[1] A disease that is very fatal to sheep.

I was Republican, I was Republican, and it was good in some ways, the Republic. There was so little to pay in taxes, and we knew how to manage the black folk; but now I am English, I am English. I know the English Government means good money and safety, and if there isn't a " Raad " [assembly] now, well, what does it matter? Almighty, how they used to talk there!—clack, clack, clack! just like an old black koran [species of bustard] at sunset. And where did they run the waggon of the Republic to—Burghers and those damned Hollanders of his, and the rest of them? Why, into the sluit—into a sluit with peaty banks; and there it would have stopped till now, or till the flood came down and swept it away, if old Shepstone—ah! what a tongue that man has, and how fond he is of the kinderchies! [little children]—had not come and pulled it out again. But look here, Captain, the volk round here don't think like that. It's the " ver-domde Britische Gouvernment " here and the " verdomde Britische Gouvernment " there, and " bymakaars " [meet-ings] here and "bymakaars " there. Silly folk, they all run one after the other like sheep. But there it is, Cap-tain, and I tell you there will be fighting before long, and then our people will shoot those poor rooibaatjes [red jackets] of yours like buck, and take the land back. Poor things! I could weep when I think of it.'

John smiled at this melancholy prognostication, and was about to explain what a poor show all the Boers in the Transvaal would make in front of a few British regi-ments, when he was astonished by a sudden change in his friend's manner. Dropping his enormous paw on to his shoulder, Coetzee broke into a burst of somewhat forced merriment, the cause of which, though John did not guess it at the moment, was that he had just perceived Frank Muller, who was in Wakkerstroom with a waggon-load of corn to grind at the mill, standing within five yards, and apparently intensely interested in flipping at the flies with a cowrie made of the tail of a vilderbeeste, but in reality listening to Coetzee's talk with all his ears.

'Ha, ha! "nef"' [nephew], said old Coetzee to the astonished John, 'no wonder you like Mooifontein—there are other mooi [pretty] things there beside the water. How often do you "opsit" [sit up at night] with Uncle Croft's pretty girl, eh? I'm not quite as blind as an ant-bear yet. I saw her blush when you spoke to her just now. I saw her. Well, well, it is a pretty game for a young man, isn't it, "nef" Frank?' (this was addressed to Muller). 'I'll be bound the Captain here "burns a long candle" with pretty Bessie every night. eh, Frank? I hope you ain't jealous, "nef"? My vrouw told me some time ago that you were sweet in that direction yourself;' and he stopped at last, out of breath, looking anxiously towards Muller for an answer, while John, who had been somewhat overwhelmed at this flood of bucolic chaff, gave a sigh of relief. As for Muller, he behaved in a curious manner. Instead of laughing, as the jolly old Boer had intended that he should, although Coetzee could not see it, his face had been growing blacker and blacker; and now that the flow of language ceased, with a savage ejacula-tion which John could not catch, but which he appeared to throw at his (John's) head, he turned on his heel and went off towards the courtyard of the inn.

'Almighty!' said old Hans, wiping his face with a red cotton pocket-handkerchief; 'I have put my foot into a big hole. That stink-cat Muller heard all that I was saying to you, and I tell you he will save it up and save it up, and one day he will bring it all out to the volk, and call me a traitor to the "land" and ruin me. I know him. He knows how to balance a long stick on his little finger so that the ends keep even. Oh, yes, he can ride two horses at once, and blow hot and blow cold. He is a devil of a man, a devil of a man! And what did he mean by swearing at you like that? Is it about the missie [girl], I wonder? Almighty! who can say? Ah! that reminds me—though I'm sure I don't know why it should—the Kafirs tell me that there is a big herd of buck—vilderbeeste and blesbok—on my outlying place about an hour and a half [ten miles] from Mooifontein. Can you hold a rifle, Captain? You look like a bit of a hunter.'

'Oh, yes, Meinheer!' said John, delighted at the prospect of some shooting.

'Ah, I thought so. All you English are sportsmen, though you don't know how to kill buck. Well now, you take Oom Croft's light Scotch cart and two good horses, and come over to my place—not to-morrow, for my wife's cousin is coming to see us, and an old cat she is, but rich; she has a thousand pounds in gold in the waggon-box under her bed—nor the next day, for it is the Lord's day, and one can't shoot creatures on the Lord's day—but Monday, yes, Monday. You be there by eight o'clock, and you shall see how to kill vilderbeeste. Almighty! now what can that jackal Frank Muller have meant? Ah! he is the devil of a man,' and, shaking his head ponderously, the jolly old Boer departed, and presently John saw him riding away upon a fat little shooting-pony which cannot have weighed much more than himself, but that cantered off with him on his fifteen-mile journey as though he were a feather-weight.

CHAPTER IX

JANTJÉ'S STORY

SHORTLY after the old Boer had gone, John went into the yard of the hotel to see to the inspanning of the Cape cart, where his attention was at once arrested by the sight of a row in active progress—at least, from the crowd of Kafirs and idlers and the angry sounds and curses which proceeded from them, he judged that it was a row. Nor was he wrong in his conclusion. In the corner of the yard, close by the stable-door, surrounded by the aforesaid crowd, stood Frank Muller; a heavy sjambock in his raised hand, as though in the act to strike. Before him, a very picture of drunken fury, his lips drawn up like a snarling dog's, so that the two lines of white teeth gleamed like polished ivory in the sunlight, his small eyes all shot with blood and his face working convulsively, was the Hottentot Jantjé. Nor was this all. Across his face was a blue wheal where the whip had fallen, and in his hand a heavy white-handled knife which he always carried.

'Hullo! what is all this?' said John, shouldering his way through the crowd.

'The swartsel [black creature] has stolen my horse's forage, and given it to yours!' shouted Muller, who was evidently almost off his head with rage, making an attempt to hit Jantjé with the whip as he spoke. The latter avoided the blow by jumping behind John, with the result that the tip of the sjambock caught the Englishman on the leg.

'Be careful, sir, with that whip,' said John to Muller, restraining his temper with difficulty. 'Now, how do you know that the man stole your horse's forage; and what business have you to touch him? If there was anything wrong, you should have reported it to me.'

'He lies, Baas, he lies!' yelled out the Hottentot in tremulous, high-pitched tones. 'He lies; he has always been a liar, and worse than a liar. Yah! yah! I can tell things about him. The land is English now, and Boers can't kill the black people as they like. That man—that Boer, Muller, he shot my father and my mother—my father first, then my mother; he gave her two bullets— she did not die the first time.'

'You yellow devil!—You black-skinned, black-hearted, lying son of Satan!' roared the great Boer, his very beard curling with fury. 'Is that the way you talk to your masters? Out of the light, rooibaatje' [soldier] —this was to John—'and I will cut his tongue out of him. I'll show him how we deal with a yellow liar;' and without further ado he made a rush for the Hottentot.

As he came, John, whose blood was now thoroughly up, put out his open hand, and, bending forward, pushed with all his strength on Muller's advancing chest. John was a very powerfully made man, though not a large one, and the push sent Muller staggering back.

'What do you mean by that, rooibaatje?' shouted Muller, his face livid with fury. 'Get out of my road or I will mark that pretty face of yours. I owe you for some goods as it is, Englishman, and I always pay my debts. Out of the path, curse you!' and he again rushed for the Hottentot.

This time John, who was now almost as angry as his

assailant, did not wait for the man to reach him, but, springing forward, hooked his arm around Muller's throat and, before he could close with him, with one tremendous jerk managed not only to stop his wild career, but to reverse the motion, and then, by interposing his foot with considerable neatness, to land him—powerful as he was —on his back in a pool of drainage that had collected from the stable in a hollow of the inn-yard. Down he went with a splash, amid a shout of delight from the crowd, who always like to see an aggressor laid low, his head bumping with considerable force against the lintel of the door. For a moment he lay still, and John was afraid that the man was really hurt. Presently, however, he rose, and, without attempting any further hostile demonstration or saying a single word, tramped off towards the house, leaving his enemy to compose his ruffled nerves as best he could. Now John, like most gentlemen, hated a row with all his heart, though he had the Anglo-Saxon tendency to go through with it un-flinchingly when once it began. Indeed, the incident irritated him almost beyond bearing, for he knew that the story with additions would go the round of the country-side, and what is more, that he had made a powerful and implacable enemy.

'This is all your fault, you drunken little blackguard!' he said, turning savagely on the Tottie, who, now that his excitement had left him, was snivelling and drivelling in an intoxicated fashion, and calling him his preserver and his Baas in maudlin accents.

'He hit me, Baas; he hit me, and I did not take the forage. He is a bad man, Baas Muller.'

'Be off with you and get the horses inspanned; you are half-drunk,' John growled, and, having seen that opera-tion advancing to a conclusion, he went to the sitting-room of the hotel, where Bessie was waiting in happy ignorance of the disturbance. It was not till they were well on their homeward way that he told her what had passed, whereat, remembering the scene she had herself gone through with Frank Muller, and the threats that he **had then made use of, she looked** very grave. Her old uncle, too, was very much put out when he heard the story on their arrival home that evening.

'You have made an enemy, Niel,' he said, as they sat upon the verandah after breakfast on the following morning, 'and a bad one. Not but what you were right to stand up for the Hottentot. I would have done as much myself had I been there and ten years younger, but Frank Muller is not the man to forget being put upon his back before a lot of Kafirs and white folk too. Perhaps that Jantjé is sober by now. I will go and call him, and we will hear what this story is about his father and his mother.'

Presently he returned followed by the ragged, dirty-faced little Hottentot, who, looking very miserable and ashamed of himself, took off his hat and squatted down on the drive, in the full glare of the African sun, to the effects of which he appeared to be totally impervious.

'Now, Jantjé, listen to me,' said the old man. 'Yesterday you got drunk again. Well, I'm not going to talk about that now, except to say that if I hear of your being drunk once more—you leave this place.'

'Yes, Baas,' said the Hottentot meekly. 'I was drunk, though not very; I only had half a bottle of Cape smoke.'

'By getting drunk you made a quarrel with Baas Muller, so that blows passed between Baas Muller and the Baas here on your account, which was more than you are worth. Now when Baas Muller had struck you,

you said that he had shot your father and your mother.
Was that a lie, or what did you mean by saying it?'

'It was no lie, Baas,' answered the Hottentot excitedly.
'I have said it once, and I will say it again. Listen,
Baas, and I will tell you the story. When I was young
—so tall'—and he held his hand high enough to indi-
cate a Tottie of about fourteen years of age—'we, that is,
my father, my mother, my uncle—a very old man, older
than the Baas' (pointing to Silas Croft)—'were bijwoners
[authorised squatters] on a place belonging to old Jacob
Muller, Baas Frank's father, down in Lydenburg yonder.
It was a bush-veldt farm, and old Jacob used to come
down there with his cattle from the High veldt in the
winter when there was no grass in the High veldt, and
with him came the Englishwoman, his wife, and the
young Baas Frank—the Baas we saw yesterday.'

'How long was all this ago?' asked Mr. Croft.

Jantjé counted on his fingers for some seconds, and
then held up his hand and opened it four times in succession. 'So,' he said, 'twenty years last winter. Baas
Frank was young then, he had only a little down upon
his chin. One year when Oom Jacob went away, after
the first rains, he left six oxen that were too poor [thin]
to go, with my father, and told him to look after them as
though they were his children. But the oxen were
bewitched. Three of them took the lung-sick and died,
a lion got one, a snake killed one, and one ate " tulip "
and died too. So when Oom Jacob came back the next
year all the oxen were gone. He was very angry with
my father, and beat him with a yoke-strap till he was all
blood, and though we showed him the bones of the oxen,
he said that we had stolen them and sold them.

'Now Oom Jacob had a beautiful span of black oxen
that he loved like children. Sixteen of them there were,

and they would come up to the yoke when he called them and put down their heads of themselves. They were tame as dogs. These oxen were thin when they came down, but in two months they grew fat and began to want to trek about as oxen do. At this time there was a Basutu, one of Sequati's people, resting in our hut, for he had hurt his foot with a thorn. When Oom Jacob found that the Basutu was there he was very angry, for he said that all Basutus were thieves. So my father told the Basutu that the Baas said that he must go away, and he went that night. Next morning the span of black oxen were gone too. The kraal-gate was down, and they had gone. We hunted all day, but we could not find them. Then Oom Jacob went mad with rage, and the young Baas Frank told him that one of the Kafir boys had said to him that he had heard my father sell them to the Basutu for sheep which he was to pay to us in the summer. It was a lie, but Baas Frank hated my father because of something about a woman—a Zulu girl.

'Next morning when we were asleep, just at daybreak, Oom Jacob Muller and Baas Frank and two Kafirs came into the hut and pulled us out, the old man my uncle, my father, my mother, and myself, and tied us up to four mimosa-trees with buffalo-hide reims. Then the Kafirs went away, and Oom Jacob asked my father where the cattle were, and my father told him that he did not know. Then Oom Jacob took off his hat and said a prayer to the Big Man in the sky, and when he had done Baas Frank came up with a gun and stood quite close and shot my father dead, and he fell forward and hung quiet over the reim, his head touching his feet. Then he loaded the gun again and shot the old man my uncle, and he slipped down dead, and his hands stuck up in the air against the reim. Next he shot my mother, but the bullet did not kill her, and cut the reim, and she ran away, and he ran after her and killed her. When that was done he came back to shoot me; but I was young then, and did not know that it is better to be dead than to live like a dog, and I cried and prayed for mercy while he was loading the gun.

'But the Baas only laughed, and said he would teach Hottentots how to steal cattle, and old Oom Jacob prayed out loud to the Big Man and said he was very sorry for me, but it was the dear Lord's will. And then, just as Baas Frank lifted the gun, he dropped it again, for there, coming softly, softly over the brow of the hill, in and out between the bushes, were all the sixteen oxen! They had got out in the night and strayed away into some kloof for a change of pasture, and came back when they were full and tired of being alone. Oom Jacob turned quite white and scratched his head, and then fell upon his knees and thanked the dear Lord for saving my life; and just then the Englishwoman, Baas Frank's mother, came down from the waggon to see what the firing was at, and when she saw all the people dead and me weeping, tied to the tree, and learnt what it was about, she went quite mad, for sometimes she had a kind heart when she was not drunk, and said that a curse would fall on them, and that they would all die in blood. And she took a knife and cut me loose, though Baas Frank wanted to kill me, so that I might tell no tales; and I ran away, travelling by night and hiding by day, for I was very much frightened, till I reached Natal, and there I stopped, working in Natal till this land became English, when Baas Croft hired me to drive his cart up from Maritzburg; and living by here I found Baas Frank, looking bigger but just the same except for his beard.

'There, Baas, that is the truth, and all the truth, and that is why I hate Baas Frank, because he shot my father and mother, and why Baas Frank hates me, because he cannot forget that he did it and because I saw him do it, for, as our people say, " one always hates a man one has wounded with a spear." '

Having finished his narrative, the miserable-looking little man picked up his greasy old felt hat that had a leather strap fixed round the crown, in which were stuck a couple of frayed ostrich feathers, and jammed it down over his ears. Then he fell to drawing circles on the soil with his long toes. His auditors only looked at one another. Such a ghastly tale seemed to be beyond comment. They never doubted its truth; the man's way of telling it carried conviction with it; indeed, two of them at any rate had heard such stories before. Most people have who live in the wilder parts of South Africa, though they are not all to be taken for gospel.

' You say,' remarked old Silas at last, ' that the Englishwoman said that a curse would fall on them, and that they would die in blood ? She was right. Twelve years ago Oom Jacob and his wife were murdered by a party of Mapoch's Kafirs down on the edge of that very Lydenburg veldt. There was a great noise about it at the time, I remember, but nothing came of it. Baas Frank was not there. He was away shooting buck, so he escaped, and inherited all his father's farms and cattle, and came to live here.'

' So ! ' said the Hottentot, without showing the slightest interest or surprise. ' I knew it would be so, but I wish I had been there to see it. I saw that there was a devil in the woman, and that they would die as she said. When there is a devil in people they always speak the truth, because they can't help it. Look, Baas, I draw a circle in the sand with my foot, and I say some words so, and at last the ends touch. There, that is the circle of Oom Jacob and his wife the Englishwoman. The ends have touched and they are dead. An old witch-doctor taught me how to draw the circle of a man's life and what words to say. And now I draw another of Baas Frank. Ah! there is a stone sticking up in the way. The ends will not touch. But now I work and work and work with my foot, and say the words and say the words, and so—the stone comes up and the ends touch now. Thus it is with Baas Frank. One day the stone will come up and the ends will touch, and he too will die in blood. The devil in the Englishwoman said so, and devils cannot lie or speak half the truth only. And now, look, I rub my foot over the circles and they are gone, and there is only the path again. That means that when they have died in blood they will be quite forgotten and stamped out. Even their graves will be flat,' and Jantjé wrinkled up his yellow face into a smile, or rather a grin, and then added in a matter-of-fact way :

'Does the Baas wish the grey mare to have one bundle of green forage or two ? '

D

CHAPTER X

JOHN HAS AN ESCAPE

On the following Monday, John, taking Jantjé to drive him, departed in a rough Scotch cart, to which were harnessed two of the best horses at Mooifontein, to shoot buck at Hans Coetzee's.

He reached the place at about half-past eight, and concluded, from the fact of the presence of several carts and horses, that he was not the only guest. Indeed, the first person whom he saw as the cart pulled up was his late enemy, Frank Muller.

'Kek [look], Baas,' said Jantjé, 'there is Baas Frank talking to his servant Hendrik, that ugly Basutu with one eye.'

John, as may be imagined, was not best pleased at this meeting. He had always disliked the man, and since Muller's conduct on the previous Friday, and Jantjé's story of the dark deed of blood in which he had been the principal actor, positively he loathed the sight of him. He jumped out of the cart, and was going to walk round to the back of the house in order to avoid him, when Muller, suddenly seeming to become aware of his presence, advanced to meet him with the utmost cordiality.

'How do you do, Captain?' he said, holding out his hand, which John just touched. 'So you have come to

shoot buck with Oom Coetzee; going to show us Transvaalers how to do it, eh? There, Captain, don't look as
stiff as a rifle barrel. I know what you are thinking of:
that little business at Wakkerstroom on Friday, is it not?
Well, now, I tell you what it is, I was in the wrong, and I
am not afraid to say so as between man and man. I had
had a glass, that was the fact, and did not quite know
what I was about. We have got to live as neighbours
here, so let us forget all about it and be brothers again.
I never bear malice, not I. It is not the Lord's will that
we should bear malice. Hit out from the shoulder, I
say, and then forget all about it. If it hadn't been for
that little monkey,' he added, jerking his thumb in the
direction of Jantjé, who was holding the horses' heads, ' it
would never have happened, and it is not nice that two
Christians should quarrel about such as he.'

Muller jerked out this long speech in a succession of
sentences, something as a schoolboy repeats a hardly
learnt lesson, fidgeting his feet and letting his restless
eyes travel about the ground as he spoke. It was evident to John, who stood quite still and listened to it in
icy silence, that his address was by no means extem-
porary; clearly it had been composed for the occasion.

' I do not wish to quarrel with anybody, Meinheer
Muller,' he answered at length. ' I never do quarrel
unless it is forced on me, and then,' he added grimly, ' I
do my best to make it unpleasant for my enemy. The
other day you attacked first my servant and then myself.
I am glad that you now see that this was an improper
thing to do, and, so far as I am concerned, there is an
end of the matter,' and he turned to enter the house.

Muller accompanied him as far as where Jantjé was
standing at the horses' heads. Here he stopped, and,
putting his hand in his pocket, took out a two-shilling

piece and threw it to the Hottentot, calling to him to catch it.

Jantjé was holding the horses with one hand. In the other he held his stick—a long walking kerrie that he always carried, the same on which he had shown Bessie the notches. In order to secure the piece of money he dropped the stick, and Muller's quick eye catching sight of the notches beneath the knob, he stooped down, picked it up, and examined it.

'What do these mean, boy?' he asked, pointing to the line of big and little notches, some of which had evidently been cut years ago.

Jantjé touched his hat, spat upon the 'Scotchman,' as the natives of that part of Africa call a two-shilling piece,[1] and pocketed it before he answered. The fact that the giver had murdered all his near relations did not make the gift less desirable in his eyes. Hottentot moral sense is not very elevated.

'No, Baas,' he said with a curious grin, 'that is how I reckon. If anybody beats Jantjé, Jantjé cuts a notch upon the stick, and every night before he goes to sleep he looks at it and says, "One day you will strike that man twice who struck you once," and so on, Baas. Look what a line of them there are, Baas. One day I shall pay them all back again, Baas Frank.'

Muller abruptly dropped the stick, and followed John towards the house. It was a much better building than the Boers generally indulge in, and the sitting-room, though innocent of flooring—unless clay and cowdung mixed can be called a floor—was more or less covered with mats made of springbuck skins. In the centre of

---

[1] Because once upon a time a Scotchman made a great impression on the simple native mind in Natal by palming off some thousands of florins among them at the nominal value of half a crown.

the room stood a table made of the pretty ' buckenhout '
wood, which has the appearance of having been indus-
triously pricked all over with a darning-needle, and
round it were chairs and couches of stinkwood, and
seated with rimpis or strips of hide.

In one big chair at the end of the room, busily employed in doing nothing, sat Tanta [Aunt] Coetzee, the
wife of Old Hans, a large and weighty woman, who evidently had once been rather handsome; and on the
couches were some half-dozen Boers, their rifles in their
hands or between their knees.

It struck John as he entered that some of these did
not look best pleased to see him, and he thought he
heard one young fellow, with a hang-dog expression of
face, mutter something about the ' damned Englishman '
to his neighbour rather more loudly than was necessary
to convey his sentiments. However, old Coetzee came
forward to greet him heartily enough, and called to his
daughters—two fine girls, very smartly dressed for Dutch
women—to give the Captain a cup of coffee. Then John
made the rounds after the Boer fashion, and beginning
with the old lady in the chair, received a lymphatic shake
of the hand from every single soul in the room. They
did not rise—it is not customary to do so—they merely
extended their paws, all of them more or less damp, and
muttered the mystic monosyllable ' Daag,' short for good-
day. It is a very trying ceremony till one gets used to
it, and John pulled up panting, to be presented with a
cup of hot coffee that he did not want, but which it would
be rude not to drink.

' The Captain is a rooibaatje ? ' said the old lady
' Aunt ' Coetzee interrogatively, and yet with the certainty
of one who states a fact.

John signified that he was.

'What does the Captain come to the "land" for? Is it to spy?'

The whole audience listened attentively to their hostess's question, and then turned their heads to listen for the answer.

'No. I have come to farm with Silas Croft.'

There was a general smile of incredulity. Could a rooibaatje farm? Certainly not.

'There are three thousand men in the British army,' announced the old vrouw oracularly, and casting a severe glance at the wolf in sheep's clothing, the man of blood who pretended to farm.

Everybody looked at John again, and awaited his answer in dead silence.

'There are more than a hundred thousand men in the regular British army, and as many more in the Indian army, and twice as many more volunteers,' he said, in a rather irritated voice.

This statement also was received with the most discouraging incredulity.

'There are three thousand men in the British army,' repeated the old lady, in a tone of certainty that was positively crushing.

'Yah, yah!' chimed in some of the younger men in chorus.

'There are three thousand men in the British army,' she repeated for the third time in triumph. 'If the Captain says that there are more he lies. It is natural that he should lie about his own army. My grandfather's brother was at Cape Town in the time of Governor Smith, and he saw the whole British army. He counted them; there were exactly three thousand. I say that there are three thousand men in the British army.'

'Yah, yah!' said the chorus; and John gazed at this terrible person in bland exasperation.

'How many men do you command in the British army?' she interrogated after a solemn pause.

'A hundred,' said John sharply.

'Girl,' said the old woman, addressing one of her daughters, 'you have been to school and can reckon. How many times does one hundred go into three thousand?'

The young lady addressed giggled confusedly, and looked for assistance to a sardonic Boer whom she was going to marry, who shook his head sadly, indicating thereby that these were mysteries into which it was not well to pry. Thrown on her own resources, she plunged into the recesses of an intricate calculation, in which her fingers played a considerable part, and finally, with an air of triumph, announced that it went twenty-six times exactly.

'Yah, yah!' said the chorus, 'it goes twenty-six times exactly.'

'The Captain,' said the oracular old lady, who was rapidly driving John mad, 'commands a twenty-sixth part of the British army, and he says that he comes here to farm with Uncle Silas Croft. He says,' she went on, with withering contempt, 'that he comes here to farm when he commands a twenty-sixth part of the British army. It is evident that he lies.'

'Yah, yah!' said the chorus.

'It is natural that he should lie!' she continued; 'all Englishmen lie, especially the rooibaatje Englishmen, but he should not lie so badly. It must vex the dear Lord to hear a man lie so badly, even though he be an Englishman and a rooibaatje.'

At this point John burst from the house, and swore

frantically to himself as soon as he was outside. It is to be hoped that he was forgiven, for the provocation was not small. It is not pleasant to be universally set down not only as a 'leugenaar' [liar], but as one of the very feeblest order.

In another minute old Hans Coetzee came out and patted him warmly on the shoulder, in a way that seemed to say that, whatever others might think of the insufficiency of his powers of falsehood, he, for one, quite appreciated them, and announced that it was time to be moving.

Accordingly the party climbed into their carts or on to their shooting-horses, as the case might be, and started. Frank Muller, John noticed, was mounted as usual on his fine black horse. After driving for more than half an hour along an indefinite kind of waggon track, the leading cart, in which were old Hans Coetzee himself, a Malay driver, and a coloured Cape boy, turned to the left across the open veldt, and the others followed in turn. This went on for some time, till at last they reached the crest of a rise that commanded a large sweep of open country, and here Hans halted and held up his hand, whereon the others halted too. On looking out over the vast plain before him John discovered the reason. About half a mile beneath them was a great herd of blesbuck feeding, three hundred or more of them, and beyond them another herd of some sixty or seventy much larger and wilder-looking animals with white tails, which John at once recognised as vilderbeeste. Nearer to them again, dotted about here and there on the plain, were a couple of dozen or so of graceful yellow springbuck.

Now a council of war was held, which resulted in the men on horseback—among whom was Frank Muller—being despatched to circumvent the herds and drive them towards the carts, that took up their stations at various points, towards which the buck were likely to run.

Then came a pause of a quarter of an hour or so, till suddenly, from the far ridge of the opposite slope, John saw a couple of puffs of white smoke float up into the air, and one of the vilderbeeste below rolled over on his back, kicking and plunging furiously. Thereon the whole herd of buck turned and came thundering towards them, stretched in a long line across the wide veldt; the springbuck first, then the blesbuck, looking for all the world like a herd of great bearded goats, owing to their peculiar habit of holding their long heads down as they galloped. Behind and mixed up with them were the vilderbeeste, who twisted and turned, and jumped into the air as though they had gone clean off their heads and were next second going clean on to them. It is very difficult, owing to his extraordinary method of progression, to distinguish one part of a galloping vilderbeeste from another; now it is his horns, now his tail, and now his hoofs that present themselves to the watcher's bewildered vision, and now again they all seem to be mixed up together. On came the great herd, making the ground shake beneath their footfall: and after them galloped the mounted Boers, from time to time jumping off their horses to fire a shot into the line of game, which generally resulted in some poor animal being left sprawling on the ground, whereon the sportsmen would remount and continue the chase.

Presently the buck were within range of some of the guns in the carts, and a regular fusillade began. About twenty blesbuck turned and came straight past John, at a distance of forty yards. Springing to the ground he fired both barrels of his 'Express' at them as they tore along—alas and alas! without touching them. The first

bullet struck under their bellies, the second must have
shaved their backs. Reloading rapidly, he fired again at
about two hundred yards' range, and this time one fell to
his second barrel. But he knew that it was a chance
shot: he had fired at the last buck, and he had killed one
ten paces in front of it. In fact this sort of shooting is
exceedingly difficult till the sportsman understands it.
The inexperienced hand firing across a line of buck will
not kill once in twenty shots, as an infinitesimal difference in elevation, or the slightest error in judging distance—in itself no easy art on those great plains—will
spoil his aim. A Boer almost invariably gets immediately
behind a herd of running buck, and fires at one about
half-way down the line. Consequently if his elevation is
a little wrong, or if he has misjudged his sighting, the
odds are that he will hit one either in front of or behind
the particular animal fired at. All that is necessary is
that the line of fire should be good. This John soon
learnt, and when he had mastered the fact he became as
good a game shot as the majority of Boers, but it being
his first attempt, much to his vexation, he did not particularly distinguish himself that day, with the result
that his friends the Dutchmen went home firmly con-
vinced that the English rooibaatje shot as indifferently
as he lied.

Jumping into the cart again, and leaving the dead
blesbuck to look after itself for the present—not a very
safe thing to do in a country where there are so many
vultures—John, or rather Jantjé, put the horses into a
gallop, and away they went at full tear. It was a most
exciting mode of progression, bumping along furiously
with a loaded rifle in his hands over a plain on which
antheaps as large as an armchair were scattered like burnt
almonds on a cake. Then there were the antbear holes

to reckon with, and the little swamps in the hollows, and other agreeable surprises. But the rush and exhilaration of the thing were too great to allow him much time to think of his neck, so away they flew, hanging on to the cart as best they could, and trusting to Providence to save them from complete disaster. Now they were bounding over an antheap, now one of the horses was on his nose, but somehow they always escaped the last dire catastrophe, thanks chiefly to the little Hottentot's skilful driving.

Whenever the game was within range they pulled up, and John would spring from the cart and let drive, then jump in and follow on again. This went on for nearly an hour, in which time he had fired twenty-seven cartridges and killed three blesbuck and wounded a vilderbeeste, which they proceeded to chase. But the vilderbeeste was struck in the rump, and an antelope so wounded will travel far, and go very fast also, so that some miles of ground had been covered before it began to rest, only to start on again as they drew near. At last, on crossing the crest of a little rise, John saw what at first he took to be his vilderbeeste, dead. A second look, however, showed him that, although it was a dead vilderbeeste, most undoubtedly it was not the one which he had wounded, for that animal was standing, its head hanging, about one hundred and twenty yards beyond the other buck, which, no doubt, had fallen to somebody else's rifle, or else had been hit farther back and come here to die. Now this vilderbeeste lay within a hundred yards of them, and Jantjé pointed out to John that his best plan would be to get out of the cart and creep on his hands and knees up to the dead animal, from the cover of which he would get a good shot at his own wounded bull.

Accordingly Jantjé having withdrawn with the cart

and horses out of sight under the shelter of the rise, John crouched upon his hands and knees and proceeded to carry out his stalk. All went well till he was quite close to the dead cow, and was congratulating himself on the prospect of an excellent shot at the wounded bull, when suddenly something struck the ground violently just beneath his body, throwing up a cloud of earth and dust. He stopped amazed, and at that instant heard the report of a rifle somewhat to his right and knew that a bullet had passed beneath him. Scarcely had he realised this when there was a sudden commotion in his hair, and the soft black felt hat that he was wearing started from his head, apparently of its own accord, and, after twirling round twice or thrice in the air, fell gently to the earth, just as the sound of a second report reached his ears. It was now evident that somebody was firing at him; so, jumping up from his crouching position, John tossed his arms into the air and sprang and shouted in a way that left no mistake as to his whereabouts. In another minute he saw a man on horseback, cantering easily towards him, in whom he had little difficulty in recognising Frank Muller. He picked up his hat; there was a bullet-hole right through it. Then, full of wrath, he advanced to meet Frank Muller.

'What the devil do you mean by firing at me?' he asked.

'Allemachter, carle!' [Almighty, my dear fellow] was the cool answer, 'I thought that you were a vilderbeeste calf. I galloped the cow and killed her, and she had a calf with her, and when I got the cartridges out of my rifle—for one stuck and took me some time—and the new ones in, I looked up, and there, as I thought, was the calf. So I got my rifle on and let drive, first with one barrel and then with the other, and when I saw you jump up like that and shout, and that I had been firing at a man, I nearly fainted. Thank the Almighty I did not hit you.'

John listened coldly. ' I suppose that I am bound to believe you, Meinheer Muller,' he said. ' But I have been told that you have the most wonderful sight of any man in these parts, which makes it odd that at three hundred yards you should mistake a man upon his hands and knees for a vilderbeeste calf.'

' Does the Captain think, then, that I wished to murder him ; especially,' he added, ' after I took his hand this morning ? '

' I don't know what I think,' answered John, looking straight into Muller's eyes, which fell before his own. ' All I know is that your curious mistake very nearly cost me my life. Look here ! ' and he took a lock of his brown hair out of the crown of his perforated hat and showed it to the other.

' Ay, it was very close. Let us thank God that you escaped.'

' It could not well have been closer, Meinheer. I hope that, both for your own sake and for the sake of the people who go out shooting with you, you will not make such a mistake again. Good-morning ! '

The handsome Boer, or Anglo-Boer, sat on his horse stroking his beautiful beard and gazing curiously after John Niel's sturdy English-looking figure as he marched towards the cart, for, of course, the wounded vilderbeeste had long ago vanished.

' I wonder,' he said to himself aloud, as he turned his horse's head and rode leisurely away, ' if the old volk are right after all, and if there is a God.' Frank Muller was sufficiently impregnated with modern ideas to be a free-thinker. ' It almost seems like it,' he went on, ' else how did it come that the one bullet passed under his

belly and the other just touched his head without harming
him? I aimed carefully enough too, and I could make
the shot nineteen times out of twenty and not miss.
Bah, a God! I snap my fingers at Him. Chance is the
only god. Chance blows men about like the dead grass,
till death comes down like the veldt fire and devours
them. But there are men who ride chance as one rides a
young colt—ay, who turn its headlong rushing and rearing to their own ends—who let it fly hither and thither
till it is weary, and then canter it along the road that
leads to triumph. I, Frank Muller, am one of those men.
I never fail in the end. I will kill that Englishman.
Perhaps I will kill old Silas Croft and the Hottentot too.
Bah! they do not know what is coming. I know; I
have helped to lay the mine; and unless they bend to
my will I shall be the one to fire it. I will kill them all,
and I will take Mooifontein, and then I will marry Bessie.
She will fight against it, but that will make it all the
sweeter. She loves that rooibaatje; I know it; and I
will kiss her over his dead body. Ah! there are the
carts. I don't see the Captain. Driven home, I suppose,
on account of the shock to his nerves. Well, I must
talk to those fools. Lord, what fools they are with their
chatter about the "land," and the "verdomde Britische
Gouvernment." They don't know what is good for them.
Silly sheep, with Frank Muller for a shepherd! Ay, and
they shall have Frank Muller for a president one day,
and I will rule them too. Bah! I hate the English; but
I am glad that I am half English for all that, for that is
where I get the brains! But these people—fools, fools!
Well, I shall pipe and they shall dance!'

'Baas,' said Jantjé to John, as they were driving
homewards, 'Baas Frank shot at you.'

'How do you know that?' asked John.

'I saw him. He was stalking the wounded bull, and not looking for a calf at all. There was no calf. He was just going to fire at the wounded bull when he turned and saw you, and he knelt down on one knee and covered you, and before I could do anything he fired, and then when he saw that he had missed you he fired again, and I don't know how it was he did not kill you, for he is a wonderful shot with a rifle—he never misses.'

'I will have the man tried for attempted murder,' said John, bringing the butt-end of his rifle down with a bang on to the bottom of the cart. 'A villain like that shall not go scot-free.'

Jantjé grinned. 'It is no use, Baas. He would get off, for I am the only witness. A jury won't believe a black man in this country, and they would never punish a Boer for shooting at an Englishman. No, Baas! you should lie up one day in the veldt where he is going to pass and shoot *him*. That is what I would do if I dared.'

CHAPTER XI

ON THE BRINK

For a few weeks after John Niel's adventure at the shooting-party no event of any importance occurred at Mooifontein. Day followed day in charming monotony, for, whatever 'gay worldlings' may think, monotony is as full of charm as a dreamy summer afternoon. 'Happy is the country that has no history,' says the voice of wisdom, and the same remark may be made with even more truth of the individual. To get up in the morning conscious of health and strength, to pursue the common round and daily task till evening comes, and finally to go to bed pleasantly tired and sleep the sleep of the just, is the true secret of happiness. Fierce excitements, excursions, and alarms do not conduce either to mental or physical well-being, and it is for this reason that we find that those whose lives have been chiefly concerned with them crave the most after the quiet round of domestic life. When they get it, often, it is true, they pant for the ardours of the fray whereof the dim and distant sounds are echoing through the spaces of their heart, in the same way that the countries without a history are sometimes anxious to write one in their own blood. But that is a principle of Nature, who will allow of no standing still among her subjects, and who has ordained that strife of one sort or another shall be the absolute condition of existence.

On the whole, John found that the life of a South African farmer came well up to his expectations. He had ample occupation; indeed, what between ostriches, horses, cattle, sheep, and crops, he was rather over than under occupied. Nor was he much troubled by the lack of civilised society, for he was a man who read a great deal, and books could be ordered from Durban and Cape Town, while the weekly mail brought with it a sufficient supply of papers. On Sundays he always read the political articles in the ' Saturday Review' aloud to Silas Croft, who, as he grew older, found that the print tried his eyes, an attention which the old gentleman greatly appreciated. Silas was a well-informed man, and notwithstanding his long life spent in a half-civilised country, had never lost his hold of affairs or his interest in the wide and rushing life of the world in one of whose side eddies he lived apart. This task of reading the ' Saturday Review' aloud had formerly been a part of Bessie's Sunday service, but her uncle was very glad to effect an exchange. Bessie's mind was not quite in tune with the profundities of that learned journal, and her attention was apt to wander at the most pointed passages.

Thus it came about, what between the ' Saturday Review' and other things, that a very warm and deep attachment sprang up betwixt the old man and his younger partner. John was a taking man, especially to the aged, for whom he was never tired of performing little services. One of his favourite sayings was that old people should be ' let down easy,' and he acted up to it. Moreover, there was a quiet jollity and a bluff honesty about him which was undoubtedly attractive both to men and women. Above all, he was a well-informed, experienced man, and a gentleman, in a country in which both were rare. Each week Silas Croft came to rely more and more on him, and allowed things to pass more and more into his hands.

'I'm getting old, Niel,' he said to him one night; 'I'm getting very old; the grasshopper is becoming a burden to me: and I'll tell you what it is, my boy,' laying his hand affectionately upon John's shoulder, 'I have no son of my own, and you must be a son to me, as my dear Bessie has been a daughter.'

John looked up into the kindly, handsome face, crowned with its fringe of snowy hair, and at the keen eyes set deep in it beneath the overhanging brows, and thought of his old father who was long since dead; and somehow he was moved, and his own eyes filled with tears.

'Ay, Mr. Croft,' he said, taking the old man's hand, 'that I will to the best of my ability.'

'Thank you, my boy, thank you. I don't like talking much about these things, but, as I said, I am getting old, and the Almighty may require my account any hour, and if He does I rely on you to look after these two girls. It is a wild country this, and one never knows what will happen in it from day to day, and they may want help. Sometimes I wish I were clear of the place. And now I'm going to bed. I am beginning to feel as though I had done my day's work in the world. I'm getting feeble. John, this is the fact of it.'

After that he always called him John.

Of Jess they heard but little. She wrote every week, it is true, and gave an accurate account of all that was going on at Pretoria and of her daily doings, but she was one of those people whose letters tell one absolutely nothing of themselves and of what is passing in their minds. They ought to have been headed ' Our Pretoria Letter,' as Bessie said disgustedly after reading through three sheets in Jess's curious, upright handwriting. ' Once you lose sight of Jess,' she went on, ' she might as well be dead for all you learn about her. Not that one learns very much when she is here,' she added reflectively.

' She is a peculiar woman,' said John thoughtfully. At first he had missed her very much, for, strange as she undoubtedly was, she had touched a new string in him, of the existence of which he had not till then been himself aware. And what is more, it had answered strongly enough for some time ; but now it was slowly vibrating itself into silence again, much as a harp does when the striker takes his fingers from the strings. Had she stayed on another week or so the effect might have been more enduring.

But although Jess had gone away Bessie had not. On the contrary, she was always about him, surrounding him with that tender care a woman, however involuntarily, cannot prevent herself from lavishing on the man she loves. Her beauty moved about the place like a beam of light about a garden, for she was indeed a lovely woman, and as pure and good as she was lovely. Nor could John long remain in ignorance of her liking for himself. He was not a vain man—very much the reverse, indeed—but neither was he a fool. And it must be said that, though Bessie never overstepped the bounds of maidenly reserve, neither did she take particular pains to hide her preference. Indeed, it was too strong to permit her so to do. Not that she was animated by the half-divine, soul-searing breath of passion, such as animated her sister, which is a very rare thing, and, take it altogether, as undesirable and unsuitable to the ordinary

conditions of this prosaic and work-a-day life as it is rare.
But she was tenderly and truly in love after the usual
young-womanly fashion ; indeed, her passion, measured
by the everyday standard, would have proved to be a deep
one.   However this might be, she was undoubtedly prepared to make John Niel a faithful and a loving wife if
he chose to ask her to marry him.

And as the weeks went on—though, of course, he
knew nothing of all this—it became a very serious question to John whether he should not ask her.   It is not
good for man to live alone, especially in the Transvaal,
and it was not possible for him to pass day by day at the
side of so much beauty and so much grace without
thinking that it would be well to draw the bond of union
closer.   Indeed, had John been a younger man or one of
less experience, he would have succumbed to the temptation much sooner than he did.   But he was neither very
young nor very inexperienced.   Ten years or more ago,
in his green and gushing youth, as has been said, he had
burnt his fingers to the bone, and a lively recollection
of this incident in his career heretofore had proved a
very efficient warning.   Also, he had reached that period
of life when men think a great many times before
they commit themselves wildly to the deep matrimonial
waters.   At three-and-twenty, for the sake of a pretty
face, most of us are willing to undertake the serious and
in many cases overwhelming burdens, risks, and cares of
family life, and the responsibility of the parentage of a
large and healthy brood, but at three-and-thirty we take
a different view of the matter.   The temptation may be
great, but the per contra list is so very alarming, and we
never know even then if we see all the liabilities.   Such
are the black thoughts that move in the breasts of selfish
men, to the great disadvantage of the marriage market ;

and however it may lower John Niel in the eyes of those who take the trouble to follow this portion of his life's history, in the interests of truth it must be confessed that he was not free from them.

In short, sweet and pretty as Bessie might be, he was not violently in love with her; and at thirty-four a man must be violently in love to rush into the near risk of matrimony. But, however commendably cautious that man may be, he is always liable to fall into temptation sufficiently strong to sweep away his caution and make a mockery of his plans. However strong the rope, it has its breaking strain; and in the same way our power of resistance to any given course depends entirely upon the power of the temptation to draw us into it. Thus it was destined to be with our friend John Niel.

It was about a week after his conversation with old Silas Croft that it occurred to John that Bessie's manner had grown rather strange of late. It seemed to him that she had avoided his society instead of showing a certain partiality for it, if not of courting it. Also, she had looked pale and worried, and evinced a tendency to irritation that was quite foreign to her natural sweetness of character. Now, when a person on whom one is accustomed to depend for most of that social intercourse and those pleasant little amenities which members of one sex value from another, suddenly cuts off the supply without any apparent rhyme or reason, it is enough to induce a feeling of wonder, not to say of vexation, in the breast. It never occurred to John that the reason might be that Bessie was truly fond of him, and perhaps unconsciously disappointed that he did not show a warmer interest in her. If, however, we were to examine into the facts of the case we should probably discover that here was the real explanation of this change. Bessie was a straightforward young woman, whose mind and purposes were as clear as running water. She was vexed with John— though she would probably not have owned it even to herself in so many words—and her manner reflected the condition of her mind.

'Bessie,' said John one lovely day, just as the afternoon was merging into evening, 'Bessie'—he always called her Bessie now—'I am going down to the black wattle plantation by the big mealie patch. I want to see how those young trees are doing. If you have done your cooking'—for she had been engaged in making a cake, as young ladies, to their souls' health, often have to do in the Colonies—'I wish you would put on your hat and come with me. I don't believe that you have been out to-day.'

'Thank you, Captain Niel, I don't think that I want to come out.'

'Why not?' he said.

'Oh, I don't know—because there is too much to do. If I go out that stupid girl will burn the cake,' and she pointed to a Kafir intombi [young girl], who, arrayed in a blue smock, a sweet smile, and a feather stuck in her wool, was vigorously employed in staring at the flies on the ceiling and sucking her black fingers. 'Really,' she added with a little stamp, 'one needs the patience of an angel to put up with that idiot's stupidity. Yesterday she smashed the biggest dinner-dish and then brought me the pieces with a broad grin on her face, and asked me to "make them one" again. The white people were so clever, she said, it would be no trouble to me. If they could make the china plate once, and could cause flowers to grow on it, it would surely be easy to make it whole again. I did not know whether to laugh or cry or throw the pieces at her.'

'Look here, young woman,' said John, taking the sin-ning girl by the arm and leading her solemnly to the oven, which was opened to receive the cake ; ' look here, if you let that cake burn while the inkosikaas [lady chieftain] is away, when I come back I will cram you into the oven to burn with it. I cooked a girl like that in Natal last year, and when she came out she was quite white ! '

Bessie translated this fiendish threat, whereat the girl grinned from ear to ear and murmured ' Koos ' [chief] in cheerful acquiescence. A Kafir maid on a pleasant afternoon is not troubled by the prospect of being baked at nightfall, which is a long way off, especially when it was John Niel who threatened the baking. The natives about Mooifontein had taken the measure of John's foot by this time with accuracy. His threats were awful, but his performances were not great. Once, indeed, he was forced to engage in a stand-up fight with a great fellow who thought that he could be taken advantage of on this account, but after he had succeeded in administering a sound hiding to that champion he was never again troubled in this respect.

' Now,' he said, ' I think we have provided for the safety of your cake, so come on.'

' Thank you, Captain Niel,' answered Bessie, looking at him in a bewitching little way she well knew how to assume, ' thank you, but I think I had rather not go out walking.' This was what she said, but her eyes added, ' I am offended with you ; I want to have nothing to do with you.'

' Very well,' said John ; ' then I suppose I must go alone,' and he took up his hat with the air of a martyr.

Bessie looked through the open kitchen door at the lights and shadows that chased each other across the swelling bosom of the hill behind the house.

' It certainly is very fine,' she said ; ' are you going far?'

'No, only round the plantation.'

'There are so many puff-adders down there, and I hate snakes,' suggested Bessie, by way of finding another excuse for not coming.

'Oh, I'll look after the puff-adders—come along.'

'Well,' she said at last, as she slowly unrolled her sleeves, which had been tucked up during the cake-making, and hid her beautiful white arms, 'I will come, not because I want to come, but because you have over-persuaded me. I don't know what has happened to me,' she added, with a little stamp and a sudden filling of her blue eyes with tears, 'I do not seem to have any will of my own left. When I want to do one thing and you want me to do another it is I who have to do what you want; and I tell you I don't like it, Captain Niel, and I shall be very cross out walking;' and sweeping past him, on her way to fetch her hat, in that peculiarly graceful fashion which angry women can sometimes assume, she left John to reflect that he never saw a more charming or taking lady in Europe or out of it.

He had half a mind to risk it and ask her to marry him. But then, perhaps, she might refuse him, and that was a contingency which he did not quite appreciate. After their first youth few men altogether relish the idea of putting themselves in a position that gives a capricious woman an opportunity of first figuratively 'jumping' on them, and then perhaps holding them up to the scorn and obloquy of her friends, relations, and other admirers. For, unfortunately, until the opposite is clearly demonstrated, many men are apt to believe that not a few women are by nature capricious, shallow, and unreliable; and John Niel, owing, possibly, to that unhappy little experience of his youth, must be reckoned among their misguided ranks.

CHAPTER XII

OVER IT

On leaving the house Bessie and John took their way down the long avenue of blue gums. This avenue was old Silas Croft's particular pride, since although it had only been planted for about twenty years, the trees, which in the divine climate and virgin soil of the Transvaal grow at the most extraordinary rate, were for the most part very lofty, and as thick in the stem as English oaks of a hundred and fifty years' standing. The avenue was not over wide, and the trees were planted quite close one to another, with the result that their brown, pillar-like stems shot up for many feet without a branch, whilst high overhead the boughs crossed and intermingled in such a way as to form a leafy tunnel, through which the landscape beyond appeared as though through a telescope.

Down this charming avenue John and Bessie walked, and on reaching its limit they turned to the right and followed a little footpath winding in and out of the rocks that built up the plateau on the hillside whereon the house stood. Presently this led them through the orchard; then came a bare strip of veldt, a very dangerous spot in a thunderstorm, but a great safeguard to the stead and trees round it, for the ironstone cropped up here, and from the house one might often see flash after flash striking down on to it, and even running and zigzagging about its

surface. To the left of this ironstone were some cultivated lands, and in front of them the plantation, in which
John was anxious to inspect the recently planted wattles.

They walked up to the copse without saying a word.
It was surrounded by a ditch and a low sod wall, whereon
Bessie seated herself, remarking that she would wait there
till he had looked at the trees, as she was afraid of the
puff-adders, whereof a large and thriving family were
known to live in this plantation.

John assented, observing that the puff-adders were
brutes, and that he must have some pigs turned in to
destroy them, which the pigs effect by munching them up,
apparently without unpleasant consequences to themselves.
Then he departed on his errand, wending his way gingerly
through the feathery black wattles. It did not take long,
and he saw no puff-adders. When he had finished looking at the young trees, he returned, still walking delicately
like Agag. On reaching the border of the plantation, he
paused to look at Bessie, who was some twenty paces
from him, perched sideways on the low sod wall, and
framed, as it were, in the full rich light of the setting sun.
Her hat was off, for the sun had lost its burning force, and
the hand that held it hung idly by her, while her eyes
were fixed on the horizon flaming with all the varied
glories of an African sunset. He gazed at her sweet face
and lissom form, and some lines that he had read years
before floated into his mind—

> The little curls about her head
> Were all her crown of gold,
> Her dèlicate arms drooped downwards
> In slender mould,
> As white-veined leaves of lilies
> Curve and fold.
> She moved to measure of music,
> As a swan sails the stream—

He had got thus far when she turned and saw him, and he abandoned poetry in the presence of one who might well have inspired it.

'What are you looking at?' she said with a smile; 'the sunset?'

'No; I was looking at you.'

'Then you might have been better employed with the sky,' she answered, turning her head quickly. 'Look at it! Did you ever see such a sunset? We sometimes get them like that at this time of year when the thunder-storms are about.'

She was right; it was glorious. The heavy clouds which a couple of hours before had been rolling like celestial hearses across the azure deeps were now aflame with glory. Some of them glowed like huge castles wrapped in fire, others with the dull red heat of burning coal. The eastern heaven was one sheet of burnished gold that slowly grew to red, and higher yet to orange and the faintest rose. To the left departing sunbeams rested lovingly on grey Quathlamba's crests, even firing the eternal snows that lay upon his highest peak, and writing once more upon their whiteness the record of another day fulfilled. Lower down the sky floated little clouds, flame-flakes fallen from the burning mass above, and on the earth beneath lay great depths of shadow barred with the brightness of the dying light.

John stood and gazed at it, and its living, glowing beauty seemed to fire his imagination, as it fired earth and heaven, in such sort that the torch of love lit upon his heart like the sunbeams on the mountain tops. Then from the celestial beauty of the skies he turned to look at the earthly beauty of the woman who sat there before him, and found that also fair. Whether it was the con-templation of the glories of Nature—for there is always a suspicion of melancholy in beautiful things—or whatever it was, her face had a touch of sadness on it that he had never seen before, and which certainly added to its charm as a shadow adds to the charm of the light.

' What are you thinking of, Bessie ? ' he asked.

She looked up, and he saw that her lips were quivering a little. ' Well, do you know,' she said, ' oddly enough, I was thinking of my mother. I can only just recall her, a woman with a thin, sweet face. I remember one evening she was sitting in front of a house while the sun was setting as it is now, and I was playing by her, when suddenly she called me to her and kissed me, then pointed to the red clouds that were gathered in the sky, and said, " I wonder if you will ever think of me, dear, when I have passed through those golden gates ? " I did not understand what she meant, but somehow I have remembered the words, and though she died so long ago, I do often think of her ; ' and two large tears rolled down her face as she spoke.

Few men can bear to see a sweet and pretty woman in tears, and this little incident was too much for John, whose caution and doubts all went to the winds together.

' Bessie,' he said, ' don't cry, dear ; please, don't ! I can't bear to see you cry.'

She looked up as though to remonstrate at his words, then she looked down again.

' Listen, Bessie,' he went on awkwardly enough, ' I have something to say to you. I want to ask you if —if, in short, you will marry me. Wait a bit, don't say anything yet ; you know me pretty well by now. I am no chicken, dear, and I have knocked about the world a good deal, and had one or two love affairs like other people. But, Bessie, I never met such a sweet woman, or, if you will let me say it, such a lovely woman as you are, and if you will have me, dear, I think that I shall be the luckiest man in South Africa ; ' and he stopped, not knowing exactly what else to say, and feeling that the time had not come for action, if indeed it was to come at all.

When first she understood the drift of his talk Bessie had flushed up to the eyes, then the blood sank back to her breast, and left her as pale as a lily. She loved the man, and they were happy words to her, and she was satisfied with them, though perhaps some women might have thought that they left a good deal to be desired. But Bessie was not of an exacting nature.

At last she spoke.

'Are you sure,' she asked, 'that you mean all this ? You know sometimes people say things of a sudden, upon an impulse, and afterwards they wish that they never had been said. Then it would be rather awkward supposing I were to say "yes," would it not ? '

' Of course I am sure,' he said indignantly.

' You see,' went on Bessie, poking at the sod wall with the stick she held in her hand, ' perhaps in this place you might be putting an exaggerated value on me. You think I am pretty because you see nobody but Kafir and Boer women, and it would be the same with everything. I'm not fit to marry such a man as you,' she went on, with a sudden burst of distress ; ' I have never seen anything or anybody. I am nothing but an ignorant, half-educated farmer girl, with nothing to recommend me, and no fortune except my looks. You are different to me ; you are a man of the world, and if ever you went back to England I should be a drag on you, and you would be ashamed of me and my colonial ways. If it had been Jess now, it would have been different, for she has more brains in her little finger than I have in my whole body.'

Somehow this mention of Jess jarred upon John's nerves, and chilled him like a breath of cold wind on a hot day. He wanted to put Jess out of his mind just now.

'My dear Bessie,' he broke in, 'why do you suppose such things? I can assure you that, if you appeared in a London drawing-room, you would put most of the women into the shade. Not that there is much chance of my frequenting London drawing-rooms again,' he added.

'Oh, yes! I may be good-looking; I don't say that I am not; but can't you understand, I do not want you to marry me just because I am a pretty woman, as the Kafirs marry their wives? If you marry me at all I want you to marry me because you care for *me*, the real *me*, not my eyes and my hair. Oh, I don't know what to answer you! I don't, indeed!' and she began to cry softly.

'Bessie, dear Bessie!' said John, who was pretty well beside himself by this time, 'just tell me honestly—do you care about me? I am not worth much, I know, but if you do all this goes for nothing,' and he took her hand and drew her towards him, so that she half slipped, half rose from the sod wall and stood face to face with him, for she was a tall woman, and they were very nearly of a height.

Twice she raised her beautiful eyes to his to answer, and twice her courage failed her; then at last the truth broke from her almost with a cry:

'Oh, John, I love you with all my heart!'

And now it will be well to drop a veil over the rest of these proceedings, for there are some things that should be sacred, even from the pen of the historian, and the first transport of the love of a good woman is one of them.

Suffice it to say that they sat there side by side on the sod wall, and were happy as people ought to be under such circumstances, till the glory departed from the western sky and the world grew cold and pale, till the night came down and hid the mountains, and only the stars and they were left to look out across the dusky distances of the wilderness of plain.

Meanwhile a very different scene was being enacted up at the house half a mile away.

Not more than ten minutes after John and his lady-love had departed on that fateful walk to look at the young trees, Frank Muller's stalwart form, mounted on his great black horse, was to be seen leisurely advancing towards the blue-gum avenue. Jantjé was lurking about between the stems of the trees in the peculiar fashion that is characteristic of the Hottentot, and which doubtless is bred into him after tens of centuries of tracking animals and hiding from enemies. There he was, slipping from trunk to trunk, and gazing round him as though he expected each instant to discover the assegai of an ambushed foe or to hear the footfall of some savage beast of prey. Absolutely there was no reason why he should behave in this fashion; he was simply indulging his natural instincts where he thought nobody would observe him. Life at Mooifontein was altogether too tame and civilised for Jantjé's taste, and he needed periodical recreations of this sort. Like a civilised child he longed for wild beasts and enemies, and if there were none at hand he found a reflected satisfaction in making a pretence of their presence.

Presently, however, whilst they were yet a long way off, his quick ear caught the sound of the horse's footfalls, and he straightened himself and listened. Not satisfied with the results, he laid himself down, put his ear to the earth, and gave a guttural grunt of satisfaction.

'Baas Frank's black horse,' Jantjé muttered to himself. 'The black horse has a cracked heel, and one foot hits the ground more softly than the others. What is Baas Frank coming here for? After Missie [Bessie] I think. He would be mad if he knew that Missie went down to the plantation with Baas Niel just now. People go into plantations to kiss each other' (Jantjé was not far out there), 'and it would make Baas Frank mad if he knew that. He would strike me if I told him, or I would tell him.'

The horse's hoofs were drawing near by now, so Jantjé slipped as easily and naturally as a snake into a thick tuft of rank grass which grew between the blue gums, and waited. Nobody would have guessed that this tuft of grass hid a human being; not even a Boer would have guessed it, unless he had happened to walk right on to the spy, and then it would have been a chance but that the Hottentot managed to avoid being trodden on and escaped detection. Again there was no reason why he should hide himself in this fashion, except that it pleased him to do so.

Presently the big horse approached, and the snakelike Hottentot raised his head ever so little and peered out with his beady black eyes through the straw-like grass stems. They fell on Muller's cold face. It was evident that he was in a reflective mood—in an angrily reflective mood. So absorbed was he that he nearly let his horse, which was also absorbed by the near prospect of a comfortable stall, put his foot into a big hole that a wandering antbear had amused himself on the previous night by digging exactly in the centre of the road.

'What is Baas Frank thinking of, I wonder?' said Jantjé to himself as horse and man passed within four feet of him. Then rising, he crossed the road, and slipping round by a back way like a fox from a covert, was standing at the stable-door with a vacant and utterly unobservant expression of face some seconds before the black horse and its rider had reached the house.

'I will give them one more chance, just one more,' thought the handsome Boer, or rather half-breed—for it will be remembered that his mother was English—'and if they won't take it, then let their fate be upon their own heads. To-morrow I go to the bÿmakaar [meeting] at Paarde Kraal to take counsel with Paul Krüger and Pretorius, and the other "fathers of the land," as they call themselves. If I throw in my weight against rebellion there will be no rebellion; if I urge it there will be, and if Oom Silas will not give me Bessie, and Bessie will not marry me, I will urge it even if it plunge the whole country in war from the Cape to Waterberg. Patriotism! Independence! Taxes!—that is what they all cry till they begin to believe it themselves. Bah! those are not the things that I would go to war for; but ambition and revenge, ah! that is another matter. I would kill them all if they stood in my way, all except Bessie. If war breaks out, who will hold up a hand to help the "verdomde Englesmann"? They would all be afraid. And it is not my fault. Can I help it if I love that woman? Can I help it if my blood dries up with longing for her, and if I lie awake hour by hour of nights, ay, and weep—I, Frank Muller, who saw the murdered bodies of my father and my mother and shed no tear—because she hates me and will not look favourably upon me?

E

'Oh, woman! woman! They talk of ambition and of avarice and of self-preservation as the keys of character and action, but what force is there to move us like a woman? A little thing, a weak fragile thing—a toy from which the rain will wash the paint and of which the rust will stop the working, and yet a thing that can shake the world and pour out blood like water, and bring down sorrow like the rain. So! I stand by the boulder. A touch and it will go crashing down the mountain-side so that the world hears it. Shall I send it? It is all one to me. Let Bessie and Oom Silas judge. I would slaughter every Englishman in the Transvaal to gain Bessie—ay! and every Boer too, and throw all the natives in;' and he laughed aloud, and struck the great black horse, making it plunge and caper gallantly.

'And then,' he went on, giving his ambition wing, 'when I have won Bessie, and we have kicked all these Englishmen out of the land, in a very few years I shall rule this country, and what next? Why, then I will stir up the Dutch feeling in Natal and in the old Colony, and we will push the Englishmen back into the sea, make a clean sweep of the natives, only keeping enough for servants, and have a united South Africa, like that poor silly man Burgers used to prate of, but did not know how to bring about. A united Dutch South Africa, and Frank Muller to rule it! Well, such things have been, and may be again. Give me forty years of life and strength, and we shall see——'

Just then he reached the verandah of the house, and, dismissing his secret ambitions from his mind, Frank Muller dismounted and entered. In the sitting-room he found Silas Croft reading a newspaper.

'Good-day, Oom Silas,' he said, extending his hand.

'Good-day, Meinheer Frank Muller,' replied the old

man very coldly, for John had told him of the incident at the shooting-party which so nearly ended fatally, and though he made no remark he had formed his own conclusions.

'What are you reading in the "Volkstem," Oom Silas —about the Bezuidenhout affair?'

'No; what was that?'

'It was that the volk are rising against you English, that is all. The sheriff seized Bezuidenhout's waggon in execution of taxes, and put it up to sale at Potchefstroom. But the volk kicked the auctioneer off the waggon and hunted him round the town; and now Governor Lanyon is sending Raaf down with power to swear in special constables and enforce the law at Potchefstroom. He might as well try to stop a river by throwing stones. Let me see, the big meeting at Paarde Kraal was to have been on the fifteenth of December, now it is to be on the eighth, and then we shall know if it will be peace or war.'

'Peace or war?' answered the old man testily. 'That has been the cry for years. How many big meetings have there been since Shepstone annexed the country? Six, I think. And what has come of it all? Just nothing but talk. And what can come of it? Suppose the Boers did fight, what would the end of it be? They would be beaten, and a lot of people would be killed, and that would be the end of it. You don't suppose that England would give in to a handful of Boers, do you? What did General Wolseley say the other day at the dinner at Potchefstroom? Why, that the country would never be given up, because no Government, Conservative, Liberal, or Radical, would dare to do it. And now this new Gladstone Government has telegraphed the same thing, so what is the use of all the talk and childishness? Tell me that, Frank Muller.'

Muller laughed as he answered, ' You are all very simple people, you English. Don't you know that a government is like a woman who cries " No, no, no," and kisses you all the time ? If there is noise enough your British Government will eat its words and give Wolseley, and Shepstone, and Bartle Frere, and Lanyon, and all of them the lie. This is a bigger business than you think for, Oom Silas. Of course all these meetings and talk are got up. The people are angry because of the English way of dealing with the natives, and because they have to pay taxes ; and they think, now that you British have paid their debts and smashed up Sikukuni and Cetewayo, that they would like to have the land back. They were glad enough for you to take it at first ; now it is another matter. But still that is not much. If they were left to themselves nothing would come of it except talk, for many of them are very glad that the land should be English. But the men who pull the strings are down in the Cape. They want to drive every Englishman out of South Africa. When Shepstone annexed the Transvaal he turned the scale against the Dutch element and broke up the plans they have been laying for years to make a big anti-English republic of the whole country. If the Transvaal remains British there is an end of their hopes, for only the Free State is left, and it is hemmed in. That is why they are so angry, and that is why their tools are stirring up the people. They mean to make them fight now, and I think that they will succeed. If the Boers win the day, they will declare themselves ; if not, you will hear nothing of them, and the Boers will bear the brunt of it. They are very cunning people the Cape " patriots," but they look well after themselves.'

Silas Croft looked troubled, but made no answer, and Frank Muller rose and stared out of the window.

CHAPTER XIII

FRANK MULLER SHOWS HIS HAND

PRESENTLY Muller turned round. ' Do you know why I have told you all this, Oom Silas? ' he asked.

' No.'

' Because I want you to understand that you and all the Englishmen in this country are in a very dangerous position. The war is coming, and whether it goes for you or against you, you must suffer. You Englishmen have many enemies. You have got all the trade and own nearly half the land, and you are always standing up for the black people, whom the Boers hate. It will go hard with you if there is a war. You will be shot and your houses will be burnt, and if you lose the day those who escape will be driven out of the country. It will be the Transvaal for the Transvaalers, then, and Africa for the Africanders.'

' Well, Frank Muller, and if all this should come to pass, what of it? What are you driving at, Frank Muller? You don't show me your hand like this for nothing.'

The Boer laughed. ' Of course I don't, Oom Silas. Well, if you want to know, I will tell you what I mean. I mean that I alone can protect you and your place and people in the bad times which are coming. I have more influence in the land than you know of. Perhaps even, I could stave off the war, and if it suited me to do so I would do it. At the least I could keep you from being harmed, that I know. But I have my price, Oom Silas, as we all have, and it must be money down and no credit.'

'I don't understand you and your dark sayings,' said the old man coldly. 'I am a straightforward man, and if you will tell me what you mean I will give you my answer; if not, I don't see the good of our going on talking.'

'Very well; I will tell you what I mean. I mean *Bessie*. I mean that I love your niece and want to marry her—ay, I mean to marry her by fair means or foul—and that she will have nothing to say to me.'

'And what have I to do with that, Frank Muller? The girl is her own mistress. I cannot dispose of her in marriage, even if I wished it, as though she were a colt or an ox. You must plead your own suit and take your own answer.'

'I have pleaded my suit and I have got my answer,' replied the Boer with passion. 'Don't you understand, she will have nothing to say to me? She is in love with that damned rooibaatje Niel whom you have brought up here. She is in love with him, I say, and will not look at me.'

'Ah,' replied Silas Croft, calmly, 'is it so? Then she shows very good taste, for John Niel is an honest man, Frank Muller, and you are not. Listen to me,' he went on, with a sudden outburst of passion; 'I tell you that you are a dishonourable man and a villain. I tell you that you murdered the Hottentot Jantjé's father, mother, and uncle in cold blood when you were yet a lad. I tell you that the other day you tried to murder John Niel, pretending to mistake him for a buck! And now you, who petitioned for this country to be taken over by the Queen, and have gone round singing out your loyalty at the top of your voice, come and tell me that you are plotting to bring about an insurrection, and to plunge the land into war, and ask me for Bessie as the price of your protection! But I will tell you something in answer, Frank Muller,' and the old man rose up, his keen eyes flashing in wrath, and, straightening his bent frame, he pointed towards the door. ' Go out of that door and never come through it again. I rely upon God and the English nation to protect me, and not on such as you, and I would rather see my dear Bessie dead in her coffin than married to a knave and traitor and a murderer like Frank Muller. Go ! '

The Boer turned white with fury as he listened. Twice he tried to speak and failed, and when the words did come they were so choked and laden with passion as to be scarcely audible. When thwarted he was liable to these accesses of rage, and, speaking figuratively, they spoilt his character. Could he have kept his head, he would have been a perfect and triumphant villain, but as it was, the carefully planned and audacious rascality of years was always apt to be swept away by the sudden gale of his furious passion. It was in such an outburst of rage that he had assaulted John in the inn yard at Wakkerstroom, and thereby put him on his guard against him, and now it mastered him once more.

' Very well, Silas Croft,' he said at last, ' I will go ; but mark this, I will come back, and when I come it shall be with men armed with rifles. I will burn this pretty place of yours, that you are so proud of, over your head, and I will kill you and your friend the Englishman, and take Bessie away, and very soon she shall be glad enough to marry Frank Muller ; but then I will not marry her—no, not if she goes on her knees to me—and she shall go on her knees often enough. We will see then what God and the English nation will do to protect you. God and the English nation! Call on the sheep and the horses; call on the rocks and the trees, and you will get a better answer.'

'Go!' thundered the old man, 'or by the God you blaspheme I will put a bullet through you,' and he reached towards a rifle that hung over the mantelpiece, 'or my Kafirs shall whip you off the place.'

Frank Muller waited for no more. He turned and went. It was dark now, but there was still some light in the sky at the end of the blue-gum avenue, and against it, as he rode away, he discovered Bessie's tall and graceful form softly outlined upon the darkening night. John had left her to see about some pressing matter connected with the farm, and there she stood, filled with the great joy of a woman who has found her love, and loth as yet to break its spell by entering again into the daily round of common life.

There she stood, a type and symbol of all that is beautiful and gracious in this rough world, the lovelights shining in her blue eyes and thoughts of happy gratitude to the Giver of all good rising from her heart to Heaven, drawn up thither, as it were, by the warmth of her pure passion, as the dew mists of the morning are drawn upward by the sun. There she was, so good, so happy, and so sweet; an answer to the world's evil, a symbol of the world's joy, and an incarnation of the world's beauty! Who but a merciful and almighty Father can create children such as she, so lovely, so lovable, and set them on the world as He sets the stars upon the sky to light it and make beholders think of holy things, and who but man could have the heart to turn such as she to the base uses whereto they are daily turned?

Presently she heard the horse's hoofs, and looked up, so that the faint light fell full upon her face, idealising it, and making its passion-breathing beauty seem more of Heaven than of earth. There was some look upon it, some indefinable light that day—such is the power that Love has to infuse all human things with the tint of his own splendour—that it went even to the heart of the wild and evil man who adored her with the deep and savage force of his dark nature. For a moment he paused half regretful, half afraid. Was it well to meddle with her, and to build up plans for her overthrow and that of all to whom she clung? Would it not be better to let her be, to go his way and leave her to go hers in peace? She did not look quite like a woman standing there, but more like something belonging to another world, some subject of a higher rule. Men of powerful but undisciplined intellect like Frank Muller are never entirely free from superstition, however free they may be from religion, and he grew superstitious as he was apt to do. Might there not be an unknown penalty for treading such a flower as that into the mire—into mire mixed perchance with the blood of those she loved?

For a few seconds he hesitated. Should he throw up the whole affair, leave the rebellion to look after itself, marry one of Hans Coetzee's daughters, and trek to the old colony, or Bechuanaland, or anywhere? His hand began to tighten on his bridle-rein and the horse to answer to the pressure. As a first step towards it he would turn away to the left and avoid her, when suddenly the thought of his successful rival flashed into his mind. What, leave her with that man? Never! He had rather kill her with his own hand. In another second he had sprung from his horse, and, before she guessed who it was, he was standing face to face with her. The strength of his jealous desire overpowered him.

'Ah, I thought he had come after missie,' said Jantjé, who, pursuing his former tactics, was once more indulging his passion for slinking about behind trees and in tufts of grass. 'Now what will missie say?'

'How are you, Bessie?' said Muller in a quiet voice, but she, looking into his face, saw that it belied the voice. It was alive with evil passions that seemed to make it positively lurid, an effect that its undoubted beauty only intensified.

'I am quite well, thank you, Mr. Muller,' she answered as she began to move homewards, commanding her voice as well as she could, but feeling dreadfully frightened and lonely. She knew something of her admirer's character, and feared to be left alone with him so far from any help, for nobody was about now, and they were more than three hundred yards from the house.

He stood before her so that she could not pass without actually pushing by him. 'Why are you in such a hurry?' he said. 'You were standing still enough just now.'

'It is time for me to be going in. I want to see about the supper.'

'The supper can wait awhile, Bessie, and I cannot wait. I am starting for Paarde Kraal to-morrow at daybreak, and I want to say good-bye to you first.'

'Good-bye,' she said, more frightened than ever at his curious constrained manner, and she held out her hand.

He took it and retained it.

'Please let me go,' she said.

'Not till you have heard what I have to say. Look here, Bessie, I love you with all my heart. I know you think I am only a Boer, but I am more than that. I have been to the Cape and seen the world. I have brains, and can see and understand things, and if you will marry me I will lift you up. You shall be one of the first ladies in Africa, though I am only plain Frank Muller now. Great things are going to happen in the country, and I shall be at the head of them, or near it. No, don't try to get away. I tell you I love you, you don't know how. I am dying for you. Oh! can't you believe me? my darling! my darling! Yes, I *will* kiss you,' and in an agony of passion, that her resistance only fired the more, he flung his strong arms round her and drew her to his breast, fight as she would.

But at this opportune moment an unexpected diversion occurred, of which the hidden Jantjé was the cause. Seeing that matters were becoming serious, and being afraid to show himself lest Frank Muller should kill him then and there, as indeed he would have been quite capable of doing, he hit upon another expedient, to the service of which he brought a ventriloquistic power that is not uncommon among natives. Suddenly the silence was broken by a frightful and prolonged wail that seemed to shape itself into the word ' Frank,' and to proceed from the air just above the struggling Bessie's head. The effect produced upon Muller was something wonderful.

' Allemachter! ' he cried, looking up, ' it is my mother's voice! '

' *Frank!* ' wailed the voice again, and he let go of Bessie in his perplexity and fear, and turned round to try and discover whence the sound proceeded—a circumstance of which that young lady took advantage to beat a rapid if not very dignified retreat.

' *Frank! Frank! Frank!* ' wailed and howled the voice, now overhead, now on this side, now on that, till at last Muller, thoroughly mystified and feeling his super-stitious fears rising apace as the moaning sound flitted about beneath the dark arch of the gum-trees, made a rush for his horse, which was snorting and trembling in every limb. It is almost as easy to work upon the superstitious fears of a dog or a horse as upon those of a man, but Muller, not being aware of this, took the animal's alarm as a clear indication of the uncanny nature of the voice. With a single bound he sprang into his saddle, and as he did so the woman's voice wailed out once more—

'*Frank*, thou shalt die in blood as I did, Frank!'

Muller turned livid with fear, and the cold perspiration streamed from his face. He was a bold man enough physically, but this was too much for his nerves.

'It is my mother's voice, they are her very words!' he called out aloud, then, dashing his spurs into his horse's flanks, he went like a flash far from the accursed spot; nor did he draw rein till he came to his own place ten miles away. Twice the horse fell in the darkness, for there was no moon, the second time throwing him heavily, but he only dragged it up with an oath, and springing into the saddle again fled on as before.

Thus the man who did not hesitate to plot and to execute the cruel slaughter of unoffending men cowered beneath the fancied echo of a dead woman's voice! Truly human nature is full of contradictions.

When the thunder of the horse's hoofs grew faint Jantjé emerged from one of his hiding-places, and, throwing himself down in the centre of the dusty road, kicked and rolled with delight, shaking all the while with an inward joy to which his habits of caution would not permit him to give audible vent. 'His mother's voice, his mother's words,' he quoted to himself. 'How should he know that Jantjé remembers the old woman's voice— ay, and the words that the devil in her spoke too? Hee! hee! hee!'

Finally he departed to eat his supper of beef, which he had cut off an unfortunate ox which that morning had expired of a mysterious complication of diseases, filled with a happy sense that he had not lived that day in vain.

Bessie fled without stopping till she reached the orange-trees in front of the verandah, where, reassured by the lights from the windows, she paused to consider. Not that she was troubled by Jantjé's mysterious howling; indeed, she was too preoccupied to give it a second thought. What she debated was whether she should say anything about her encounter with Frank Muller. Young ladies are not, as a rule, too fond of informing their husbands or lovers that somebody has kissed them; first, because they know it will force them to make a disturbance and possibly to place themselves in a ridiculous position; and, secondly, because they fear lest suspicious man might take the story with a grain of salt, and suggest even that they, the kissed, were themselves to blame. Both these reasons presented themselves to Bessie's practical mind, also a further one, namely, that he had not kissed her after all. So on a rapid review of the whole case she came to the decision to say nothing to John about it, and only enough to her uncle to make him forbid Frank Muller the house—an unnecessary precaution, as the reader will remember. Then, after pausing for a few seconds to pick a branch of orange blossom and to recover herself generally, which, not being hysterically inclined, she very soon did, she entered the house quietly as though nothing had happened. The very first person she met was John himself, who had come in by the back way. He laughed at her orange-blossom bouquet, and said that it was most appropriate, then proceeded to embrace her tenderly in the passage; and indeed he would have been a poor sort of lover if he had not. It was exactly at this juncture that old Silas Croft happened to open the sitting-room door and became the spectator of this surprising and attractive tableau.

'Well, I never!' said the old gentleman. 'What is the meaning of all this, Bessie?'

Of course there was nothing for it but to advance and explain the facts of the case, which John did with much humming and ha-ing and a general awkwardness of manner that baffles description, while Bessie stood by, her hand upon her lover's shoulder, blushing as red as any rose.

Mr. Croft listened in silence till John had finished, a smile upon his face and a kindly twinkle in his keen eyes.

'So,' he said, 'that is what you young people have been after, is it? I suppose that you want to enlarge your interests in the farm, eh, John? Well, upon my word, I don't blame you; you might have gone farther and fared worse. These sort of things never come singly, it seems. I had another request for your hand, my dear, only this afternoon, from that scoundrel Frank Muller, of all men in the world,' and his face darkened as he said the name. 'I sent him off with a flea in his ear, I can tell you. Had I known then what I know now, I should have referred him to John. There, there! He is a bad man, and a dangerous man, but let him be. He is taking plenty of rope, and he will hang himself one of these days. Well, my dears, this is the best bit of news that I have heard for many a long year. It's time you got married, both of you, for it is not right for man to live alone, or woman either. I have done it all my life, and that is the conclusion I have come to after thinking the matter over for somewhere about fifty years. Yes, you have my consent and my blessing too, and you will have something more one day before so very long. Take her, John, take her. I have led a rough life, but I have seen somewhat of women for all that, and I tell you that there is not a sweeter or a better or a prettier girl in South Africa than Bessie Croft, and in wanting to marry her you have shown your sense. God bless you both, my dears; and now, Bessie, come and give your old uncle a kiss. I hope that you won't let John quite drive me out of your head, that's all, for you see, my dear, having no children of my own, I have managed to grow very fond of you in the last twelve years or so.'

Bessie kissed the old man tenderly.

'No, uncle,' she answered, 'neither John nor anybody nor anything in the world can do that,' and it was evident from her manner that she meant what she said. Bessie had a large heart, and was not at all the person to let her lover drive her uncle and benefactor out of his share thereof.

CHAPTER XIV

JOHN TO THE RESCUE

THE important domestic events described in the last
chapter took place on December 7, 1880, and for the next
twelve days or so everything went as happily at Mooifontein as things should go under the circumstances. Every
day Silas Croft beamed with an enlarged geniality in his
satisfaction at the turn that matters had taken, and every
day John found cause to congratulate himself more and
more on the issue of his bold venture towards matrimony.
Now that he came to be on such intimate terms with his
betrothed, he perceived a hundred charms and graces
in her nature which before he had never suspected.
Bessie was like a flower: the more she basked in the
light and warmth of her love the more her character
opened and unfolded, shedding perfumed sweetness
around her and revealing unguessed charms. It is so
with all women, and more especially with a woman of
her stamp, whom Nature has made to love and be loved
as maid and wife and mother. Her undoubted personal
beauty shared also in this development, her fair face
taking a richer hue and her eyes an added depth and
meaning. She was in every respect, save one, all that
a man could desire in his wife, and even the exception
would have stood to her credit with many men. It was
this; she was not an intellectual person, although cer-

tainly she possessed more than the ordinary share of intelligence and work-a-day common sense. Now John was a decidedly intellectual man, and, what is more, he highly appreciated that rare quality in the other sex. But, after all, when one is just engaged to a sweet and lovely woman, one does not think much about her intellect. Those reflections come afterwards.

And so they sauntered hand in hand through the sunny days and were happy exceedingly. Least of all did they allow the rumours which reached them from the great Boer gathering at Paarde Kraal to disturb their serenity. There had been so many of these reports of rebellion that folk were beginning to regard them as a chronic state of affairs.

' Oh, the Boers ! ' said Bessie with a pretty toss of her golden head, as they were sitting one morning on the verandah. ' I am sick to death of hearing about the Boers and all their got-up talk. I know what it is ; it is just an excuse for them to go away from their farms and wives and children and idle about at these great meetings, and drink " square-face " with their mouths full of big words. You see what Jess says in her last letter. People in Pretoria believe that it is all nonsense from beginning to end, and I think they are perfectly right.'

' By the way, Bessie,' asked John, ' have you written to Jess telling her of our engagement ? '

' Oh yes, I wrote some days ago, but the letter only went yesterday. She will be pleased to hear about it. Dear old Jess, I wonder when she means to come home again. She has been away long enough.'

John made no answer, but went on smoking his pipe in silence, wondering if Jess would be pleased. He did not understand her yet. She had gone away just as he was beginning to understand her,

Presently he observed Jantjé sneaking about between the orange-trees as though he wished to call attention to himself. Had he not wanted to do so he would have moved from one to the other in such a way that nobody could have seen him. His partial and desultory appearances indicated that he was on view.

'Come out of those trees, you little rascal, and stop slipping about like a snake in a stone wall!' shouted John. 'What is it you want—wages?'

Thus adjured, Jantjé advanced and sat down on the path, as usual in the full glare of the sun.

'No, Baas,' he said, 'it is not wages. They are not due yet.'

'What is it, then?'

'No, Baas, it is this. The Boers have declared war on the English Government, and they have eaten up the rooibaatjes at Bronker's Spruit, near Middelburg. Joubert shot them all there the day before yesterday.'

'What!' shouted John, letting his pipe fall in his astonishment. 'Stop, though, that must be a lie. You say near Middelburg, the day before yesterday: that would be December 20. When did you hear this?'

'At daybreak, Baas. A Basutu told me.'

'Then there is an end of it. The news could not have reached here in thirty-eight hours. What do you mean by coming to me with such a tale?'

The Hottentot smiled. 'It is quite true, Baas. Bad news flies like a bird,' and he picked himself up and slipped off to his work.

Notwithstanding the apparent impossibility of the thing, John was considerably disturbed, knowing the extraordinary speed with which tidings do travel among Kafirs, more swiftly, indeed, than the fleetest mounted messenger can bear them. Leaving Bessie, who was also somewhat alarmed, he went in search of Silas Croft, and, finding him in the garden, told him what Jantjé had said. The old man did not know what to make of the tale, but, remembering Frank Muller's threats, he shook his head.

'If there is any truth in it, that villain Muller has a hand in it,' he said. 'I'll go to the house and see Jantjé. Give me your arm, John.'

He obeyed, and, on arriving at the top of the steep path, they perceived the stout figure of old Hans Coetzee, who had been John's host at the shooting-party, ambling along on his fat little pony.

'Ah,' said Silas, 'here is the man who will tell us if there is anything in it all.'

'Good-day, Oom Coetzee, good-day!' he shouted out in his stentorian tones. 'What news do you bring with you?'

The jolly-looking Boer rolled awkwardly off his pony before answering, and, throwing the reins over its head, came to meet them.

'Allemachter, Oom Silas, it is bad news. You have heard of the "bÿmakaar" [meeting] at Paarde Kraal. Frank Muller wanted me to go, but I would not, and now they have declared war on the British Government and sent a proclamation to Lanyon. There will be fighting, Oom Silas, the land will run with blood, and the poor rooibaatjes will be shot down like buck.'

'The poor Boers, you mean,' growled John, who did not like to hear her Majesty's army talked of in terms of regretful pity.

Oom Coetzee shook his head with the air of one who knew all about it, and then turned an attentive ear to Silas Croft's version of Jantjé's story.

'Allemachter!' groaned Coetzee, 'what did I tell you? The poor rooibaatjes shot down like buck, and the land running with blood! And now that Frank Muller will draw me into it, and I shall have to go and shoot the poor rooibaatjes; and I can't miss, try as hard as I will, I *can't* miss. And when we have shot them all I suppose that Burgers will come back, and he is "kransick" [mad]. Yes, yes; Lanyon is bad, but Burgers is worse,' and the comfortable old gentleman groaned aloud at the troubles in which he foresaw he would be involved, and finally took his departure by a bridle-path over the mountain, saying that, as things had turned out, he would not like it to be known that he had been calling on an Englishman. 'They might think that I was not loyal to the "land,"' he added in explanation; 'the land which we Boers bought with our blood, and which we shall win back with our blood, whatever the poor "pack oxen" of rooibaatjes try to do. Ah, those poor, poor rooibaatjes, one Boer will drive away twenty of them and make them run across the veldt, if they can run in those great knapsacks of theirs, with the tin things hanging round them like the pots and kettles to the bed-plank of a waggon. What says the Holy Book? "One thousand shall flee at the rebuke of one, and at the rebuke of five shall ye flee," at least I think that is it. The dear Lord knew what was coming when He wrote it. He was thinking of the Boers and the poor rooibaatjes,' and Coetzee departed, shaking his head sadly.

'I am glad that the old gentleman has made tracks,' said John, 'for if he had gone on much longer about the poor English soldiers he would have fled "at the rebuke of one," I can tell him.'

'John,' said Silas Croft suddenly, 'you must go up to Pretoria and fetch Jess. Mark my words, the Boers will besiege Pretoria, and if we don't get her down at once she will be shut up there.'

' Oh no,' cried Bessie, in sudden alarm, ' I cannot let John go.'

' I am sorry to hear you talk like that, Bessie, when your sister is in danger,' answered her uncle rather sternly; ' but there, I dare say that it is natural. I will go myself. Where is Jantjé? I shall want the Cape cart and the four grey horses.'

' No, uncle dear, John shall go. I was not thinking what I was saying. It seemed—a little hard at first.'

' Of course I must go,' said John. ' Don't fret, dear, I shall be back in five days. Those four horses can go sixty miles a day for that time, and more. They are fat as butter, and there is lots of grass along the road if I can't get forage for them. Besides, the cart will be nearly empty, so I can carry a muid of mealies and fifty bundles of forage. I will take that Zulu boy, Mouti, with me. He does not know very much about horses, but he is a plucky fellow, and would stick by one at a pinch. One can't rely on Jantjé; he is always sneaking off somewhere, and would be sure to get drunk just as one wanted him.'

' Yes, yes, John, that's right, that's right,' said the old man. ' I will go and see about having the horses got up and the wheels greased. Where is the castor-oil, Bessie? There is nothing like castor-oil for these patent axles. You ought to be off in an hour. You had better sleep at Luck's to-night; you might get farther, but Luck's is a good place to stop, and they will look after you well there, and you can be off by three in the morning, reaching Heidelberg by ten o'clock to-morrow night, and Pretoria by the next afternoon,' and he bustled away to make the necessary preparations.

' Oh, John,' said Bessie, beginning to cry, ' I don't like your going at all among all those wild Boers. You are an English officer, and if they find you out they will shoot you. You don't know what brutes some of them are when they think it safe to be so. Oh, John, John, I can't endure your going.'

'Cheer up, my dear,' said John, 'and for Heaven's sake stop crying, for I cannot bear it. I must go. Your uncle would never forgive me if I did not, and, what is more, I should never forgive myself. There is nobody else to send, and we can't leave Jess to be shut up there in Pretoria—for months perhaps. As for the risk, of course there is a little risk, but I must take it. I am not afraid of risks—at least I used not to be, but you have made a bit of a coward of me, Bessie dear. There, give me a kiss, old girl, and come and help me to pack my things. Please God I shall get back all right, and Jess with me, in a week from now.'

Whereon Bessie, being a sensible and eminently practical young woman, dried her tears, and with a cheerful face, albeit her heart was heavy enough, set to work with a will to make every possible preparation.

The few clothes John was to take with him were packed in a Gladstone bag, the box fitted underneath the movable seat in the Cape cart was filled with the tinned provisions which are so much used in South Africa, and all the other little arrangements, small in themselves, but of such infinite importance to the traveller in a wild country, were duly attended to by her careful hands. Then came a hurried meal, and before it was swallowed the cart was at the door, with Jantjé hanging as usual on to the heads of the two front horses, and the stalwart Zulu, or rather Swazi boy, Mouti, whose sole luggage appeared to consist of a bundle of assegais and sticks wrapped up in a grass mat, and who, hot as it was, was enveloped in a vast military great-coat, lounging placidly alongside.

'Good-bye, John, dear John,' said Bessie, kissing him again and again, and striving to keep back the tears that, do what she could, would gather in her blue eyes. 'Good-bye, my love.'

'God bless you, dearest,' he said simply, kissing her in answer; 'good-bye, Mr. Croft. I hope to see you again in a week,' and he was in the cart and had gathered up the long and intricate-looking reins. Jantjé let go the horses' heads and uttered a whoop. Mouti, giving up star-gazing, suddenly became an animated being and scrambled into the cart with surprising alacrity; the horses sprang forward at a hand gallop, and were soon hidden from Bessie's dim sight in a cloud of dust. Poor Bessie, it was a hard trial, and now that John had gone and her tears could not distress him, she went into her room and gave way to them freely enough.

John reached Luck's, a curious establishment on the Pretoria road, such as are to be met with in sparsely populated countries, combining the characteristics of an inn, a shop, and a farm-house. It was not an inn and not a farm-house, strictly speaking, nor was it altogether a shop, though there was a 'store' attached. If the traveller is anxious to obtain accommodation for man and beast at a place of this stamp he has to proceed warily, so to say, lest he should be requested to move on. He must advance, hat in hand, and ask to be taken in as a favour, as many a stiff-necked wanderer, accustomed to the obsequious attentions of 'mine host,' has learnt to his cost. There is no such dreadful autocrat as your half-and-half innkeeper in South Africa, and then he is so completely master of the situation. 'If you don't like it, go and be d—d to you,' is his simple answer to the remonstrances of the infuriated voyager. Then you must either knock under and look as though you liked it, or

trek on into the 'unhostelled' wilderness. But on this
occasion John fared well enough. To begin with, he
knew the owners of this place, who were very civil
people if approached in a humble spirit, and, further-
more, he found everybody in such a state of unpleasurable
excitement that they were only too glad to get another
Englishman with whom to talk over matters. Not that
their information amounted to much, however. There
was a rumour of the Bronker's Spruit disaster and other
rumours of the investment of Pretoria, and of the advance of large bodies of Boers to take possession of the
pass over the Drakensberg, known as Laing's Nek, but
there was no definite intelligence.

'You won't get into Pretoria,' said one melancholy
man, ' so it's no use trying. The Boers will just catch
you and kill you, and there will be an end of it. You had
better leave the girl to look after herself and go back to
Mooifontein.'

But this was not John's view of the matter. 'Well,'
he answered, ' at any rate I'll have a try.' Indeed, he had a
sort of bull-dog nature about him which led him to believe
that if he made up his mind to do a thing, he would do it
somehow, unless he should be physically incapacitated by
circumstances beyond his own control. It is wonderful
how far a mood of the kind will take a man. Indeed, it
is the widespread possession of this sentiment that has
made England what she is. Now it is beginning to die
down and to be legislated out of our national character,
and the results are already commencing to appear in the
incipient decay of our power. We cannot govern Ireland.
It is beyond us ; let Ireland have Home Rule ! We
cannot cope with our Imperial responsibilities ; let them
be cast off: and so on. The Englishmen of fifty years
ago did not talk in this ' weary Titan ' strain.

Well, every nation becomes emasculated sooner or later, that seems to be the universal fate; and it appears that it is our lot to be emasculated, not by the want of law but by a plethora thereof. This country was made, not by Governments, but for the most part in despite of them, by the independent efforts of generations of individuals. The tendency nowadays is to merge the individual in the Government, and to limit and even forcibly to destroy personal enterprise and responsibility. Everything is to be legislated for or legislated against. As yet the system is only in its bud. When it blooms, if it is ever allowed to bloom, the Empire will lose touch of its constituent atoms and become a vast soulless machine, which will first get out of order, then break down, and, last of all, break up. We owe more to sturdy, determined, unconvinceable Englishmen like John Niel than we know, or, perhaps, should be willing to acknowledge in these enlightened days. ' Long live the Caucus!' that is the cry of the nineteenth century. But what will Englishmen cry in the twentieth?[1]

John resumed his perilous journey more than an hour before dawn on the following morning. Nobody was stirring, and as it was practically impossible to arouse the slumbering Kafirs from the various holes and corners where they were taking their rest—for a native hates the cold of the dawning—Mouti and he were obliged to harness the horses and inspan them without assistance—an awkward job in the dark. At last,

---

[1] These words were written some ten years ago; but since then, with all gratitude be it said, a change has come over the spirit of the nation, or rather, the spirit of the nation has re-asserted itself. Though the 'Little England' party still lingers, it exists upon the edge of its own grave. The dominance and responsibilities of our Empire are no longer a question of party politics, and among the Radicals of to-day we find some of the most ardent Imperialists. So may it ever be!—H. R. H. 1896.

however, everything was ready, and, as the bill had been
paid overnight, there was nothing to wait for, so they
clambered into the cart and made a start. But before
they had proceeded forty yards, however, John heard a
voice calling to him to stop. He did so, and presently,
holding a lighted candle which burnt without a flicker in
the still damp air, and draped from head to foot in a
dingy-looking blanket, appeared the male Cassandra of
the previous evening.

He advanced slowly and with dignity, as became a
prophet, and at length reached the side of the cart,
where the sight of his illuminated figure and of the dirty
blanket over his head nearly made the horses run away.

'What is it?' said John testily, for he was in no
mood for delay.

'I thought I'd just get up to tell you,' replied the
draped form, 'that I am quite sure that I was right, and
that the Boers will shoot you. I should not like you to
say afterwards that I have not warned you,' and he held
up the candle so that the light fell on John's face, and
gazed at it in fond farewell.

'Curse it all,' said John in a fury, 'if that was all you
had to say you might have kept in bed,' and he brought
down his lash on the wheelers and away they went with
a bound, putting out the prophet's candle and nearly
knocking the prophet himself backwards into the sluit.

CHAPTER XV

A ROUGH JOURNEY

THE four greys were fresh horses, in good condition and
with a light load behind them, so, notwithstanding the
bad state of the tracks which they call roads in South
Africa, John made good progress.

By eleven o'clock that day he had reached Standerton,
a little town upon the Vaal, not far from which, had he
but known it, he was destined to meet with a sufficiently
striking experience. Here he obtained confirmation of
the Bronker's Spruit disaster, and listened with set face
and blazing eyes to the tale of treachery and death which
was, as he said, without a parallel in the annals of civilised war. But, after all, what does it matter?—a little
square of graves at Bronker's Spruit, a few more widows
and a hundred or so of orphans. England, by her
Government, answered the question plainly—it matters
very little.

At Standerton John was again warned that it would be
impossible for him to make his way through the Boers
at Heidelberg, a town about sixty miles from Pretoria,
where the Triumvirate, Krüger, Pretorius, and Joubert,
had proclaimed the Republic. But he answered as before,
that he must go on till he was stopped, and inspanning
his horses set forward again, a little comforted by the
news that the Bishop of Pretoria, who was hurrying up

to rejoin his family, had passed through a few hours before, also intent upon running the blockade, and that if he drove fast he might overtake him.

On he went, hour after hour, over the great deserted plain, but he did not succeed in catching up the Bishop. About forty miles from Standerton he saw a waggon standing by the roadside, and halted to try if he could obtain any information from its driver. But on investigation it became clear that the waggon had been looted of the provisions and goods with which it was loaded and the oxen driven off. Nor was this the only evidence of violence. Across the disselboom of the waggon, its hands still clasping a long bamboo whip, as though he had been trying to defend himself with it, lay the dead body of the native driver. His face, John noticed, was so composed and peaceful, that had it not been for the attitude and a neat little blue hole in the forehead, one might have thought he was asleep, not dead.

At sunset John outspanned his now flagging horses by the roadside, and gave them each a couple of bundles of forage from the store that he had brought with him. Whilst they were eating it, leaving Mouti to keep an eye to them, he strolled away and sat down on a big ant-heap to think. It was a wild and melancholy scene that stretched before and behind him. Miles upon miles of plain, rolling east and west and north and south like the billows of a frozen sea, only broken, far along the Heidelberg road, by some hills, known as Rooi Koppies. Nor was this all. Overhead was blazing and burning one of those remarkable sunsets which are sometimes seen in the South African summer time. The sky was full of lowering clouds, and the sullen orb of the setting sun had stained them perfectly blood-red. Blood-red they floated through the ominous sky, and blood-red

their shadows lay upon the grass. Even the air seemed
red. It looked as though earth and heaven had been
steeped in blood ; and, fresh as John was from the sight
of the dead driver, his ears yet tingling with the tale of
Bronker's Spruit, it is not to be wondered at that the
suggestive sight oppressed him, seated in that lonely
waste, with no company except the melancholy ' *kakara-
kakara* ' of an old black koran hidden away somewhere
in the grass. He was not much given to such reflections, but he did begin to wonder whether this was the
last journey of all the many he had made during the past
twenty years, and if for him a Boer bullet was about to
solve the mystery of life and death.

Then he sank to the stage of depression that most
people have made acquaintance with at some time or
another, when a man begins to ask, ' What is the use of it ?
Why were we born ? What good do we do here ? Why
should we—as the majority of mankind doubtless are—
mere animals be laden up with sorrows till at last our poor
backs break ? Is God powerful or powerless ? If powerful, why did He not let us sleep in peace, without setting
us here to taste of every pain and mortification, to
become acquainted with every grief, and then to perish
miserably ? ' Old questions these, which the sprightly
critic justly condemns as morbid and futile, and not
to be dangled before a merry world of make-believe.
Perhaps he is right. It is better to play at marbles on
a sepulchre than to lift the lid and peep inside. But, for
all that, they *will* arise when we sit alone at even in
our individual wildernesses, surrounded, perhaps, by me-
mentoes of our broken hopes and tokens of our beloved
dead, strewn about us like the bleaching bones of the
wild game on the veldt, and in spirit watch the red sun
of our existence sinking towards its vapoury horizon.

They *will* come even to the sanguine successful man.
One cannot always play at marbles; the lid of the
sepulchre will sometimes slip aside of itself, and we
must see.   True, it depends upon individual disposition.
Some people can, metaphorically, smoke cigarettes and
make puns by the death-beds of their dearest friends,
or even on their own.   We should pray for a disposition
like that—it makes life more pleasant.

By the time that the horses had eaten their forage and
Mouti had forced the bits into their reluctant mouths, the
angry splendour of the sunset faded, and the quiet night
was falling over the glowing veldt like the pall on one
scarce dead.   Fortunately for the travellers, there was
a bright half moon, and by its light John managed to
direct the cart over many a weary mile.   On he went for
hour after hour, keeping his tired horses to the collar as
best he could, till at last, about eleven o'clock, he saw
the lights of Heidelberg before him, and knew that the
question of whether or no his journey was at an end
would speedily be decided for him.   However, there was
nothing for it but to go on and take his chance of slipping
through.   Presently he crossed a little stream, and dis-
tinguished the shape of a cart just ahead, around which
men and a couple of lanterns were moving.   No doubt,
John thought to himself, it was the Bishop, who had been
stopped by the Boers.   He was quite close to the cart
when it moved on, and in another second he was greeted
by the rough challenge of a sentry, and caught sight of
the cold gleam of a rifle barrel.

' Wie da ? ' [Who's there ?]

' Friend ! ' he answered cheerfully, though feeling far
from cheerful.

There was a pause, during which the sentry called to
another man, who came up yawning, and saying some-

thing in Dutch. Straining his ears he caught the words, ' Bishop's man,' and this gave him an idea.

' Who are you, Englishman ? ' asked the second man gruffly, holding up a lantern to look at John, and speaking in English.

' I am the Bishop's chaplain, sir,' he answered mildly trying desperately to look like an unoffending clergyman, ' and I want to get on to Pretoria with him.'

The man with the lantern inspected him closely. Fortunately John wore a dark coat and a clerical-looking black felt hat ; the same that Frank Muller had put a bullet through.

' He is a preacher fast enough,' said the one man to the other. ' Look, he is dressed like an old crow ! What did Oom Krüger's pass say, Jan ? Was it two carts or one that we were to let through ? I think that it was one.'

The other man scratched his head.

' I think it was two,' he said. He did not like to confess to his comrade that he could not read. ' No, I am sure that it was two.'

' Perhaps we had better send up to Oom Krüger and ask ? ' suggested the first man.

' Oom Krüger will be in bed, and he puts up his quills like a porcupine if one wakes him,' was the answer.

' Then let us keep the damned preaching Englishman till to-morrow.'

' Pray let me go on, gentlemen,' said John, still in his mildest voice. ' I am wanted to preach the Word at Pretoria, and to watch by the wounded and dying.'

' Yes, yes,' said the first man, ' there will soon be plenty of wounded and dying there. They will all be like the rooibaatjes at Bronker's Spruit. Lord, what a sight that was! But they will get the Bishop, so they won't want you. You can stop and look after our wounded if the rooibaatjes manage to hit any of us.' And he beckoned to him to come out of the cart.

'Hullo!' said the other man, 'here is a bag of mealies. We will commandeer that, anyhow.' And he took his knife and cut the line with which the sack was fastened to the back of the cart, so that it fell to the ground. 'That will feed our horses for a week,' he said with a chuckle, in which the other man joined. It was pleasant to become so easily possessed of an unearned increment in the shape of a bag of mealies.

'Well, are we to let the old crow go?' said the first man.

'If we don't let him go we shall have to take him up to headquarters, and I want to sleep.' And he yawned.

'Well, let him go,' answered the other. 'I think you are right. The pass said two carts. Be off, you damned preaching Englishman!'

John did not wait for any more, but laid the whip across the horses' backs with a will.

'I hope we did right,' said the man with the lantern to the other as the cart bumped off. 'I am not sure he was a preacher after all. I have half a mind to send a bullet after him.' But his companion, who was very sleepy, gave no encouragement to the idea, so it dropped.

On the following morning when Commandant Frank Muller—having heard that his enemy John Niel was on his way up with the Cape cart and four grey horses—ascertained that a vehicle answering to that description had been allowed to pass through Heidelberg in the dead of night, his state of mind may better be imagined than described.

As for the two sentries, he tried them by court-martial and sent them to make fortifications for the rest of the rebellion. Now they can neither of them hear the name of a clergyman mentioned without breaking out into a perfect flood of blasphemy.

Luckily for John, although he had been delayed for five minutes or more, he managed to overtake the cart in which he presumed the Bishop was ensconced. His lordship had been providentially delayed by the breaking of a trace; otherwise, it is clear that his self-nominated chaplain would never have got through the steep streets of Heidelberg that night. The town was choked up with Boer waggons, full of sleeping Boers. Over one batch of waggons and tents John saw the Transvaal flag fluttering idly in the night breeze, marking, no doubt, the headquarters of the Triumvirate, and emblazoned with the appropriate emblem of an ox-waggon and an armed Boer. Once the cart ahead of him was stopped by a sentry, and some conversation ensued. Then it went on again; and so did John, unmolested. It was weary work, that journey through Heidelberg, and full of terrors for John, who every moment expected to be stopped and dragged off ignominiously to gaol. The horses, too, were dead beat, and made frantic attempts to turn and stop at every house. But, somehow, they won through the little place, and then were halted once more. Again the first cart passed on, but this time John was not so lucky.

'The pass said one cart,' said a voice.

'Yah, yah, one cart,' answered another.

John again put on his clerical air and told his artless tale; but neither of the men could understand English, so they went to a waggon that was standing about fifty yards away, to fetch somebody who could.

F

'Now, Inkoos,' whispered the Zulu Mouti, 'drive on! drive on!'

John took the hint and lashed the horses with his long whip; while Mouti, bending forward over the splashboard, thrashed the wheelers with a sjambock. Off went the team in a spasmodic gallop, and it had covered a hundred yards of ground before the two sentries realised what had happened. Then they began to run after the cart shouting, but were soon lost in the darkness.

John and Mouti did not spare the whip, but pressed on up the stony hills on the Pretoria side of Heidelberg without a halt. They were, however, unable to keep up with the cart ahead of them, which was evidently more freshly horsed. About midnight, too, the moon vanished altogether, and they must creep on as best they could through the darkness. Indeed, so dark was it, that Mouti was obliged to get out and lead the exhausted horses, one of which would now and again fall down, to be cruelly flogged before it rose. Once, too, the cart very nearly upset; and on another occasion it was within an inch of rolling down a precipice.

This went on till two in the morning, when John found that it was impossible to force the wearied beasts a yard farther. So, having luckily come to some water about fifteen miles out of Heidelberg, he halted, and after the horses had drunk, gave them as much forage as they could eat. One lay down at once, and refused to touch anything—a sure sign of great exhaustion; a second ate lying down; but the other two filled themselves in a satisfactory way. Then came a weary wait for the dawn. Mouti slept a little, but John did not dare to do so. All he could do was to swallow a little ' biltong ' [dried game flesh] and bread, drink some square-face and water, and then sit down in the cart, his rifle between his knees, and wait for the light. At last it came, lying on the eastern sky like a promise, and he once more fed the horses. And now a new difficulty arose. The animal that would not eat was clearly too weak to pull, so the harness had to be altered, and the three sound animals arranged unicorn fashion, while the sick one was fastened to the rear of the cart. Then they started again.

By eleven o'clock they reached an hotel, or wayside house, known as Ferguson's, situate about twenty miles from Pretoria. It was empty, except for a couple of cats and a stray dog. The inhabitants had evidently fled from the Boers. Here John stabled and fed his horses, giving them all that remained of the forage; and then, once more, inspanned for the last stage. The road was dreadful; and he knew that the country must be full of hostile Boers, but fortunately he met none. It took him four hours to cover the twenty miles of ground; but it was not until he reached the 'Poort,' or neck running into Pretoria, that he saw a vestige of a Boer. Then he perceived two mounted men riding along the top of a precipitous stone-strewn ridge, six hundred yards or so from him. At first he thought that they were going to descend it, but presently they changed their minds and got off their horses.

While he was still wondering what this might portend, he saw a puff of white smoke float up from where the men were, and then another. Next came the sharp unmistakable 'ping' of a bullet passing, as far as he could judge, within some three feet of his head, followed by a second 'ping,' and a cloud of dust beneath the belly of the first horse. The two Boers were firing at him.

John did not wait for any more target practice, but, thrashing the horses to a canter, drove the cart round a projecting bank before they could load and fire again. After that, they troubled him no more.

At last he reached the mouth of the Poort, and saw the prettiest of the South African towns, with its red and white houses, its tall clumps of trees, and pink lines of blooming rose hedges lying on the plain before him, all set in the green veldt, made beautiful by the golden light of the afternoon, and he thanked God for the sight. John knew that he was safe now, and let his tired horses walk slowly down the hillside and across the space of plain beyond.   To his left were the gaol and the barrack-sheds, and gathered about them stood hundreds of waggons and tents, towards which he drove.   Evidently the town was deserted and its inhabitants were in laager.   When he was within half a mile or so, a picket of mounted men rode out to meet him, followed by a miscellaneous crowd on horseback and on foot.

' Who goes there ? ' shouted a voice in honest English.

' A friend who is uncommonly glad to see you,' John answered, with that feeble jocosity in which we are all apt to indulge when at length a great weight is lifted from our nerves.

CHAPTER XVI

JESS was not very happy at Pretoria previous to the unexpected outbreak of hostilities. Most people who have made a great moral effort, and after some severe mental struggle have entered on the drear path of self-sacrifice, experience the reaction that will follow as certainly as the night follows the day. It is one thing to renounce the light, to stand in the full glow of the setting beams of our imperial joy and chant out our farewell, and quite another to live alone in the darkness. For a little while memory may support us, but memory grows faint. On every side is the thick, cheerless pall and that stillness through which no sound comes. We are alone, quite alone, cut off from the fellowship of the day, unseeing and unseen. More especially is this so when the dungeon is of our own making, and we ourselves have shot its bolts. There is a natural night that comes to all, and in its unwavering course swallows every mortal hope and fear, for ever and for ever. To this we can more easily resign ourselves, for we recognise the universal lot and bow ourselves beneath the all-effacing hand. The earth does not pine when the daylight passes from its peaks ; it only sleeps.

But Jess had buried herself and she knew it. There was no absolute need for her to have sacrificed her affection to her sister's : she had done so of her own will, and at times not unnaturally she was regretful. Self-denial is a stern-faced angel. If only we hold him fast and wrestle with him long enough he will speak us soft words of happy sound, just as, if we wait long enough in the darkness of the night, stars will come to share our loneliness. Still this is one of those things that Time hides from us and only reveals at his own pleasure ; and, so far as Jess was concerned, his pleasure was not yet. Outwardly, however, she showed no sign of her distress and of the passion which was eating at her heart. She was pale and silent, it is true, but then she had always been remarkable for her pallor and silence. Only she gave up her singing.

So the weeks passed very drearily for the poor girl, who was doing what other people did—eating and drinking, riding, and going to parties like the rest of the Pretoria world, till at last she began to think that she had better be turning home again, lest she should wear out her welcome. And yet she dreaded to do so, mindful of her daily prayer to be delivered from temptation. As to what was happening at Mooifontein she was in almost complete ignorance. Bessie wrote to her, of course, and so did her uncle once or twice, but they did not tell her much of what she wanted to know. Bessie's letters were, it is true, full of allusions to what Captain Niel was doing, but she did not go beyond that. Her reticence, however, told her observant sister more than her words. Why was she so reticent ? No doubt because things still hung in the balance. Then Jess would think of what it all meant for her, and now and again give way to an outburst of passionate jealousy which would have been painful enough to witness if anybody had been there to see it.

Thus the time went on towards Christmas, for Jess, having been warmly pressed to do so, had settled to stay over Christmas and return to the farm with the new year. There had been a great deal of talk in the town about the Boers, but she was too much preoccupied with her own affairs to pay much attention to it. Nor, indeed, was the public mind greatly moved; they were so much accustomed to Boer scares at Pretoria, and hitherto these had invariably ended in smoke. But all of a sudden, on the morning of the eighteenth of December, came the news of the proclamation of the Republic. The town was thrown into a ferment, and there arose a talk of going into laager, so that, anxious as she was to get away, Jess could see no hope of returning to the farm till the excitement was over. Then, a day or two later, Conductor Egerton came limping into Pretoria from the scene of the disaster at Bronker's Spruit, with the colours of the 94th Regiment tied round his middle, and such a tale to tell that the blood went to her heart and seemed to stagnate there as she listened.

After that there was confusion worse confounded. Martial law having been proclaimed, the town, which was large, straggling, and incapable of defence, was abandoned, the inhabitants being ordered into laager on the high ground overlooking the city. There they were, young and old, sick and well, delicate women and little children, all crowded together in the open under the cover of the fort, with nothing but canvas tents, waggons, and sheds to shelter them from the fierce summer suns and rains. Jess shared a waggon with her friend and her friend's sister and mother, and found it rather a tight fit even to lie down. Sleep with all the noises of the camp going on round her was almost impossible.

It was about three o'clock on the day following that first miserable night in the laager when, by the last mail that passed into Pretoria, she received Bessie's letter, announcing her engagement to John. She took her letter and went some way from the camp to the side of Signal Hill, where she was not likely to be disturbed, and, finding a nook shaded by mimosa-trees, sat down and broke the envelope. Before she had reached the foot of the first page she saw what was coming and set her teeth. Then she read the long epistle through from beginning to end without flinching, though the words of affection seemed to burn her. So it had come at last. Well, she expected it, and had plotted to bring it about, so really there was no reason in the world why she should feel disappointed. On the contrary, she ought to rejoice, and for a little while she really did rejoice in her sister's happiness. It made her glad to think that Bessie, whom she so dearly loved, was happy.

And yet she felt angry with John with that sort of anger which we feel against those who have blindly injured us. Why should it be in his power to hurt her so cruelly? Still she hoped that he would be happy with Bessie, and then she hoped that these wretched Boers would take Pretoria, and that she would be shot or otherwise put out of the way. She had no heart for life; all the colour had faded from her sky. What was she to do with her future? Marry somebody and busy herself with rearing a pack of children? It would be a physical impossibility to her. No, she would go away to Europe and mix in the great stream of life and struggle with it, and see if she could win a place for herself among the people of her day. She had it in her, she knew that; and now that she had put herself out of the reach of passion she would be more likely to succeed, for success is to the impassive, who are also the strong. She would not stop on the farm after John and Bessie were married; she was quite determined as to that; nor, if she could avoid it, would she return there before they were married. She would see him no more, no more! Alas, that she had ever seen him.

Feeling somewhat happier, or at any rate calmer, in this decision, she rose to return to the noisy camp, extending her walk, however, by a détour towards the Heidelberg road, for she was anxious to be alone as long as she could. She had been walking some ten minutes when she caught sight of a cart that seemed familiar to her, with three horses harnessed in front of it and one tied behind, which were also familiar. There were many men walking alongside the cart all talking eagerly.

Jess halted to let the little procession go by, when suddenly she perceived John Niel among these men and recognised the Zulu Mouti on the box. *There* was the man whom she had just vowed never to see again, and the sight of him seemed to take all her strength out of her, so that she felt inclined to sink down upon the veldt. His sudden appearance was almost uncanny in the sharpness of its illustration of her impotence in the hands of Fate. She felt it then; all in an instant it seemed to be borne in upon her mind that she could not help herself, but was only the instrument in the hands of a superior power whose will she was fulfilling through the workings of her passion, and to whom her individual fate was a matter of little moment. It was inconclusive reasoning and perilous doctrine, but it must be allowed that the circumstances gave it a colour of truth. And, after all, the border-line between fatalism and free-will has never been quite authoritatively settled, even by St. Paul, so perhaps she was right. Mankind does not like to admit it, but it is, at the least, a question whether we can oppose our little wills against the forces of an universal law, or derange the details of an unvarying plan to suit the petty wants and hopes of individual mortality. Jess was a clever woman, but it would take a wiser head than hers to know where or when to draw that red line across the writings of our lives.

On came the cart and the knot of men, then suddenly John looked up and saw her gazing at him with those dark eyes that at times did indeed seem as though they were the windows of her soul. He turned and said something to his companions and to the Zulu Mouti, who went on with the cart, then he came towards her smiling and with outstretched hand.

'How do you do, Jess?' he said. 'So I have found you all right?'

She took his hand and answered, almost angrily, 'Why have you come? Why did you leave Bessie and my uncle?'

'I came because I was sent, also because I wished it. I wanted to bring you back home before Pretoria was besieged.'

'You must have been mad! How could you expect to get back? We shall both be shut up here together now.'

'So it appears. Well, things might be worse,' he added cheerfully.

'I do not think that anything could be worse,' she answered with a stamp of her foot, then, quite thrown off her balance, she burst incontinently into a flood of tears.

John Niel was a very simple-minded man, and it never struck him to attribute her grief to any other cause than anxiety at the state of affairs and at her incarcera-

tion for an indefinite period in a besieged town that ran
the daily risk of being taken *vi et armis*. Still he was a
little hurt at the manner of his reception after his long
and most perilous journey, which is not, perhaps, to be
wondered at.

'Well, Jess,' he said, 'I think that you might speak a
little more kindly to me, considering—considering all
things.   There, don't cry, they are all right at Mooifontein,
and I dare say that we shall win back there somehow
some time or other.   I had a nice business to get here at
all, I can tell you.'

Suddenly she stopped weeping and smiled, her tears
passing away like a summer storm.   'How did you get
through?' she asked.   'Tell me all about it, Captain
Niel,' and accordingly he did.

She listened in silence while he sketched the chief
events of his journey, and when he had done she spoke
in quite a changed tone.

'It is very good and kind of you to have risked your
life like this for me.   Only I wonder that you did not all
of you see that it would be of no use.   We shall both be
shut up here together now, that is all, and that will be
very sad for you and Bessie.'

'Oh! So you have heard of our engagement?' he
said.

'Yes, I read Bessie's letter about a couple of hours
ago, and I congratulate you both very much.   I think
that you will have the sweetest and loveliest wife in
South Africa, Captain Niel; and I think that Bessie will
have a husband any woman might be proud of;' and she
half bowed and half curtseyed to him as she said it, with
a graceful little air of dignity that was very taking.

'Thank you,' he answered simply; 'yes, I think I am
a very lucky fellow.'

'And now,' she said, 'we had better go and see
about the cart. You will have to find a stand for it
in that wretched laager. You must be very tired and
hungry.'

A few minutes' walk brought them to the cart, which
Mouti had outspanned close to Mrs. Neville's waggon,
where Jess and her friends were living, and the first
person they saw was Mrs. Neville herself. She was a
good, motherly colonial woman, accustomed to a rough
life, and one not easily disturbed by emergencies.

'My goodness, Captain Niel!' she cried, as soon as
Jess had introduced him. 'Well, you are plucky to have
forced your way through all those horrid Boers! I am
sure I wonder that they did not shoot you or beat you
to death with sjambocks, the brutes. Not that there is
much use in your coming, for you will never be able to
take Jess back till Sir George Colley relieves us, and that
can't be for two months, they say. Well, there is one
thing; Jess will be able to sleep in the cart now, and you
can have one of the patrol-tents and camp alongside. It
won't be quite proper, perhaps, but in these times we
can't stop to consider propriety. There, there, you go off
to the Governor. He will be glad enough to see you, I'll
be bound; I saw him at the other end of the camp
five minutes ago. We will have the cart unpacked and
arrange about the horses.'

Thus adjured, John departed, and when he returned
half an hour afterwards, having told his eventful tale,
which did not, however, convey any information of general
value, he was rejoiced to find that the process of 'getting
things straight' was almost complete. What was better
still, Jess had fried him a beefsteak over the camp fire,
and was now employed in serving it on a little table
by the waggon. He sat down on a stool and ate his

meal heartily enough, while Jess waited on him and
Mrs. Neville chattered incessantly.

'By the way,' she said, 'Jess tells me that you are
going to marry her sister. Well, I wish you joy. A
man wants a wife in this country. It isn't like England, where in five cases out of six he might as well go
and cut his throat as get married. It saves him money
here, and children are a blessing, as Nature meant them
to be, and not a burden, as civilisation has made them.
Lord, how my tongue does run on! It isn't delicate to
talk about children when you have only been engaged a
couple of weeks; but, you see, that's what it comes to
after all. She's a pretty girl, Bessie, and a good one too
—I don't know her much—though she hasn't got the
brains of Jess here. That reminds me; as you are
engaged to Bessie, of course you can look after Jess, and
nobody will think anything of it. Ah! if you only knew
what a place this is for talk, though their talk is pretty
well scared out of them now, I'm thinking. My husband
is coming round presently to the cart to help to get Jess's
bed into it. Lucky it's big. We are such a tight fit in
that waggon that I shall be downright glad to see the
last of the dear girl; though, of course, you'll both come
and take your meals with us.'

Jess heard all this in silence. She could not well
insist upon stopping in the crowded waggon; it would be
asking too much; and, besides, she had passed one night
there, and that was quite enough for her. Once she
suggested that she should try to persuade the nuns to
take her in at the convent, but Mrs. Neville suppressed
the notion instantly.

'Nuns!' she said; 'nonsense. When your own
brother-in-law—at least he will be your brother-in-law if
the Boers don't make an end of us all—is here to take

care of you, don't talk about going to a parcel of nuns. It will be as much as they can do to look after themselves, I'll be bound.'

As for John, he ate his steak and said nothing. The arrangement seemed a very proper one to him.

CHAPTER XVII

THE TWELFTH OF FEBRUARY

JOHN soon settled down into the routine of camp life in Pretoria, which, after one became accustomed to it, was not so disagreeable as might have been expected, and possessed, at any rate, the merit of novelty. Although he was an officer of the army, having several horses to ride, and his services not being otherwise required, John preferred, on the whole, to enrol himself in the corps of mounted volunteers, known as the Pretoria Carbineers. This, in the humble capacity of a sergeant, he obtained leave to do from the officer commanding the troops. He was an active man, and his duties in connection with the corps kept him fully employed during most of the day, and sometimes, when there was outpost duty to be done, during a good part of the night too. For the rest, whenever he returned to the cart—by which he had stipulated he should be allowed to sleep in order to protect Jess in case of any danger—he always found her ready to greet him, and every little preparation made for his comfort that was possible under the circumstances. Indeed, as time went on, they thought it more convenient to set up their own little mess instead of sharing that of their friends. So every day they used to sit down to breakfast and dine together at a little table contrived out of a packing-case, and placed under an extemporised tent, for all the world like a young couple picnicking on their honeymoon. Of course, the situation was very irksome in a way, but it is not to be denied that it had a charm of its own.

To begin with, once thoroughly known, Jess was one of the most delightful companions possible to a man like John Niel. Never, till this long *tête-à-tête* at Pretoria, had he guessed how powerful and original was her mind, or how witty she could be when she liked. There was a fund of dry and suggestive humour about her, which, although it would no more bear being written down than champagne will bear standing in a tumbler, was very pleasant to listen to, more especially as John soon discovered that he was the only person so privileged. Her friends and relations had never suspected that Jess was humorous. Another thing which struck him as time went on, was that she was growing quite handsome. She had been very pale and thin when he reached Pretoria, but before a month was over she had become, comparatively speaking, stout, which was an enormous gain to her appearance. Her pale face, too, gathered a faint tinge of colour that came and went capriciously, like star-light on the water, and her beautiful eyes grew deeper and more beautiful than ever.

'Who would ever have thought that it was the same girl!' said Mrs. Neville to him, holding up her hands as she watched Jess solemnly surveying a half-cooked mutton chop. 'Why, she used to be such a poor creature, and now she's quite a fine woman. And that with this life too, which is wearing me to a shadow and has half-killed my dear daughter.'

'I suppose it is being in the open air,' said John, it having never occurred to him that the medicine that was doing Jess so much good might be happiness. But so it was.   After her first struggles came a lull, and then an idea.   Why should she not enjoy his society while she could?   He had been thrown into her way through no wish of hers.   She had no desire to wean him from Bessie; or, if she had the desire, it was one which she was far too honourable a woman to entertain. He was perfectly innocent of the whole story; to him she was the young lady who happened to be the sister of the woman he was going to marry, that was all. Why should she not pluck her innocent roses whilst she might?   Jess forgot that the rose is a flower with a dangerous perfume, and one that is apt to confuse the senses and turn the head.   So she gave herself full swing, and for some weeks went nearer to knowing what happiness really meant than she ever had before.   What a wonderful thing is the love of a woman in its simplicity and strength, and how it gilds all the poor and common things of life and even finds a joy in service!   The prouder the woman the more delight does she extract from her self-abasement before her idol. Only not many women can love like Jess, and when they do almost invariably they make some fatal mistake, whereby the wealth of their affection is wasted, or, worse still, becomes a source of misery or shame to themselves and others.

It was after they had been incarcerated in Pretoria for a month that a bright idea occurred to John.   About a quarter of a mile from the outskirts of the camp stood a little house known, probably on account of its diminutive size, as 'The Palatial.'   This cottage, like almost every other house in Pretoria, had been abandoned to its fate, its owner, as it happened, being away from the town.   One day, in the course of a walk, John and Jess crossed the little bridge that spanned the sluit and went in to inspect the place. Passing down a path lined on either side with young blue gums, they reached the little tin-roofed cottage. It consisted of two rooms—a bedroom and a good-sized sitting-room, in which still stood a table and a few chairs, with a stable and a kitchen at the back. They went in, sat down by the open door and looked out. The garden of the cottage sloped down towards a valley, on the farther side of which rose a wooded hill. To the right, too, was a hill clothed in deep green bush. The grounds themselves were planted with vines, just now loaded with bunches of ripening grapes, and surrounded by a beautiful hedge of monthly roses that formed a blaze of bloom. Near the house, too, was a bed of double roses, some of them exceedingly lovely, and all flowering with a profusion unknown in this country. Altogether it was a delightful spot, and, after the noise and glare of the camp, seemed a perfect heaven. So they sat there and talked a great deal about the farm and old Silas Croft and a little about Bessie.

'This *is* nice,' said Jess presently, putting her hands behind her head and looking out at the bush beyond.

'Yes,' said John. 'I say, I've got a notion. I vote we take up our quarters here—during the day, I mean. Of course we shall have to sleep in camp, but we might eat here, you know, and you could sit here all day; it would be as safe as a church, for those Boers will never try to storm the town, I am sure of that.'

Jess reflected, and soon came to the conclusion that it would be a charming plan. Accordingly, next day she set to work and made the place as clean and tidy as circumstances would allow, and they commenced housekeeping.

The upshot of this arrangement was that they were

thrown more together even than before. Meanwhile the siege dragged its slow length along. No news whatever reached the town from outside, but this did not trouble the inhabitants very much, as they were sure that Colley was advancing to their relief, and even got up sweepstakes as to the date of his arrival. Now and then a sortie took place, but, as the results attained were very small, and were not, on the whole, creditable to our arms, perhaps the less said about them the better. John, of course, went out on these occasions, and then Jess would endure agonies that were all the worse because she was forced to conceal them. She lived in constant terror lest he should be among the killed. However, nothing happened to him, and things went on as usual till the twelfth of February, when an attack was made on a place called the Red House Kraal, which was occupied by Boers near a spot known as the Six-mile Spruit.

The force, which was a mixed one, left Pretoria before daybreak, and John went with it. He was rather surprised when, on going to the cart in which Jess slept, to get some little thing before saddling up, he found her sitting on the box in the night dews, a cup of hot coffee which she had prepared for him in her hand.

' What do you mean by this, Jess ? ' he asked sharply. ' I will not have you getting up in the middle of the night to make coffee for me.'

' I have not got up,' she answered quietly; ' I have not been to bed.'

' That makes matters worse,' he exclaimed ; but, nevertheless, he drank the coffee and was glad of it, while she sat on the box and watched him.

' Put on your shawl and wrap something over your head,' he said, ' the dew will soak you through. Look, your hair is all wet.'

Presently she spoke. 'I wish you would do something for me, John,' for she called him John now. 'Will you promise?'

'How like a woman,' he said, 'to ask one to promise a thing without saying what it is.'

'I want you to promise for Bessie's sake, John.'

'Well, what is it, Jess?'

'Not to go on this sortie. You know you can easily get out of it if you like.'

He laughed. 'You little silly, why not?'

'Oh, I don't know. Don't laugh at me because I am nervous. I am afraid that—that something might happen to you.'

'Well,' he remarked consolingly, 'every bullet has its billet, and if it does I don't see that it can be helped.'

'Think of Bessie,' she said again.

'Look here, Jess,' he answered testily, 'what is the good of trying to take the heart out of a fellow like this? If I am going to be shot I can't help it, and I am not going to show the white feather, even for Bessie's sake; so there you are, and now I must be off.'

'You are quite right, John,' she said quietly. 'I should not have liked to hear you say anything different, but I could not help speaking. Good-bye, John; God bless you!' and she stretched out her hand, which he took, and went.

'Upon my word, she has given me quite a turn,' reflected John to himself, as the troop crept on through the white mists of dawn. 'I suppose she thinks that I am going to be plugged. Perhaps I am! I wonder how Bessie would take it. She would be awfully cut up, but I expect that she would get over it pretty soon. Now I don't think that Jess would shake off a thing of that sort in a hurry.   That is just the difference between the two ; the one is all flower and the other is all root.'

Then he fell to wondering how Bessie was, and what she was doing, and if she missed him as much as he missed her, and so on, till his mind came back to Jess, and he reflected what a charming companion she was, and how thoughtful and kind, and breathed a secret hope that she would continue to live with them after they were married.   Unconsciously they had arrived at that point of intimacy, innocent in itself, when two people become absolutely necessary to each other's daily life. Indeed, Jess had travelled a long way farther, but of this John was of course ignorant.   He was still at the former stage, and was not himself aware how large a proportion of his daily thoughts were occupied by this dark-eyed girl or how completely her personality overshadowed him.   He only knew that she had the knack of making him feel thoroughly happy in her company.   When he was talking to her, or even sitting silently by her, he became aware of a sensation of restfulness and reliance that he had never before experienced in the society of a woman.   Of course to a large extent this was the natural homage of the weaker nature to the stronger, but it was also something more.   It was a shadow of the utter sympathy and complete accord that is the surest sign of the presence of the highest forms of affection, which, when it accompanies the passion of men and women, as it sometimes though rarely does, being more often to be found in perfection in those relations from which the element of sexuality is excluded, raises it almost above the level of the earth.   For the love where that sympathy exists, whether it is between mother and son, husband and wife, or those who, whilst desiring it, have no hope of that relationship, is an undying love, and will endure till the night of Time has swallowed all things.

Meanwhile, as John reflected, the force to which he was attached was moving into action, and soon he found it necessary to come down to the unpleasantly practical details of Boer warfare. More particularly did this come home to his mind when, shortly afterwards, the man next to him was shot dead, and a little later he himself was slightly wounded by a bullet which passed between the saddle and his thigh. Into the details of the fight that ensued it is not necessary to enter here. They were, if anything, more discreditable than most of the episodes of that unhappy war in which the holding of Potchefstroom, Lydenburg, Rustenburg, and Wakkerstroom are the only bright spots. Suffice it to say that they ended in something very like an utter rout of the English at the hands of a much inferior force, and that, a few hours after he had started, the ambulance being left in the hands of the Boers, John found himself on the return road to Pretoria, with a severely wounded man behind his saddle, who, as they went painfully along, mingled curses of shame and fury with his own. Meanwhile exaggerated accounts of the English defeat had reached the town, and, amongst other things, it was said that Captain Niel had been shot dead. One man who came in stated that he saw him fall, and that he was shot through the head. This Mrs. Neville heard with her own ears, and, greatly shocked, started to communicate the intelligence to Jess.

As soon as it was daylight, as was customary with her, Jess had gone over to the little house which she and John occupied, 'The Palatial,' as it was called ironically, and settled herself there for the day. First she tried to work and could not, so she took a book that she had brought with her and began to read, but it was a failure also. Her eyes would wander from the page and her ears strain to catch the distant booming of the big guns that came from time to time floating across the hills. The fact of the matter was that the poor girl was the victim of a presentiment that something was going to happen to John. Most people of imaginative mind have suffered from this kind of thing at one time or other in their lives, and have lived to see the folly of it; and there was more in the circumstances of the present case to excuse indulgence in the luxury of presentiments than is usual. Indeed, as it happened, she was not far out— only a sixteenth of an inch or so—for John was very *nearly* killed.

Not finding Jess in camp, Mrs. Neville made her way across to 'The Palatial,' where she knew the girl sat, crying as she went, at the thought of the news that she had to communicate, for the good soul had grown very fond of John Niel. Jess, with that acute sense of hearing which often accompanies nervous excitement, caught the sound of the little gate at the bottom of the garden almost before her visitor had passed through it, and ran round the corner of the house to see who was there.

One glance at Mrs. Neville's tear-stained face was enough for her. She knew what was coming, and clasped at one of the young blue gum trees that grew along the path to prevent herself from falling.

'What is it?' she said faintly. 'Is he dead?'

'Yes, my dear, yes; shot through the head, they say.'

Jess made no answer, but clung to the sapling, feeling as though she were going to die herself, and faintly hoping that she might do so. Her eyes wandered vaguely from the face of the messenger of evil, first up to the sky, then down to the cropped and trodden veldt. Past the gate of 'The Palatial' garden ran a road, which, as it happened, was a short cut from the scene of the fight, and down this road came four Kafirs and half-castes, bearing something on a stretcher, behind which rode three or four carbineers. A coat was thrown over the face of the form on the stretcher, but its legs were visible. They were booted and spurred, and the feet fell apart in that peculiarly lax and helpless way of which there is no possibility of mistaking the meaning.

' *Look !* ' she said, pointing.

' Ah, poor man, poor man ! ' said Mrs. Neville, ' they are bringing him here to lay him out.'

Then Jess's beautiful eyes closed, and down she went with the bending tree. Presently the sapling snapped, and she fell senseless with a little cry, and as she fell the men with the corpse passed on.

Two minutes afterwards, John Niel, having heard the rumour of his own death on arrival at the camp, and greatly fearing lest it should have reached Jess's ears, cantered up hurriedly, and, dismounting as well as his wound would allow, limped up the garden path.

' Great heavens, Captain Niel ! ' exclaimed Mrs. Neville, looking up ; ' why—we thought that you were dead ! '

' And that is what you have been telling her, I suppose,' he said sternly, glancing at the pale and deathlike face ; ' you might have waited till you were sure. Poor girl ! it must have given her a turn ! ' and, stooping down, he placed his arms under Jess, and, lifting her with some difficulty, staggered to the house, where he laid her down upon the table and, assisted by Mrs. Neville, began to do all in his power to revive her. So obstinate was her faint, however, that their efforts were unavailing, and at last Mrs. Neville started for the camp to get some brandy, leaving him to go on rubbing her hands and sprinkling water on her face.

The good lady had not been gone more than two or three minutes when Jess suddenly opened her eyes and sat up, slipping her feet to the ground. Her eyes fell upon John and dilated with wonder; he thought that she was about to faint again, for even her lips blanched, and she began to shake and tremble all over in the extremity of her agitation.

'Jess, Jess,' he said, 'for God's sake don't look like that, you frighten me!'

'I thought you were—I thought you were——' she said slowly, then suddenly burst into a passion of tears and fell forward upon his breast and lay there sobbing her heart out, her brown curls resting against his face.

It was an awkward and a most moving position. John was only a man, and the spectacle of this strange woman, to whom he had lately grown so much attached, plunged into intense emotion, awakened, apparently, by anxiety about his fate, stirred him very deeply—as it would have stirred anybody. Indeed, it struck some chord in him for which he could not quite account, and its echoes charmed and yet frightened him. What did it mean?

'Jess, dear Jess, pray stop; I can't bear to see you cry so,' he said at last.

She lifted her head from his shoulder and stood looking at him, her hand resting on the edge of the table behind her. Her face was wet with tears and looked like a dew-washed lily, and her beautiful eyes were alight with a flame that he had never seen in the eyes of woman before. She said nothing, but her whole face was more eloquent than any words, for there are times when the features can convey a message in that language of their own which is more suitable than any tongue we talk. There she stood, her breast heaving with emotion as the sea heaves when the fierceness of the storm has passed—a very incarnation of the intensest love of woman. And as she stood something seemed to pass before her eyes and blind her; a spirit took possession of her that absorbed all her doubts and fears, and she gave way to a force that was of her and yet compelled her, as, when the wind blows, the sails compel a ship. Then, for the first time, where her love was concerned, she put out all her strength. She knew, and had always known, that she could master him, and force him to regard her as she regarded him, did she but choose. How she knew it she could not say, but so it was. Now she yielded to an unconquerable impulse and chose. She said nothing, she did not even move, she only looked at him.

'Why were you in such a fright about me?' he stammered.

She did not answer, but kept her eyes upon his face, and it seemed to John as though power flowed from them; for, while she looked, he felt the change come. Everything melted away before the almost spiritual intensity of her gaze. Bessie, honour, his engagement—all were forgotten; the smouldering embers broke into flame, and he knew that he loved this woman as he had never loved any living creature before—that he loved her even as she loved him. Strong man as he was, he shook like a leaf before her.

'Jess,' he said hoarsely, 'God forgive me! I love you!' and he bent forward to kiss her.

She lifted her face towards him, then suddenly changed her mind, and laid her hand upon his breast.

'You forget,' she said almost solemnly, 'you are going to marry Bessie.'

Crushed by a deep sense of shame, and by a knowledge of the calamity that had overtaken him, John turned and limped from the house.

CHAPTER XVIII

AND AFTER

In front of the door of ' The Palatial ' was a garden-bed filled with weeds and flowers mixed up together like the good and evil in the heart of a man, and to the right-hand side of this bed stood an old and backless wooden chair. No sooner had John limped outside the door of the cottage than he became sensible that, what between one thing and another—weariness, loss of blood from his wound, and intense mental emotion—if he did not sit down somewhere quickly, he should follow the example set by Jess and faint away. Accordingly he steered for the old chair and sank into it with gratitude. Presently he saw Mrs. Neville running up the path with a bottle of brandy in her hand.

' Ah ! ' he thought to himself, ' that will just come in handy for me. If I don't have a glass of brandy soon I shall roll off this infernal chair—I am sure of it.'

' Where is Jess ? ' panted Mrs. Neville.

' In there,' he said; ' she has recovered. It would have been better for us both if she hadn't,' he added to himself.

' Why, bless me, Captain Niel, how queer you look ! ' said Mrs. Neville, fanning herself with her hat; ' and there is such a row going on at the camp there; the volunteers swear that they will attack the military for deserting them, and I don't know what all; and they simply wouldn't believe me when I said you were not shot. Why, I never! Look! your boot is full of blood! So you were hit after all.'

'Might I trouble you to give me some brandy, Mrs. Neville?' said John faintly.

She filled a glass she had brought with her half full of water from a little irrigation furrow that ran down from the main sluit by the road, and then topped it up with brandy. He drank it, and felt decidedly better.

'Dear me!' said Mrs. Neville, 'there are a pair of you now. You should just have seen that girl go down when she saw the body coming along the road! I made sure that it was you; but it wasn't. They say that it was poor Jim Smith, son of old Smith of Rustenburg. I tell you what it is, Captain Niel, you had better be careful; if that girl isn't in love with you she is something very like it. A girl does not pop over like that for Dick, Tom, or Harry. You must forgive an old woman like me for speaking out plain, but she is an odd girl is Jess, just like ten women rolled into one so far as her mind goes, and if you don't take care you will get into trouble, which will be rather awkward, as you are going to marry her sister. Jess isn't the one to have a bit of a flirt to pass away the time and have done with it, I can tell you;' and she shook her head solemnly, as though she suspected him of trifling with his future sister-in-law's young affections, then, without waiting for an answer, she turned and went into the cottage.

As for John, he only groaned. What could he do but groan? The thing was self-evident, and if ever a man felt ashamed of himself that man was John Niel. He

was a strictly honourable individual, and it cut him
to the heart to think that he had entered on a course
which, considering his engagement to Bessie, was not
honourable. When a few minutes before he had told
Jess he loved her he had said a disgraceful thing, however true it might be. And that was the worst of it; it
was true; he did love her. He felt the change come
sweeping over him like a wave as she stood looking at
him in the room, utterly drowning and overpowering his
affection for Bessie, to whom he was bound by every tie
of honour. It was a new and a wonderful experience
this passion that had arisen within him, as a strong
man armed, driving every other affection away into the
waste places of his mind; and, unfortunately, as he
already guessed, it was overmastering and enduring.
He cursed himself in his shame and anger as he sat
recovering his equilibrium on the broken chair and
tying a handkerchief tightly round his wounded leg.
What a fool he had been! Why had he not waited to
see which of the two he really loved? Why had Jess
gone away like that and thrown him into temptation with
her pretty sister? He was sure now that she had cared
for him all along. Well, there it was, and a bad business
too! One thing he was clear about; it should go no
farther. He would not break his engagement to Bessie;
it was not to be thought of. But, all the same, he felt
sorry for himself, and sorry for Jess too.

Just then, however, the bandage on his leg slipped,
and the wound began to bleed so fast that he was fain to
hobble into the house for assistance.

Jess, who had apparently quite recovered from her
agitation, was standing by the table talking to Mrs.
Neville, who was persuading her to swallow some of the
brandy she had been at such pains to fetch. The moment

she caught sight of John's face, which had now turned ghastly white, and saw the red line trickling down his boot, she took up her hat that was lying on the table.

'You had better lie down on the old bedstead in the little room,' she said ; 'I am going for the doctor.'

Assisted by Mrs. Neville he was only too glad to take this advice, but long before the doctor arrived John had followed Jess's example, and gone off into a dead faint, to the intense alarm of Mrs. Neville, who was vainly endeavouring to check the flow of blood, which had now become copious. On the arrival of the doctor it appeared that the bullet had grazed the walls of one of the arteries on the inside of his thigh without actually cutting them, which had now given way, rendering it necessary to tie the artery. This operation, with the assistance of chloroform, he proceeded to carry out successfully, announcing afterwards that a great deal of blood had already been lost.

When at last it was over Mrs. Neville asked about John being moved up to the hospital, but the doctor declared that he must lie where he was, and that Jess must stop and help to nurse him, with the assistance of a soldier's wife whom he would send to her.

'Dear me,' said Mrs. Neville, 'that is very awkward.'

'It will be more awkward if you try to move him at present,' was the grim reply, 'for the silk may slip, in which case the artery will probably break out again, and he will bleed to death.'

As for Jess, she said nothing, but set to work to make preparations for her task of nursing. As Fate had once more thrown them together she accepted the position gladly, though it is only fair to say that she would not have sought it.

In about an hour's time, just as John was beginning
to recover from the painful effects of the chloroform, the
soldier's wife who was to assist her in nursing arrived.
As Jess soon discovered, she was not only a low stamp of
woman, but both careless and ignorant into the bargain,
and all that she could be relied on to do was to carry out
some of the rougher work of the sick-room. When John
woke up and learned whose was the presence that was
bending over him, and whose the cool hand that lay
upon his forehead, he groaned again and went to sleep.
But Jess did not go to sleep. She sat by him there
throughout the night, till at last the cold lights of the
dawn came gleaming through the window and fell upon
the white face of the man she loved. He was still sleeping soundly, and, as the night was exceedingly hot and
oppressive, she had left nothing but a sheet over him.
Before she went to rest a little herself she turned to look
at him once more, and as she looked saw the sheet
grow suddenly red with blood. The artery had broken
out fresh.

Calling to the soldier's wife to run across to the
doctor, Jess shook her patient till he awoke, for he
was sleeping quite soundly, and would, no doubt, have
continued to do so till he glided away into a still deeper
sleep ; and then between them they did what they could
to quench that dreadful pumping flow, Jess knotting her
handkerchief round his leg and twisting it with a stick,
while he pressed his thumb upon the severed artery.
But, strive as they would, they were only partially
successful, and Jess began to think that he would die
in her arms from loss of blood. It was agonising to
wait there minute after minute and see his life ebbing
away.

'I don't think I shall last much longer, Jess. God

bless you, dear ! ' he said.   ' The place is beginning to go
round and round.'

Poor soul ! she could only set her teeth and wait for
the end.

Presently John's pressure on the wounded artery
relaxed, and he fainted off, and, oddly enough, just then
the flow of blood diminished considerably.   Another five
minutes, and she heard the quick step of the doctor
coming up the path.

' Thank God you have come ! He has bled dreadfully.'

' I was out attending a poor fellow who was shot
through the lung, and that fool of a woman waited for
me to come back instead of following me. I have brought
you an orderly in place of her. By Jove, he has bled ! I
suppose the silk has slipped. Well, there is only one
thing for it. Orderly, the chloroform.'

Then followed another long half-hour of slashing
and tying and horror, and when at last the unfortunate
John opened his eyes again he was too weak to speak,
and could only smile feebly. For three days after this he
lay in a dangerous state, for if the artery had broken out
for the third time the chances were that, having so little
blood left in his veins, he would die before anything could
be done for him. At times he was very delirious from
weakness, and these were the critical hours, for it was
almost impossible to keep him still, and every moment
threw Jess into an agony of terror lest the silk fastenings
of the artery should break away. Indeed there was only
one fashion in which she could quiet him, and that
was by placing her slim white hand upon his forehead
or giving it to him to hold. Oddly enough, this had
more effect upon his fevered mind than anything else.
For hour after hour she would sit thus, though her

arm ached, and her back felt as if it were about to break in two, till at last she was rewarded by seeing his wild eyes cease their wanderings and close in peaceful sleep.

Yet with it all that week was perhaps the happiest time in her life. There he lay : the man she loved with all the intensity of her deep nature, and she ministered to him, and felt that he loved her, and depended on her as a babe upon its mother. Even in his delirium her name was continually on his lips, and generally with some endearing term before it. She felt in those dark hours of doubt and sickness as though they two were growing life to life, knit up in a divine identity she could not analyse or understand. She felt that it was so, and she believed that, once being so, whatever her future might be, that communion could never be dissolved, and therefore was she happy, though she knew that his recovery meant their lifelong separation. For though Jess, when thrown utterly off her balance, had once given her passion way, it was not a thing she meant to repeat. She had, she knew, injured Bessie enough already in taking her future husband's heart. That she could not help now, but she would take no more. John should go back to her sister.

And so she sat and gazed at that sleeping man through the long watches of the night, and was happy. There lay her joy. Soon they must part and she would be left desolate ; but whilst he lay there he was hers. It was passing sweet to her woman's nature to place her hand upon him and see him sleep, for this desire to watch the sleep of a beloved object is one of the highest and strangest manifestations of passion. Truly, and with a keen insight into the human heart, has the poet said that there is no joy like the joy of a woman watching what she loves asleep. As Jess sat and gazed

G

those beautiful and tender lines came floating into her
mind, and she thought how true they were :

> For there it lies, so tranquil, so beloved,
> All that it hath of life with us is living ;
> So gentle, stirless, helpless, and unmoved,
> And all unconscious of the joy 'tis giving ;
> All it hath felt, inflicted, passed and proved,
> Hushed into depths beyond the watcher's diving ;
> There lies the thing we love with all its errors
> And all its charms, like death without its terrors.

Ay ! there lay the thing she loved.

The time went on, and the artery broke out no more.
Then at last came a morning when John opened his
eyes and watched the pale earnest face bending over him
as though he were trying to remember something. Presently he shut them again.   He had remembered.

' I have been very ill, Jess,' he said after a pause.

' Yes, John.'

' And you have nursed me ? '

' Yes, John.'

' Am I going to recover ? '

' Of course you are.'

He closed his eyes again.

' I suppose there is no news from outside ? '

' No more ; things are just the same.'

' Nor from Bessie ? '

' None : we are quite cut off.'

Then came a pause.

' John,' said Jess, ' I want to say something to you.
When people are delirious, or when delirium is coming
on, they sometimes say things that they are not responsible for, and which had better be forgotten.'

' Yes,' he said, ' I understand.'

' So,' she went on, in the same measured tone, ' we

will forget everything you may fancy that you said, or that I did, since the time when you came in wounded and found that I had fainted.'

'Quite so,' said John. 'I renounce them all.'

'*We* renounce them all,' she corrected, and gave a solemn little nod of her head and sighed, and thus they ratified that audacious compact of oblivion.

But it was a lie, and they both knew that it was a lie. If love had existed before, was there anything in his helplessness and her long and tender care to make it less? Alas! no; rather was their companionship the more perfect and their sympathy the more complete. 'Propinquity, sir, propinquity,' as the wise man said;—we all know the evils of it.

It was a lie, and a very common and everyday sort of lie. Who, being behind the scenes, has not laughed in his sleeve to see it acted?—Who has not admired and wondered at the cold and formal bow and shake of the hand, the tender inquiries after the health of the maiden aunt and the baby, the carelessly expressed wish that we may meet somewhere—all so palpably overdone? *That* the heroine of the impassioned scene at which we had unfortunately to assist an hour ago! Where are the tears, the convulsive sobs, the heartbroken grief? And *that* the young gentleman who saw nothing for it but flight or a pistol bullet! There, all the world's a stage, and fortunately most of us can act at a pinch.

Yes, we can act; we can paint the face and powder the hair, and summon up the set smile and the regulation joke and make pretence that things are as things were, when they are as different as the North Pole from the Torrid Zone. But unfortunately, or fortunately—I do not know which—we cannot bedeck our inner selves and make them mime as the occasion pleases, and sing the old song when their lips are set to a strange new chant. Of a surety there is within us a spark of the Eternal Truth, for in our own hearts we cannot lie. And so it was with these two. From that day forward they forgot that scene in the sitting-room of 'The Palatial,' when Jess put out her strength and John bent and broke before it like a reed before the wind. Surely it was a part of the delirium! They forgot that now, alas! they loved each other with a love which did but gather force from its despair. They talked of Bessie, and of John's marriage, and discussed Jess's plans to go to Europe, just as though these were not matters of spiritual life and death to each of them. In short, however for one brief moment they might have gone astray, now, to their honour be it said, they followed the path of duty with unflinching feet, nor did they complain when the stones cut them.

But it was all a living lie, and they knew it. For behind them stood the irrevocable Past, who for good or evil had bound them together in his unchanging bonds, and with cords that never can be broken

CHAPTER XIX

HANS COETZEE COMES TO PRETORIA

ONCE he had turned the corner, John's recovery was rapid. Naturally of a vigorous constitution, when the artery had reunited, he soon made up for the great loss of blood which he had undergone, and in a little more than a month from the date of his wound physically, was almost as good a man as ever.

One morning—it was the 20th of March—Jess and he were sitting in 'The Palatial' garden. John was lying in a long cane deck chair that Jess had borrowed or stolen out of one of the deserted houses, and smoking a pipe. By his side, in a hole in the flat arm of the chair, fashioned originally to receive a soda-water tumbler, was a great bunch of purple grapes which she had gathered for him ; and on his knees lay a copy of that journalistic curiosity, the 'News of the Camp,' which was chiefly remarkable for its utter dearth of news. It is not easy to run a journal in a beleaguered town.

They sat in silence : John puffing away at his pipe, and Jess, her work—one of his socks—lying idly upon her knees, her hands clasped over it, and her eyes fixed upon the lights and shadows that played with broad fingers upon the wooded slopes beyond.

So silently did they sit that a great green lizard came and basked himself in the sun within a yard of them, and

a beautiful striped butterfly perched deliberately upon
the purple grapes! It was a delightful day and a
delightful spot. They were too far from the camp to be
disturbed by its rude noise, and the only sounds that
reached their ears were the rippling of running water and
the whispers of the wind, odorous with the breath of
mimosa blooms, as it stirred the stiff grey leaves on the
blue gums.

They were seated in the shade of the little house
that Jess had learned to love as she had never loved a
spot before, but around them lay the flood of sunshine
shimmering like golden water; and beyond the red line
of the fence at the end of the garden, where the rich
pomegranate bloom tried to blush the roses down, the
hot air danced merrily above the rough stone wall like a
million microscopic elves at play. Peace! everywhere
was peace! and in it the full heart of Nature beat out in
radiant life. Peace in the voice of the turtle-doves among
the willows! peace in the play of the sunshine and the
murmur of the wind! peace in the growing flowers and
hovering butterfly! Jess looked out at the wealth and
glory which were spread about her, and thought that
it was like heaven; then, giving way to the melancholy
strain in her nature, she began to wonder idly how many
human beings had sat and thought the same things, and
had been gathered up into the azure of the past and forgotten; and how many would sit and think there when
she in her turn had been utterly swept away into that
gulf whence no echo ever comes! But what did it
matter? The sunshine would still flood the earth with
gold, the water would ripple, and the butterflies hover;
and there would be other women to sit and fold their
hands and consider them, thinking the same identical
thoughts, beyond which our human intelligence cannot

travel.   And so on for thousands upon thousands of centuries, till at last the old world reaches its journey's appointed end, and, passing from the starry spaces, is swallowed up with those it bore.

And she—where would she be ?   Would she still live on, and love and suffer elsewhere, or was it all a cruel myth ?   Was she merely a creature bred of the teeming earth, or had she an individuality beyond the earth ? What awaited her after sunset ?—Sleep.   She had often hoped that it was sleep, and nothing but sleep.   But now she did not hope that.   Her life had centred itself around a new interest, and one that she felt could never die while that life lasted.   She hoped for a future now ; for if there was a future for her, there would be one for *him*, and then her day would come, and where he was there she would be also.   Oh, sweet mockery, old and unsubstantial thought, bright dream set halowise about the dull head of life !   Who has not dreamt it, but who can believe in it ?   And yet, who shall say that it is not true ? Though philosophers and scientists smile and point in derision to the gross facts and freaks that mark our passions, is it not still possible that there may be a place where the love shall live when the lust has died; and where Jess will find that she has not sat in vain in the sunshine, throwing out her pure heart towards the light of a happiness and a visioned glory whereof, for some few minutes, the shadow seemed to lie within her?

John had finished his pipe, and, although she did not know it, was watching her face, which, now when she was off her guard, was no longer impassive, but seemed to mirror the tender and glorious hope that was floating through her mind.   Her lips were slightly parted, and her wide eyes were full of a soft strange light, while on the whole countenance was stamped a look of eager thought and spiritualised desire such as he had known portrayed in ancient masterpieces upon the face of the Virgin Mother. Except as regards her eyes and hair, Jess was not even a good-looking person. But, at that moment, John thought that her face was touched with a diviner beauty than he had yet seen on the face of woman. It thrilled him and appealed to him, not as Bessie's beauty had appealed, but to that other side of his nature, of which Jess alone could turn the key. It was more like the face of a spirit than that of a human being, and it almost frightened him to see it.

'Jess,' he said at last, 'what are you thinking of?'

She started, and her face resumed its normal expression. It was as though a mask had been suddenly set upon it.

'Why do you ask?' she said.

'Because I want to know. I never saw you look like that before.'

She laughed a little.

'You would call me foolish if I told you what I was thinking about. Never mind, it has gone wherever thoughts go. I will tell you what I am thinking about now, which is—that it is about time we got out of this place. My uncle and Bessie must be half distracted.'

'We've had more than two months of it now. The relieving column can't be far off,' suggested John; for these foolish people in Pretoria laboured under a firm belief that one fine morning they would be gratified with a vision of the light dancing down a long line of British bayonets, and of Boers evaporating in every direction like storm clouds before the sun.

Jess shook her head. She was beginning to lose faith in relieving columns that never came.

'If we don't help ourselves, my opinion is that we may stop here till we are starved out, which in fact we are. However, it's no use talking about it, so I'm off to fetch our rations. Let's see, have you everything you want?'

'Everything, thanks.'

'Well, then, mind you stop quiet till I come back.'

'Why,' laughed John, 'I am as strong as a horse.'

'Possibly; but that is what the doctor said, you know. Good-bye!' And Jess took her big basket and started on what John used feebly to call her 'rational undertaking.'

She had not gone fifty paces from the door before she suddenly caught sight of a familiar form seated on a familiar pony. The form was fat and jovial-looking, and the pony was small but also fat. It was Hans Coetzee—none other!

Jess could hardly believe her eyes. Old Hans in Pretoria! What could it mean?

'Oom Coetzee! Oom Coetzee!' she called, as he came ambling past her, evidently heading for the Heidelberg road.

The old Boer pulled up his pony, and gazed around him in a mystified fashion.

'Here, Oom Coetzee! Here!'

'Allemachter!' he said, jerking his pony round. 'It's you, Missie Jess, is it? Now who would have thought of seeing you here?'

'Who would have thought of seeing *you* here?' she answered.

'Yes, yes; it seems strange; I dare say that it seems strange. But I am a messenger of peace, like Uncle Noah's dove in the ark, you know. The fact is,' and he glanced round to see if anybody was listening, 'I have been sent by the Government to arrange about an exchange of prisoners.'

'The Government! What Government?'

'What Government? Why, the Triumvirate, of course—whom may the Lord bless and prosper as He did Jonah when he walked on the wall of the city.'

'Joshua, when he walked round the wall of the city,' suggested Jess. 'Jonah walked down the whale's throat.'

'Ah! to be sure, so he did, and blew a trumpet inside. I remember now; though I am sure I don't know how he did it. The fact is that our glorious victories have quite confused me. Ah! what a thing it is to be a patriot! The dear Lord makes strong the arm of the patriot, and takes care that he hits his man well in the middle.'

'You have turned wonderfully patriotic all of a sudden, Oom Coetzee,' said Jess tartly.

'Yes, missie, yes; I am a patriot to the bone of my back! I hate the English Government; damn the English Government! Let us have our land back and our Volksraad. Almighty! I saw who was in the right at Laing's Nek there. Ah, those poor rooibaatjes! I killed four of them myself; two as they came up, and two as they ran away, and the last one went head-over-heels like a buck. Poor man! I cried for him afterwards. I did not like going to fight at all, but Frank Muller sent to me and said that if I did not go he would have me shot. Ah, he is a devil of a man, that Frank Muller! So I went, and when I saw how the dear Lord had put it into the heart of the English general to be a bigger fool even that day than he is every day, and to try and drive us out of Laing's Nek with a thousand of his poor rooibaatjes, then, I tell you, I saw where the right lay, and I said, "Damn the English Government! What is the English Government doing here?" and after Ingogo I said it again.'

'Never mind all that, Oom Coetzee,' broke in Jess.

'I have heard you tell a different tale before, and perhaps you will again. How are my uncle and my sister? Are they at the farm?'

'Almighty! you don't suppose that I have been there to see, do you? But, yes, I have heard they are there. It is a nice place, that Mooifontein, and I think that I shall buy it when we have turned all you English people out of the land. Frank Muller told me that they were there. And now I must be getting on, or that devil of a man, Frank Muller, will want to know what I have been about.'

'Oom Coetzee,' said Jess, 'will you do something for me? We are old friends, you know, and once I persuaded my uncle to lend you five hundred pounds when all your oxen died of the lungsick.'

'Yes, yes, it shall be paid back one day—when we have hunted the damned Englishmen out of the country.' And he began to gather up his reins preparatory to riding off.

'Will you do me a favour?' said Jess, catching the pony by the bridle.

'What is it? What is it, missie? I must be getting on. That devil of a man, Frank Muller, is waiting for me with the prisoners at the Rooihuis Kraal.'

'I want a pass for myself and Captain Niel, and an escort. We wish to go home.'

The old Boer held up his fat hands in amazement.

'Almighty!' he said, 'it is impossible. A pass!— who ever heard of such a thing? Come, I must be going.'

'It is not impossible, Uncle Coetzee, as you know,' said Jess. 'Listen! If I get that pass I will speak to my uncle about the five hundred pounds. Perhaps he would not want it all back again.'

'Ah!' said the Boer. 'Well, we are old friends, missie, and "never desert a friend," that is my saying. Almighty! I must ride a hundred miles—I will swim through blood for a friend. Well, well, I must see. It depends upon that devil of a man, Frank Muller. Where are you to be found—in the white house yonder? Good. To-morrow the escort will come in with the prisoners, and if I can get it they will bring the pass. But, missie, remember the five hundred pounds. If you do not speak to your uncle about that I shall be even with him. Almighty! what a thing it is to have a good heart, and to love to help your friends! Well, good-day, good-day,' and off he cantered on his fat pony, his broad face shining with a look of unutterable benevolence.

Jess cast a look of contempt after him, and then went on towards the camp to fetch the rations.

When she returned to 'The Palatial' she told John what had taken place, and suggested that it would be as well, in case there should be a favourable reply to her request, to have everything prepared for a start. Accordingly, the cart was brought down and stood outside 'The Palatial,' where John unscrewed the patent caps and filled them with castor-oil, and ordered Mouti to keep the horses, which were all in health, though 'poor' from want of proper food, well within hail.

Meanwhile, old Hans pursued the jerky tenour of his way for an hour or so, till he came in sight of a small red house.

Presently, from the shadow in front of the red house emerged a rider, mounted on a powerful black horse. The horseman—a stern, handsome, bearded man—put his hand above his eyes to shade them from the sun, and gazed up the road. Then he seemed suddenly to strike his spurs into the horse, for the animal bounded forward swiftly, and came sweeping towards Hans at a hand gallop.

' Ah ! it is that devil of a man, Frank Muller ! ' ejaculated Coetzee. ' Now I wonder what he wants ? I always feel cold down the back when he comes near me.'

By this time the plunging black horse was being reined up alongside of his pony so sharply that it reared till its great hoofs were pawing the air within a few inches of Hans' head.

' Almighty ! ' said the old man, tugging his pony round. ' Be careful, nephew, be careful; I do not wish to be crushed like a beetle.'

Frank Muller—for it was he—smiled. He had made his horse rear purposely, in order to frighten the old man, whom he knew to be an arrant coward.

' Why have you been so long? and what have you done with the Englishmen ? You should have been back half an hour ago.'

' And so I should, nephew, and so I should, if I had not been detained. Surely you do not suppose that I would linger in the accursed place ? Bah,' and he spat upon the ground, ' it stinks of Englishmen. I cannot get the taste of them out of my mouth.'

' You are a liar, Uncle Coetzee,' was the cool answer. ' English with the English, Boer with the Boer. You blow neither hot nor cold. Be careful lest I show you up. I know you and your talk. Do you remember what you were saying to the Englishman Niel in the inn-yard at Wakkerstroom when you turned and saw me ? I heard, and I do not forget. You know what happens to a " land betrayer " ? '

Hans' teeth positively chattered, and his florid face blanched with fear.

' What do you mean, nephew ? ' he asked.

'I—ah!—I mean nothing. I was only speaking a word of warning to you as a friend. I have heard things said about you by——' and he dropped his voice and whispered a name, at the sound of which poor Hans turned whiter than ever.

'Well,' went on his tormentor, when he had sufficiently enjoyed his terror, 'what sort of terms did you make in Pretoria?'

'Oh, good, nephew, good,' he gabbled, delighted to find a fresh subject. 'I found the Englishmen supple as a tanned skin. They will give up their twelve prisoners for our four. The men are to be in by ten to-morrow. I told their commandant about Laing's Nek and Ingogo, and he would not believe me. He thought I lied like himself. They are getting hungry there now. I saw a Hottentot I knew, and he told me that their bones were beginning to show.'

'They will be through the skin before long,' muttered Frank. 'Well, here we are at the house. The General is there. He has just come up from Heidelberg, and you can make your report to him. Did you find out about the Englishman—Captain Niel? Is it true that he is dead?'

'No, he is not dead. By the way, I met Oom Croft's niece—the dark one. She is shut up there with the Captain, and she begged me to try and get them a pass to go home. Of course I told her that it was nonsense, and that they must stop and starve with the others.'

Muller, who had been listening to this last piece of information with intense interest, suddenly checked his horse and answered:

'Did you? Then you are a bigger fool than I thought you. Who gave you authority to decide whether they should have a pass or not?'

CHAPTER XX

THE GREAT MAN

COMPLETELY overcome by this last remark, Hans collapsed like a jelly-fish out of water, and reflected in his worthless old heart that Frank Muller was indeed 'a devil of a man.' By this time they had reached the door of the little house, and were dismounting, and in another minute Hans found himself in the presence of one of the leaders of the rebellion.

He was a short, ugly person of about fifty-five, with a big nose, small eyes, straight hair, and a stoop. The forehead, however, was good, and the whole face betrayed a keenness and ability far beyond the average. The great man was seated at a plain deal table, writing something with evident difficulty upon a dirty sheet of paper, and smoking a very large pipe.

'Sit, Heeren, sit,' he said when they entered, waving the stem of his pipe towards a deal bench. Accordingly they sat down without even removing their hats, and, pulling out their pipes, proceeded to light them.

'How, in the name of God, do you spell "Excellency"?' asked the General presently. 'I have spelt it in four different ways, and each one looks worse than the last.'

Frank Muller gave the required information. Hans in his heart thought he spelt it wrong, but he did not dare to say so. Then came another pause, only interrupted by the slow scratching of a quill across the dirty paper, during which Hans nearly went to sleep; for the weather was very hot, and he was tired with his ride.

'There!' said the writer presently, gazing at his handwriting with an almost childish air of satisfaction, 'that is done. A curse on the man who invented writing! Our fathers did very well without it; why should not we? Though, to be sure, it is useful for treaties with the Kafirs. I don't believe you have told me right now about that "Excellency," nephew. Well, it will have to serve. When a man writes such a letter as that to the representative of the English Queen he needn't mind his spelling; it will be swallowed with the rest,' and he leaned back in his chair and laughed softly.

'Now, Meinheer Coetzee, what is it? Ah, I know; the prisoners. Well, what did you do?'

Hans told his story, and was rambling on when the General cut him short.

'So, cousin, so! You talk like an ox-waggon—rumble and creek and jolt, a devil of a noise and turning of wheels, but very little progress. They will give up their twelve prisoners for our four, will they? That is about a fair proportion. No, it is not, though: four Boers are better than twelve Englishmen any day—ay, better than forty!' and he laughed again. 'Well, the men shall be sent in as you arranged; they will help to eat up their last biscuits. Good-day, cousin. Stop, though; one word before you go. I have heard about you at times, cousin. I have heard it said that you cannot be trusted. Now, I don't know if that is so. I don't believe it myself. Only, listen: if it should be true, and I should

find you out, by God! I will have you cut into rimpis
with afterox sjambocks, and then shoot you and send
in your carcase as a present to the English.' As he
spoke thus he leaned forward, brought down his fist
upon the deal table with a bang that produced a most
unpleasant effect upon poor Hans's nerves, and a cold
gleam of sudden ferocity flickered in the small eyes, very
discomforting for a timid man to behold, however innocent he knew himself to be.

'I swear——' he began to babble.

'Swear not at all, cousin; you are an elder of the
church. There is no need for it, besides. I told you I did
not believe it of you; only I have had one or two cases
of this sort of thing lately. No, never mind who they
were. You will not meet them about again. Good-day,
cousin, good-day. Forget not to thank the Almighty
God for our glorious victories. He will expect it from
an elder of the church.'

Poor Hans departed crestfallen, feeling that the days
of him who tries, however skilfully and impartially, to
sit upon two stools at once are not happy days, and
sometimes threaten to be short ones. And supposing
that the Englishmen should win after all—as in his heart
he hoped they might—how should he then prove that he
had hoped it? The General watched him waddle through
the door from under his pent brows, a half-humorous,
half-menacing expression on his face.

'A windbag; a coward; a man without a heart for good
or for evil. Bah! nephew, that is Hans Coetzee. I
have known him for years. Well, let him go. He would
sell us if he could, but I have frightened him now, and,
what is more, if I see reason, he shall find I never bark
unless I mean to bite. Well, enough of him. Let me
see, have I thanked you yet for your share in Majuba?

Ah! that was a glorious victory! How many were there of you when you started up the mountain?'

'Eighty men.'

'And how many at the end?'

'One hundred and seventy—perhaps a few more.'

'And how many of you were hit?'

'Three—one killed, two wounded, and a few scratches.'

'Wonderful, wonderful! It was a brave deed, and because it was so brave it was successful. He must have been mad, that English general. Who shot him?'

'Breytenbach. Colley held up a white handkerchief in his hand, and Breytenbach fired, and down went the general of a heap, and then they all ran helter-skelter down the hill. Yes, it was a wonderful thing! They could have beat us back with their left hand. That is what comes of having a righteous cause, uncle.'

The General smiled grimly. 'That is what comes of having men who can shoot, and who understand the country, and are not afraid. Well, it is done, and well done. The stars in their courses have fought for us, Frank Muller, and so far we have conquered. But how is it to end? You are no fool; tell me, how will it end?'

Frank Muller rose and walked twice up and down the room before he answered. 'Shall I tell you?' he asked, and then, without waiting for a reply, went on: 'It will end in our getting the country back. That is what this armistice means. There are thousands of rooibaatjes there at the Nek; they cannot therefore be waiting for soldiers. They are waiting for an opportunity to yield, uncle. We shall get the country back, and you will be President of the Republic.'

The old man took a pull at his pipe. 'You have a long head, Frank, and it has not run away with you.

The English Government is going to give in. The stars in their courses continue to fight for us. The English Government is as mad as its officers. They will give in. But it means more than that, Frank; I will tell you what it means. It means '—and again he let his heavy hand fall upon the deal table—' the triumph of the Boer throughout South Africa. Bah! Burgers was not such a fool after all when he talked of his great Dutch Republic. I have been twice to England now, and I know the Englishman. I could measure him for his veldtschoens [shoes]. He knows nothing—nothing. He understands his shop; he is buried in his shop, and can think of nothing else. Sometimes he goes away and starts his shop in other places, and buries himself in it, and makes it a big shop, because he understands shops. But it is all a question of shops, and if the shops abroad interfere with the shops at home, or if it is thought that they do, which comes to the same thing, then the shops at home put an end to the shops abroad. Bah! they talk a great deal there in England, but, at the bottom of it, it is shop, shop, shop. They talk of honour, and patriotism too, but they both give way to the shop. And I tell you this, Frank Muller: it is the shop that has made the English, and it is the shop that will destroy them. Well, so be it. We shall have our slice: Africa for the Africanders. The Transvaal for the Transvaalers first, then the rest. Shepstone was a clever man; he would have made it all into an English shop, with the black men for shop-boys. We have changed all that, but we ought to be grateful to Shepstone. The English have paid our debts, they have eaten up the Zulus, who would otherwise have destroyed us, and they have let us beat them, and now we are going to have our turn again, and, as you say, I shall be the first President.'

'Yes, uncle,' replied the younger man calmly, 'and I shall be the second.'

The General looked at him. 'You are a bold man,' he said; 'but boldness makes the man and the country. I dare say you will. You have the head; and one clear head can turn many fools, as the rudder does the ship, and guide them when they are turned. I dare say that you will be President one day.'

'Yes, I shall be President, and when I am I will drive the Englishmen out of South Africa. This I will do with the help of the Natal Zulus. Then I will destroy the natives, as T'Chaka destroyed, keeping only enough for slaves. That is my plan, uncle; it is a good one.'

'It is a big one; I am not certain that it is a good one. But good or bad, who shall say? You may carry it out, nephew, if you live. A man with brains and wealth may carry out anything if he lives. But there is a God. I believe, Frank Muller, that there is a God, and I believe that God sets a limit to a man's doings. If he is going too far, God kills him. *If you live*, Frank Muller, you will do these things, but perhaps God will kill you. Who can say? You will do what God wills, not what *you* will.'

The elder man was speaking seriously now. Muller felt that this was none of the whining cant people in authority among the Boers find it desirable to adopt. It was what he thought, and it chilled Muller in spite of his pretended scepticism, as the sincere belief of an intellectual man, however opposite to our own, is apt to chill us into doubt of ourselves and our opinions. For a moment his slumbering superstition awoke, and he felt half afraid. Between him and that bright future of blood and power lay a dark gulf. Suppose that gulf should be death, and the future nothing but a dream—or worse! His face fell as the idea occurred to him, and the General noticed it.

'Well,' he went on, 'he who lives will see. Meanwhile you have done good service to the State, and you shall have your reward, cousin. If I am President'—he laid emphasis on this, the meaning of which his listener did not miss—'if by the support of my followers I become President, I will not forget you. And now I must up-saddle and ride back. I want to be at Laing's Nek in sixty hours, to wait for General Wood's answer. You will see about the sending in of those prisoners;' and he knocked out his pipe and rose.

'By the way, Meinheer,' said Muller, suddenly adopting a tone of respect, 'I have a favour to ask.'

'What is it, nephew?'

'I want a pass for two friends of mine—English people—in Pretoria to go down to their relations in Wakkerstroom district. They sent a message to me by Hans Coetzee.'

'I don't like giving passes,' answered the General with some irritation. 'You know what it means, letting out messengers. I wonder you ask me.'

'It is a small favour, Meinheer, and I do not think that it will matter. Pretoria will not be besieged much longer; I am under an obligation to the people.'

'Well, well, as you like; but, if any harm comes of it, you will be held responsible. Write the pass; I will sign it.'

Frank Muller sat down and wrote and dated the paper. Its contents were simple: 'Pass the bearers unharmed.'

'That is big enough to drive a waggon along,' said the General, when it was handed to him to sign. 'It might mean all Pretoria.'

'I am not certain if there are two or three of them,' answered Muller carelessly.

'Well, well, you are responsible. Give me the pen;' and he scrawled his big coarse signature on the paper.

'I propose, with your permission, to escort the cart down with two other men. As you are aware, I go to take over the command of the Wakkerstroom district to-morrow.'

'Very good. It is your affair; you are responsible. I shall ask no questions, provided your friends do no hurt to the cause;' and he left the room without another word.

When the great man had gone, Frank Muller sat down again on the bench and looked at the pass, and communed with himself, for he was far too wise to commune with anybody else. 'The Lord hath delivered mine enemy into mine hand,' he said with a smile, and stroked his golden beard. 'Well, well, I will not waste His merciful opportunities as I did that day out buck-shooting. And then for Bessie. I suppose I shall have to kill old Croft too. I am sorry for that, but it can't be helped; besides, if anything should happen to Jess, Bessie will take Mooifontein, and that is worth having. Not that I want more land; I have enough. Yes, I will marry her. It would serve her right if I didn't; but, after all, marriage is more respectable; also one has more hold of a wife. Nobody will interfere for her. Then, she will be of use to me by-and-by, for a beautiful woman is a power even among these fellow-countrymen of mine, if only a man knows how to bait his lines with her. Yes, I shall marry her. Bah! that is the way to win a woman—by capture; and, what is more, they like it. It makes her worth winning too. It will be a courtship of blood. Well, the kisses will be the sweeter, and in the end she will love me the more for what I have dared for her.

'So, Frank Muller, so! Ten years ago you said to yourself: "There are three things worth having in the world—first, wealth; secondly, women, if they take your fancy, or, better still, one woman, if you desire her above all others; thirdly, power." Now, you have got the wealth, for one way and another you are the richest man in the Transvaal. In a week you will have the woman you love, and who is sweeter to you than all the world besides. In five years' time you will have the power—absolute power. That old man is clever; he will be President. But I am cleverer. I shall soon take his seat, thus'—and he rose and seated himself in the General's chair—'and he will go down a step and take mine. Ay, and then I will reign. My tongue shall be honey and my hand iron. I will pass over the land like a storm. I will drive these English out with the help of the Kafirs, and then I will kill the Kafirs and take their country. Ah!'—and his eyes flashed and his nostrils dilated as he said it to himself—'then life will be worth living! What a thing is power! What a thing it is to be able to destroy! Take that Englishman, my rival: to-day he is well and strong; in three days he will be gone utterly, and I—I shall have sent him away. That is power. But when the time comes that I have only to stretch out my hand to send thousands after him!—that will be absolute power; and then with Bessie I shall be happy.'

And so he dreamed on for an hour or more, till at last the fumes of his untutored imagination actually drowned his reason in a spiritual drunkenness. Picture after picture rose and unrolled itself before his mind's eye. He saw himself as President addressing the Volksraad, and compelling it to his will. He saw himself, the supreme general of a great host, defeating the forces of England with awful carnage, and driving them before him; ay, he even selected the battle-ground on the slopes of the Biggarsberg in Natal. Then he saw himself again, sweeping the natives out of South Africa with the relentless besom of his might, and ruling unquestioned over a submissive people. And, last of all, he saw something glittering at his feet—it was a crown!

This was the climax of his dream. Then there came an anticlimax. The rich imagination which had been leading him on as a gaudy butterfly does a child, suddenly changed colour and dropped to earth; and there rose up in his mind the memory of the General's words: 'God sets a limit to a man's doings. If he is going too far, *God kills him.*'

The butterfly had settled on a coffin!

CHAPTER XXI

JESS GETS A PASS

ABOUT half-past ten on the morning following her interview with Hans Coetzee, Jess was at 'The Palatial' as usual, and John was just finishing packing the cart with such few goods as they possessed. There was little chance of his labour proving of material use, for he did not in the slightest degree expect that they would get the pass; but, as he said cheerfully, it was as good an amusement as any other.

'I say, Jess,' he called out presently, 'come here.'

'What for?' asked Jess, who was seated on the door-step mending something, and looking at her favourite view.

'Because I want to speak to you.'

She rose and went, feeling rather angry with herself for going.

'Well,' she said tartly, 'here I am. What is it?'

'I have finished packing the cart, that's all.'

'And you mean to tell me that you have brought me round here to say that?'

'Yes, of course I have; exercise is good for the young.' Then he laughed, and she laughed too.

It was all nothing—nothing at all—but somehow it was very delightful. Certainly mutual affection, even when unexpressed, has a way of making things go happily, and can find entertainment anywhere.

Just then, who should arrive but Mrs. Neville, in a great state of excitement, and, as usual, fanning herself with her hat?

'What do you think, Captain Niel? The prisoners have come in, and I heard one of the Boers in charge say that he had a pass signed by the Boer general for some English people, and that he was coming over to see about them presently. Who can it be?'

'It is for us,' said Jess quickly. 'We are going home. I saw Hans Coetzee yesterday, and begged him to try and get us a pass, and I suppose he has.'

'My word! going to get out: well, you are lucky! Let me sit down and write a letter to my great-uncle at the Cape. You must post it when you can. He is ninety-four, and rather soft, but I dare say he will like to hear from me,' and she hurried into the house to give her aged relative—who, by the way, laboured under the impression that she was still a little girl of four years of age—as minute an account of the siege of Pretoria as time would allow.

'Well, John, you had better tell Mouti to put the horses in. We shall have to start presently,' said Jess.

'Ay,' he said, pulling his beard thoughtfully, 'I suppose that we shall;' adding, by way of an afterthought, 'Are you glad to go?'

'No,' she said, with a sudden flash of passion and a stamp of the foot. Then she turned and entered the house again.

'Mouti,' said John to the Zulu, who was lounging about in a way characteristic of that intelligent but unindustrious race, 'inspan the horses. We are going back to Mooifontein.'

'Koos!' [chief], said the Zulu unconcernedly, and
started on the errand as though it were the most everyday
occurrence to drive off home out of a closely beleaguered
town. That is another beauty of the Zulu race : you
cannot astonish them. No doubt they consider that
extraordinary mixture of wisdom and insanity, the white
man, to be '*capable de tout*,' as the agnostic French critic
said in despair of the prophet Zerubbabel.

John stood and watched the inspanning absently.
In truth, he, too, was conscious of a sensation of regret.
He felt ashamed of himself for it, but there it was ; he
was sorry to leave the place. For the last week or so
he had been living in a dream, and everything outside
that dream was blurred, indistinct as a landscape in a
fog. He knew the objects were there, but he could not
quite appreciate their relative size and position. The
only real thing was his dream ; all else was as vague as
those far-off people and events that we lose in infancy
and find again in old age.

Now there would be an end of dreaming; the fog
would lift, and he must face the facts. Jess, with whom
he had dreamed, would go away to Europe and he would
marry Bessie, and all this Pretoria business would glide
away into the past like a watch in the night. Well,
it must be so ; it was right and proper that it should be
so, and he for one would not flinch from his duty ;
but he must have been more than human had he not
felt the pang of awakening. It was all so very unfortunate.

By this time Mouti had got up the horses, and asked
if he was to inspan.

'No; wait a bit,' said John. 'Very likely it is all
nonsense,' he added to himself.

Scarcely were the words out of his mouth when he

caught sight of two armed Boers of a peculiarly unpleasant type and rough appearance, riding across the veldt towards 'The Palatial' gate. With them was an escort of four carbineers. At the gate they all stopped, and one of the Boers dismounted and walked to where John was standing by the stable-door.

'Captain Niel?' he said interrogatively, in English.

'That is my name.'

'Then here is a letter for you;' and he handed him a folded paper.

John opened it—it had no envelope—and read as follows:

'Sir,—The bearer of this has with him a pass which it is understood that you desire, giving you and Miss Jess Croft a safe-conduct to Mooifontein, in the Wakkerstroom district of the Republic. The only condition attached to the pass, which is signed by one of the honourable Triumvirate, is that you must carry no despatches out of Pretoria. Upon your giving your word of honour to the bearer that you will not do this he will hand you the pass.'

This letter, which was fairly written and in good English, had no signature.

'Who wrote this?' asked John of the Boer.

'That is no affair of yours,' was the curt reply. 'Will you pass your word about the despatches?'

'Yes.'

'Good. Here is the pass;' and he handed over that document to John. It was in the same handwriting as the letter, but signed by the Boer general.

John examined it, and then called to Jess to come to translate it, who, having heard the voice of the Boer, was on her way round the corner of the house.

'It means, "Pass the bearers unharmed,"' she said,

' and the signature is genuine. I have seen Paul Krüger's signature before.'

' When must we start ? ' asked John of the Boer.

' At once, or not at all.'

'I must drive round by the headquarter camp to explain my departure. They will think that I have run away.'

To this the Boer demurred, but finally, after going to the gate to consult his companion, he consented and the two rode back to the headquarter camp, saying that they would wait for the cart there, whereupon the horses were inspanned.

In five minutes everything was ready, and the cart was standing on the roadway in front of the little gate. After he had looked to all the straps and buckles, and seen that the baggage was properly packed, John went to call Jess. He found her by the doorstep, looking out at her favourite view. Her hand was placed side-ways against her forehead, as though to shade her eyes from the sun. But where she was standing there was no sun, and John could not help guessing why she was shading her eyes. She was crying at leaving the place in that quiet and harrowing way which some women indulge in ; that is to say, a few big tears were rolling down her face. John felt a lump rise in his own throat at the sight, and not unnaturally relieved his feelings by rough language.

' What the deuce are you after ? ' he asked. ' Are you going to keep the horses standing all day ? '

Jess did not resent this. The probability is that she guessed its reason. Besides, it is a melancholy fact that women rather like being sworn at than otherwise, provided that the swearer is the man whom they are attached to. But he must only swear on state occasions.

At this moment, too, Mrs. Neville plunged out of the house, licking an envelope as she ran.

'There,' she said, 'I hope you weren't waiting for me. I haven't told the old gentleman half the news; in fact, I've only taken him down to the time when the communications were cut, and I dare say he has seen all that in the papers. But he won't understand anything about it, and if he does he will guess the rest; besides, for all I know, he may be dead and buried by now. I shall have to owe you for the stamp. I think it's threepence. I'll pay you when we meet again—that is, if we ever do meet again. I'm beginning to think that this siege will go on for all eternity. There, good-bye, my dear! God bless you! When you get out of it, mind you write to the "Times," in London, you know. There, don't cry. I am sure I should not cry if I were going to get out of this place;' for at this point Jess took the opportunity of Mrs. Neville's fervent embrace to burst out into a sob or two.

In another minute they were in the cart, and Mouti was scrambling up behind.

'Don't cry, old girl,' said John, laying his hand upon her shoulder. 'What can't be cured must be endured.'

'Yes, John,' she answered, and dried her tears.

At the headquarter camp John went in and explained the circumstances of his departure. At first the officer who was temporarily in command—the Commandant having been wounded at the same time that John was hit—rather demurred to his going, especially when he learned that he had passed his word not to carry despatches. Presently, however, he thought better of it, and said he supposed that it was all right, as he could not see that their departure could do the garrison any harm: 'rather the reverse, in fact, because you can tell people how we are getting on in this God-forsaken hole. I only wish that somebody would give me a pass, that's all.' So John shook hands with him and left, to find an eager crowd gathered outside.

The news of their good luck had gone abroad, and everybody was running down to hear the truth of it. Such an event as a departure out of Pretoria had not happened for a couple of months and more, and the excitement was proportionate to its novelty.

' I say, Niel, is it true you are going?' halloed a burly farmer.

' How the deuce did you get a pass?' put in another man with a face like a weasel. He was what is known as a ' Boer vernuker ' (literally a ' Boer cheater '), that is, a travelling trader whose business it is to beguile the simple-minded Dutchman by selling him worthless goods at five times their value. ' I have loads of friends among the Boers. There is hardly a Boer in the Transvaal who does not know me '—(' To his cost,' put in a bystander with a grunt)—' and yet I have tried all I know '—(' And you know a good deal,' said the same rude man)—' and *I* can't get a pass.'

' You don't suppose those poor Boers are going to let you out when once they have got you in?' went on the tormentor. ' Why, man, it's against human nature. You've got all their wool : now do you think they want you to have their skin too?'

Whereupon the weasel-faced individual uttered a howl of wrath, and pretended to make a rush at the author cf these random gibes, waiting halfway for somebody to stop him and prevent a breach of the peace.

' Oh, Miss Croft!' cried out a woman in the crowd, who, like Jess, had been trapped in Pretoria while on a fly-ing visit, ' if you can, do send a line to my husband at

Maritzburg, to tell him that I am well, except for the
rheumatism, from sleeping on the wet ground ; and tell
him to kiss the twins for me.'

'I say, Niel, tell those Boers that we will give them
a d—d good hiding yet, when Colley relieves us,' sang out
a jolly young Englishman in the uniform of the Pretoria
Carbineers.   He little knew that poor Colley—kind-
hearted English gentleman that he was—lay sleeping
peacefully under six feet of ground with a Boer bullet
through his brain.

'Now, Captain Niel, if you are ready, we must trek,'
said one of the Boers in Dutch, suiting the action to the
word by giving the near wheeler a sharp cut with his
riding sjambock that made him jump nearly out of the
traces.

Away started the horses with a plunge, scattering the
crowd to the right and left, and, amid a volley of farewells,
they were off upon their homeward journey.

For more than an hour nothing particular happened.
John drove at a fair pace, and the two Boers cantered
along behind.   At the end of this time, however, just as
they were approaching the Red House, where Frank
Muller had obtained the pass from the General on the
previous day, one of the Boers rode up and told them,
roughly enough, that they were to outspan at the house,
where they would find some food.   As it was past
one o'clock, they were by no means sorry to hear
this, and John drew up the cart about fifty yards from
the place, where they outspanned the horses, and,
having watched them roll and drink, they went up to the
house.

The two Boers, who had also off-saddled, were already
sitting on the verandah, and when Jess looked inquiringly
towards them one of them pointed with his pipe towards

the little room. Taking the hint, they entered, and found a Hottentot woman just setting some food upon the table.

'Here is dinner : let us eat it,' said John ; ' goodness knows when we shall get any more ; ' and accordingly he sat down.

As he did so the two Boers came in, and one of them made some sneering remark that caused the other to look at them and laugh insultingly.

John flushed, but took no notice. Indeed he thought it safest not, for, to tell the truth, he did not much like the appearance of these two worthies. One of them was a big, smooth, pasty-faced man, with a peculiarly villainous expression of countenance and a prominent tooth that projected in ghastly isolation over his lower lip. The other was a small man, with a sardonic smile, a profusion of black beard and whiskers on his face, and long hair hanging on to his shoulders. Indeed, when he smiled more vigorously than usual, his eyebrows came down and his whiskers advanced, and his moustache went up till there was scarcely any face left, and he looked more like a great bearded monkey than a human being. This man was a Boer of the wildest type from the far borders of Zoutpansberg, and did not understand a word of English. Jess nicknamed him the Vilderbeeste, from his likeness to that ferocious-looking and hairy animal. His companion, on the contrary, understood English perfectly, for he had passed many years of his life in Natal, having left that colony on account of some little indiscretion about thrashing Kafirs which had brought him into collision with the penal laws. Jess named him the Unicorn, on account of his one gleaming tusk.

The Unicorn was an unusually pious person, and on arriving at the table, to John's astonishment, gently

H

but firmly he grasped the knife with which he was about
to cut the meat.

'What's the matter?' said John.

The Boer shook his head sadly. 'No wonder you
English are an accursed race, and have been given over
into our hands as the great king Agag was given into the
hands of the Israelites, so that we have hewed you to
pieces. You sit down to meat and give no thanks to
the dear Lord,' and he threw back his head and sang out
a portentously long Dutch grace through his nose. Not
content with this, he set to work to translate it into
English, which took a good time; nor was the rendering
a very finished one in the result.

The Vilderbeeste grinned sardonically and put in a
pious 'Amen,' and then at last they were allowed to
proceed with their dinner, which, on the whole, was
not a pleasant meal. But they could not expect much
pleasure under the circumstances, so they ate their food
and made the best of a bad business. After all, it might
have been worse: they might have had no dinner to eat.

CHAPTER XXII.

JOHN and Jess had finished their meal, and were about to leave the table, when suddenly the door opened, and who should appear at it but Frank Muller himself! Mistake was impossible; there he stood, stroking his long golden beard, as big, as handsome, and, to Jess's mind, as evil-looking as ever. The cold eyes fell upon John with a glance of recognition, and something like a smile began to play around the corners of the finely cut cruel mouth. Suddenly, however, his gaze lit upon the two Boers, one of whom was picking his teeth with a steel fork and the other lighting his pipe within a few inches of Jess's head, and instantly his face grew stern and angry.

'Did I not tell you two men,' he said, 'that you were not to eat with the prisoners?'—this word struck awkwardly on Jess's ear. 'I told you that they were to be treated with all respect, and here I find you sprawling over the table and smoking in their faces. Be off with you!'

The smooth-faced man with the tusk rose at once with a sigh, put down the steel fork with which he had been operating, and departed, recognising that Meinheer Muller was not a commanding officer to be trifled with, but his companion, the Vilderbeeste, demurred. 'What,' he said, tossing his head so as to throw the long black hair out of his eyes, 'am I not fit to sit at meat with a couple of accursed English—a rooibaatje and a woman ? If I had my way he should clean my boots and she should cut up my tobacco ; ' and he grinned at the notion till eyebrows, whiskers, and moustache nearly met round his nose, causing him to look for all the world like a hairy-faced baboon.

Frank Muller made no answer in words. He simply took one step forward, pounced upon his insubordinate follower, and with a single swing of his athletic frame sent him flying headlong through the door, so that this free and independent burgher lit upon his head in the passage, smashing his pipe and considerably damaging his best feature—his nose. 'There,' said Muller, shutting the door after him, 'that is the only way to deal with such a fellow. And now let me bid you good-day, Miss Jess,' and he extended his hand, which Jess took, rather coldly it must be owned.

'It has given me great pleasure to be able to do you this little service,' he added politely. ' I had considerable difficulty in obtaining the pass from the General—indeed I was obliged to urge my personal services before he would give it to me. But never mind that, I got it, as you know, and it will be my care to escort you safely to Mooifontein.'

Jess bowed, and Muller turned to John, who had risen from his chair and was standing some two paces away, and addressed him. 'Captain Niel,' he said, ' you and I have had some differences in the past. I hope that the service I am doing you will prove that I, for one, bear no malice. I will go farther. As I told you before, I was to blame in that affair in the inn-yard at Wakkerstroom. Let us shake hands and end what we cannot mend,' and he stepped forward and extended his hand.

Jess turned to see what would happen. She knew the whole story, and hoped he would not take the man's hand; next, remembering their position, she hoped that he would.

John turned colour a little, then he drew himself up deliberately and put his hand behind his back.

'I am very sorry, Mr. Muller,' he said, 'but even in our present position I cannot shake hands with you; you will know why.'

Jess saw a flush, bred of the furious passion which was his weak point, spread itself over the Boer's face.

'I do *not* know, Captain Niel. Be so good as to explain.'

'Very well, I will,' said John calmly. 'You tried to assassinate me.'

'What do you mean?' thundered Muller.

'What I say. You shot at me twice under pretence of firing at a buck. Look here!'—and he took up his soft black hat, which he still wore—'here is the mark of one of your bullets! I did not know about it then; I do now, and I decline to shake hands with you.'

By this time Muller's fury had got the better of him. 'You shall answer for that, you English liar!' he said, at the same time clapping his hand to his belt, in which his hunting-knife was placed. Thus for a few seconds they stood face to face. John never flinched or moved. There he stood, quiet and strong as some old stubby tree, his plain honest face and watchful eye affording a strange contrast to the beautiful but demoniacal countenance of the great Dutchman. Presently he spoke in measured tones.

'I have proved myself a better man than yourself once, Frank Muller, and if necessary I will again, notwithstanding that knife of yours. But, in the meantime, I wish to remind you that I have a pass signed by your own General guaranteeing our safety. And now, Mr. Muller,' with a flash of the blue eyes, 'I am ready.' The Dutchman drew the knife, but replaced it in its sheath. For a moment he was minded to end the matter then and there, but suddenly, even in his rage, he remembered that there was a witness.

'A pass from the General!' he said, forgetting his caution in his fury. 'Much good a pass from the General is likely to be to you. You are in my power, man! If I choose to close my hand I can crush you. But there— there,' he added, checking himself, 'perhaps I ought to make allowances. You are one of a defeated people, and no doubt are sore, and say what you do not mean. Anyhow, there is an end of it, especially in the presence of a lady. Some day we may be able to settle our trouble like men, Captain Niel; till then, with your permission, we will let it drop.'

'Quite so, Mr. Muller,' said John, 'only you must not ask me to shake hands with you.'

'Very good, Captain Niel; and now, if you will allow me, I will tell the boy to get your horses in; we must be getting on if we are to reach Heidelberg to-night.' And he bowed himself out, feeling that once more his temper had endangered the success of his plans. 'Curse the fellow!' he said to himself: 'he is what those English call a gentleman. It was brave of him to refuse to take my hand when he is in my power.'

'John,' said Jess, as soon as the door had closed, 'I am afraid of that man. If I had understood that he had anything to do with the pass I would not have taken it,

I thought that the writing was familiar to me. Oh dear!
I wish we had stopped at Pretoria.'

'What can't be cured must be endured,' said John
again. 'The only thing to do is to make the best of it
and get on as we can. You will be all right anyhow, but
he hates me like poison. I suppose that it is on account
of Bessie.'

'Yes, that's it,' said Jess : 'he is, or was, madly in
love with Bessie.'

'It is curious to think that a man like that can be in
love,' remarked John as he lit his pipe, 'but it only shows
what queer mixtures people are. I say, Jess, if this
fellow hates me so much, what made him give me the
pass, eh ? What's his game ?'

Jess shook her head as she answered, 'I don't know,
John ; I don't like it.'

'I suppose he can't mean to murder me ; he did try
it on once, you know.'

'Oh no, John,' she answered with a sort of cry, 'not
that.'

'Well, I don't know that it would matter much,' he
said, with an approach to cheerfulness which was rather
a failure. 'It would save one a deal of worry, and only
anticipate things a bit. But there, I frightened you, and
I dare say that, for the present at any rate, he is an
honest man, and has no intentions on my person. Look !
there is Mouti calling us. I wonder if those brutes have
given him anything to eat ! We'll secure the rest of this
leg of mutton on chance. At any rate, Mr. Frank Muller
sha'n't starve me to death,' and with a cheerful laugh he
left the room.

In a few minutes they were on their road again. As
they started Frank Muller came up, took off his hat, and
informed them that probably he would join them on the

morrow below Heidelberg, in which town they would find every preparation to enable them to spend the night comfortably. If he did not join them it would be because he was detained on duty. In that case the two men had his orders to escort them safely to Mooifontein, and, he added significantly, 'I do not think that you will be troubled with any further impoliteness.'

In another moment he had galloped off on his great black horse, leaving the pair considerably mystified and not a little relieved.

' Well,' said John, ' at any rate that does not look like foul play, unless, indeed, he has gone on to prepare a warm reception for us.'

Jess shrugged her shoulders, she could not understand it ; and then they settled themselves down to their long lonely drive. They had forty odd miles to cover, but the guides, or rather the guard, would only consent to their outspanning once, which they did on the open veldt a little before sunset. At sundown they inspanned again, and started across the darkening veldt. The road was in a shocking state, and until the moon rose, which it did about nine o'clock, the journey was both difficult and dangerous. After that things were a little better ; and at last, about eleven o'clock, they reached Heidelberg. The town seemed almost deserted. Evidently the great body of the Boers were at the front, and had only left a guard at their seat of government.

' Where are we to outspan ? ' asked John of the Unicorn, who was jogging on alongside, apparently half asleep.

' At the hotel,' was the short reply, and thither they went. Thankful enough they were to reach it, and to find, from the lights in the windows, that people were still about.

Notwithstanding the awful jolting of the cart, Jess had been asleep for the last two hours. Her arm was hooked round the back of the seat, and her head rested against John's great-coat, which he had fixed up in such a way as to make a pillow. 'Where are we?' she asked, waking up with a start as the cart stopped. 'I have had such a bad dream! I dreamt that I was travelling through life, and that suddenly everything stopped, and I was dead.'

'I don't wonder at it,' laughed John; 'the road for the last ten miles has been as rough as anybody's life. We are at the hotel. Here come the boys to take the horses,' and he clambered stiffly out of the cart and helped or rather lifted her down, for she was almost too cramped to move.

Standing at the inn-door, holding a light above her head, they found a pleasant-looking Englishwoman, who welcomed them heartily.

'Frank Muller was here three hours ago, and told me to expect you,' she said; 'and very glad I am to see an English face again, I can tell you. My name is Gooch. Tell me, is my husband all right in Pretoria? He went up there with his waggon just before the siege began, and I have not heard a word from him since.'

'Yes,' said John, 'he is all right. He was slightly wounded in the shoulder a month ago, but he has quite recovered.'

'Oh, thank God!' said the poor woman, beginning to cry; 'those devils told me that he was dead—to torment me, I suppose. Come in, miss: there is some hot supper ready when you have washed your hands. The boys will see to the horses.'

Accordingly they entered, and were made as happy as

a good supper, a hearty welcome, and comfortable beds could make people in their condition.

In the early morning one of their estimable escort sent in a message to say that they were not to start before half-past ten, as the horses required more rest, so they enjoyed some hours longer in bed than they had expected, and anybody who has ever made a journey in a post-cart in South Africa can understand the blessing thereof. At nine they breakfasted, and as the clock struck half-past ten Mouti brought the cart round, and with it came the two Boers.

'Well, Mrs. Gooch,' said John, 'what do we owe you?'

'Nothing, Captain Niel, nothing. If you only knew what a weight you have taken off my mind! Besides, we are quite ruined; the Boers have looted all my husband's cattle and horses, and until last week six of them were quartered on me without paying a farthing, so it makes no odds to me.'

'Never mind, Mrs. Gooch,' said John cheerfully, 'the Government will compensate you when this business is over, no doubt.'

Mrs. Gooch shook her head prophetically. 'Never a halfpenny do I expect to see,' she said. 'If only I can get my husband back, and we can escape out of this wicked place with our lives, I shall be thankful. And look here, Captain Niel, I have put up a basketful of food—bread, meat, and hard-boiled eggs, with a bottle of three-star brandy. It may be useful to you and the young lady before you reach home. I don't know where you will sleep to-night, for the English are still holding Standerton, so you won't be able to stop there, and you can't drive right through. No, don't thank me, I could not do less. Good-bye—good-bye, miss; I hope you will get

through all right. You had better look out, though.
Those two men you have with you are very bad lots. I
heard say, rightly or wrongly, that that fat-faced man with
the tooth shot two wounded soldiers through the head
after the fight at Bronker's Spruit, and I know no good
of the other. They were laughing and talking together
about you in the kitchen this morning ; one of my boys
overheard them, and the Boer with the long hair said
that, at any rate, they would not be troubled with you
after to-night. I don't know what he meant ; perhaps
they are going to change the escort ; but I thought that
I had better tell you.'

John looked grave, and his suspicions re-arose, but at
that moment one of the men in question rode up and
told him that he must start at once, and so off they
went.

This second day's journey was in many respects a
counterpart of the first. The road was utterly deserted,
and they saw neither Boer, Englishman, nor Kafir upon
it ; nothing, indeed, except a few herds of game grazing
on the ridges. About two o'clock, however, just as
they had started after a short outspan, a little incident
occurred. Suddenly the Vilderbeeste's horse put his foot
into an ant-bear hole and fell heavily, throwing his rider
on to his head. He was up in a minute, but his forehead
had struck against the jawbone of a dead buck, and the
blood was pouring from it down his hairy face. His
companion laughed brutally at the accident, for there are
some natures in the world to which the sight of pain is
irresistibly comical, but the injured man cursed aloud,
trying to staunch the flow with the lappet of his coat.

'Waacht een beeche' [Wait a bit], said Jess, 'there
is some water in that pool,' and telling John to pull up
she sprang from the trap and led the man, who was half-

blinded with blood, to the spring. Here she made him
kneel down and bathed the wound, which was not a very
deep one, till it stopped bleeding, and then, having first
placed a pad of cotton-wool, some of which she happened
to have in the cart, upon it, she bound her handkerchief
tightly round his head. The man, brute as he was,
appeared to be much touched at her kindness.

'Almighty,' he said, 'but you have a kind heart and
soft fingers ; my own wife could not have done it better ;
it is a pity that you are a damned Englishwoman.'

Jess climbed back into the cart, making no reply, and
they started on, the Vilderbeeste looking more savage
and unhuman than ever with the discoloured handkerchief
round his head, and his dense beard and hair matted
with gore which he would not take the trouble to wash
out of them.

After this nothing further occurred till, by the orders
of their escort, they outspanned, an hour or so before
sunset, at a spot in the veldt where a faint track forked
from the Standerton road.

CHAPTER XXIII

IN THE DRIFT OF THE VAAL

THE day had been intensely hot, and our travellers sa&
in the shade of the cart overpowered and gasping.
During the afternoon a faint breeze blew, but this had
now died away, and the stifling air felt as thick as though
they were breathing cream. Even the two Boers seemed
to feel the heat, for they lay outstretched on the grass a
few paces to the left, to all appearance fast asleep. As
for the horses, they were thoroughly done up—too much
so to eat—and hobbled along as well as their knee-halters
would allow, daintily picking a mouthful here and a
mouthful there. The only person who did not seem to
mind was the Zulu Mouti, who sat on an ant-heap near
the horses, in full glare of the setting sun, and comfortably droned out a little song of his own invention,
for Zulus seem as clever at improvising as are the
Italians.

'Have another egg, Jess?' said John. 'It will do
you good.'

'No, thank you ; the last one stuck in my throat. It
is impossible to eat in this heat.'

'You had better. Goodness knows when and where
we shall stop again. I can get nothing out of our
delightful escort; either they don't know or they won't
say.'

'I can't, John. There is a thunderstorm coming up, I feel it in my head, and I can never eat before a thunderstorm—and when I am tired,' she added by an afterthought.

After that the conversation flagged for a while.

'John,' said Jess at last, 'where do you suppose we are going to camp to-night? If we follow the main road we shall reach Standerton in an hour.'

'I don't think that they will go near Standerton,' he answered, 'I suppose that we shall cross the Vaal by another drift and have to "veldt" it.'

Just then the two Boers woke up and began to talk earnestly together, as though they were debating something hotly.

Slowly the huge red ball of the sun sank towards the horizon, steeping the earth and sky in blood. About a hundred yards from where they sat the little bridle path that branched from the main road crossed the crest of one of the great landwaves which rolled away in every direction towards the far horizon. John watched the sun sinking behind it till something called off his attention for a minute. When he looked up again there was a figure on horseback, standing quite still upon the crest of the ridge, and in full glow of the now disappearing sun. It was Frank Muller. John recognised him in a moment. His horse was halted sideways, so that even at that distance every line of his features, and even the trigger-guard of the rifle which rested on his knee, showed distinctly against the background of smoky red. Nor was that all. Both he and his horse had the appearance of being absolutely on fire. The effect produced was so wild and extraordinary that John called his companion's attention to it. Jess looked and shuddered involuntarily.

'He looks like a devil in hell,' she said; 'the fire seems to be running all up and down him.'

'Well,' said John, 'he is certainly a devil, but I am sorry to say that he has not yet reached his destination. Here he comes, like a whirlwind.'

In another twenty seconds Muller had reined the great black horse on to his haunches alongside of them, and was smiling sweetly and taking off his hat.

'You see I have managed to keep my word,' he said. 'I can tell you that I had great difficulty in doing so; indeed I was nearly obliged to give the thing up at the last moment. However, here I am.'

'Where are we to outspan to-night?' asked Jess. 'At Standerton?'

'No,' he said; 'I am afraid that is more than I could manage for you, unless you can persuade the English officers there to surrender. What I have arranged is, that we should cross the Vaal at a drift I know of about two hours (twelve miles) from here, and outspan at a farm on the other side. Do not trouble, I assure you you shall both sleep well to-night,' and he smiled, a somewhat terrifying smile, as Jess thought.

'But how about this drift, Mr. Muller?' said John. 'Is it safe? I should have thought the Vaal would have been in flood after all the rain that we have had.'

'The drift is perfectly safe, Captain Niel. I crossed it myself about two hours ago. I know you have a bad opinion of me, but I suppose you do not think that I would guide you to an unsafe drift?' Then with another bow he rode on to speak to the two Boers, saying, as he went, 'Will you tell the Kafir to put the horses in?'

With a shrug of the shoulders John rose and went to Mouti, to help him to drive up the four greys, which were now standing limply together, biting at the flies, that,

before a storm, sting more sharply than at any other time.
The two horses belonging to the escort were some fifty
paces to the left. It was as though they appreciated the
position of affairs, and declined to mix with the animals
of the discredited Englishman.

The Boers rose as Muller came and walked towards
their horses, Muller slowly following them. As they
drew near, the horses hobbled away for twenty or thirty
yards. Then they lifted up their heads, and, as a conse-
quence, their forelegs, to which the heads were tied, and
stood looking defiantly at their captors, just as though
they were trying to make up their minds whether or
no to shake hands with them.

Frank Muller was alongside the two men now, and
they were alongside the horses.

'Listen!' he said sternly.

The men looked up.

'Go on loosening the reims, and listen.'

They obeyed, and slowly began to fumble at the knee-
halters.

'You understand what our orders are. Repeat them
—you!'

The man with the tooth, who was addressed, still
handling the reim, began as follows: 'To take the two
prisoners to the Vaal, to force them into the water where
there is no drift, at night, so that they drown: if they do
not drown, to shoot them.'

'Those are the orders,' said the Vilderbeeste, grin-
ning.

'You understand them?'

'We understand, Meinheer; but, forgive us, the matter
is a big one. You gave the orders—we wish to see the
authority.'

'Yah, yah,' said the other, 'show us the authority.'

These are two harmless people enough. Show us the
authority for killing them. People must not be killed so,
even if they are English folk, without proper authority,
especially when one is a pretty girl who would do for a
man's wife.'

Frank Muller set his teeth. 'Nice fellows you are to
have under one!' he said. 'I am your officer; what
other authority do you want? But I thought of this.
See here!' and he drew a paper from his pocket. 'Here,
you—read it! Careful now—do not let them see from
the waggon.'

The big flabby-faced man took the paper and, still
bending down over the horse's knee, read aloud:

'The two prisoners and their servant (an Englishman,
an English girl, and a Zulu Kafir) to be executed in pur-
suance of our decree, as your commanding officer shall
order, as enemies to the Republic. For so doing this
shall be your warrant.'

'You see the signature,' said Muller, 'and you do not
dispute it?'

'Yah, we see it, and we do not dispute it.'

'Good. Give me back the warrant.'

The man with the tooth was about to obey when his
companion interposed.

'No,' he said, 'the warrant must remain with us. I
do not like the job. If it were only the man and the
Kafir now—but the girl, the girl! If we give you back
the warrant, what shall we have to show for the deed of
blood? The warrant must remain with us.'

'Yah, yah, he is right,' said the Unicorn; 'the
warrant must remain with us. Put it in your pocket,
Jan.'

'Curse you, give it me!' said Muller between his
teeth.

'No, Frank Muller, no!' answered the Vilderbeeste, patting his pocket, while the two or three square inches of skin round his nose wrinkled up in a hairy grin that, owing to the cut on his head, was even more curious than usual. 'If you wish to have the warrant you shall have it, but then we shall up-saddle and go, and you can do your murdering yourself. There, there! take your choice; we shall be glad enough to get home, for we do not care for the job. If I go out shooting I like to shoot buck or Kafirs, not white people.'

Frank Muller reflected a moment, then he laughed a little.

'You are funny folk, you home-bred Boers,' he said; 'but perhaps you are right. After all, what does it matter who keeps the warrant, provided the thing is well done? Mind that there is no bungling, that is all.'

'Yah, yah,' said the fat-faced man, 'you can trust us for that. It won't be the first that we have toppled over. If I have my warrant I ask nothing better than to go on shooting Englishmen all night, one down the other come on. I know no prettier sight than an Englishman toppling over.'

'Stop that talk and saddle up, the cart is waiting. You fools can never understand the difference between killing when it is necessary to kill and killing for killing's sake. These people must die because they have betrayed the land.'

'Yah, yah,' said the Vilderbeeste, 'betrayed the land; we have heard that before. Those who betray the land must manure it; that is a good rule!' and he laughed and passed on.

Frank Muller watched his retreating form with a smile of peculiar malignity on his handsome face. 'Ah, my friend,' he said to himself in Dutch, 'you and that warrant will part company before you are many hours older. Why, it would be enough to hang me, even in this happy land of patriots. Old —— would not forgive even me for taking that little liberty with his name. Dear me, what a lot of trouble it is to be rid of a single enemy ! Well, it must be done, and Bessie is well worth the pains ; but if it had not been for this war I could never have managed it. Yes ! I did well to give my voice for war. I am sorry for the girl Jess, but it is necessary ; there must be no living witness left. Ah ! we are going to have a storm. So much the better. Such deeds are best done in a storm.'

Muller was right ; the storm was coming up fast, throwing a veil of inky cloud across the star-spangled sky. In South Africa there is but little twilight, and the darkness follows hard upon the heels of the day. No sooner had the angry ball of the setting sun disappeared than the night swept with all her stars across the sky. And now after her came the great storm, covering up her beauty with his blackness. The air was stiflingly hot. Above was a starry space, to the east the black bosom of the storm, in which the lightnings were already playing with an incessant flickering movement, and to the west a deep red glow, reflected from the sunken sun, yet lingered on the horizon.

On toiled the horses through the gathering gloom. Fortunately, the road was almost level and free from mud-holes, and Frank Muller rode just ahead to show the way, his strong athletic form standing out clearly against the departing western glow. Silent was the earth, silent as death. No bird or beast, no blade of grass or breath of air stirred upon its surface. The only sign of life was the continual flickering of those awful tongues of light as they licked the lips of the storm. On for mile after mile,

on through the desolation! They were not far from
the river now, and could hear the distant growling of
the thunder, echoing down it solemnly.

It was an awful night. Great pillars of mud-coloured
cloud came creeping across the surface of the veldt
towards them, seemingly blown along without a wind.
Now, too, a ghastly-looking ringed moon arose throwing an unholy and distorted light upon the blackness that
seemed to shudder in her rays as though with a pre-
science of the advancing terror. On crept the mud-
coloured columns, and on above them, and resting on
them, came the muttering storm. The cart was quite
close to the river now, and they could distinguish the
murmur of its waters. To their left stood a koppie,
covered with white, slab-like stones, on which the sickly
moonbeams danced.

'Look, John, look!' cried Jess with an hysterical
laugh; 'it is like a huge graveyard, and the dark shadows
between are the ghosts of the buried.'

'Nonsense,' said John sternly; 'why do you talk
such rubbish?'

He felt that her mind had lost its balance, and, what
is more, his own nerves were shaken. Therefore he was
naturally the angrier with her, and the more determined
to be perfectly matter-of-fact.

Jess made no answer, but she was frightened, she
could not tell why. The scene resembled that of some
awful dream, or of one of Doré's pictures come to life.
No doubt, also, the near presence of the tempest exercised
a physical effect upon her. Even the wearied horses
snorted and shook themselves uneasily.

They crept over the ridge of a wave of land, and the
wheels rolled softly on the grass.

'Why, we are off the road!' shouted John to Muller,

who was still guiding them, fifteen or twenty paces ahead.

'All right! all right! it is a short cut to the ford!' he called in answer, and his voice rang strange and hollow through the great depths of the silence.

Below them, a hundred yards away, the light, such as it was, gleamed faintly upon the wide surface of the river. Another five minutes and they were on the bank, but in the gathering gloom they could not see the opposite shore.

'Turn to the left!' shouted Muller; 'the ford is a few yards up. It is too deep here for the horses.'

John turned accordingly, and followed Muller's horse some three hundred yards up the bank till they came to a spot where the water ran with an angry music, and there was a great swirl of eddies.

'Here is the place,' said Muller; 'you must make haste through. The house is just the other side, and it will be better to get there before the tempest breaks.'

'It is all very well,' said John, 'but I cannot see an inch before me; I don't know where to drive.'

'Drive straight ahead; the water is not more than three feet deep, and there are no rocks.'

'I am not going, and that is all about it.'

'You must go, Captain Niel. You cannot stop here, and if you can we will not. Look there, man!' and he pointed to the east, which now presented a truly awful and magnificent sight.

Down, right on to them, its centre bowed out like the belly of a sail by the weight of the wind behind, swept the great storm-cloud, while over all its surface the lightning played unceasingly, appearing and disappearing in needles of fire, and twisting and writhing serpentwise round and about its outer edges. So brilliant was the intermittent light that it appeared to fire the revolving pillars of mud-coloured cloud beneath, and gave ghastly peeps of river and bank and plain, miles upon miles away. But perhaps its most awful circumstance was the preternatural silence. The distant boom and muttering of thunder had died away, and now the great storm swept on in voiceless majesty, like the passage of a ghostly host, from which there arose no sound of feet or of rolling wheels. Only before it sped the swift angels of the wind, and behind it swung the curtain of the rain.

Even as Muller spoke a gust of icy air caught the cart and tilted it, and the lightning needles began to ply more dreadfully than ever. The tempest was breaking upon them.

'Come, drive on, drive on!' he shouted, 'you will be killed here; the lightning always strikes along the water;' and as he said it he struck one of the wheelers sharply with his whip.

'Climb over the back of the seat, Mouti, and stand by to help me with the reins!' called out John to the Zulu, who obeyed, scrambling between him and Jess.

'Now, Jess, hold on and say your prayers, for it strikes me that we shall have need of them. So, horses, so!'

The horses backed and plunged, but Muller on the one side and the smooth-faced Boer on the other lashed them without mercy, and at last they went into the river with a rush. The gust had passed now, and for a few moments the heavy quiet was renewed, except for the whirl of the water and the snake-like hiss of the coming rain.

For some yards, ten or fifteen perhaps, all went well, and then John discovered suddenly that they were driving into deep water; the two leaders were evidently almost off their legs, and could scarcely stand against the current of the flooded river.

Damn you!' he shouted back, 'there is no drift here.'

'Go on, go on, it is quite safe!' came Muller's voice in answer.

John said no more, but, putting out all his strength, he tried to drag the horses round. Jess turned herself on the seat to look, and just then a blaze of lightning flamed which revealed Muller and his two companions standing dismounted on the bank, the muzzles of their rifles pointing straight at the cart.

'O God!' she screamed, 'they are going to shoot us.'

Even as the words passed her lips three tongues of fire flared from the rifles' mouths, and the Zulu Mouti, sitting by her side, pitched heavily forward on to his head into the bottom of the cart, while one of the wheelers reared straight up into the air with a shriek of agony, and fell with a splash into the river.

Then followed a scene of horror indescribable. Overhead the storm burst in fury, and flash after flash of fork, or rather chain lightning, leapt into the river. The thunder, too, began to crack like the trump of doom; the wind rushed down, tearing the surface of the water into foam, and, catching under the tent of the cart, lifted it quite off the wheels, so that it began to float. Then the two leaders, made mad with fear by the fury of the storm and the dying struggles of the off-wheeler, plunged and tore at the traces till at last they rent themselves loose and vanished between the darkness overhead and the boiling water beneath. Away floated the cart, now touching the bottom and now riding on the river like a boat, oscillating this way and that, and slowly turning round and round. With it floated the dead horse, dragging down the other wheeler beneath the water. It was awful to see his struggles in the glare of the lightning, but at last he sank and choked.

Meanwhile, sounding sharp and clearly through the din and hubbub of the storm, came the cracking of the three rifles whenever the flashes showed the position of the cart to the murderers on the bank. Mouti was lying still in the bottom of it on the bed-plank, a bullet between his broad shoulders and another in his skull: but John felt that his life was yet whole in him, though something had hissed past his face and stung it. Instinctively he reached across the cart and drew Jess on to his knee, and cowered over her, thinking dimly that perhaps his body would protect her from the bullets.

Rip! rip! through the wood and canvas; *phut! phut!* through the air: but some merciful power protected them, and though one cut John's coat and two passed through the skirt of Jess's dress, not a bullet struck them. Very soon the shooting began to grow wild, then that dense veil of rain came down and wrapped them so closely that even the lightning could not reveal their whereabouts to the assassins on the bank.

' Stop shooting,' said Frank Muller; ' the cart has sunk, and there is an end of them. No human being can have lived through that fire and the Vaal in flood.'

The two Boers ceased firing, and the Unicorn shook his head softly and remarked to his companion that the damned English people in the water could not be much wetter than they were on the bank. It was a curious thing to say at such a moment, but probably the spirit that caused the remark was not so much callousness as that which animated Cromwell, who flipped the ink in his neighbour's face when he signed the death-warrant of his king.

The Vilderbeeste made no reply. His conscience was

oppressed ; he had a touch of imagination. He thought of the soft fingers which had bound up his head that morning : the handkerchief—her handkerchief !—was still around it. Now those fingers would be gripping at the slippery stones of the Vaal in a struggle for life, or more probably they were already limp in death, with little grains of gravel sticking beneath the nails. It was a painful thought, but he consoled himself by remembering the warrant, also by the reflection that whoever had shot the people he had not, for he had been careful to fire wide of the cart every time.

Muller was also thinking of the warrant which he had forged. He must get it back somehow, even if——

' Let us take shelter under the shore. There is a flat place, about fifty yards up, where the bank hangs over. This rain is drowning us. We can't up-saddle till it clears. I must have a nip of brandy, too. Almighty ! I can see that girl's face still ! the lightning shone on it just as I shot. Well, she will be in heaven now, poor thing, if English people ever go to heaven.'

It was the Unicorn who spoke, and the Vilderbeeste made no reply, but advanced with him to where the horses stood. They caught the patient brutes that were waiting for their masters, their heads well down and the water streaming from their flanks, and led them along with them. Frank Muller stood by his own horse still thinking, and watched them vanish into the gloom. How was he to win that warrant back without dyeing his hands even redder than they were ?

As he thought an answer came. For at that moment, accompanied by a fearful thunderclap, there shot from the storm overhead, which had now nearly passed away, one of those awful flashes that sometimes end an African tempest. It lit up the scene with a light vivid as that of day, and in the white heart of it Muller saw his two companions in crime and their horses as the great king saw the men in the furnace. They were about forty paces from him on the crest of the bank. He saw them, one moment erect; the next—men and horses falling this way and that prone to the earth. Then it was dark again.

Muller staggered with the shock, and when it had passed he rushed to the spot, calling the men by name; but no answer came except the echo of his voice. He was there alone now, and the moonlight began to struggle faintly through the rain. Its pale beams lit upon two outstretched forms—one lying on its back, its distorted features gazing up to heaven, the other on its face. By them, the legs of the nearer sticking straight into the air, lay the horses. They had all gone to their account. The lightning had killed them, as it kills many a man in Africa.

Frank Muller looked; then, forgetting about the warrant and everything else in the horror of what he took to be a visible judgment, he rushed to his horse and galloped wildly away, pursued by all the terrors of hell.

CHAPTER XXIV

THE SHADOW OF DEATH

THE firing from the bank had ceased, and John, who still
kept his head, being a rather phlegmatic specimen of the
Anglo-Saxon race, knew that, for the moment at any
rate, all danger from this source was ended. Jess lay
perfectly still in his arms, her head upon his breast.
A horrible idea struck him that she might be shot,
perhaps already dead!

'Jess, Jess,' he shouted, through the turmoil of the
storm, ' are you hit?'

She lifted her head an inch or two—'I think not,' she
said. 'What is going on?'

'God only knows, I don't. Sit still, it will be all
right.'

But in his heart he knew it was not 'all right,'
and that they stood in imminent danger of death by
drowning. They were whirling down a raging river in a
cart. In a few moments it was probable that the cart
would upset, and then——

Presently the wheel bumped against something, the
cart gave a great lurch, and scraped along a little.

' Now for it,' thought John, for the water was pouring
over the flooring. Then came a check, and the cart
leant still farther to one side.

Crack! The pole had gone, and the cart swung round bows, or rather box, on to the stream. What had happened was this : they had drifted across a rock that projected from the bed of the river, the force of the current having washed the dead horses to the one side of it and the cart to the other. Consequently they were anchored to the rock, as it were, the anchor being the dead horses, and the cable the stout traces of untanned leather. So long as these traces and the rest of the harness held, they were safe from drowning ; but of course they did not know this.

Indeed, they knew nothing. Above them rolled the storm ; about them the river seethed and the rain hissed. They knew nothing except that they were helpless living atoms tossing between the wild waters and the wilder night, with imminent death staring them in the face, around, above, and below. To and fro they rocked, locked fast in each other's arms, and as they swung came that awful flash that, though they guessed it not, sent two of the murderers to their account, and for an instant, even through the sheet of rain, illumined the space of boiling water and the long lines of the banks on either side. It showed the point of rock to which they were fixed, it glared upon the head of one of the poor horses tossed up by the driving current as though it were still trying to escape its watery doom, and revealed the form of the dead Zulu, Mouti, lying on his face, one arm hanging over the edge of the cart and dabbling in the water that ran level with it, in ghastly similarity to some idle passenger in a pleasure boat, who lets his fingers slip softly through the stream.

In a second it was gone, and once more they were in darkness. Then by degrees the storm passed off and the moon began to shine, feebly indeed, for the sky was not clear washed of clouds, which still trailed along in the tracks of the tempest, sucked after it by its mighty draught. Still it was lighter and the rain thinned gradually till at last it stopped. The storm had rolled in majesty down the ways of night, and there was no sound round them save the sound of rushing water.

'John,' said Jess presently, 'can we do anything?'

'Nothing, dear.'

'Shall we escape, John?'

He hesitated. 'It is in God's hands, dear. We are in great danger. If the cart upsets we shall be drowned. Can you swim?'

'No, John.'

'If we can hang on here till daylight we may get ashore, if those devils are not there to shoot us. I do not think that our chance is a good one.'

'John, are you afraid to die?'

He hesitated. 'I don't know, dear. I hope to meet it like a man.'

'Tell me what you truly think. Is there any hope for us at all?'

Once more he paused, reflecting whether or no he should speak the truth. Finally he decided to do so.

'I can see none, Jess. If we are not drowned we are sure to be shot. They will wait about the bank till morning, and for their own sakes they will not dare to let us live.'

He did not know that all which was left of two of them would indeed wait for many a long year, while the third had fled aghast.

'Jess, dear,' he went on, 'it is of no good to tell lies. Our lives may end any minute. Humanly speaking, they must end before the sun is up.'

The words were awful enough—if the reader can by an

effort of imagination throw himself for a moment into the position of these two, he will understand how awful.

It is a dreadful thing, when in the flow of health and youth, suddenly to be placed face to face with the certainty of violent death, and to know that in a few more minutes your course will have been run, and that you will have commenced to explore a future, which may prove to be even worse, because more enduring, than the life you are now quitting in agony. It is a dreadful thing, as any who have ever stood in such a peril can testify, and John felt his heart sink within him at the thought of it—for Death is very strong. But there is one thing stronger, a woman's perfect love, against which Death himself cannot prevail. And so it came to pass that now as he fixed his cold gaze upon Jess's eyes they answered him with a strange unearthly light. She feared not Death, so that she might meet him with her beloved. Death was her hope and opportunity. Here she had nothing; there she might have all. The fetters had fallen from her, struck off by an overmastering hand. Her duty was satisfied, her trust fulfilled, and she was free —free to die with her beloved. Ay! her love was indeed a love deeper than the grave; and now it rose in eager strength, standing expectant upon the earth, ready, when dissolution had lent it wings, to soar to its own predestined star.

'You are sure, John?' she asked again.

'Yes, dear, yes. Why do you force me to repeat it? I can see no hope.'

Her arms were round his neck, her soft curls rested on his cheek, and the breath from her lips played upon his brow. Indeed it was only by speaking into each other's ears that conversation was possible, owing to the rushing sound of the waters.

'Because I have something to tell you which I cannot tell unless we are going to die. You know it, but I want to say it with my own lips before I die. I love you, John, *I love you, I love you*; and I am glad to die because I can die with you, and go away with you.'

He heard, and such was the power of her love, that his, which had been put out of mind in the terror of that hour, reawoke and took the colour of her own. He too forgot the imminence of death in the warm presence of his down-trodden passion. She was in his arms as he had taken her during the firing, and he bent his head to look at her. The moonlight played upon her pallid, quivering face, and showed that in her eyes which no man could look upon and turn away. Once more—yes, even then—there came over him that feeling of utter surrender to the sweet mastery of her will which had possessed him in the sitting-room of ' The Palatial.' Only all earthly considerations having faded into nothingness now, he no longer hesitated, but pressed his lips to hers and kissed her again and yet again. It was perhaps as wild and pathetic a love scene as ever the old moon above has witnessed. There they clung, those two, in the actual shadow of death experiencing the fullest and acutest joy that our life has to offer. Nay, death was present with them, for, beneath their very feet, half-hidden by the water, lay the stiffening corpse of the Zulu.

To and fro swung the cart in the rush of the swollen river, up and down beside them the carcases of the horses rose and fell with the surge of the water, on whose surface the broken moonbeams played and quivered. Overhead was the blue star-sown depth through which they were waiting presently to pass, and to the right and left the long broken outlines of the banks stretched away till at last they appeared to grow together in the gloom.

But they heeded none of these things ; they remembered nothing except that they had found each other's hearts, and were happy with a wild joy it is not often given to us to feel. The past was forgotten, the future loomed at hand, and between the one and the other was spanned a bridge of passion made perfect and sanctified by its approaching earthly end. Bessie was forgotten, all things were forgotten, for they were alone with Love and Death.

Let those who would blame them pause awhile. Why not ? They had kept the faith. They had denied themselves and run straightly down the path of duty. But the compacts of life end with life. No man may bargain for the beyond ; even the marriage service shrinks from it. And now that hope had gone and life was at its extremest ebb, why should they not take their joy before they passed to the land where, perchance, such things will be forgotten ? So it seemed to them ; if indeed they were any longer capable of reason.

He looked into her eyes and she laid her head upon his heart in that mute abandonment of worship which is sometimes to be met with in the world, and is redeemed from vulgar passion by an indefinable quality of its own. He looked into her eyes and was glad to have lived, ay, even to have reached this hour of death. And she, lost in the abyss of her deep nature, sobbed out her love-laden heart upon his breast, and called him her own, her own, her very own !

Thus the long hours passed unheeded, till at last a new-born freshness in the air told them that they were not far from dawn. The death they were awaiting had not found them. It must now be very near at hand.

'John,' she whispered in his ear, 'do you think that they will shoot us?'

'Yes,' he answered hoarsely; 'they must for their own safety.'

'I wish it were over,' she said.

Suddenly she started back from his arms with a little cry, causing the cart to rock violently.

'I forgot,' she said; 'you can swim, though I cannot. Why should you not swim to the bank and escape under cover of the darkness? It is only fifty yards, and the current is not so very swift.'

The idea of flight without Jess had never occurred to John, and now that she suggested it, it struck him as so absurd that he broke into a ghost of a laugh.

'Don't be foolish, Jess,' he said.

'Yes, yes, I will. Go! You *must* go! It does not matter about me now. I know that you love me, and I can die happy. I will wait for you. Oh, John! wherever I am, if I have any individual life and any remembrance I will wait for you. Never forget that all your days. However far I may seem away, if I live at all, I shall be waiting for you. And now go; you *shall* go, I say. No, I will not be disobeyed. If you will not go I will throw myself into the water. Oh, the cart is turning over!'

'Hold on, for God's sake!' shouted John. 'The traces have broken.'

He was right; the tough leather was at length worn through by constant rubbing against the rock, and the strain and sway of the dead horses on the one side, and of the cart upon the other. Round it spun, broadside on to the current, and immediately began to heave over, till at last the angle was so sharp that the dead body of poor Mouti slid out with a splash and vanished into the darkness. This relieved the cart, and it righted

I

for a moment, but now being no longer held up by the bodies of the horses or by the sustaining power of the wind it began to fill and sink, and at the same time to revolve swiftly. John understood that all was finished, and that to stop in the cart would only mean certain death, because they would be held under water by the canvas tent. So with a devout aspiration for assistance he seized Jess round the waist with one arm and sprang off into the river. As he leapt the cart filled and sank.

'Lie still, for Heaven's sake!' he shouted, when they rose to the surface.

In the dim light of the dawn which was now creeping over the earth he could discover the line of the left bank of the Vaal, the same from which they had driven into the river on the previous night. It appeared to be about forty yards away, but the current was running quite six knots, and he saw that, burdened as he was, it would be quite impracticable for him to reach it. The only thing to do was to keep afloat. Luckily the water was warm and he was a strong swimmer. In a minute or so he saw that about fifty paces ahead some rocks jutted out twenty yards into the bed of the stream. Then catching Jess by the hair with his left hand he made his effort, and a desperate one it was. The broken water boiled furiously round the rocks. Presently he was in it, and, better still, his feet touched the ground. Next second he was swept off them and rolled over and over at the bottom of the river, to be sadly knocked about against the boulders. Somehow he struggled to his legs, still retaining his hold of Jess. Twice he fell, and twice he struggled up again. One more effort—so. The water was only up to his thighs now, and he was obliged to half carry his companion.

As he lifted her he felt a deadly sickness come over

him, but still he staggered on, till at last they both fell of a heap upon a big flat rock, and for a while he remembered no more.

When he came to himself again it was to see Jess, who had recovered sooner than he had, standing over him and chafing his hands. Indeed, as the sun was up he guessed that he must have lost his senses for some time. He rose with difficulty and shook himself. Except for some bruises he was sound enough.

'Are you hurt?' he asked of Jess, who, pale, faint and bruised, her hat gone, her dress torn by bullets and the rocks, and dripping water at every step, looked an exceedingly forlorn object.

'No,' she said feebly, 'not very much.'

He sat down on the rock in the sun, for they were both shivering with cold. 'What is to be done?' he asked.

'Die,' she said fiercely; 'I meant to die—why did you not let me die? Ours is a position that only death can set straight.'

'Don't be alarmed,' he said, 'your desire will soon be gratified: those murdering villains will hunt us up presently.'

The bed and banks of the river were clothed with thin layers of mist, but as the sun gathered power these lifted. The spot at which they had climbed ashore was about three hundred yards below that where the two Boers and their horses had been destroyed by the lightning on the previous night. Seeing the mist thin, John insisted upon Jess crouching with him behind a rock so that they could look up and down the river without being seen themselves. Presently he made out the forms of two horses grazing about a hundred yards away.

'Ah,' he said, 'I thought so; the devils have off-saddled

there. Thank Heaven I have still got my revolver, and the cartridges are watertight. I mean to sell our lives as dearly as I can.'

'Why, John,' cried Jess, following the line of his out-stretched hand, 'those are not the Boers' horses, they are our two leaders that broke loose in the water. Look, their collars are still on.'

'By Jove! so they are. Now if only we can catch them without being caught ourselves we have a chance of getting out of this.'

'Well, there is no cover about, and I can't see any signs of Boers. They must have been sure of having killed us, and gone away,' Jess answered.

John looked round, and for the first time a sense of hope began to creep into his heart. Perhaps they would survive after all.

'Let's go up and look. It is no good stopping here; we must get food somewhere, or we shall faint.'

She rose without a word, and taking his hand they advanced together along the bank. They had not gone twenty yards before John uttered an exclamation of joy, and rushed at something white that had lodged in the reeds. It was the basket of food which was given to them by the innkeeper's wife at Heidelberg that had been washed out of the cart, and as the lid was fastened nothing was lost out of it. He undid it. There was the bottle of three-star brandy untouched, also most of the eggs, meat, and bread, the last, of course, sodden and worthless. It did not take long to draw the cork, and then John filled a broken wineglass there was in the basket half full of water and half of brandy, and made Jess drink it, with the result that she began to look a little less like a corpse. Next, he repeated the process twice on his own account, and instantly felt as though new life were flowing into him. Then they went on cautiously.

The horses allowed themselves to be caught without trouble, and did not appear to be any the worse for their adventure, although the flank of one was grazed by a bullet.

'There is a tree yonder where the bank shelves over; we had better tie the horses up, dress, and eat some breakfast,' said John, almost cheerfully; and accordingly they proceeded towards it. Suddenly John, who was ahead, started back with an exclamation of fear, and the horses began to snort, for there, stark and stiff in death, already swollen and discoloured by decomposition—as is sometimes the case with people killed by lightning—the rifles in their hands twisted and fused, their clothes cut and blown from the bodies by the explosion of cartridges in their bandoliers—lay the two Boer murderers. It was a terrifying sight, and, taken in conjunction with their own remarkable escape, one to make the most careless and sceptical reflect.

'And yet there are people who say that there is no God, and no punishment for wickedness,' said John aloud.

CHAPTER XXV

MEANWHILE

JOHN, it will be remembered, left Mooifontein for Pretoria towards the end of December, and with him went all the life and light of the place.

'Dear me, Bessie,' said old Silas Croft on the evening after he had started, 'the house seems very dull without John'—a remark in which Bessie, who was weeping secretly in the corner, heartily concurred.

Then, a few days afterwards, came the news of the investment of Pretoria, but no news of John. They ascertained that he had passed Standerton in safety, but beyond that nothing could be heard of him. Day after day passed, but without tidings, and at last, one evening, Bessie broke into a passion of hysterical tears.

'What did you send him for?' she asked of her uncle. 'It was ridiculous—I knew that it was ridiculous. He could not help Jess or bring her back; the most that could happen was that they would be both shut up together. Now he is dead—I know that those Boers have shot him—and it is all your fault! And if he is dead I will never speak to you again.'

The old man retreated, somewhat dismayed at this outburst, which was not at all in Bessie's style.

'Ah, well,' he said to himself, 'that is the way of women; they turn into tigers about a man!'

There may have been truth in this reflection, but a tiger is not a pleasant domestic pet, as poor old Silas discovered during the next two months. The more Bessie thought about the matter the more incensed she grew because he had sent her lover away. Indeed, in a little while she quite forgot that she had herself acquiesced in his going. In short, her temper gave way completely under the strain, so that at last her uncle scarcely dared to mention John's name.

Meanwhile, things had been going as ill without as within. First of all—that was the day after John's departure—two or three loyal Boers and an English store-keeper from Lake Chrissie, in New Scotland, outspanned on the place and came and implored Silas Croft to fly for his life into Natal while there was yet time. They said that the Boers would certainly shoot any Englishman who might be sufficiently defenceless. But the old man would not listen.

'I am an Englishman—*civis Romanus sum*,' he said in his sturdy fashion, 'and I do not believe that they will touch me, who have lived among them for twenty years. At any rate, I am not going to run away and leave my place at the mercy of a pack of thieves. If they shoot me they will have to reckon with England for the deed, so I expect that they will leave me alone. Bessie can go if she likes, but I shall stop here and see the row through, and there's an end of it.'

Whereon, Bessie having flatly declined to budge an inch, the loyalists departed in a hurry, metaphorically wringing their hands at such an exhibition of ill-placed confidence and insular pride. This little scene occurred at dinner-time, and after dinner old Silas proceeded to hurl defiance at his foes in another fashion. Going to a cupboard in his bedroom, he extracted an exceedingly large Union Jack, and promptly advanced with it to an open spot between two of the orange-trees in front of the house, where in such a position that it could be seen for miles around a flagstaff was planted, formed of a very tall young blue gum. Upon this flagstaff it was Silsa's habit to hoist the large Union Jack on the Queen's birthday, Christmas Day, and other State occasions.

' Now, Jantjé,' he said, when he had bent on the bunting, ' run her up, and I'll cheer ! ' and accordingly, as the broad flag floated out on the breeze, he took off his hat and waved it, and gave such a ' hip, hip, hoorah ! ' in his stentorian tones that Bessie ran out from the house to see what was the matter. Nor was he satisfied with this, but, having obtained a ladder, he placed it against the post and sent Jantjé up it, instructing him to fasten the rope on which the flag was bent at a height of about fifteen feet from the ground, so that nobody should get at it to haul it down.

' There,' he said, ' I've nailed my colours to the mast. That will show these gentry that an Englishman lives here.

> Confound their politics,
> Frustrate their knavish tricks,
> God save the Queen.'

' Amen,' said Bessie, but she had her doubts about the wisdom of that Union Jack, which, whenever the wind blew, streamed out, a visible defiance not calculated to soothe the breasts of excited patriots.

Indeed, two days after that, a patrol of three Boers, spying the ensign whilst yet a long way off, galloped up in hot haste to see what it meant. Silas saw them coming, and, taking his rifle in his hand, went and stood beneath the flag, for which he had an almost superstitious veneration, feeling sure that they would not dare to meddle either with him or it.

'What is the meaning of this, Oom Silas?' asked the leader of the three men, with all of whom he was perfectly acquainted.

'It means that an Englishman lives here, Jan,' was the answer.

'Haul the dirty rag down!' said the man.

'I will see you damned first!' replied old Silas.

Thereon the Boer dismounted and made for the flag-staff, only to find 'Uncle Croft's' rifle in a direct line with his chest.

'You will have to shoot me first, Jan,' he said, and thereon, after some consultation, they left him and went away.

In truth, his British nationality notwithstanding, Silas Croft was very popular with the Boers, most of whom had known him since they were children, and to whose Volksraad he had twice been elected. It was to this personal popularity he owed the fact that he was not turned out of his house, and forced to choose between serving against his countrymen or being imprisoned and otherwise maltreated at the very commencement of the rebellion.

For a fortnight or more after this flag episode nothing of any importance happened, and then came the tidings of the crushing defeat at Laing's Nek. At first, Silas Croft would not believe it. 'No general could have been so mad,' he said; but soon the report was amply confirmed from native sources.

Another week passed, and with it came the news of the British defeat at Ingogo. The first they heard of it was on the morning of February 8, when Jantjé brought a Kafir up to the verandah at breakfast-time. This

Kafir said that he had been watching the fight from a mountain ; that the English were completely hemmed in and fighting well, but that 'their arms were tired,' and they would all be killed at night-time. The Boers, he said, were not suffering at all—the English could not 'shoot straight.' After hearing this they passed a sufficiently miserable day and evening. About twelve o'clock that night, however, a native spy despatched by Mr. Croft returned with the report that the English general had won safely back to camp, having suffered heavily and abandoned his wounded, many of whom had died in the rain, for the night after the battle was wet.

Then came another long pause, during which no reliable news reached them, though the air was thick with rumours, and old Silas was made happy by hearing that large reinforcements were on their way from England.

'Ah, Bessie, my dear, they will soon sing another song now,' he said in great glee ; 'and what's more, it's about time they did. I can't understand what the soldiers have been about—I can't indeed.'

And so the time wore heavily along till at last there came a dreadful day, which Bessie will never forget so long as she lives. It was the 20th of February—just a week before the final disaster at Majuba Hill. Bessie was standing idly on the verandah, looking down the long avenue of blue gums, where the shadows formed a dark network to catch the wandering rays of light. The place looked very peaceful, and certainly no one could have known from its appearance that a bloody war was being waged within a few miles. The Kafirs came and went about their work as usual, or made pretence to ; but now and then a close observer might see them stop, look towards the Drakensberg, and then say a few words to their neighbour about the wonderful thing which had come to pass, that the Boers were beating the great white people, who came out of the sea and shook the earth with their tread. Whereon the neighbour would take the opportunity to relax from toil, squat down, have a pinch of snuff, and relate in what particular collection of rocks on the hillside he and his wives slept the last night—for when the Boers are out on commando the Kafirs will not sleep in their huts for fear of being surprised and shot down. Then the pair would spend half an hour or so in speculating on what would be their fate when the Boer had eaten up the Englishman and taken back the country, and finally come to the conclusion that they had better emigrate to Natal.

Bessie, on the verandah, noted all this going on, every now and again catching snatches of the lazy rascals' talk, which chimed in but too sadly with her own thoughts. Turning from them impatiently, she began to watch the hens marching solemnly about the drive, followed by their broods. This picture, also, had a sanguinary background, for under an orange-tree two rival cocks were fighting furiously. They always did this about once a week, nor did they cease from troubling till each retired, temporarily blinded, to the shade of a separate orange-tree, where they spent the rest of the week in recovering, only to emerge when the cure was effected and fight their battle over again. Meanwhile, a third cock, young in years but old in wisdom, who steadily refused to retaliate when attacked, looked after the hens in dispute. To-day the fray was particularly ferocious, and, fearing that the combatants would have no eyes left at all if she did not interfere, Bessie called to the old Boer hound who was lying in the sun on the verandah.

'Hi, Stomp, Stomp—hunt them, Stomp!'

Up jumped Stomp and made a prodigious show of furiously attacking the embattled cocks; it was an operation to which he was used, and which afforded him constant amusement. Suddenly, however, as he dashed towards the trees, the dog stopped midway, his simulated wrath ceased, and instead of it, an expression of real disgust grew upon his honest face. Then the hair along his backbone stood up like the quills upon the fretful porcupine, and he growled.

' A strange Kafir, I expect,' said Bessie to herself.

Stomp hated strange Kafirs. She had scarcely uttered the words before they were justified by the appearance of a native. He was a villainous-looking fellow, with one eye, and nothing on but a ragged pair of trousers fastened round the middle with a greasy leather strap. In his wool, however, were stuck several small distended bladders such as are generally worn by medicine-men and witch-doctors. With his left hand he held a long stick, cleft at one end, and in the cleft was a letter.

' Come here, Stomp,' said Bessie, and as she spoke a wild hope shot across her heart like a meteor across the night : perhaps the letter was from John.

The dog obeyed her unwillingly enough, for evidently he did not like that Kafir ; and when he saw that Stomp was well out of the way the Kafir himself followed. He was an insolent fellow, and took no notice of Bessie beyond squatting himself down upon the drive in front of her.

' What is it ? ' said Bessie in Dutch, her lips trembling as she spoke.

' A letter,' answered the man.

' Give it to me.'

' No, missie, not till I have looked at you to see if it is right. Light yellow hair that curls—*one*,' checking it on his fingers, ' yes, that is right; large blue eyes – *two*, that is right; big and tall, and fair as a star—yes, the letter is for you, take it,' and he poked the long stick almost into her face.

' Where is it from ? ' asked Bessie, with sudden suspicion and recoiling a step.

' Wakkerstroom last.'

' Who is it from ? '

' Read it, and you will see.'

Bessie took the letter, which was wrapped in a piece of old newspaper, from the cleft of the stick and turned it over and over doubtfully. Most of us have a mistrust of strange-looking letters, and this letter was unusually strange. To begin with, it had no address whatever on the dirty envelope, which seemed curious. In the second place, that envelope was sealed, apparently with a threepenny bit.

' Are you sure it is for me ? ' asked Bessie.

' Yah, yah—sure, sure,' answered the native, with a rude laugh. ' There are not many such white girls in the Transvaal. I have made no mistake. I have " smelt you out." ' And he began to go through his catalogue— ' Yellow hair that curls,' &c.—again.

Then Bessie opened the letter. Inside was an ordinary sheet of paper written over in a bold, firm, yet slightly unpractised writing that she knew well enough, and the sight of which filled her with a presentiment of evil. It was Frank Muller's.

She turned sick and cold, but could not choose but read as follows :

' Camp, near Pretoria. 15 February.

' Dear Miss Bessie,—I am sorry to have to write to you, but though we have quarrelled lately, and also your good uncle, I think it my duty to do so, and send this to your hand by special runner. Yesterday was a sortie made by the poor folk in Pretoria, who are now as thin with hunger as the high veldt oxen just before spring. Our arms were again victorious; the redcoats ran away and left their ambulance in our hands, carrying with them many dead and wounded. Among the dead was the Captain Niel——'

Here Bessie uttered a sort of choking cry, and let the letter fall over the verandah, to one of the posts of which she clung with both her hands.

The ill-favoured native below grinned, and, picking the paper up, handed it to her.

She took it, feeling that she must know all, and read on like one reads in some ghastly dream:

' who has been staying on your uncle's farm. I did not see him killed myself, but Jan Vanzyl shot him, and Roi Dirk Oosthuizen, and Carolus, a Hottentot, saw them pick him up and carry him away. They say that he was quite dead. For this I fear you will be sorry, as I am, but it is the chance of war, and he died fighting bravely. Make my obedient compliments to your uncle. We parted in anger, but I hope in the new circumstances that have arisen in the land to show him that I, for one, bear no anger.—Believe me, dear Miss Bessie, your humble and devoted servant,

                                    ' FRANK MULLER.'

Bessie thrust the letter into the pocket of her dress, then again she caught hold of the verandah post, and supported herself by it, while the light of the sun appeared to fade visibly out of the day before her eyes and to replace itself by a cold blackness in which there was no break. He was dead!—her lover was dead! The glow had gone from her life as it seemed to be going from the day, and she was left desolate. She had no knowledge of how long she stood thus, staring with wide eyes at the sunshine she could not see. She had lost her count of time; things were phantasmagorical and unreal; all that she could realise was this one overpowering, crushing fact—John was dead!

'Missie,' said the ill-favoured messenger below, fixing his one eye upon her poor sorrow-stricken face, and yawning.

There was no answer.

'Missie,' he said again, 'is there any answer? I must be going. I want to get back in time to see the Boers take Pretoria.'

Bessie looked at him vaguely. 'Yours is a message that needs no answer,' she said. 'What is, is.'

The brute laughed. 'No, I can't take a letter to the Captain,' he said; 'I saw Jan Vanzyl shoot him. He fell *so*,' and suddenly he collapsed all in a heap on the path, in imitation of a man struck dead by a bullet. 'I can't take *him* a message, missie,' he went on, rising, 'but one day you will be able to go and look for him yourself. I did not mean that; what I meant was that I could take a letter to Frank Muller. A live Boer is better than a dead Englishman; and Frank Muller will make a fine husband for any girl. If you shut your eyes you won't know the difference.'

'Go!' said Bessie, in a choked voice, and pointing her hand towards the avenue.

Such was the suppressed energy in her tone that the man sprang to his feet, and while he rose, interpreting her gesture as an encouragement to action, the old dog, Stomp, who had been watching him all the time, and occasionally giving utterance to a low growl of animosity, flew straight at his throat from the verandah. The dog, which was a heavy one, struck the man full in the chest and knocked him backwards. Down came dog and man on the drive together, and then ensued a terrible scene, the man cursing and shrieking and striking out at the dog, and the dog worrying the man in a fashion that he was not likely to forget for the remainder of his life.

Bessie, whose energy seemed again to be exhausted, took absolutely no notice of the fray, and it was at this juncture that her old uncle arrived upon the scene, together with two Kafirs—the same whom Bessie had seen idling.

'Hullo! hullo!' he halloed in his stentorian tones, 'what is all this about? Get off, you brute!' and what between his voice and the blows of the Kafirs the dog was persuaded to let go his hold of the man, who staggered to his feet, severely mauled, and bleeding from half a dozen bites.

For a moment he did not say anything, but picked up his sticks. Then, however, having first made sure that the dog was being held by the Kafirs, he turned, his face streaming with blood, his one eye blazing with fury, and, shaking both his clenched fists at poor Bessie, broke into a scream of cursing.

'You shall pay for this—Frank Muller shall make you pay for it. I am his servant. I——'

'Get out of this, whoever you are,' thundered old Silas, 'or by Heaven I will let the dog on you again!' and he pointed to Stomp, who was struggling wildly with the two Kafirs.

The man paused and looked at the dog, then, with a final shake of the fist, he departed at a run down the avenue, turning once only to look if the dog were coming.

With empty eyes Bessie watched him go, taking no more notice of him than she had of the noise of the fighting. Then, as though struck by a thought, she turned and went into the sitting-room.

'What is all this, Bessie?' said her uncle, following her. 'What does the man mean about Frank Muller?'

'It means, uncle dear,' she said at last, in a voice that was something between a sob and a laugh, 'that I am a widow before I am married. John is dead!'

'Dead! dead!' said the old man, putting his hand to his forehead and turning round in a dazed sort of fashion, 'John dead!'

'Read the letter,' said Bessie, handing him Frank Muller's missive.

The old man took and read it. His hand shook so much that he was a long while in mastering its contents.

'Good God!' he said at last, 'what a blow! My poor Bessie,' and he drew her into his arms and kissed her. Suddenly a thought struck him. 'Perhaps it is all one of Frank Muller's lies,' he said, 'or perhaps he made a mistake.'

But Bessie did not answer. For the time, at any rate, hope had left her.

CHAPTER XXVI

FRANK MULLER'S FAMILIAR

THE study of the conflicting elements which go to make up a character like that of Frank Muller, however fascinating it might prove, is not one which can be attempted in detail here. Such a character in its developed form is fortunately well nigh impossible in a highly civilised country, for the dead weight of the law would crush it back to the level of the human mass around it. But those who have lived in the wild places of the earth will be acquainted with its prototypes, more especially in the countries where a handful of a superior race rule over the dense thousands of an inferior. Solitudes are favourable to the production of strongly marked individualities. The companionship of highly developed men, on the contrary, whittles individualities away; the difference between their growth being the difference between the growth of a tree on a plain and a tree in the forest. On the plain the tree takes the innate bend of its nature. It springs in majesty towards the skies; it spreads itself around, or it slants along the earth, just as Nature intended that it should, and in accordance with the power of the providential breath which bends it. In the forest it is different. There the tree grows towards the light wherever the light may be. Forced to modify its natural habit in obedience to the pressure of circumstances over which it has no command, it takes such form and height as its neighbours will allow to it, all its energies being directed to the preservation of life in any shape and at any sacrifice.

Thus is it with us all. Left to ourselves, or surrounded only by the scrub of humanity, we become outwardly that which the spirit within would fashion us to, but, placed among our fellows, shackled by custom, restrained by law, pruned and bent by the force of public opinion, we grow as like one to another as the fruit bushes on a garden wall. The sharp angles of our characters are fretted away by the friction of the crowd, and we become round, polished, and, superficially, at any rate, identical. We no longer resemble a solitary boulder on a plain, but are as a worked stone built into the great edifice of civilised society.

The place of a man like Frank Muller is at the junction of the waters of civilisation and barbarism. Too civilised to possess those savage virtues which, such as they are, represent the quantum of innate good Nature has thought fit to allow in the mixture, Man ; and too barbarous to be subject to the tenderer restraints of cultivated society, he is at once strong in the strength of both and weak in their weaknesses. Animated by the spirit of barbarism, Superstition ; and almost entirely destitute of the spirit of civilisation, Mercy, he stands on the edge of both and an affront to both, as terrific a moral spectacle as the world can afford.

Had he been a little more civilised, with his power of evil trained by education and cynical reflection to defy the attacks of those spasms of unreasoning spiritual terror and unrestrainable passion that have their natural dwelling-place in the raw strong mind of uncultivated man, Frank Muller might have broken upon the world as a Napoleon. Had he been a little more savage, a little farther removed from the unconscious but present influence of a progressive race, he might have ground his fellows down and ruthlessly destroyed them in the madness of his rage and lust, like an Attila or a T'Chaka. As it was he was buffeted between two forces he did not realise, even when they swayed him, and thus at every step in his path towards a supremacy of evil an unseen power made stumbling-blocks of weaknesses which, if that path had been laid along a little higher or a little lower level in the scale of circumstances, would themselves have been deadly weapons of overmastering force.

See him as, with his dark heart filled up with fears, he thunders along from that scene of midnight death and murder which his brain had not feared to plan and his hand to execute. Onward his black horse strides, companioned by the storm, like a dark thought travelling on the wings of Night. He does not believe in any God, and yet the terrible fears that spring up in his soul, born fungus-like from a dew of blood, take shape and form, and seem to cry aloud, ' *We are the messengers of the avenging God.*' He glances up. High on the black bosom of the storm the finger of the lightning is writing that awful name, and again and again the voice of the thunder reads it aloud in spirit-shaking accents. He shuts his dazed eyes, and even the falling rhythm of his horse's hoofs beats out, ' *There is a God! there is a God!*' from the silent earth on which they strike.

And so, on through the tempest and the night, flying from that which no man can leave behind.

It was near midnight when Frank Muller drew rein at a wretched and lonely mud hut built on the banks of the Vaal, and flanked by an equally miserable shed. The place was silent as the grave; not even a dog barked.

'If that beast of a Kafir is not here,' he said aloud, 'I will have him flogged to death. Hendrik, Hendrik!'

As he called, a form rose up at his very feet, causing the weary horse to start back so violently that he almost threw his rider to the ground.

'What in the name of the devil are you?' almost shrieked Frank Muller, whose nerves, indeed, were in no condition to bear fresh shocks.

'It is I, Baas,' said the form, at the same time throwing off a grey blanket in which it was enveloped, and revealing the villainous countenance of the one-eyed witch-doctor, who had taken the letter to Bessie. For years this man had been Muller's body-servant, who followed him about like a shadow.

'Curse you, you dog! What do you mean by hiding up like that? It is one of your infernal tricks; be careful'—tapping his pistol case—'or I shall one day put an end to you and your witchcraft together.'

'I am very sorry, Baas,' said the man in a whine, 'but half an hour ago I heard you coming. I don't know what is the matter with the air to-night, but it sounded as though twenty people were galloping after you. I could hear them all quite clearly; first the big black horse, and then all those who followed, just as though they were hunting you. So I came out and lay down to listen, and it was not till you were quite close that one by one the others stopped. Perhaps it was the devils who galloped.'

'Damn you, stop that wizard's talk,' said Muller, his teeth chattering with fear and agitation. 'Take the horse, groom and feed him well; he has galloped far,

and we start at dawn. Stop, tell me, where are the
lights and the brandy? If you have drunk the brandy I
will flog you.'

'They are on the shelf to the left as you go in, Baas,
and there is flesh too, and bread.'

Muller swung himself from the saddle and entered
the hut, pushing open the cranky, broken-hinged door
with a kick. He found the box of Tandstickör matches,
and, after one or two attempts — due chiefly to his
shaking hand—succeeded in striking fire and lighting a
coarse dip such as the Boers make out of mutton fat.
Near the candle were a bottle of peach brandy two-thirds
full, a tin pannikin and a jug of river water. Seizing
the pannikin, he half filled it with spirit, added a little
water, and drank off the mixture. Then he took the
meat and bread from the same shelf, and, cutting some
of each with his clasp-knife, tried to eat. But he could
not swallow much, and soon gave up the attempt, con-
soling himself instead with the brandy.

'Bah!' he said, 'the stuff tastes like hell fire;' and
he filled his pipe and sat smoking.

Presently Hendrik came in to say that the horse
was eating well, and turned to go out again, when his
master beckoned him to stop. The man was surprised,
for generally his master was not fond of his society, except
when he wanted to consult him or persuade him to exercise his pretended art of divination. The truth was, however, that at the moment Frank Muller would have been
glad to consort with a dog. The events of the night had
brought this terrible man, steeped in iniquity from his
youth up, down to the level of a child frightened at the
dark. For a while he sat in silence, the Kafir squatting on
the ground at his feet. Presently, however, the doses of
powerful spirit took effect on him, and he began to talk

more unguardedly than was his custom, even with his black ' familiar ' Hendrik.

' How long have you been here ? ' he asked of his retainer.

' About four days, Baas.'

' Did you take my letter to Oom Croft's ? '

' Yah, Baas. I gave it to the missie.'

' What did she do ? '

' She read it, and then stood like this, holding on to the verandah pole ; ' and he opened his mouth and one eye, twisting up his hideous countenance into a ghastly imitation of Bessie's sorrow-stricken face, and gripping the post that supported the hut to give verisimilitude to his performance.

' So she believed it ? '

' Surely.'

' What did she do, then ? '

' She set the dog on me.   Look here ! and here ! and here ! ' and he pointed to the half-healed scars left by Stomp's sharp fangs.

Muller laughed a little.   ' I should like to have seen him worry you, you black cheat; it shows her spirit, too.   I suppose you are angry, and want to have a revenge ? '

' Surely.'

' Well, who knows?   Perhaps you shall ; we are going there to-morrow.'

' So, Baas !   I knew that before you told me.'

' We are going there, and we are going to take the place ; and we are going to try Uncle Silas by court-martial for flying an English flag, and if he is found guilty we are going to shoot him, Hendrik.'

' So, Baas,' said the Kafir, rubbing his hands in glee, ' but will he be found guilty ? '

'I don't know,' murmured the white man, stroking his golden beard; 'that will depend upon what missie has to say; and upon the verdict of the court,' he added, by way of an afterthought.

'On the verdict of the court, ha! ha!' chuckled his wicked satellite; 'on the verdict of the court, yes! yes! and the Baas will be president, ha! ha! One needs no witchcraft to guess that verdict. And if the court finds Uncle Silas guilty, who will do the shooting, Baas?'

'I have not thought of that; the time has not come to think of it. It does not matter; anybody can carry out the sentence of the law.'

'Baas,' said the Kafir, 'I have done much for you, and had little pay. I have done ugly things. I have read omens and made medicines, and "smelt out" your enemies. Will you grant me a favour? Will you let me shoot Oom Croft if the court finds him guilty? It is not much to ask, Baas. I am a clever wizard, and deserve my pay.'

'Why do you want to shoot him?'

'Because he flogged me once, years ago, for being a witch-doctor, and the other day he hunted me off the place. Beside, it is nice to shoot a white man. I should like it better,' he went on, with a smack of the lips, 'if it were missie, who set the dog on me. I would——'

In a moment Muller had seized the astonished ruffian by the throat, and was kicking and shaking him as though he were a toy. His brutal talk of Bessie appealed to such manliness as he had in him, and, whatever his own wickedness may have been, he was too madly in love with the woman to let her name be taken in vain by a man whom, though he held his 'magic' in superstitious reverence, he yet ranked lower than a dog. With his nerves strung to the highest possible state of tension, and half drunk as he was, Frank Muller was no more to be played with or irritated than is a mad bull.

' You black beast ! ' he yelled, ' if ever you dare to mention her name again like that I will kill you, for all your witchcraft ; ' and he hurled him with such force against the wall of the hut that the whole place shook.   The man fell and lay for a moment groaning ; then he crept from the hut on his hands and knees.

Muller sat scowling from under his bent brows, and watched him go.   When he was gone, he rose and fastened the door behind him, then suddenly he burst into tears, the result, no doubt, of the mingled effects of drink, mental and physical exhaustion, and the never-resting passion—one can scarcely call it love—which ate at his heart, like the worm that dieth not.

' Oh, Bessie, Bessie ! ' he groaned, ' I have done it all for you.   Surely you cannot be angry when I have killed them all for you ?   Oh, my darling, my darling !   If you only knew how I love you !   Oh, my darling, my darling ! ' and in an agony of passion he flung himself on to the rough pallet in the corner of the hut and sobbed himself to sleep.

It would seem that Frank Muller's evil-doing did not make him happy, the truth being that to enjoy wickedness a man must be not only without conscience, but also without passion.   Now Frank Muller was tormented with a very effective substitute for the first—superstition, and by the latter his life was overshadowed, since the beauty of a girl possessed the power to dominate his wildest moods and to inflict upon him torments that she herself was incapable even of imagining.

At the first light of dawn Hendrik crept humbly into the hut to wake his master, and within half an hour they were across the Vaal and on the road to Wakker-stroom.

As the light increased so did Muller's spirits rise, till at last, when the red sun came up in glory and swept away the shadows, he felt as though all the load of guilt and fear that lay upon his heart had departed with them. He could see now that the death of the two Boers by lightning was a mere accident—a happy accident, indeed; for, had it not so chanced, he would have been forced to kill them himself, if he could not have obtained possession of the warrant by other means. As it was, he had for-gotten this document; but it did not matter much, he reflected. Nobody would be likely to find the bodies of the two men and horses under that lonely bank. Certainly they would not be found before the aasvögels had picked them clean, and these would be at work upon them now. And if they were found, the paper would have rotted or been blown away, or, at the worst, rendered so discoloured as to be unreadable. For the rest, there was nothing to connect him with the murder, now that his confederates were dead. Hendrik would prove an alibi for him. He was a useful man, Hendrik. Besides, who would believe that it was a murder? Two men were escorting an Englishman to the river; they became involved in a quarrel; the Englishman shot them, and they shot the Englishman and his companion. Then the horses plunged into the Vaal upsetting the cart, and there was an end of it. He could see now how well things had gone for him. Events had placed him be-yond suspicion.

Then he fell to thinking of the fruits of his honest labours, and Muller's cheek grew warm with the mount-ing blood, and his eyes flashed with the fire of youth. In two days—forty-eight hours—at the outside, Bessie

would be in his arms. He could not miscarry now, for
was he not in absolute command? Besides, Hendrik
had read it in his omens long ago.[1] Mooifontein should
be stormed on the morrow, if that were necessary, and
Oom Silas Croft and Bessie should be taken prisoners;
and then he knew how to deal with them. His talk
about shooting on the previous night had been no idle
threat. She should yield herself to him, or the old man
must die, and then he would take her. There could be
no legal consequences now that the British Government
was in the act of surrender. It would be a meritorious
deed to execute a rebel Englishman.

Yes, it was all plain sailing now. How long had it
needed to win her—three years? He had loved her
for three years. Well, he would have his reward; and
then, his passion satisfied, he would turn his mind to
those far-reaching, ambitious schemes, whereof the end
was something like a throne.

[1] It is not a very rare thing to meet white men in South Africa
who believe more or less in the efficacy of native witchcraft, and,
although such a proceeding is forbidden by law, who at a pinch will
not hesitate to consult the witch-doctors.—AUTHOR.

CHAPTER XXVII

SILAS IS CONVINCED

At first Bessie was utterly prostrated by the blow that had fallen on her, but as time went on she revived a little, for hers was an elastic and a sanguine nature. Troubles sink into the souls of some like water into a sponge, and weigh them down almost to the grave. From others they run off as the water does if poured upon marble, merely wetting the surface.

Bessie belonged to neither of these classes, but was of a substance between the two—a healthy, happy-hearted woman, full of beauty and vigour, made to bloom in the sunshine, not to languish in the shadow of some old grief. Women of her stamp do not die of broken hearts or condemn themselves to life-long celibacy as a sacrifice to the shade of the departed. If unfortunately No. 1 is removed, as a general rule they shed many a tear and suffer many a pang, and after a decent interval very sensibly turn their attention to No. 2.

Still it was but a pale-faced, quiet Bessie who went to and fro about the place after the visit of the one-eyed Kafir. All her irritability had left her now; she no longer reproached her uncle because he had despatched John to Pretoria. Indeed, on that very evening after the evil tidings came, he began to blame himself bitterly in her presence for having sent her lover away, when she stopped him.

'It is God's will, uncle,' she said quietly. 'You only did what it was ordained that you should do.' Then she came and laid her sunny head upon the old man's shoulder and cried a little, and said that they two were all alone in the world now; and he comforted her in the best fashion that he could. It was a curious thing that they neither of them thought much of Jess when they talked thus of being alone. Jess was an enigma, a thing apart even from them. When she was there she was loved and allowed to go her own way, when she was not there she seemed to fade into outer darkness. A veil came down between her and her belongings. Of course they were both very fond of her, but simple-natured people are apt to shrink from what they cannot understand, and these two were no exception to the rule. For instance, Bessie's affection for her sister was a poor thing compared to the deep and self-sacrificing, though often secret love that her sister showered upon her. She loved her old uncle far more dearly than she loved Jess, and it must be owned that he returned her attachment with interest, and in those days of heavy trouble they drew nearer to each other than ever they were before.

But as time went on they both began to hope again. No confirmation of John's death reached them. Was it not possible then, after all, that the story was an invention? They knew that Frank Muller was not a man to hesitate at a lie if he had a purpose to gain, and they could guess in this case what that purpose was. His furious passion for Bessie was no secret from either of them, and it occurred to them as possible that the tale of John's death might have been invented to forward it. This was scarcely probable, it is true, but it might be so, and however cruel suspense may be, it is at least less absolutely crushing than the dead weight of certainty.

One Sunday—it was just a week since the letter came —Bessie was sitting after dinner on the verandah, when her quick ears caught what she took to be the booming of heavy guns far away on the Drakensberg. She rose, and leaving the house, climbed the hill behind it. On reaching its top she stood and looked at the great solemn stretch of mountains. Away, a little to her right, was a square precipitous peak called Majuba, which was generally clothed in clouds. To-day, however, there was no mist, and it seemed to her that it was from the direction of this peak that the faint rolling sounds came floating on the breeze. But she could see nothing; the mountain seemed as tenantless and devoid of life as on the day when it first towered up upon the face of things created. Presently the sounds died away, and she returned, thinking that she must have been deceived by the echoes of some distant thunderstorm.

Next day they learnt from the natives that what she had heard was the roar of the big guns covering the flight of the British troops down the precipitous sides of Majuba Mountain. After these tidings old Silas Croft began to lose heart a little. The run of disaster was so unrelieved that even his robust faith in the invincibility of the English arms was shaken.

'It is very strange, Bessie,' he said, 'very strange; but, never mind, it is bound to come right at last. Our Government is not going to knock under because it has suffered a few reverses.'

Then followed a long four weeks of uncertainty. The air was thick with rumours, most of them brought by natives, and one or two by passing Boers, to which Silas

Croft declined to pay any attention. Soon, however, it became abundantly clear that an armistice was concluded between the English and the Boers, but what were its terms or its object they were quite unable to decide. Silas Croft thought that the Boers, overawed by the advance of an overwhelming force, meant to give in without further fighting ;[1] but Bessie shook her head.

One day—it was the same on which John and Jess left Pretoria—a Kafir brought the news that the armistice was at an end, that the English were advancing up to the Nek in thousands, and were going to force it on the morrow and relieve the garrisons—a piece of intelligence that brought some of the old light back to Bessie's eyes. As for her uncle, he was jubilant.

'The tide is going to turn, at last, my love,' he said, 'and we shall have our innings. Well, it is time we should, after all the disgrace, loss and agony of mind we have gone through. Upon my word, for the last two months I have been ashamed to call myself an Englishman. However, there is an end of it now. I knew that they would never give in and desert us,' and the old man straightened his crooked back and slapped his chest, looking as proud and gallant as though he were five-and-twenty instead of seventy years of age.

The rest of that day passed without any further news, and so did the following two days, but on the third, which was March 23, the storm broke.

About eleven o'clock in the forenoon Bessie was employed upon her household duties as usual, or rather she had just finished them. Her uncle had returned from his usual after-breakfast round upon the farm, and was standing in the sitting-room, his broad felt hat

[1] This is said on good authority to have been their intention had not Mr. Gladstone surprised them by his sudden surrender.—AUTHOR.

in one hand and a red pocket-handkerchief in the other, with which he was polishing his bald head, while he chatted to Bessie through the open door.

'No news of the advance, Bessie dear?'

'No, uncle,' she replied with a sigh, her blue eyes filling with tears, for she was thinking of one of whom there was also no news.

'Well, never mind. These things take a little time, especially with our soldiers, who move so slowly. I dare say that there was some delay waiting for guns or ammunition or something. I expect that we shall hear by to-night——'

He had got thus far when suddenly the figure of Jantjé appeared, flying up the passage in an extremity of terror and haste.

'De Booren, Baas, de Booren!' [the Boers, master, the Boers] he shouted. 'The Boers are coming with a waggon, twenty of them or more, with Frank Muller at their head on his black horse, and Hans Coetzee, and the one-eyed Basutu wizard with him. I was hiding behind a tree at the end of the avenue, and I saw them riding over the rise. They are going to take the place;' and, without waiting to give any further explanations, he slipped through the house and hid himself up somewhere out of the way at the back, for Jantjé, like most Hotten-tots, was a sad coward.

The old man stopped rubbing his head and stared at Bessie, who stood pale and trembling in the doorway. Just then he heard the patter of running feet on the drive outside, and looked out of the window. It was caused by the passing of some half-dozen Kafirs who were working on the place, and who, on catching sight of the Boers, had promptly thrown down their tools and were flying to the hills. Even as they passed a shot was fired somewhere from the direction of the avenue, and the last of the Kafirs, a lad of about twelve, suddenly threw up his hands and pitched forward on to his face, with a bullet between his shoulder-blades.

Bessie heard the shout of 'Good shot, good shot!' the brutal laughter that greeted his fall, and the tramping of the ho: ses as they came up the drive.

' Oh, uncle ! ' she said, ' what shall we do ? '

The old man made no answer at the moment, but going to a rack upon the wall, he reached down a Wesley-Richards falling-block rifle that hung there. Then he sat down in a wooden armchair that faced the French window opening on to the verandah, and beckoned to her to come to him.

' We will meet them so,' he said. ' They shall see that we are not afraid of them. Don't be frightened, dear, they will not dare to harm us ; they will be afraid of the consequences of harming English people.'

The words were scarcely out of his mouth when the cavalcade began to appear in front of the window, led, as Jantjé had said, by Frank Muller on his black horse, accompanied by Hans Coetzee on the fat pony, and the villainous-looking Hendrik, mounted on a nondescript sort of animal, and carrying a gun and an assegai in his hand. Behind these were a body of about fifteen or sixteen armed men, among whom Silas Croft recognised most of his neighbours, by whose side he had lived for years in peace and amity.

Opposite the house they stopped and began looking about. They could not see into the room at once, on account of the bright light outside and the shadow within.

' I fancy you will find the birds flown, nephew,' said

K

the fat voice of Hans Coetzee. 'They have got warning of your little visit.'

'They cannot be far off,' answered Muller. 'I have had them watched, and know that they have not left the place. Get down, uncle, and look in the house, and you too, Hendrik.'

The Kafir obeyed with alacrity, tumbling out of his saddle with all the grace of a sack of coals, but the Boer hesitated.

'Uncle Silas is an angry man,' he ventured; 'he might shoot if he found me poking about his house.'

'Don't answer me!' thundered Muller; 'get down and do as I bid you!'

'Ah, what a devil of a man!' murmured the unfortunate Hans as he hurried to obey.

Meanwhile, Hendrik the one-eyed had jumped upon the verandah and was peering through the windows.

'Here they are, Baas; here they are!' he sung out; 'the old cock and the pullet too!' and he gave a kick to the window, which, being unlatched, swung wide, revealing the old man sitting in his wooden armchair, his rifle on his knees, and holding by the hand his fair-haired niece, who was standing at his side. Frank Muller dismounted and came on to the verandah, and behind him crowded a dozen or more of his followers.

'What is it that you want, Frank Muller, that you come to my house with all these armed men?' asked Silas Croft from his chair.

'I call upon you, Silas Croft, to surrender to take your trial as a land betrayer and a rebel against the Republic,' was the answer. 'I am sorry,' he added, with a bow towards Bessie, on whom his eyes had been fixed all the time, 'to be obliged to take you prisoner in the presence of a lady, but my duty gives me no choice.'

'I do not know what you mean,' said the old man.
'I am a subject of Queen Victoria and an Englishman.
How, then, can I be a rebel against any republic? I am
an Englishman, I say,' he went on with rising anger,
speaking so high that his powerful voice rang till every
Boer there could hear it, ' and I acknowledge the authority of no republics. This is my house, and I order
you to leave it. I claim my rights as an Englishman ——'

' Here,' interrupted Muller coldly, 'Englishmen have
no rights, except such as we choose to allow to them.'

' Shoot him ! ' cried a voice.

'Treat him as Buskes treated Van der Linden at
Potchefstroom ! ' cried another.

' Yes, make him swallow the same pill that we gave
to Dr. Barber,' put in a third.

' Silas Croft, are you going to surrender?' asked
Muller in the same cold voice.

' *No !* ' thundered the old man in his English pride.
'I surrender to no rebels in arms against the Queen. I
will shoot the first man who tries to lay a finger on me ! '
and he rose to his feet and lifted his rifle.

' Shall I shoot him, Baas?—shall I shoot him?'
asked the one-eyed Hendrik, smacking his lips at the
thought. and fiddling with the rusty lock of the old
fowling-piece he carried.

Muller, by way of answer, struck him across the face
with the back of his hand. ' Hans Coetzee,' he said, ' go
and arrest that man.'

Poor Hans hesitated, as well he might. Nature had
not endowed him with any great amount of natural
courage, and the sight of his old neighbour's rifle-barrel
made him feel positively sick. He hesitated and began
to stammer excuses.

'Are you going, uncle, or must I denounce you to the General as a sympathiser with Englishmen?' asked Muller in malice, for he knew the old fellow's weaknesses and cowardice, and was playing on them.

'I am going. Of course I am going, nephew. Excuse me, a little faintness took me—the heat of the sun,' he babbled. 'Oh, yes, I am going to seize the rebel. Perhaps one of those young men would not mind engaging his attention on the other side. He is an angry man—I know him of old—and an angry man with a gun, you know, dear cousin——'

'Are you going?' said his terrible master once more.

'Oh, yes! yes, certainly, yes. Dear Uncle Silas, pray put down that gun, it is so dangerous. Don't stand there looking like a wild ox, but come up to the yoke. You are old, Uncle Silas, and I don't want to have to hurt you. Come now, come, come,' and he held out his hand towards him as though he were a shy horse that he was endeavouring to beguile.

'Hans Coetzee, traitor and liar that you are,' said the old man, 'if you draw a single step nearer, by God! I will put a bullet through you!'

'Go on, Hans, chuck a riem over his head; get him by the tail; knock him down with a yokeskei; turn the old bull on his back!' shouted the crowd of scoffers from the window, taking very good care, however, to clear off to the right and left in order to leave room for the expected bullet.

Hans positively burst into tears, and Muller, who was the only one who held his ground, caught him by the arm, and putting out all his strength, swung him towards Silas Croft.

For reasons of his own, he was anxious that the latter

should shoot one of them, and he chose Hans Coetzee, whom he disliked and despised, for the sacrifice.

Up went the rifle, and at that moment Bessie, who had been standing bewildered, made a dash at it, knowing that bloodshed could only make matters worse. As she did so it exploded, but not before she had shaken her uncle's arm, for, instead of killing Hans, as it undoubtedly would otherwise have done, the bullet only cut his ear and then passed out through the open window-place. In an instant the room was filled with smoke. Hans Coetzee clapped his hand to his head, uttering yells of pain and terror, and in the confusion that ensued three or four men, headed by the Kafir Hendrik, rushed into the room and sprang upon Silas Croft, who had retreated to the wall and was standing with his back against it, his rifle, which he had clubbed in both his hands, raised above his head.

When his assailants were close to him they hesitated, for, aged and bent as he was, the old man looked dangerous. He stood there like a wounded lion, and swung the rifle-stock about. Presently one of the men struck at him and missed him, but before he could retreat Silas brought down the stock of the rifle on his head, and down he went like an ox beneath a poleaxe. Then they closed on him, but for a while he kept them off, knocking down another man in his efforts. At that moment the witch-doctor Hendrik, who had been watching his opportunity, brought down the barrel of his old fowling-piece upon Silas's bald head and felled him. Fortunately the blow was not a very heavy one, or it would have broken in his skull. As it was, it only cut his scalp open and knocked him down. Thereon the whole mass of Boers, with the exception of Muller, who stood watching, seeing that he was now defenceless, fell upon

Silas, and would have kicked him to death had not Bessie precipitated herself upon him with a cry, and thrown her arms about his body to protect him.

Then Frank Muller interfered, fearing lest she should be hurt. Plunging into the fray with a curse, he exercised his great strength, throwing the men this way and that like ninepins, and finally dragging Silas to his feet again.

'Come!' he shouted, 'take him out of this;' and accordingly, with taunts, curses and obloquy, the poor old man, whose fringe of white locks was red with blood, was kicked and pushed on to the verandah, then off it on to the drive. Here he fell over the body of the murdered Kafir boy, but finally he was dragged to the open space by the flagstaff, on which the Union Jack that he had hoisted there some two months before still waved bravely in the breeze. There he sank down upon the grass, his back against the flagstaff, and asked faintly for some water. Bessie, who was weeping bitterly, and whose heart felt as though it were bursting with anguish and indignation, pushed her way through the men, and, running to the house, filled a glass and brought it to him. One of the brutes tried to knock it out of her hand, but she avoided him and gave it to her uncle, who drank it greedily.

'Thank you, love, thank you,' he said; 'don't be frightened, I ain't much hurt. Ah! if only John had been here, and we had had an hour's notice, we would have held the place against them all.'

Meanwhile one of the Boers, climbing on to the shoulders of another, had succeeded in untying the cord on which the Union Jack was bent, and hauled it down. Then they reversed it and hoisted it half-mast high, and began to cheer for the Republic.

'Perhaps Uncle Silas does not know that we are a

Republic again now,' said one of the men, a near neighbour of his own, in mockery.

'What do you mean by a Republic?' asked the old man. 'The Transvaal is a British colony.'

There was a hoot of derision at this. 'The English Government has surrendered,' said the same man. 'The country is given up, and the British are to evacuate it in six months.'

'It is a lie!' said Silas, springing to his feet, 'a cowardly lie! Whoever says that the English have given up the country to a few thousand blackguards like you, and deserted its subjects and the loyals and the natives, is a liar—a liar from hell!'

There was another howl of mockery at this outburst, and when it had subsided Frank Muller stepped forward.

'It is no lie, Silas Croft,' he said, 'and the cowards are not we Boers, who have beaten you again and again, but your soldiers, who have done nothing but run away, and your Mr. Gladstone, who follows the example of your soldiers. Look here'—and he took a paper out of his pocket—'you know that signature, I suppose? It is that of one of the Triumvirate. Listen to what he says,' and he read aloud :—

'" WELL-BELOVED HEER MULLER,—This is to inform you that, by the strength of our arms fighting for the right and freedom, and also by the cowardice of the British Government, generals, and soldiers, we have by the will of the Almighty concluded this day a glorious peace with the enemy. The Heer Gladstone surrenders nearly everything except in the name. The Republic is to be re-established, and the soldiers who are left will leave the land within six months. Make this known to everyone, and forget not to thank God for our glorious victories." '

The Boers shouted aloud, as well they might, and Bessie wrung her hands. As for the old man, he leant against the flagstaff, and his gory head sank upon his breast as though he were about to faint. Then suddenly he lifted it, and with clenched and quivering fists, held high in the air, he broke out into such a torrent of blasphemy and cursing that even the Boers fell back for a moment, dismayed into silence by the force of the fury wrung from his utter humiliation.

It was an appalling sight to see this good and God-fearing old man, his face bruised, his grey hairs dabbled with blood, and his clothes nearly rent from his body, stamp and reel to and fro, blaspheming his Maker and the day that he was born ; hurling execrations at his beloved country and the name of Englishman, and the Government of Britain that had deserted him, till at last nature gave out, and he fell in a fit, there, in the very shadow of his dishonoured flag.

CHAPTER XXVIII

BESSIE IS PUT TO THE QUESTION

MEANWHILE another little tragedy was being enacted at the back of the house. After the one-eyed witch-doctor Hendrik had knocked Silas Croft down and assisted in the pleasing operation of dragging him to the flagstaff, it occurred to his villainous heart that the present would be a good opportunity to profit personally by the confusion, and possibly to add to the Englishman's misfortunes by doing him some injury on his own account. Accordingly, just before Frank Muller began to read the despatch announcing the British surrender, he slipped away into the house, which was now totally deserted, to see what he could steal. Passing into the sitting-room, he annexed Bessie's gold watch and chain, which was lying on the mantelpiece, a present that her uncle had made her on the Christmas Day before the last. Having pocketed this he proceeded to the kitchen, where, lying on the dresser ready to be put away, there was a goodly store of silver forks and spoons which Bessie had been busily engaged in cleaning that morning. These he also transferred, to the extent of several dozens, to the capacious pockets of the tattered military great-coat that he wore. Whilst thus employed he was much disturbed by the barking of the dog Stomp, the same animal that had mauled him so severely a few weeks before, and was now, as it happened,

tied up to his kennel—an old wine-barrel—just outside
the kitchen door. Hendrik peeped out of the window,
and having ascertained that the dog was secured, he proceeded, with a diabolical chuckle, to settle his account
with the poor animal. He had left his gun behind on the
grass, but he still held his assegai in his hand, and going
out of the kitchen door with it, he showed himself within
a few feet of the kennel. The dog recognised him instantly, and went nearly mad with fury, making the most
desperate efforts to break its chain and get at him. For
some moments he stood exciting the animal by derisive
gestures and pelting it with stones, till at last, fearing that
the clamour would attract attention, he suddenly trans-
fixed it with his spear, and then, thinking he was quite
unobserved, sat down, snuffed and enjoyed the luxury of
watching the poor beast's last agonies.

But, as it happened, he was not quite alone, for, creeping along in the grass and rubbish that grew on the farther side of the wall, his brown body squeezed tightly
against the brown stones—so tightly that an unpractised
eye would certainly have failed to observe it at a distance
of a dozen paces—was the Hottentot Jantjé. Occasionally, too, he would lift his head above the level of the wall
and observe the proceedings of the one-eyed man. Apparently he was undecided what to do, for he hesitated a
little, and whilst he did so Hendrik killed the dog.

Now Jantjé had all a Hottentot's natural love for
animals, which is, generally speaking, as marked as is
the Kafir's callousness towards them, and he was particularly fond of the dog Stomp, which always went out
with him on those rare occasions when he thought it
safe or desirable to walk like an ordinary man instead of
creeping from bush to bush like a panther, or wriggling
through the grass like a snake. The sight of the animal's

death, therefore, raised in his yellow breast a very keen
desire for vengeance on the murderer, if vengeance could
be safely accomplished ; and he paused to reflect how this
might be done. As he thought Hendrik rose, gave the
dead dog a kick, withdrew his assegai from the carcase,
and then, as though struck by a sudden desire to conceal
the murder, he undid the collar and, lifting the dog in
his arms, carried him with difficulty into the house and
laid him under the kitchen-table. This done, he came
out again to the wall, which was built of unmortared
stones, pulled one out without trouble, deposited the
watch and the silver he had stolen in the cavity, and replaced the stone. Next, before Jantjé could guess what
he meant to do, he proceeded to make it practically impossible for his robbery to be discovered, or at any rate
very improbable, by lighting a match, and, having first
glanced round to see that nobody was looking, reaching
up and applying it to the thick thatch wherewith the house
itself was roofed, the fringe of which just at this spot
was not more than nine feet from the ground. No rain
had fallen at Mooifontein for several days, and there
had been a hot sun with wind. As a result the thatch
was dry as tinder. The light caught in a second, and
in two more a thin line of fire was running up the roof.

Hendrik paused, stepped a few paces back, resting his
shoulders against the wall, immediately the other side of
which was Jantjé, and began to chuckle aloud and rub
his hands as he admired the results of his labours. This
proved too much for the Hottentot behind him. The
provocation was overmastering, and so was the opportunity. Jantjé carried with him the thick stick on which
he was so fond of cutting notches. Raising it in both
hands he brought the heavy knob down with all his
strength upon the one-eyed villain's unprotected skull.

It was a thick skull, but the knob prevailed against it, and fractured it, and down went the estimable witch-doctor as though he were dead.

Next, taking a leaf out of his fallen enemy's book, Jantjé slipped over the wall, and, seizing the senseless man, he dragged him by one arm into the kitchen and rolled him under the table to keep company with the dead dog. Then, filled with a fearful joy, he crawled out, shutting and locking the door behind him, and crept round to a point of vantage in a little plantation seventy or eighty yards to the right of the house, whence he could see what the Boers were doing and watch the conflagration that he knew must ensue, for the fire had taken instant and irremediable hold.

Ten minutes or so afterwards that amiable character Hendrik partially regained his senses, to find himself surrounded by a sea of fire, in which he perished miserably, not having power to move, and his feeble cries being totally swallowed up and lost in the fierce roaring of the flames. Such was the very appropriate end of Hendrik and of the magic of Hendrik.

Down by the flagstaff the old man lay in his fit, while Bessie tended him and a posse of Boers stood round, smoking and laughing or lounging about with an air of lordly superiority, well worthy of victors in possession.

'Will none of you help me to take him to the house?' she cried.   'Surely you have ill treated an old man enough.'

Nobody stirred, not even Frank Muller, who was gazing at her tear-stained face with a fierce smile playing round the corners of his clean-cut mouth, which his beard was trimmed to show.

'It will pass, Miss Bessie,' he said; 'it will pass. I have often seen such fits. They come from too much excitement, or too much drink——'

Suddenly he broke off with an exclamation, and pointed to the house, from the roof of which pale curls of blue smoke were rising.

'Who has fired the house?' he shouted. 'By Heaven! I will shoot the man.'

The Boers wheeled round staring in astonishment, and as they gazed the tinderlike roof burst into a red sheet of flame that grew and gathered breadth and height with an almost marvellous rapidity. Just then, too, a light breeze sprang up from over the hill at the rear of the house, as it sometimes did at this time of the day, and bent the flames over towards them in an immense arch of fire, so that the fumes and heat and smoke began to beat upon their faces.

'Oh, the house is burning down!' cried Bessie, utterly bewildered by this new misfortune.

'Here, you!' shouted Muller to the gaping Boers, 'go and see if anything can be saved. Phew! we must get out of this,' and, stooping down, he lifted Silas Crcft in his arms and walked away with him, followed by Bessie, towards the plantation on their left, the same spot where Jantjé had taken refuge. In the centre of this plantation was a little glade surrounded by young orange and blue-gum trees. Here he laid the old man down upon a bed of dead leaves and soft springing grass, and then hurried away without a word to the fire, only to find that the house was already utterly unapproachable. Such was the rapidity with which the flames did their work upon the mass of dry straw and the wooden roof and floorings beneath, that in fifteen minutes the whole of the interior of the house was a glowing incandescent pile, and in half an hour it was completely gutted, nothing being left standing but the massive outer walls of stone, over which a dense column of smoke hung like a pall. Mooifontein was a blackened ruin; only the stables and out-houses, which were roofed with galvanised iron, remained uninjured.

Frank Muller had not been gone five minutes when, to Bessie's joy, her uncle opened his eyes and sat up.

'What is it? what is it?' he said. 'Ah! I recollect. What is all this smell of fire? Surely they have not burnt the place?'

'Yes, uncle,' sobbed Bessie, 'they have.'

Silas groaned aloud. 'It took me ten years to build, bit by bit, almost stone by stone, and now they have destroyed it. Well, why not? God's will be done. Give me your arm, love; I want to get to the water. I feel faint and sick.'

She did as he bade her, sobbing bitterly. Within fifteen yards, on the edge of the plantation, was a little spruit or runnel of water, and of this he drank copiously, and bathed his wounded head and face.

'There, love,' he said, 'don't fret; I feel quite myself again. I fear I made a fool of myself. I haven't learnt to bear misfortune and dishonour as I should yet, and, like Job, I felt as though God had forsaken us. But, as I said, His will be done. What is the next move, I wonder? Ah! we shall soon know, for here comes our friend Frank Muller.'

'I am glad to see that you have recovered, uncle,' said Muller politely, 'and I am sorry to have to tell you that the house is beyond help. Believe me, if I knew who fired it I would shoot him. It was not my wish or intention that the property should be destroyed.'

The old man merely bowed his head and made no answer. His fiery spirit seemed to be crushed out of him.

'What is it your pleasure that we should do, sir?'

said Bessie at last. 'Perhaps, now that we are ruined, you will allow us to go to Natal, which, I suppose, is still an English country?'

'Yes, Miss Bessie, Natal is still English—for the present; soon it will be Dutch; but I am sorry that I cannot let you go there now. My orders are to keep you both prisoners and to try your uncle by court-martial. The waggon-house,' he went on quickly, 'with the two little rooms on each side of it, have not been touched by the fire. They shall be made ready for you, and as soon as the heat is less you can go there;' and, turning to the men who had followed him, he gave some rapid orders, which two of them departed to carry out.

Still the old man made no comment; he did not even seem indignant or surprised; but poor Bessie was utterly prostrated, and stood helpless, not knowing what to say to this terrible, remorseless man, who stood so calm and unmoved before them.

Frank Muller paused awhile to think, stroking his golden beard, then he turned again and addressed the two other men who stood behind him.

'You will keep guard over the prisoner,' indicating Silas Croft, 'and suffer none to communicate with him by word or sign. As soon as it is ready you will place him in the little room to the left of the waggon-house, and see that he is supplied with all he wants. If he escapes or converses, or is ill treated, I will hold you responsible. Do you understand?'

'Yah, Meinheer,' was the answer.

'Very good; be careful you do not forget. And now, Miss Bessie, I shall be glad if you can give me a word alone——'

'No,' said Bessie; 'no, I will not leave my uncle.'

'I fear you will have to do that,' he said, with his

cold smile. 'I beg you to think again. It will be very much to your advantage to speak to me, and to your uncle's advantage also. I should advise you to come.'

Bessie hesitated. She hated and mistrusted the man, as she had good reason to do, and feared to trust herself alone with him.

While she still hesitated, the two Boers, under whose watch and ward Muller had placed her uncle, advanced and stood between him and her, cutting her off from him. Muller turned and walked a few paces—ten or so—to the right, and in desperation she followed him. He halted behind a bushy orange-tree of some eight years' growth. Overtaking him, she stood silent, waiting for him to begin. They were quite close to the others, but the roaring of the flames of the burning house was still sufficiently loud to have drowned a much more audible conversation.

'What is it you have to say to me?' she said at length, pressing her hand against her heart to still its beating. Her woman's instinct told her what was coming, and she was trying to nerve herself to meet it.

'Miss Bessie,' he said slowly, 'it is this. For years I have loved you and wanted to marry you. I again ask you to be my wife.'

'Mr. Frank Muller,' she answered, her spirit rising to the occasion, 'I thank you for your offer, and the only answer that I can give you is that I once and for all decline it.'

'Think,' he said; 'I love you as women are not often loved. You are always in my mind, by day and by night too. Everything I do, every step I go up the ladder, I have said and say to myself, "I am doing it for Bessie Croft, whom I mean to marry." Things have changed in this country. The rebellion has been successful. It was I who gave the casting vote for it that I might win you. I am now a great man, and shall one day be a greater. You will be great with me. Think what you say.'

'I have thought, and I will not marry you. You dare to come and ask me to marry you over the ashes of my home, out of which you have dragged me and my poor old uncle. I hate you, I tell you, and I will not marry you! I had rather marry a Kafir than marry you, Frank Muller, however great you may be.'

He smiled. 'Is it because of the Englishman Niel that you will not marry me? He is dead. It is useless to cling to a dead man.'

'Dead or alive, I love him with all my heart, and if he is dead it is at the hands of your people, and his blood rises up between us.'

'His blood has sunk down into the sand. He is dead, and I am glad that he is dead. Once more, is that your last word?'

'It is.'

'Very good. Then I tell you that you shall marry me or——'

'Or what?'

'Or your uncle, the old man you love so much, shall *die!*'

'What do you mean?' she said in a choked voice.

'What I say; no more and no less. Do you think that I will let one old man's life stand between me and my desire? Never. If you will not marry me, Silas Croft shall be put upon his trial for attempted murder and for treason within an hour from this. Within an hour and a half he shall be condemned to die, and to-morrow at dawn he shall be shot, by warrant under my hand. I am commandant here, with power of life and

death, and I tell you that he shall certainly die—and his
blood will be on your head.'

Bessie grasped at the tree for support. 'You dare
not,' she said; 'you dare not murder an innocent old
man.'

'Dare not!' he answered; 'you must understand me
very ill, Bessie Croft, when you talk of what I dare not
do for you. There is nothing,' he added, with a thrill of
his rich voice, 'that I dare not do to gain you. Listen:
promise to marry me to-morrow morning. I will bring
a clergyman here from Wakkerstroom, and your uncle
shall go free as air, though he is a traitor to the
land, and though he has tried to shoot a burgher after
the declaration of peace. Refuse, and he dies. Choose
now.'

'I have chosen,' she answered with passion. 'Frank
Muller, perjured traitor—yes, murderer that you are, I
will *not* marry you!'

'Very good, very good, Bessie; as you will. But
now one more thing. You shall not say that I have not
warned you. If you persist in this your uncle shall die,
but you shall not escape me. You will not marry me?
Well, even in this country, where I can do most things,
I cannot force you to do that. But I can force you to be
my wife in all but the name, without marriage; and this,
when your uncle is stiff in his bloody grave, I will do.
You shall have one more chance after the trial, and one
only. If you refuse he shall die, and then, after his
death, I shall take you away by force, and in a week's
time you will be glad enough to marry me to cover up
your shame, my pretty!'

'You are a devil, Frank Muller, a wicked devil, but I
will not be frightened into dishonour by you. I had
rather kill myself. I trust to God to help me. I will

have nothing to do with you ; ' and she put her hands before her face and burst into tears.

' You look lovely when you weep,' he said with a laugh ; ' to-morrow I shall be able to kiss away your tears. As you will. Here, you ! ' he shouted to some men, who could be seen watching the progress of the dying fire, ' come here.'

Some of the men obeyed, and to them he gave instructions in the same terms that he had given to the other two men who were watching old Silas, ordering Bessie to be instantly incarcerated in the corresponding little room on the other side of the waggon-house, and kept strictly from all communication with the outside world, adding, however, these words :

' Bid the burghers assemble in the waggon-house for the trial of the Englishman, Silas Croft, for treason against the State, and attempted murder of one of the burghers of the State in the execution of the commands of the Triumvirate.'

The two men advanced and seized Bessie by both arms. Then, faint and overpowered, she was led through the little plantation, over a gap in the garden wall, down past the scorched syringa-trees which lined the roadway that ran along the hillside at the back of the still burning house, till they reached the waggon-house with the two little rooms which served respectively as a store and a harness room. There she was thrust into the store-room, which was half full of loose potatoes and mealies in sacks, and the door locked upon her.

There was no window to this room, and the only light in it was such as found its way through the chinks of the door and an air-hole in the masonry of the back wall. Bessie sank on a half-emptied sack of mealies and tried to reflect. Her first thought was of escape, but soon she came to the conclusion that this was a practical impossibility. The stout yellow wood door was locked upon her, and a sentry stood before it. She rose and looked through the air-hole in the rear wall, but there another sentry was posted. Then she turned her attention to the side wall that divided the room from the waggon-house. It was built of fourteen-inch green brickwork, and had cracked from the shrinkage of the bricks, so that she could hear everything that went on in the waggon-house, and even see anybody who might be moving about in it. But it was far too strong for her to hope to be able to break through, and even if she did, it would be useless, for armed men were there also. Besides, how could she run away and leave her old uncle to his fate?

CHAPTER XXIX

CONDEMNED TO DEATH

HALF an hour passed in silence, which was broken only
by the footsteps of the sentries as they tramped, or rather
loitered, up and down, or by the occasional fall of some
calcined masonry from the walls of the burnt-out house.
What between the smell of smoke and dust, the heat of
the sun on the tin roof above, and the red-hot embers of
the house in front, the little room where Bessie was shut
up grew almost unbearable, and she felt as though she
should faint upon the sacks. Through one of the cracks
in the waggon-house wall there blew a slight draught,
and by this crack Bessie placed herself, leaning her head
against the wall so as to get the full benefit of the air and
to command a view of the place. Presently several of the
Boers came into the waggon-house and pulled some of
carts and timber out of it, leaving one buck-waggon, however, placed along the wall on the side opposite to the
crack through which Bessie was looking. Then they
pulled the Scotch cart over to her side, laughing about
something among themselves as they did so, and arranged
it with its back turned towards the waggon, supporting
the shafts upon a waggon-jack. Next, out of the farther
corner of the place, they extracted an old saw-bench, and
set it at the top of the open space. Then Bessie understood what they were doing: they were arranging a court,

and the saw-bench was the judge's chair. So Frank Muller meant to carry out his threat!

Shortly after this all the Boers, except those who were keeping guard, filed into the place and began to clamber on to the buck-waggon, seating themselves with much rough joking in a double row upon the broad side rails. Next appeared Hans Coetzee, his head bound up in a bloody handkerchief. He was pale and shaky, but Bessie could see that he was but little the worse for his wound. Then came Frank Muller himself, looking white and very terrible, and as he came the men stopped their jokes and talking. Indeed it was curious to observe how strong was his ascendency over them. As a rule, the weak part of Boer organisation is that it is practically impossible to persuade one Boer to pay deference to or obey another; but this was certainly not the case where Frank Muller was concerned.

Muller advanced without hesitation to the saw-bench at the top of the open space, and sat down on it, placing his rifle between his knees. After this there was a pause, and then Bessie saw her old uncle led forward by two armed Boers, who halted in the middle of the space, about three paces from the saw-bench, and stood one on either side of their prisoner. At the same time Hans Coetzee climbed into the Scotch cart, and Muller drew a note-book and a pencil from his pocket.

'Silence!' he said. 'We are assembled here to try the Englishman, Silas Croft, by court-martial. The charges against him are that by word and deed, notably by continuing to fly the British flag after the country had been surrendered to the Republic, he has traitorously rebelled against the Government of this country. Further, that he has attempted to murder a burgher of the Republic by shooting at him with a loaded rifle. If these charges are proved against him he will be liable to death, by martial law. Prisoner Croft, what do you answer to the charges against you ? '

The old man, who seemed very quiet and composed, looked up at his judge, and then replied :

' I am an English subject. I only defended my house after you had murdered one of my servants. I deny your jurisdiction over me, and I refuse to plead.'

Frank Muller made some notes in his pocket-book, and then said, ' I overrule the prisoner's objection as to the jurisdiction of the court. As to the charges, we will now take evidence. Of the first charge no evidence is needed, for we all saw the flag flying. As to the second, Hans Coetzee, the assaulted burgher, will now give evidence. Hans Coetzee, do you swear, in the name of God and the Republic, to speak the truth, the whole truth, and nothing but the truth ? '

' Almighty, yes,' answered Hans from the cart on which he had enthroned himself, ' so help me the dear Lord.'

' Proceed, then.'

' I was entering the house of the prisoner to arrest him, in obedience to your worshipful commands, when the prisoner lifted a gun and fired at me. The bullet from the gun struck me upon the ear, cutting it and putting me to much pain and loss of blood. That is the evidence I have to give.'

' That's right ; that is not a lie,' said some of the men on the waggon.

' Prisoner, have you any question to ask the witness ? ' said Muller.

' I have no question to ask ; I deny your jurisdiction,' said the old man with spirit.

' The prisoner declines to question the witness, and

again pleads to the jurisdiction, a plea which I have over-ruled. Gentlemen, do you desire to hear any further evidence?'

'No, no.'

'Do you find the prisoner guilty of the charges laid against him?'

'Yes, yes,' from the waggon.

Muller made a further note in his book, and went on:

'Then, the prisoner having been found guilty of high treason and attempted murder, the only matter that remains is the question of the punishment required to be meted out by the law to such wicked and horrible offences. Every man will give his verdict, having duly considered if there is any way by which, in accordance with the holy dictates of his conscience, and with the natural promptings to pity in his heart, he can extend mercy to the prisoner. As commandant and president of the court, the first vote lies with me; and I must tell you, gentlemen, that I feel the responsibility a very heavy one in the sight of God and my country; and I must also warn you not to be influenced or overruled by my decision, who am, like you, only a man, liable to err and be led away.'

'Hear, hear,' said the voices on the waggon as he paused to note the effect of his address.

'Gentlemen and burghers of the State, my natural promptings in this case are towards pity. The prisoner is an old man, who has lived many years amongst us like a brother. Indeed, he is a " voortrekker," and, though an Englishman, one of the fathers of the land. Can we condemn such a one to a bloody grave, more especially as he has a niece dependent on him?'

'No, no!' they cried, in answer to this skilful touch upon the better strings in their nature.

'Gentlemen, those sentiments do you honour. My own heart cried but now, " No, no. Whatever his sins have been, let the old man go free." But then came reflection. True, the prisoner is old; but should not age have taught him wisdom? Is that which is not to be forgiven to youth to be forgiven to the ripe experience of many years? May a man murder and be a traitor because he is old?'

' No, certainly not ! ' answered the chorus on the waggon.

' Then there is the second point. He was a " voortrekker " and a father of the land. Should he not therefore have known better than to betray it into the hands of the cruel, godless English? For, gentlemen, though that charge is not laid against him, we must remember, as throwing light upon his general character, that the prisoner was one of those vile men who betrayed the land to Shepstone. Is it not a most cruel and unnatural thing that a father should sell his own child into slavery?— that a father of the land should barter away its freedom? Therefore on this point too does justice temper mercy.'

' That is so,' echoed the chorus with particular enthusiasm, most of them having themselves been instrumental in bringing the annexation about.

' Then one more thing : this man has a niece, and it is the care of all good men to see that the young shall not be left destitute and friendless, lest they should grow up bad and become enemies to the well-being of the State. But in this case that will not be so, for the farm will go to the girl by law; and, indeed, she will be well rid of so desperate and godless an old man.

' And now, having set my reasons towards one side and the other before you, and having warned you fully to act each man according to his conscience, I give my vote.

It is '—and in the midst of the most intense silence he
paused and looked at old Silas, who never even quailed—
'it is *death*.'

There was a little hum of conversation, and poor
Bessie, surveying the scene through the crack in the
store-room wall, groaned in bitterness and despair of
heart.

Then Hans Coetzee spoke. 'It cut his bosom in two,'
he said, ' to have to say a word against one to whom he
had for many years been as a brother. But, then, what
was he to do? The man had plotted evil against their
land, the dear land that the dear Lord had given them,
and which they and their fathers had on various occasions
watered, and were still continuing to water, with their
blood. What could be a fitting punishment for so black-
hearted a traitor, and how would it be possible to insure
the better behaviour of other damned Englishmen, unless
they inflicted that punishment? There could, alas! be
but one answer—though, personally speaking, he uttered
it with many tears—and that answer was *death*.'

After this there were no more speeches, but each man
voted, according to his age, upon his name being called
by the president. At first there was a little hesitation,
for some among them were fond of old Silas, and loth to
destroy him. But Frank Muller had played his game
very well, and, notwithstanding his appeals to their independence of judgment, they knew full surely what would
happen to him who gave his vote against the president.
So they swallowed their better feelings with all the ease
for which such swallowing is noted, and one by one
uttered the fatal word.

When they had all done Frank Muller addressed Silas :
'Prisoner, you have heard the judgment against you.
I need not now recapitulate your crimes. You have had

a fair and open trial by court-martial, such as our law directs. Have you anything to say why sentence of death should not be passed upon you in accordance with the judgment?'

Old Silas looked up with flashing eyes, and shook back his fringe of white hair like a lion at bay.

'I have nothing to say. If you will do murder, do it, black-hearted villain that you are! I might point to my grey hairs, to my murdered servant, to my home that took me ten years to build—destroyed by you! I might tell you how I have been a good citizen and lived peaceably and neighbourly in the land for more than twenty years—ay, and done kindness after kindness to many of you who are going to butcher me in cold blood! But I will not. Shoot me if you will, and may my death lie heavy on your heads. This morning I would have said that my country would avenge me; I cannot say that now, for England has deserted us, and I have no country. Therefore I leave the vengeance in the hands of God, who never fails to avenge, though sometimes He waits for long to do it. I am not afraid of you. Shoot me—now if you like. I have lost my honour, my home, and my country; why should I not lose my life also?'

Frank Muller fixed his cold eyes upon the old man's quivering face and smiled a dreadful smile of triumph.

'Prisoner, it is now my duty, in the name of God and the Republic, to sentence you to be shot to-morrow at dawn, and may the Almighty forgive you your wickedness and have mercy upon your soul.

'Let the prisoner be removed, and let a man ride full speed to the empty house on the hillside, where the Englishman with the red beard used to live, one hour this side of Wakkerstroom, and bring back with him the clergyman he will find waiting there, that the prisoner

may be offered his ministrations.   Also let two men be
set to dig the prisoner's grave in the burial-place at the
back of the house.'

The guards laid their hands upon the old man's
shoulders, and he turned and went with them without a
word.   Through her crack in the wall Bessie watched
him go till the dear old head with its fringe of white
hairs and the bent frame were no more visible.   Then at
last, benumbed and exhausted by the horrors she was
passing through, her faculties failed her, and she fell
forward in a faint there upon the sacks.

Meanwhile Muller was writing the death-warrant on
a sheet of his pocket-book.   At the foot he left a space
for his own signature, but for reasons of his own he did
not sign.   What he did do was to pass the book round to
be countersigned by all who had formed the court in this
mock trial, his object being to implicate every one there
present in the judicial murder by the direct and incontro-
vertible evidence of his sign-manual.   Now, Boers are
simple pastoral folk, but they are not quite so simple as
to be deceived by a move like this, and hereon followed
a very instructive little scene.   To a man they had been
willing enough to give their verdict for the execution of
Silas, but they were by no means prepared to record it
in black and white.   As soon as they understood the
object of their feared and respected commandant, a
general desire manifested itself to make themselves in-
dividually and collectively scarce.   Suddenly they found
that they had business outside, to which each and all of
them must attend.   Already they had escaped from their
extemporised jury-box, and, headed by the redoubtable
Hans, were approaching the entrance to the waggon-
house, when Frank Muller perceived their design, and
roared in a voice of thunder :

'Stop! Not a man leaves this place till the warrant is signed.'

Instantly they halted, and began to look innocent and converse.

'Hans Coetzee, come here and sign,' said Muller again, whereon that unfortunate advanced with as good a grace as he could muster, murmuring to himself curses, not loud but deep, upon the head of 'that devil of a man, Frank Muller.'

However, there was no help for it, so, with a sickly smile, he put his name to the fatal document in big and shaky letters. Then Muller called another man, who instantly tried to shirk on the ground that his education had been neglected, and that he could not write, an excuse which availed him little, for Frank Muller quietly wrote his name for him, leaving a space for his mark. After this there was no more trouble, and in five minutes the back of the warrant was covered with the sprawling signatures of the various members of the court.

One by one the men went, till at last Muller was left alone, seated on the saw-bench, his head sunk upon his breast, in one hand holding the warrant, while with the other he stroked his golden beard. Presently he ceased stroking his beard and sat for some minutes perfectly still—so still that he might have been carved in stone. By this time the afternoon sun had sunk behind the hill and the deep waggon-house was full of shadow that seemed to gather round him and to invest him with a sombre, mysterious grandeur. He looked like a King of Evil, for Evil has her princes as well as Good, whom she stamps with an imperial seal of power, and crowns with a diadem of her own, and among these Frank Muller was surely great. A little smile of triumph played upon his beautiful cruel face, a little light danced within his cold eyes and ran down the yellow beard. At that moment he might have sat for a portrait of his master, the devil.

Presently he awoke from his reverie. 'I have her!' he said to himself; 'I have her in a vice! She cannot escape me; she cannot let the old man die! Those curs have served my purpose well; they are as easy to play on as a fiddle, and I am a good player. Yes, and now we are getting to the end of the tune.'

CHAPTER XXX

' WE MUST PART, JOHN '

JESS and her companion stood in awed silence and gazed at the blackening and distorted corpses of the thunder-blasted Boers. Then they passed by them to the tree which grew some ten paces or more on the other side of the place of death. There was some little diffi-culty in leading the horses by the bodies, but at last they came with a wheel and a snort of suspicion, and were tied up to the tree by John. Meanwhile Jess took some of the hard-boiled eggs out of the basket and vanished, remarking that she should take her clothes off and dry them in the sun while she ate her breakfast, and that she advised him to do likewise. Accordingly, so soon as she was well out of sight behind the shelter of the rocks she set to work to free herself from her sodden garments, a task of no little difficulty. Then she wrung them out and spread them one by one on the flat water-washed stones around, which were by now thoroughly warmed with the sun. Next she climbed to a pool under the shadow of the steep bank, in the rock-bed of the river, where she bathed her bruises and washed the sand and mud from her hair and feet. Her bath finished, she returned and sat herself on a slab of flat stone out of the glare of the sun, and ate her breakfast of hard-boiled eggs, reflecting meanwhile on the position

in which she found herself. Her heart was very sore
and heavy, and almost could she wish that she were lying
deep beneath. those rushing waters. She had counted
upon death, and now she was not dead ; indeed, she
with her shame and trouble might yet live for many a
year. She was as one who in her sleep had seemed to
soar on angels' wings far into the airy depths, and then
awakened with a start to find that she had tumbled
from her bed. All the heroic scale, all the more than
earthly depth of passion, all the spiritualised desires
that sprang into being beneath the shadow of the approaching end, had come down to the common level of
an undesirable attachment, along which she must drag
her weary feet for many a year. Nor was this all. She
had been false to Bessie ; more, she had broken Bessie's
lover's troth. She had tempted him and he had fallen,
and now he was as bad as she. Death would have
justified all this ; never would she have done it had she
thought that she was doomed to live ; but now Death
had cheated her, as is his fashion with people to whom
his presence is more or less desirable, leaving her to cope
with the spirit she had invoked when his sword was
quivering over her.

What would be the end of it in the event of their
escape ? What could be the end except misery ? It
should go no farther, far as it had gone—that she swore ;
no, not if it broke her heart and his too. The conditions
were altered again, and the memory of those dreadful and
wondrous hours when they two swung upon the raging
river and exchanged their undying troth, with the grave
for an altar, must remain a memory and nothing more.
It had risen on their lives like some beautiful yet terrible
dream-image of celestial joy, and now like a dream it
must vanish. And yet it was no dream, except in so far as

all her life was a dream and a vision, a riddle of which
glimpses of the answer came as rarely as gleams of sunshine on a rainy day.   Alas ! it was no dream ; it was a
portion of the living, breathing past, that, having once
been, is immortal in its every part and moment, incar-
nating as it does the very spirit of immortality, an utter
incapacity to change.   As the act was, as the word had
been spoken, so would act and word be for ever and for
ever.   And now this undying thing must be caged and
cast about with the semblance of death and clouded over
with the shadow of an unreal forgetfulness.   Oh, it was
bitter, very bitter !   What would it be now to go away,
quite away from him, and know him married to her own
sister, the other woman with a prior right ?   What would
it be to think of Bessie's sweetness slowly creeping into
her empty place and filling it, of Bessie's gentle constant
love covering up the recollection of their wilder passion ;
pervading it and covering it up as the twilight slowly
pervades and covers up the day, till at last perhaps it
was blotted out and forgotten in the night of forgetfulness ?

And yet it must be so : she was determined that it
should be so.   Ah, that she had died then with his kiss
upon her lips !   Why had he not let her die ?   And
grieving thus the poor girl shook her damp hair over
her face and sobbed in the bitterness of her heart, as Eve
might have sobbed when Adam reproached her.

But, naked or dressed, sobbing will not mend matters
in this sad world of ours, a fact which Jess had the sense
to recognise ; so presently she wiped her eyes with her
hair, having nothing else at hand to wipe them with, and
set to work to struggle into her partially dried garments
again, a process calculated to irritate the most fortunate
and happy-minded woman in the whole wide world.

L

Certainly in her present frame of mind those damp, bullet-torn clothes drove Jess frantic, so much so that had she been a man she would probably have sworn—a consolation that her sex denied her. Fortunately she carried a travelling comb in her pocket, with which she made shift to do her curling hair, if hair can be said to be done when one has not a hairpin or even a bit of string wherewith to fasten it.

Then, after a last and frightful encounter with her sodden boots, that seemed to take almost as much out of her as her roll at the bottom of the Vaal, Jess rose and walked back to the spot where she had left John an hour before. When she reached him he was employed in saddling up the two greys with the saddles and bridles that he had removed from the carcases of the horses which the lightning had destroyed.

'Why, Jess, you look quite smart. Have you dried your clothes?' he said. 'I have after a fashion.'

'Yes,' she answered.

He looked at her. 'Dearest, you have been crying. Come, things are black enough, but it is useless to cry. At any rate, we have escaped with our lives so far.'

'John,' said Jess sharply, 'there must be no more of that. Things have changed. We were dead last night. Now we have come to life again. Besides,' she added, with a ghost of a laugh, 'perhaps you will see Bessie to-morrow. I should think that we ought to have come to the end of our misfortunes.'

John's face fell as a sense of the impossible and most tragic position in which they were placed, physically and morally, swept into his mind.

'Jess, my own Jess,' he said, 'what *can* we do?'

She stamped her foot in the bitter anguish of her heart. 'I told you,' she said, 'that there must be no

more of that. What are you thinking about? From
to-day we are dead to each other. I have done with you
and you with me. It is your own fault; you should
have let me die. Oh, John,' she wailed out, 'why did
you not let me die? Why did we not both die? We
should have been happy now, or—asleep. We must
part, John, we must part; and what shall I do without
you, how *shall* I live without you?'

Her distress was very poignant, and it affected him so
much that for a moment he could not trust himself to
answer her.

'Would it not be best to make a clean breast of it to
Bessie?' he said at last. 'I should feel a villain for the
rest of my life, but upon my word I have a mind to do it.'

'No, no,' she cried passionately, 'I will not allow it!
You shall swear to me that you will never breathe a
word to Bessie. I will not have her happiness destroyed.
We have sinned, we must suffer; not Bessie, who is
innocent, and only takes her right. I promised my dear
mother to look after Bessie and protect her, and I will
not be the one to betray her—never, never! You must
marry her and I must go away. There is no other way
out of it.'

John looked at her, not knowing what to say or do.
A sharp pang of despair went through him as he watched
the passionate pale face and the great eyes dim with
tears. How was he to part from her? He put out his
arms to take her in them, but she pushed him away
almost fiercely.

'Have you no honour?' she cried. 'Is it not all
hard enough to bear without your tempting me? I tell
you it is done with. Finish saddling that horse and let
us start. The sooner we get off the sooner it will be
over, unless the Boers catch us again and shoot us,

which for my own part I devoutly hope they may. You must make up your mind to remember that I am nothing but your sister-in-law. If you will not remember it, then I shall ride away and leave you to go your road and I will go mine.'

John said no more. Her determination was as crushing as the cruel necessity that dictated it. What was more, his own reason and sense of honour approved it, whatever his passion might prompt to the contrary. As he turned wearily to finish saddling the horses, with Jess he almost regretted that they had not both been drowned.

Of course the only saddles that they had were those belonging to the dead Boers, which was very awkward for a lady. Luckily for herself, however, from constant practice, Jess could ride almost as well as though she had been trained to the ring, and was even capable of balancing herself without a pommel on a man's saddle, having often and often ridden round the farm in that fashion. So soon as the horses were ready she astonished John by clambering into the saddle of the older and steadier animal, placing her foot in the stirrup-strap and announcing that she was ready to start.

'You had better ride some other way,' said John. 'It isn't usual, I know, but you will tumble off so.'

'You shall see,' she said with a cold little laugh, putting the horse into a canter as she spoke. John followed her on the other horse, and noted with amazement that she sat as straight and steady on her slippery seat as though she were on a hunting saddle, keeping herself from falling by an instinctive balancing of the body which was very curious to notice. When they were well on to the plain they halted to consider their route, and, turning, Jess pointed to the long lines of

vultures descending to feast on their would-be murderers.
If they went down the river it would lead them to
Standerton, and there they would be safe if they could
slip into the town, which was garrisoned by English.
But then, as they had gathered from the conversation
of their escort, Standerton was closely invested by the
Boers, and to try and pass through their lines was more
than they dared to do. It was true that they still had
the pass signed by the Boer general, but after what had
occurred not unnaturally they were somewhat sceptical
about the value of a pass, and certainly most unwilling
to put its efficacy to the proof. So after due consideration they determined to avoid Standerton and ride in the
opposite direction till they found a practicable ford of the
Vaal. Fortunately, they both of them had a very good
idea of the lay of the land ; and, in addition to this, John
possessed a small compass, fastened to his watch-chain,
which would enable him to steer a fairly correct course
across the veldt—a fact that rendered them independent
of the waggon tracks. On the roads they were exposed
to the risk, if not the certainty, of detection. But on the
wide veldt the chances were they would meet no living
creature except the wild game. Should they see houses
they could avoid them, and probably their male inhabitants
would be far away from home on business connected
with the war.

Accordingly they rode ten miles or more along the
bank without seeing a soul, till they reached a space
of bubbling, shallow water that looked fordable. Indeed,
an investigation of the banks revealed the fact that a
loaded waggon had passed the river here and at no
distant date, perhaps a week before.

'This is good enough,' said John ; 'we will try it.'
And without further ado they plunged into the rapid.

*L

In the centre of the stream the water was strong and deep, and for a few yards swept the horses off their legs, but they struck out boldly till they found their footing again ; and after that there was no more trouble. On the farther side of the river John took counsel with his compass, and they steered a course straight for Mooifontein. At midday they off-saddled the horses for an hour by some water, and ate a small portion of their remaining food. Then they up-saddled and went on across the lonely, desolate veldt. No human being did they see all that long day. The wide country was tenanted only by great herds of game that went thundering past like squadrons of cavalry, or here and there by coteries of vultures, hissing and fighting furiously over some dead buck. And so at last the twilight gathered and found them alone in the wilderness.

' Well, what is to be done now ? ' said John, pulling up his tired horse. ' It will be dark in half an hour.'

Jess slid from her saddle as she answered, ' Get off and go to sleep, I suppose.'

She was quite right ; there was absolutely nothing else that they could do ; so John set to work and hobbled the horses, tying them together for further security, for it would be a dreadful thing if they were to stray. By the time that this was done the twilight was deepening into night, and the two sat down to contemplate their surroundings with feelings akin to despair. So far as the eye could reach there was nothing to be seen but a vast stretch of lonely plain, across which the night wind blew in dreary gusts, causing the green grass to ripple like the sea. There was absolutely no shelter to be had, nor any object to break the monotony of the veldt, except two ant-heaps set about five paces apart. John sat down on one of the ant-heaps, and Jess took up her position on the other, and there they remained, like pelicans in the wilderness, watching the daylight fade out of the day.

'Don't you think that we had better sit together?' suggested John feebly. 'It would be warmer, you see.'

'No, I don't,' answered Jess snappishly. 'I am very comfortable as I am.'

Unfortunately, however, this was not the exact truth, for already poor Jess's teeth were chattering with cold. Soon, indeed, weary as they were, they found that the only way to keep their blood moving was to tramp continually up and down. After an hour and a half of this exercise, the breeze dropped and the temperature became more suitable to their lightly clad, half-starved, and almost exhausted bodies. Then the moon came up, and the hyenas, or wolves, or some such animals, came up also and howled round them—though they could not see them. These hyenas proved more than Jess's nerves would bear, and at last she condescended to ask John to share her ant-heap : where they sat, shivering in each other's arms, throughout the livelong night. Indeed, had it not been for the warmth they gathered from each other, it is probable that they might have fared even worse than they did ; for, though the days were hot, the nights were now beginning to be cold on the high veldt, especially when, as at present, the air had recently been chilled by the passage of a heavy tempest. Another drawback to their romantic situation was that they were positively soaked with the falling dew. There they sat, or rather cowered, for hour after hour without sleeping, for sleep was impossible, and almost without speaking; and yet, notwithstanding the wretchedness of their circumstances, not altogether unhappy, since they were united in their misery. At last the eastern sky began to turn grey, and John rose, shook the dew from his hat and clothes, and limped off as well as his half-frozen limbs would allow to catch the horses, which were standing together some yards away, looking huge and ghost-like in the mist. By sunrise he had managed to saddle them up, and they started once more. This time, however, he was obliged to lift Jess on to the saddle.

About eight o'clock they halted and ate their little remaining food, and then went on, slowly enough, for the horses were almost as tired as they were, and it was necessary to husband them if they were to reach Mooifontein by dark. At midday they rested for an hour and a half, and then, feeling almost worn out, continued their journey, reckoning that they could not be more than sixteen or seventeen miles from Mooifontein. It was about two hours after this that the catastrophe happened. The course they were following ran down the side of one land wave, then across a little swampy sluit, and up the opposite slope. They crossed the marshy ground, walked their horses up to the crest of the opposite rise, and found themselves face to face with a party of armed and mounted Boers.

CHAPTER XXXI

JESS FINDS A FRIEND

THE Boers swooped down on them with a shout, like hawks on a sparrow. John pulled up his horse and drew his revolver.

'Don't, don't!' cried Jess; 'our only chance is to be civil;' whereon, thinking better of the matter, he replaced it, and wished the leading Boer good-day.

'What are you doing here?' asked the Dutchman; whereon Jess explained that they had a pass—which John promptly produced—and were proceeding to Mooifontein.

'Ah, Oom Crofts!' said the Boer as he took the pass, 'you are likely to meet a burying party there,' but at the time Jess did not understand what he meant. He eyed the pass suspiciously all over, and then asked how it came to be stained with water.

Jess, not daring to tell the truth, said that it had been dropped into a puddle. The Boer was about to return it when suddenly his eye fell upon Jess's saddle.

'How is it that the girl is riding on a man's saddle?' he asked. 'Why, I know that saddle; let me look at the other side. Yes, there is a bullet-hole through the flap. That is Swart Dirk's saddle. How did you get it?'

'I bought it from him,' answered Jess without a moment's hesitation. 'I could get nothing to ride on.'

The Boer shook his head. 'There are plenty of saddles in Pretoria,' he said, 'and these are not the days when a man sells his saddle to an English girl. Ah! and that other is a Boer saddle too. No Englishman has a saddle-cloth like that. This pass is not sufficient,' he went on in a cold tone ; 'it should have been countersigned by the local commandant. I must arrest you.'

Jess began to make further excuses, but he merely repeated, 'I must arrest you,' and gave some orders to the men with him.

'We are caught again,' she said to John ; 'and there is nothing for it but to go.'

'I sha'n't mind so much if only they will give us some food,' replied John philosophically. 'I am half starved.'

'And I am half dead,' said Jess with a little laugh. 'I wish they would shoot us and have done with it.'

'Come, cheer up, Jess,' he answered ; 'perhaps the luck is going to change.'

She shook her head with the air of one who expects the worst, and then some gay young spirits among the Boers came up and made things pleasant by an exhibition of their polished wit, which they chiefly exercised at the expense of poor Jess, whose appearance, as may well be imagined, was exceedingly wretched and forlorn ; so much so that it would have moved the pity of most people. But these specimens of the golden youth of a simple pastoral folk found in it a rich mine of opportunities. They asked her if she would not like to ride straddle-legged, and if she had bought her dress from an old Hottentot who had done with it, and if she had been rolling about tipsy in the veldt to get all the mud on it; and generally availed themselves of this unparalleled occasion to be witty at the expense of an English lady in sore distress. Indeed, one gay young dog called Jacobus was proceeding from jokes linguistic to jokes practical. Perceiving that Jess only kept her seat on the man's saddle by the exercise of a faculty of balance, it occurred to him that it would be a fine thing to upset it and make her fall upon her face. Accordingly, with a sudden twist of the rein he brought his horse sharply against her wearied animal, nearly throwing it down; but she was too quick for him, and saved herself by catching at the mane. Jess said nothing; indeed, she made no answer to her tormentors, and fortunately John understood little of what they were saying. Presently, however, the young Boer made another attempt, putting out his hand to give her a slight push. As it happened John saw this, and the sight of the indignity caused the blood to boil in his veins. Before he could reflect on what he was doing he was alongside of the man, and, catching him by the throat, had hurled him backwards over his crupper with all the force he could command. Jacobus fell heavily upon his shoulders, and instantly there was a great hubbub. John drew his revolver, and the other Boers raised their rifles, so that Jess thought there was an end of it, and put her hand before her face, having first thanked John for avenging the insult with a swift flash of her beautiful eyes. And indeed in another second it would have been all over had not the elder man who inspected the pass interposed. In fact he had witnessed the proceedings which led to his follower's discomfiture, and, being a decent person at bottom, strongly disapproved of them.

'Leave them alone and put down those guns,' he

shouted. 'It served Jacobus right; he was trying to push the girl from her horse! Almighty! it is not wonderful those English call us brute beasts when you boys do such things. Put down your guns, I say, and one of you help Jacobus up. He looks as sick as a buck with a bullet through it.'

Accordingly the row passed over, and the playful Jacobus—whom Jess noted with satisfaction seemed exceedingly ill and trembled in every limb—was with difficulty hoisted on to his horse, to continue his journey with not a single bit of fun left in him.

A little while after this Jess pointed out a long low hill that lay upon the flat veldt, a dozen miles or so away, like a stone on a stretch of sand.

'Look,' she said, 'there is Mooifontein at last!'

'We are not there yet,' remarked John sadly.

Another weary half-hour passed, and then on passing over a crest suddenly they saw Hans Coetzee's homestead lying down by the water in the hollow. So that was whither they were being taken.

Within a hundred yards of the house the Boers halted and consulted, except Jacobus, who went on, still looking very green. Finally the elder man came to them and addressed Jess, at the same time handing her back the pass.

'You can go on home,' he said. 'The Englishman must stay with us till we find out more about him.'

'He says that I can go. What shall I do?' asked Jess. 'I don't like leaving you with these men.'

'Do? why, go, of course. I can look after myself; and if I can't, certainly you won't be able to help me. Perhaps you will be able to get some help from the farm. At any rate, you must go.'

'Now, Englishman,' said the Boer.

'Good-bye, Jess,' said John.   'God bless you.'

'Good-bye, John,' she answered, looking him steadily in the eyes for a moment, and then turning away to hide the tears which would gather in her own.

And thus they parted.

She knew her way now even across the open veldt, for she dared not go by the road.   There was, however, a bridle path that ran over the hill at the back of Mooifontein, and for this she shaped her course.   It was five o'clock by now, and both she and her horse were in a condition of great exhaustion, enhanced in her own case by want of food and trouble of mind.   But she was a strong woman, with a will like iron, and she held on when most girls would have died.   Jess meant to get to Mooifontein somehow, and she knew that she would get there.   If only she could reach the place and find help to send to her lover, she did not greatly care what happened to her afterwards.   The pace of the horse she was riding grew slower and slower.   From the ambling canter into which at first she managed occasionally to force it, and which is the best pace to travel at in South Africa, it relapsed continually into a rough short trot, which was agony to her, riding as she was, and from the trot into a walk.   Indeed, just before sunset, or a little after six o'clock, the walk became final.   At last they reached the rising ground that stretched up the slope to the Mooifontein hill, and here the poor beast fell down utterly worn out.   Jess slipped off and tried to drag it up, but failed.   It had no strength left in it.   So she did what she could, pulling off the bridle and undoing the girth, so that the saddle would fall off if the horse ever managed to rise.   The animal watched her go with melancholy eyes, knowing that it was being deserted. First it neighed, then with a desperate effort it struggled to its feet and trotted after her for a hundred yards or so, only to fall down again at last. Jess turned and saw it, and, exhausted as she was, she positively ran to get away from the look in those big eyes. That night there was a cold rain, in which the horse perished, as ' poor ' horses are apt to do.

It was nearly dark when at length Jess reached the top of the hill and looked down. She knew the spot well, and from it she could always see the light in the kitchen window of the house. To-night there was no light. Wondering what it could mean, and feeling a fresh chill of doubt creep round her heart, she scrambled on down the hill. When she was about half-way a shower of sparks suddenly shot into the air from the spot where the house should be, caused by the fall of a piece of wall into the smouldering embers beneath. Again Jess paused, wondering and aghast. What could have happened? Determined at all hazards to discover, she crept on very cautiously. Before she had gone another twenty yards, however, a hand was laid suddenly upon her arm. She turned quickly, too paralysed with fear to cry out, and a voice that was familiar to her whispered into her ear, ' Missie Jess, Missie Jess, is it you? I am Jantjé.'

She gave a sigh of relief, and her heart, which had stood still, began to move again. Here was a friend at last.

' I heard you coming down the hill, though you came so softly,' he said ; ' but I could not tell who it was, because you jumped from rock to rock and did not walk as usual. But I thought it was a woman with boots ; I could not see, because the light all falls dead against the hill, and the stars are not up. So I got to the left of your path—for the wind is blowing from the right—and waited till you had passed and *winded* you. Then I knew who you were for certain—either you or Missie Bessie; but Missie Bessie is shut up, so it could not be her.'

'Bessie shut up!' ejaculated Jess, not even pausing to marvel at the dog-like instinct that had enabled the Hottentot to identify her. ' What do you mean ?'

'This way, missie, come this way, and I will tell you;' and he led her to a fantastic pile of rocks in which it was his wild habit to sleep. Jess knew the place well, and had often peeped into, but never entered, the Hottentot's kennel.

'Stop a bit, missie. I will go and light a candle; I have some in there, and they can't see the light from out-side;' and accordingly he vanished. In a few seconds he returned, and, taking her by the sleeve, led her along a winding passage between great boulders till they came to a beehole in the rocks, through which she could see the light shining. Going down on his hands and knees, Jantjé crept through, and Jess followed him. She found herself in a small apartment, about six feet square by eight high, formed for the most part by the accidental falling together of big boulders, and roofed in with one great natural slab. The place, which was lighted by an end of candle stuck upon the floor, was very dirty, as might be expected of a Hottentot's den, and in it were col-lected an enormous variety of odds and ends. As, dis-carding a three-legged stool that Jantjé offered her, Jess sank down on a pile of skins in the corner, her eye fell upon a collection worthy of an old rag and bone shop. The sides of the chamber were festooned with every imaginable garment, from the white full-dress coat of an Austrian officer down to a shocking pair of corduroys 'lifted' by Jantjé from the body of a bushman, which he had discovered in his rambles. All these clothes were in various stages of decay, and obviously the result of years of patient collecting. In the corners again were sticks, kerries, and two assegais, a number of queer-shaped stones and bones, handles of broken table-knives, bits of the locks of guns, portions of an American clock, and various other articles which this human jackdaw had picked up and hidden away. Altogether it was a strange place : and vaguely it occurred to Jess, as she sank back upon the dirty skins, that, had it not been for the old clothes and the wreck of the American clock, she would have made acquaintance with a very fair example of the dwellings of primeval man.

'Stop before you begin,' she said. 'Have you any-thing to eat here ? I am nearly starving.'

Jantjé grinned knowingly, and, grubbing in a heap of rubbish in the corner, drew out a gourd with a piece of flat sheet iron, which once had formed the back plate of a stove, placed on the top of it. It contained ' maas,' or curdled buttermilk, which a woman had brought him that very morning from a neighbouring kraal, and it was destined for Jantjé's own supper. Hungry as he was himself, for he had tasted no food all day, he gave it to Jess without a moment's hesitation, together with a wooden spoon, and, squatting on the rock before her, watched her eat it with guttural exclamations of satis-faction. Not knowing that she was robbing a hungry man, Jess ate the maas to the last spoonful, and was grateful to feel the sensation of gnawing sickness leave her.

'Now,' she said, 'tell me what you mean.'

Thereon Jantjé began at the beginning and related the events of the day so far as he was acquainted with them. When he came to where the old man was dragged, with kicks and blows and ignominy, from his own house, Jess's eyes flashed, and she positively ground her teeth with indignation ; and as for her feelings when she learnt that he was condemned to death and to be shot at dawn on the morrow, they are simply indescribable. Of the Bessie complication Jantjé was quite ignorant, and could only tell her that Frank Muller had an interview with her sister in the little plantation, after which she was shut up in the store-room, where she still remained. But this was quite enough for Jess, who knew Muller's character better, perhaps, than anybody else, and was not by any means ignorant of his designs upon Bessie. A few moments' thought put the key of the matter into her hand. She saw now what was the reason of the granting of the pass, and of the determined and partially successful attempt at wholesale murder of which they had been the victims. She saw, too, why her old uncle had been condemned to death—it was to be used as a lever with Bessie ; the man was capable even of that.

Yes, she saw it all as clear as daylight ; and in her heart she swore, helpless as she seemed to be, that she would find a way to prevent it. But what way ? what way ? Ah, if only John were here ! but he was not, so she must act without him if only she could see the road to action. She thought first of all of going down boldly to face Muller and denounce him as a murderer before his men ; but a moment's reflection showed that this was impracticable. For his own safety he would be obliged to stop her mouth somehow, and the best she could expect would be to be incarcerated and rendered quite powerless. If only she could manage to communicate with Bessie ! At any rate it was absolutely necessary that she should know what was happening. She might as well be a hundred miles away as a hundred yards.

'Jantjé,' she said, 'tell me where the Boers are.'

'Some are in the waggon-house, missie, some are on

sentry, and the rest are down by the waggon they brought with them and outspanned behind the gums there. The cart is there, too, that came just before you did, with the clergyman in it.'

'And where is Frank Muller?'

'I don't know, missie; but he brought a round tent with him in the waggon, and it is pitched between the two big gums.'

'Jantjé, I must go down there and find out what is going on, and you must come with me.'

'You will be caught, missie. There is a sentry at the back of the waggon-house, and two in front. But,' he added, 'perhaps we might get near. I will go out and look at the night.'

Presently he returned and said that a 'small rain' had come on, and the clouds covered up the stars so that it was very dark.

'Well, let us go at once,' said Jess.

'Missie, you had better not go,' answered the Hottentot. 'You will get wet, and the Boers will catch you. Better let me go. I can creep about like a snake, and if the Boers catch me it won't matter.'

'You must come too, but I am going. I must find out.'

Then the Hottentot shrugged his shoulders and yielded, and, having extinguished the candle, silently as ghosts they crept out into the night.

CHAPTER XXXII

HE SHALL DIE

THE night was still and very dark. A soft cold rain, such as often falls in the Wakkerstroom and New Scotland districts of the Transvaal, and which more resembles a true north country mist than anything else, was drizzling gently but persistently. This condition of affairs was as favourable as possible to their enterprise, and under cover of it the Hottentot and the white girl crept far down the hill to within twelve or fourteen paces of the back of the waggon-house. Then Jantjé, who was leading, suddenly put back his hand and checked her, and at that moment Jess caught the sound of a sentry's footsteps as he tramped leisurely up and down. For a couple of minutes or so they stopped thus, not knowing what to do, when suddenly a man came round the corner of the building holding a lantern in his hand. On seeing the lantern Jess's first impulse was to fly, but Jantjé by a motion made her understand that she was to stop still. The man with the lantern advanced towards the other man, holding the light above his head, and looking dim and gigantic in the mist and rain. Presently he turned his face, and Jess saw that it was Frank Muller himself. He stood thus for a moment waiting till the sentry was near to him.

' You can go to your supper,' he said. ' Come back in

half an hour. I will be responsible for the prisoners till then.'

The man growled out an answer something about the rain, and then departed round the end of the building, followed by Muller.

'Now then, come on,' whispered Jantjé; 'there is a hole in the store-room wall, and you may be able to speak to Missie Bessie.'

Jess did not require a second invitation, but slipped up to the wall in five seconds. Passing her hand over the stone-work she found the air-hole, which she remembered well, for they used to play bo-peep there as children, and was about to whisper through it, when suddenly the door at the other end opened, and Frank Muller entered, bearing the lantern in his hand. For a moment he stood on the threshold, opening the slide of the lantern in order to increase the light. His hat was off, and he wore a cape of dark cloth thrown over his shoulders, which seemed to add to his great breadth. Indeed the thought flashed through the mind of Jess as she looked at him through the hole, and saw the light strike upon his face and form, glinting down his golden beard, that he was the most magnificent specimen of humanity whom she had ever seen. In another instant he had turned the lantern round and revealed her dear sister Bessie to her gaze. Bessie lay upon one of the half-empty sacks of mealies, apparently half asleep, for she opened her wide blue eyes and looked round apprehensively like one suddenly awakened. Her golden curls were in disorder and falling over her fair forehead, and her face was very pale and troubled, and marked beneath the eyes with deep blue lines. Catching sight of her visitor she rose hurriedly and retreated as far from him as the pile of sacks and potatoes would allow.

' What is it ? ' she asked in a low voice. ' I gave you my answer. Why do you come to torment me again ? '

He placed the lantern upon an upright sack of mealies, and carefully balanced it before he answered. Jess could see that he was taking time to consider.

' Let us recapitulate,' he said at length, in his full rich voice. ' The position is this. I gave you this morning the choice between consenting to marry me to-morrow and seeing your old uncle and benefactor shot. Further, I assured you that if you would not consent to marry me your uncle should be shot, and that I would then make you mine, dispensing with the ceremony of marriage. Is that not so ? '

Bessie made no answer, and he continued, his eyes fixed upon her face and thoughtfully stroking his beard.

' Silence gives consent. I will go on. Before a man can be shot according to law he must be tried and condemned according to law. Your uncle has been tried and has been condemned.'

' I heard it all, cruel murderer that you are, ' said Bessie, lifting her head for the first time.

' So ! I thought you would, through the crack. That is why I had you put into this place ; it would not have looked well to bring you before the court ; ' and he took the light and examined the crevice. ' This wall is badly built,' he went on in a careless tone ; ' look, there is another space there at the back ; ' and he actually came up to it and held the lantern close to the airhole in such fashion that its light shone through into Jess's eyes and nearly blinded her. She shut them quickly so that the gleam reflected from them should not betray her, then held her breath and remained still as the dead. In another second Muller took away the light and replaced it on the mealie bag.

So you say you saw it all. Well, it must have shown you that I was in earnest. The old man took it well, did he not? He is a brave man, and I respect him. I fancy that he will not move a muscle at the last. That comes of English blood, you see. It is the best in the world, and I am proud to have it in my veins.'

'Cannot you stop torturing me, and say what you have to say?' asked Bessie.

'I had no wish to torture you, but if you like I will come to the point. It is this. Will you now consent to marry me to-morrow morning at sun-up, or am I to be forced to carry the sentence on your old uncle into effect?'

'I will not. I will not. I hate you and defy you.'

Muller looked at her coldly, and then drew his pocket-book from his pocket and extracted from it the death-warrant and a pencil.

'Look, Bessie,' he said. 'This is your uncle's death-warrant. At present it is valueless and informal, for I have not yet signed, though, as you will see, I have been careful that everybody else should. If once I place my signature there it cannot be revoked, and the sentence must be carried into effect. If you persist in your refusal I will sign it before your eyes;' and he placed the paper on the book and took the pencil in his right hand.

'Oh, you cannot, you cannot be such a fiend,' wailed the wretched woman, wringing her hands.

'I assure you that you are mistaken. I both can and will. I have gone too far to turn back for the sake of one old Englishman. Listen, Bessie, Your lover Niel is dead—that you know.'

Here Jess behind the wall felt inclined to cry out, 'It is a lie!' but, remembering the absolute necessity of silence, she checked herself.

'And, what is more,' went on Muller, 'your sister Jess is dead too! she died two days ago.'

'Jess dead! Jess dead! It is not true. How do you know that she is dead?'

'Never mind; I will tell you when we are married. She is dead, and, except for your uncle, you are alone in the world. If you persist in this he will soon be dead too, and his blood will be upon your head, for you will have murdered him.'

'And if I were to say yes, how would that help him?' she cried wildly. 'He is condemned by your court-martial—you would only deceive me and murder him after all.'

'On my honour, no. Before the marriage I will give this warrant to the pastor, and he shall burn it as soon as the service is said. But, Bessie, don't you see that these fools who tried your uncle are only like clay in my hands? I can bend them this way and that, and whatever song I sing they will echo it. They do not wish to shoot your uncle, and will be glad indeed to get out of it. Your uncle shall go in safety to Natal, or stay here if he wills. His property shall be secured to him, and compensation paid for the burning of his house. I swear it before God.'

She looked up at him, and he could see that she was inclined to believe him.

'It is true, Bessie, it is true—I will rebuild the place myself, and if I can find the man who fired it he shall be shot. Come, listen to me, and be reasonable. The man you love is dead, and no amount of sighing can bring him to your arms. I alone am left—I who love you better than life, better than man ever loved woman before. Look at me : am I not a proper man for any maid to wed, though I be half a Boer? And I have the brains, too,

Bessie, the brains that shall make us both great. We were made for each other—I have known it for years, and slowly, slowly, I have worked my way to you till at last you are in my reach;' and he stretched out both his arms towards her.

'My darling,' he went on, in a soft, half-dreamy voice, 'my love and desire, yield, now—yield! Do not force this new crime upon me. I want to grow good for your sake, and have done with bloodshed. When you are my wife I believe that the evil will go out of me, and I shall grow good. Yield, and never shall woman have had such a husband as I will be to you. I will make your life soft and beautiful to you as women love life to be. You shall have everything that money can buy and power bring. Yield for your uncle's sake, and for the sake of the great love I bear you.'

As he spoke he was slowly drawing nearer Bessie, whose face wore a half-fascinated expression. As he came the wretched woman gathered herself together and put out her hand to repulse him. 'No, no,' she cried, 'I hate you—I cannot be false to him, living or dead. I shall kill myself—I know I shall.'

He made no answer, but only came always nearer, till at last his strong arms closed round her shrinking form and drew her to him as easily as though she were a babe. And then all at once she seemed to yield. That embrace was the outward sign of his cruel mastery, and she struggled no more, mentally or physically.

'Will you marry me, darling—will you marry me?' he whispered, with his lips so close to the golden curls that Jess, straining her ears outside, could only just catch the words—

'Oh, I suppose so; but I shall die—it will kill me.'

He strained her to his heart and kissed her beautiful

face again and again, until Jess heard the heavy footsteps of the returning sentry, and saw Muller leave go of
her. Then Jantjé caught Jess by the hand, dragging her
away from the wall, and presently she was once more
ascending the hill-side towards the Hottentot's kennel.
She had desired to find out how matters stood, and she
had found out indeed. To attempt to portray the fury,
the indignation, and the thirst to be avenged upon this
fiend who had attempted to murder her and her lover, and
had bought her dear sister's honour at the price of their
innocent old uncle's life, would be impossible. Her
weariness had left her; she was mad with all she had seen
and heard, with the knowledge of what had been done and
of what was about to be done. She even forgot her passion
in it, and swore that Muller should never marry Bessie
while she lived to prevent it. Had she been a bad woman
herein she might have seen an opportunity, for Bessie
once tied to Muller, John would be free to marry her,
but this idea never even entered her mind. Whatever
Jess's errors may have been she was a self-sacrificing,
honourable woman, and one who would have died rather
than profit thus by circumstance. At length they reached
the shelter again and crept into it.

'Light a candle,' said Jess.

Jantjé hunted for and struck a match. The piece of
candle they had been using, however, was nearly burnt
out, so from the rubbish in the corner he produced a box
full of 'ends,' some of them three or four inches long.
In the queer sort of way that trifles do strike us when
the mind is undergoing a severe strain, Jess remembered
instantly that for years she had been unable to discover
what became of the odd bits of the candles used in the
house. Now the mystery was explained.

'Go outside and leave me. I want to think,' she said.

M

The Hottentot obeyed, and seated upon the heap of skins, her forehead resting on her hand and her fingers buried in her silky rain-soaked hair, Jess began to review the position. It was evident to her that Frank Muller would be as good as his word. She knew him too well to doubt this for a moment. If Bessie did not marry him he would murder the old man, as he had tried to murder herself and John, only this time judicially, and then abduct her sister afterwards. She was the only price that he was prepared to take in exchange for her uncle's life. But it was impossible to allow Bessie to be so sacrificed; the thought was horrible to her.

How, then, was it to be prevented?

She thought again of confronting Frank Muller and openly accusing him of her attempted murder, only, however, to dismiss the idea. Who would believe her? And if they did believe what good would it do? She would only be imprisoned and kept out of harm's way, or possibly murdered out of hand. Then she thought of attempting to communicate with her uncle and Bessie, to tell them that John was, so far as she knew, alive, only to recognise the impossibility of doing so now that the sentry had returned. Besides, what object could be served? The knowledge that John was alive might, it is true, encourage Bessie to resist Muller, but then the death of the old man must certainly ensue. Dismissing this project from her mind Jess began to consider whether they could obtain assistance. Alas! it was impossible. The only people from whom she could hope for aid would be the natives, and now that the Boers had triumphed over the English— for this much she had gathered from her captors and from Jantjé—it was very doubtful if the Kafirs would dare to assist her. Besides, at the best it would take twenty-four hours to collect a force, and by then help would come too late. The situation was hopeless. Nowhere could she see a ray of light.

'What,' Jess said aloud to herself—'what is there in the world that will stop a man like Frank Muller?'

And then of an instant the answer rose up in her brain as though by inspiration—

'*Death!*'

Death, and death alone, would stay him. For a minute she held the idea in her mind till she grew familiar with it, then it was driven out by another thought that followed swiftly on its track. Frank Muller must die, and die before the morning light. By no other possible means could the Gordian knot be cut, and both Bessie and her old uncle be saved. If he were dead he could not marry Bessie, and if he died with the warrant unsigned their uncle could not be executed. That was the terrible answer to her riddle.

Yet it was most just that he should die, for had he not murdered and attempted murder? Surely if ever a man deserved a swift and awful doom that man was Frank Muller.

And so this forsaken, helpless girl, crouching upon the ground a torn and bespattered fugitive in the miserable hiding-hole of a Hottentot, arraigned the powerful leader of men before the tribunal of her conscience, and without pity, if without wrath, passed upon him a sentence of extinction.

But who was to be the executioner? A dreadful thought flashed into her mind and made her heart stand still, but she dismissed it. No, she had not come to that! Her eyes wandering round the kennel lit upon Jantjé's assegais and sticks in the corner, and these gave her another inspiration. Jantjé should do the deed.

John had told her one day when they were sitting

together in 'The Palatial' at Pretoria the whole of Jantjé's awful story about the massacre of his relatives by Frank Muller twenty years before, of which, indeed, she already knew something. It would be most fitting that this fiend should be removed from the face of the earth by the survivor of those unfortunates. That would be poetic justice, and justice is so rare in the world. But the question was, would he do it? The little man was a wonderful coward, that she knew, and had a great terror of Boers, and especially of Frank Muller.

'Jantjé,' she whispered, stooping towards the bee-hole.

'Yah, missie,' answered a hoarse voice outside, and next second the Hottentot's monkey-like face came creeping into the ring of light, followed by his even more monkey-like form.

'Sit down there, Jantjé. I am lonely here and want to talk.'

He obeyed her, with a grin. 'What shall we talk about, missie? Shall I tell you a story of the time when the beasts could speak, as I used to do years and years ago?'

'No, Jantjé. Tell me about that stick—that long stick with a knob at the top, and the nicks cut on it. Has it not something to do with Frank Muller?'

The Hottentot's face instantly grew evil. 'Yah, yah, missie!' he said, reaching out a skinny claw and seizing the stick. 'Look, this big notch, that is my father, Baas Frank shot him; and this next notch, that is my mother, Baas Frank shot her; and the next one, that is my uncle, an old, old man, Baas Frank shot him also. And these small notches, they are when he has beaten me—yes, and other things too. And now I will make more notches, one for the house that is burnt, and one for the old Baas

Croft, my own Baas, whom he is going to shoot, and one for Missie Bessie.' And Jantjé drew from his side his large white-handled hunting-knife, and began to cut them then and there upon the hard wood of the stick.

Jess knew this knife of old. It was Jantjé's peculiar treasure, the chief joy of his narrow little heart. He had bought it from a Zulu for a heifer which her uncle had given him in lieu of half a year's wage. This Zulu had it from a half-caste whose kraal was beyond Delagoa Bay. As a matter of fact it was a Somali knife, manufactured from soft native steel which takes an edge like a razor, and with a handle cut out of the tusk of a hippopotamus. For the rest, it was about a foot long, with three grooves running the length of the blade, and very heavy.

'Stop cutting notches, Jantjé, and let me look at that knife.'

He obeyed, and put it into her hand.

'That knife would kill a man, Jantjé,' she said.

'Yes, yes,' he answered : 'no doubt it has killed many men.'

'It would kill Frank Muller, now, would it not?' she went on, suddenly bending forward and fixing her dark eyes upon the little man's jaundiced orbs.

'Yah, yah,' he said starting back, 'it would kill him dead. Ah! what a thing it would be to kill him!' he added, making a fierce sound, half grunt, half laugh.

'He killed your father, Jantjé.'

'Yah, yah, he killed my father,' said Jantjé, his eyes beginning to roll with rage.

'He killed your mother.'

'Yah, he killed my mother,' he repeated after her with eager ferocity.

'And your uncle. He killed your uncle.'

'And my uncle too,' he went on, shaking his fist and twitching his long toes as his hoarse voice rose to a subdued scream. 'But he will die in blood—the old English-woman, his mother, said it when the devil was in her, and the devils never lie. Look! I draw Baas Frank's circle in the dust with my foot; and listen, I say the words—I say the words,' and he muttered something rapidly; 'an old, old witch-doctor taught me how to do it, and what to say. Once before I did it, and there was a stone in the circle, now there is no stone: look, *the ends meet*. He will die in blood; he will die *soon*. I know how to read the omen;' and he gnashed his teeth and sawed the air with his clenched fists.

'Yes, you are right, Jantjé,' she said, still holding him with her dark eyes. 'He will die in blood, and he will die to-night, and *you* will kill him, Jantjé.'

The Hottentot started, and turned pale under his yellow skin.

'How?' he said; 'how?'

'Bend forward, Jantjé, and I will tell you how;' and Jess whispered for some minutes into his ear.

'Yes! yes! yes!' he said when she had done. 'Oh, what a fine thing it is to be clever like the white people! I will kill him to-night, and then I can cut out the notches, and the spooks of my father and my mother and my uncle will stop howling round me in the dark as they do now, when I am asleep.'

CHAPTER XXXIII

VENGEANCE

For three or four minutes more Jess and Jantjé whispered together, after which the Hottentot rose and crept away to find out what was passing among the Boers below, and watch when Frank Muller retired to his tent. So soon as he had marked him down it was agreed that he was to come back and report to Jess.

When he was gone Jess gave a sigh of relief. This stirring up of Jantjé to the boiling-point of vengeance had been a dreadful thing to nerve herself to do, but now at any rate it was done, and Muller's doom was sealed. But what the end of it would be none could say. Practically she would be a murderess, and she felt that sooner or later her guilt must find her out, and then she could hope for little mercy. Still she had no scruples, for after all Frank Muller's would be a well-merited fate. But when all was said and done, it was a dreadful thing to be forced to steep her hands in blood, even for Bessie's sake. If Muller were removed Bessie would marry John, provided that John escaped the Boers, and be happy, but what would become of herself? Robbed of her love and with this crime upon her mind, what could she do even if she escaped—except die? It would be better to die and never see him again, for her sorrow and her shame were more than she could bear. Then Jess began to think of

John till all her poor bruised heart seemed to go out towards him. Bessie could never love him as she did, she felt sure of that, and yet Bessie was to have him by her all her life, and she—she must go away. Well, it was the only thing to do. She would see this deed done, and set her sister free, then if she happened to escape she would go at once—go quite away where she would never be heard of again. Thus at any rate she would have behaved like an honourable woman. She sat up and put her hands to her face. It was burning hot though she was wet through, and chilled to the bone with the raw damp of the night. A fierce fever of mind and body had taken hold of her, worn out as she was with emotion, hunger, and protracted exposure. But her brain was clear enough; she never remembered its being so clear before. Every thought that came into her mind seemed to present itself with startling strength, standing out alone against a black background of nothingness, not softened down and shaded one into another as thoughts generally are. She seemed to see herself wandering away—alone, utterly alone, alone for ever !—while in the far distance John stood holding Bessie by the hand, gazing after her regretfully. Well, she would write to him, since it must be so, and bid him one word of farewell. She could not go without that, though how her letter was to reach John she knew not, unless indeed Jantjé could find him and deliver it. She had a pencil, and in the breast of her dress was the Boer pass, the back of which, stained as it was with water, would serve the purpose of paper. She found it and, bending forward towards the light, placed it on her knees:

'Good-bye,' she wrote, 'good-bye! We can never meet again, and it is better that we never should in this world. I believe that there is another. If there is I shall wait for you there if I have to wait ten thousand years. If not, then good-bye for ever. Think of me sometimes, for I have loved you very dearly, and as nobody will ever love you again; and while I live in this or any other existence and am myself, I shall always love you and you only. Don't forget me. I never shall be really dead to you until I am forgotten.—J.'

She lifted the paper from her knee, and without even re-reading what she had written thrust the pass back into her bosom and was soon lost in thought.

Ten minutes later Jantjé, like a great snake in human form, came creeping in to where she sat, his yellow face shining with the raindrops.

'Well,' whispered Jess, looking up with a start, 'have you done it?'

'No, missie, no. Baas Frank has but now gone to his tent. He has been talking to the clergyman, something about Missie Bessie, I don't know what. I was near, but he talked low, and I could only hear the name.'

'Are all the Boers asleep?'

'All, missie, except the sentries.'

'Is there a sentry before Baas Frank's tent?'

'No, missie, there is nobody near.'

'What is the time, Jantjé?'

'About three hours and a half after sundown' (half-past ten).

'Let us wait half an hour, and then you must go.'

Accordingly they sat in silence. In silence they sat facing each other and their own thoughts. Presently Jantjé broke it by drawing the big white-handled knife and commencing to sharpen it on a piece of leather.

The sight made Jess feel sick. 'Put the knife up,' she said quickly, 'it is sharp enough.'

Jantjé obeyed with a feeble grin, and the minutes passed on heavily.

'Now, Jantjé,' she said at length, speaking huskily in her struggle to overcome the spasmodic contractions of her throat, 'it is time for you to go.'

The Hottentot fidgeted about, and at last spoke.

'Missie must come with me!'

'Come with you!' answered Jess starting, 'why?'

'Because the ghost of the old Englishwoman will be after me if I go alone.'

'You fool!' said Jess angrily; then recollecting herself she added, 'Come, be a man, Jantjé: think of your father and mother, and be a man.'

'I am a man,' he answered sulkily, 'and I will kill him like a man, but what good is a man against the ghost of a dead Englishwoman? If I put the knife into her she would only make faces, and fire would come out of the hole. I will not go without you, missie.'

'You must go,' she said fiercely; 'you shall go!'

'No, missie, I will not go alone,' he answered.

Jess looked at him and saw that Jantjé meant what he said. He was growing sulky, and the worst dispositioned donkey in the world is far, far easier to deal with than a sulky Hottentot. She must either give up the project or go with the man. Well, she was equally guilty one way or the other, and being almost callous about detection, she might as well go. She had no power left to make fresh plans. Her mind seemed to be exhausted. Only she must keep out of the way at the last. She could not bear to be near then.

'Well,' she said, 'I will go with you, Jantjé.'

'Good, missie, that is all right now. You can keep off the ghost of the dead Englishwoman while I kill Baas

Frank. But first he must be fast asleep. Fast, fast asleep.'

Theñ slowly and with the uttermost caution once more they crept down the hill. This time there was no light to be seen in the direction of the waggon-house, and no sound to be heard except the regular tramp of the sentries. But their present business did not take them to the waggon-house ; they left that on their right, and went on towards the blue-gum avenue. When they were nearly opposite to the first tree they halted in a patch of stones, and Jantjé slipped forward to reconnoitre. Presently he returned with the intelligence that all the Boers who were with the waggon had gone to sleep, but that Muller was still sitting in his tent thinking. Then they crept on, perfectly sure that if they were not heard they would not be seen, curtained as they were by the dense mist and darkness.

At length they reached the bole of the first big gum tree. Five paces from this tree Frank Muller's tent was pitched. There was a light in it which caused the wet tent to glow in the mist, as though it had been rubbed with phosphorus, and on this lurid canvas the shadow of Frank Muller was gigantically limned. He was so placed that the lamp cast a magnified reflection of his every feature and even of his expression upon the screen before them. The attitude in which he sat was his favourite one when he was plunged in thought, his hands resting on his knees and his gaze fixed on vacancy. He was thinking of his triumph, and of all that he had gone through to win it, and of all that it would bring him. He held the trump cards now, and the game lay in his own hand. He had triumphed, and yet over him hung the shadow of that curse which dogs the presence of our accomplished desires. Too often, even with the innocent, does the seed of our destruction lurk in the rich blossom of our hopes, and much more is this so with the guilty. Somehow this thought was present with him to-night, and in a rough half-educated way he grasped its truth. Once more the saying of the old Boer general rose in his mind : 'I believe that there is a God—I believe that God sets a limit to a man's doings. If he is going too far, *God kills him.*'

What a dreadful thing it would be if the old fool were right after all ! Supposing that there were a God, and God were to kill him to-night, and hurry off his soul, if he had one, to some dim place of unending fear ! All his superstitions awoke at the thought, and he shivered so violently that the shadow of the shiver caused the outlines of the gigantic form upon the canvas to tremble visibly.

Then, rising with an angry curse, Muller hastily threw off his outer clothing, and having turned down but not extinguished the rough paraffine lamp, he flung himself upon the little camp bedstead, which creaked and groaned beneath his weight like a thing in pain.

Now came silence, only broken by the drip, drip of the rain from the gum leaves overhead, and the rattling of the boughs whenever a breath of air stirred them. It was an eerie and depressing night, a night that might well have tried the nerves of any strong man who, wet through and worn out, was obliged to crouch upon the open veldt and endure it. How much more awful was it then to the unfortunate woman who, half broken-hearted, fever-stricken, and well-nigh crazed with suffering of mind and body, waited in it to see murder done ! Slowly the minutes passed, and at every raindrop or rustle of a bough her guilty conscience summoned up a host of fears. But by the mere power of her will she kept them down.

She would go through with it. Yes, she would go through with it. Surely he must be asleep by now!

They crept up to the tent and placed their ears within two inches of his head. Yes, he was asleep; the sound of his breathing rose and fell with the regularity of an infant's.

Jess turned round and touched her companion upon the shoulder. He did not move, but she felt that his arm was shaking.

'*Now*,' she whispered.

Still he hung back. It was evident to her that the long waiting had taken the courage out of him.

'Be a man,' she whispered again, so low that the sound scarcely reached his ears although her lips were almost touching them, 'go, and mind you strike home!'

Then at last she heard him softly draw the great knife from the sheath, and in another second he had glided from her side. Presently she saw the line of light that streamed upon the darkness through the opening of the tent broaden a little, and by this she knew that he was creeping in upon his dreadful errand. Then she turned her head and put her fingers in her ears. But even so she could see a long line of shadow travelling across the skirt of the tent. So she shut her eyes also, and waited sick at heart, for she did not dare to move.

Presently—it might have been five minutes or only half a minute afterwards, for she had lost count of time —Jess felt somebody touch her on the arm. It was Jantjé.

'*Is it done?*' she whispered again.

He shook his head and drew her away from the tent. In going her foot caught in one of the guy-ropes and stirred it slightly.

'I could not do it, missie,' he said. 'He is asleep and

looks just like a child. When I lifted the knife he smiled in his sleep and all the strength went out of my arm, so that I could not strike. And then before I grew strong again the spook of the old Englishwoman came and hit me in the back, and I ran away.'

If a look could have blasted a human being Jantjé would assuredly have been blasted then. The man's cowardice maddened Jess, but whilst she still choked with wrath a duiker buck, which had come down from its stony home to feed upon the rose bushes, suddenly sprang with a crash almost from their feet, passing away like a grey gleam into the utter darkness.

Jess started, then recovered herself, guessing what it was, but the miserable Hottentot, overcome with terror, fell upon the ground groaning out that it was the spook of the old Englishwoman. He had dropped the knife as he fell, and Jess, seeing the imminent peril in which they were placed, knelt down, found it, and hissed into his ear that if he were not quiet she would kill him.

This pacified him a little, but no earthly power could persuade him to enter the tent again.

What was to be done? What could she do? For two minutes or more she buried her face in her wet hands and thought wildly and despairingly.

Then a dark and dreadful determination entered her mind. The man Muller should not escape. Bessie should not be sacrificed to him. Rather than that, she would do the deed herself.

Without a word she rose, animated by the tragic agony of her purpose and the force of her despair, and glided towards the tent, the great knife in her hand. Now, ah! all too soon, she was inside of it, and stood for a second to allow her eyes to grow accustomed to the light. Presently she began to see, first the outline of the bed, then the outline of the manly form stretched upon it, then both bed and man distinctly. Jantjé had said that he was sleeping like a child. He might have been; now he was *not*. On the contrary, his face was convulsed like the face of one in an extremity of fear, and great beads of sweat stood upon his brow. It was as though he knew his danger, and yet was utterly powerless to avoid it. He lay upon his back. One heavy arm, his left, hung over the side of the bed, the knuckles of the hand resting on the ground; the other was thrown back, and his head was pillowed upon it. The clothing had slipped away from his throat and massive chest, which were quite bare.

Jess stood and gazed. 'For Bessie's sake, for Bessie's sake!' she murmured; then impelled by a force that seemed to move of itself she crept slowly, slowly, to the right-hand side of the bed.

At this moment Muller woke, and his opening eyes fell full upon her face. Whatever his dream had been, what he now saw was far more terrible, for bending over him was the *ghost of the woman he had murdered in the Vaal!* There she was, risen from her river grave, torn, dishevelled, water yet dripping from her hands and hair. Those sunk and marble cheeks, those dreadful flaming eyes could belong to no human being, but only to a spirit. It was the spirit of Jess Croft, of the woman whom he had slain, come back to tell him that there *was* a living vengeance and a hell!

Their eyes met, and no creature will ever know the agony of terror that he tasted of before the end came. She saw his face sink in and turn ashen grey while the cold sweat ran from every pore. He was awake, but fear paralysed him, he could not speak or move.

He was awake, and she could hesitate no more. . . .

He must have seen the flash of the falling steel, and——

Jess was outside the tent again, the red knife in her hand. She flung the accursed thing from her. That shriek must have awakened every soul within a mile. Already she could faintly hear the stir of men down by the waggon, and the patter of the feet of Jantjé running for his life.

Then she too turned, and fled straight up the hill. She knew not whither, she cared not where! None saw her or followed her, the hunt had broken away to the left after Jantjé. Her heart was lead and her brain a rocking sea of fire, whilst before her, around her, and behind her yelled all the conscience-created furies that run Murder to his lair.

On she flew, one sight only before her eyes, one sound only in her ears. On over the hill, far into the rain and the night!

CHAPTER XXXIV

TANTA COETZEE TO THE RESCUE

AFTER Jess had been set free by the Boers outside Hans Coetzee's place, John was sharply ordered to dismount and off-saddle his horse. This he did with the best grace that he could muster, and the horse was knee-haltered and let loose to feed. It was then indicated to him that he was to enter the house, and this he also did, closely attended by two of the Boers. The room into which he was conducted was the same that he had first become acquainted with, on the occasion of the buck hunt that had so nearly ended in his murder. There was the Buckenhout table, and there were the stools and couches made of stinkwood. Also, in the biggest chair at the other end of the room, a moderate-sized slop-basin full of coffee by her side, sat Tanta Coetzee, still actively employed in doing absolutely nothing. There, too, were the showily dressed maidens, there was the sardonic lover of one of them, and all the posse of young men with rifles. The 'sit-kammer' and its characteristics were quite unchanged, and on entering it John felt inclined to rub his eyes and wonder whether the events of the last few months had been nothing but a dream.

The only thing that had changed was his welcome. Evidently he was not expected to shake hands all round on the present occasion. Fallen indeed would that Boer have been considered who, within a few days of Majuba, offered to shake hands with a wretched English rooibaatje, picked up like a lame buck on the veldt. At the least he would have kept the ceremony for private celebration, if only out of respect to the feelings of others. On this occasion John's entry was received in icy silence. The old woman did not deign to look up, the young ones shrugged their shoulders and turned their backs, as though they had suddenly seen something that was not nice. Only the countenance of the sardonic lover softened to a grin.

John walked to the end of the room where there was a vacant chair and stood by it.

'Have I your permission to sit down, ma'am?' he said at last in a loud tone, addressing the old lady.

'Dear Lord!' said the old lady to the man next to her, 'what a voice the poor creature has! it is like a bull's. What does he say?'

The man explained.

'The floor is the right place for Englishmen and Kafirs,' said the old lady, 'but after all he is a man, and perhaps sore with riding. Englishmen always get sore when they try to ride. Then with startling energy she shouted out:

'*Sit !*'

'I will show the rooibaatje that he is not the only one with a voice,' she added by way of explanation.

A subdued sniggle followed this sally of wit, during which John took his seat with such native grace as he could command, which at the moment was not much.

'Dear me!' she went on presently, for she was a bit of a humorist, 'he looks very dirty and pale, doesn't he? I suppose the poor thing has been hiding in the ant-bear holes with nothing to eat. I am told that up in the Drakensberg yonder the ant-bear holes are full of English-

men. They had rather starve in them than come out,
for fear lest they should meet a Boer.'

This provoked another snigger, and then the young
ladies took up the ball.

'Are you hungry, rooibaatje?' asked one in English.

John was boiling with fury, but he was also starving,
so he answered that he was.

'Tie his hands behind him, and let us see if he
can catch in his mouth, like a dog,' suggested a gentle
youth.

'No, no; make him eat pap with a wooden spoon,
like a Kafir,' said another. 'I will feed him—if you have
a very long spoon.'

Here again was legitimate cause for merriment, but in
the end matters were compromised by a lump of biltong
and a piece of bread being thrown to John from the
other end of the room. He caught them and began to
eat, trying to conceal his ravenous hunger as much as
possible from the circle of onlookers who clustered round
to watch the operation.

'Carolus,' said the old lady to the sardonic affianced
of her daughter, 'there are three thousand men in the
British army.'

'Yes, my aunt.'

'There are three thousand men in the British army,'
she repeated, looking round angrily as though somebody
had questioned the truth of her statement. 'I tell you
that my grandfather's brother was at Cape Town in the
time of Governor Smith, and he counted the whole
British army, and there were three thousand of them.'

'That is so, my aunt,' answered Carolus.

'Then why did you contradict me, Carolus?'

'I did not intend to, my aunt.'

'I should hope not, Carolus; it would vex the dear

Lord to see a boy with a squint' (Carolus was slightly afflicted in this way) 'contradict his future mother-in-law. Tell me how many Englishmen were killed at Laing's Nek?'

'Nine hundred,' replied Carolus promptly.

'And at Ingogo?'

'Six hundred and twenty.'

'And at Majuba?'

'One thousand.'

'Then that makes two thousand five hundred men; yes, and the rest were finished at Bronker's Spruit. Nephews, that rooibaatje there,' pointing to John, 'is one of the last men left in the British army.'

Most of her audience appeared to accept this argument as conclusive, but some mischievous spirit put it into the breast of the saturnine Carolus to contradict her, notwithstanding the lesson he had just received.

'That is not so, my aunt; there are many damned Englishmen still sneaking about the Nek, and also at Pretoria and Wakkerstroom.'

'I tell you it is a lie,' said the old lady, raising her voice, 'they are only Kafirs and camp-followers. There were three thousand men in the British army, and now they are all killed except that rooibaatje. How dare you contradict your future mother-in-law, you dirty squint-eyed, yellow-faced monkey? There, take that!' and before the unfortunate Carolus knew where he was, he received the slop-basin with its contents full in the face. The bowl broke upon the bridge of his nose, and the coffee flew all about him, into his eyes and hair, down his throat and over his body, making such a spectacle of him as must have been seen to be appreciated.

'Ah!' went on the old lady, much soothed and gratified by the eminent and startling success of her shot, 'never you say again that I don't know how to throw a basin of coffee. I haven't practised at my man Hans for thirty years for nothing, I can tell you. Now you, Carolus, I have taught you not to contradict; go and wash your face and we will have supper.'

Carolus ventured no reply, and was led away by his betrothed half blinded and utterly subdued, while her sister set the table for the evening meal. When it was ready the men sat down to meat and the women waited on them. John was not asked to join them, but one of the girls threw him a boiled mealiecob, for which, being still very hungry, he was duly grateful, and afterwards he managed to secure a mutton bone and another bit of bread.

When supper was over, some bottles of peach brandy were produced, and the Boers began to drink freely, and then it was that matters commenced to look dangerous for the Englishman. Suddenly one of the men remembered about the young fellow whom John had thrown backwards off the horse, and who was lying very sick in the next room, and suggested that measures of retaliation should be taken, which would undoubtedly have been done if the elderly Boer who had commanded the party had not interposed. This man was getting drunk like the others, but fortunately for John he grew amiably drunk.

'Let him alone,' he said, 'let him alone. We will send him to the commandant to-morrow. Frank Muller will know how to deal with him.'

John thought to himself that he certainly would.

'Now, for myself,' the man went on with a hiccough, 'I bear no malice. We have thrashed the British and they have given up the country, so let bygones be bygones, I say, Almighty, yes! I am not proud, not I. If an Englishman takes off his hat to me I shall acknowledge it.'

This staved the fellows off for a while, but presently John's protector went away, and then the others became playful. They took their rifles and amused themselves with levelling them at him, and making sham bets as to where they would hit him. John, seeing the emergency, backed his chair well into the corner of the wall and drew his revolver, which fortunately for himself he still had.

'If any man interferes with me, by God, I'll shoot him!' he said in good English, which they did not fail to understand. Undoubtedly as the evening went on it was only the possession of this revolver and his evident determination to use it that saved his life.

At last things grew very bad indeed, so bad that John found it absolutely necessary to keep his eyes continually fixed, now on one and now on another, to prevent their putting a bullet through him unawares. He had twice appealed to the old woman, but she sat in her big chair with a sweet smile upon her fat face and refused to interfere. It is not every day that a Boer 'frau' has the chance of seeing a real live English rooibaatje baited like an ant-bear on the flat.

Presently, just as John in desperation was making up his mind to begin shooting right and left, and take his chance of cutting his way out, the saturnine Carolus, whose temper had never recovered the bowl of coffee, and who was besides very drunk, rushed forward with an oath and dealt a tremendous blow at him with the butt-end of his rifle. John dodged the blow, which fell upon the back of the chair and smashed it to bits, and in another second Carolus's gentle soul would have departed to a better sphere, had not the old frau, seeing that the game had gone beyond a joke, waddled down the room with marvellous activity and thrown herself between them.

'There, there,' she said, cuffing right and left with her fat fists, 'be off with you, every one. I can't have this noise going on here. Come, off you all go, and get the horses into the stable; they will be right away by morning if you trust them to the Kafirs.'

Carolus collapsed, and the other men also hesitated and drew back, whereupon, following up her advantage, the old woman, to John's astonishment and relief, bundled the whole tribe of them bodily out of the front door.

'Now then, rooibaatje,' said the old lady briskly when they had gone, 'I like you because you are a brave man, and were not afraid when they mobbed you. Also, I don't want to have a mess made upon my floor here, or any noise or shooting. If those men come back and find you here they will first get rather drunker and then kill you, so you had better be off while you have the chance,' and she pointed to the door.

'I really am much obliged to you, my aunt,' said John, utterly astonished to find that she possessed a heart at all, and more or less had been playing a part throughout the evening.

'Oh, as to that,' she said drily, 'it would be a great pity to kill the last English rooibaatje in the whole British army; they ought to keep you as a curiosity. Here, take a tot of brandy before you go; it is a wet night, and sometimes when you are clear of the Transvaal and remember this business, remember, too, that you owe your life to Tanta Coetzee. But I would not have saved you, not I, if you had not been so plucky. I like a man to be a man, and not like that miserable monkey Carolus. There, be off!'

John poured out and swallowed half a tumblerful of the brandy, and in another moment he was outside the house and had slipped off into the night. It was very dark and wet, for the rain-clouds had covered up the moon, and he soon learned that any attempt to look for his horse would end in failure and probably in his recapture. The only thing to do was to get away on foot in the direction of Mooifontein as quickly as he could; so off he went down the track across the veldt as fast as his stiff legs would take him. He had a ten miles trudge before him, and with that cheerful acquiescence in circumstances over which he had no control which was one of his characteristics, he set to work to make the best of it. For the first hour or so all went well, then to his intense disgust he discovered that he was off the track, a fact at which anybody who has ever had the pleasure of wandering along a so-called road on the African veldt on a dark night will scarcely be surprised.

After wasting a quarter of an hour or more in a vain attempt to find the path, John struck out boldly for a dim mass that loomed in the distance, and which he took to be Mooifontein Hill. And so it was, only instead of keeping to the left, when he would have arrived at the house, or rather where the house had stood, unwittingly he bore to the right, and thus went half round the hill before he found out his mistake. Nor would he have discovered it then had he not chanced in the mist and darkness to turn into the mouth of the great gorge known as Leuwen Kloof, where once, months ago, he had had an interesting talk with Jess just before she went to Pretoria. It was whilst he was blundering and stumbling up this gorge that at length the rain ceased and the moon revealed herself, it being then nearly midnight. Her very first rays lit upon one of the extraordinary pillars of balanced boulders, and by it he recognised the locality. As may be imagined, strong man though he was, by this time John was quite exhausted. For nearly a week he had been travelling incessantly, and for the last two nights he had not only not slept, but also had endured much mental excitement and bodily peril. Were it not for the brandy that Tanta Coetzee gave him he could never have tramped the fifteen miles or so of ground which he had covered. Now he was quite broken down, and felt that the only thing which he could do, wet through as he was, would be to lie down somewhere, and sleep or die as the case might be. Then it was that he remembered the little cave near the top of the Kloof, the same from which Jess had watched the thunder-storm. He had visited it once with Bessie after their engagement, and she had told him that it was one of her sister's favourite haunts.

If he could but reach the cave at any rate he would find shelter and a dry place to lie in. It could not be more than three hundred yards away. So he struggled on bravely through the wet grass and over the scattered boulders, till at last he came to the base of the huge column that had been shattered by the lightning before Jess's eyes.

Thirty paces more and John was in the cave.

With a sigh of utter exhaustion he flung himself down upon the rocky floor, and almost instantly was buried in a profound sleep.

CHAPTER XXXV

THE CONCLUSION OF THE MATTER

WHEN the rain ceased and the moon began to shine, Jess was still fleeing like a wild thing across the plain on the top of the mountain. She felt no sense of exhaustion now or even of weariness; her only idea was to get away, right away somewhere, where she could lose herself and nobody would ever see her again. Presently she reached the top of Leuwen Kloof, and recognising the spot in a bewildered way she began to descend it. Here was a place where she might lie till she died, for no one ever came there, except now and again some wandering Kafir herd. On she sprang, from rock to rock, a wild and eerie figure, well in keeping with the solemn and titanic sadness of the place.

Twice she fell, once right into the stream, but she took no heed, she did not even seem to feel it. At last she was at the bottom, now creeping like a black dot across the wide spaces of moonlight, and now swallowed up in the shadow. There before her gaped the mouth of the little cave; her strength was leaving her at last, and she was fain to crawl into it, broken-hearted, crazed, and —*dying*.

'Oh, God, forgive me! God forgive me!' she moaned as she sank upon the rocky floor. 'Bessie, I sinned against you, but I have washed away my sin. I did it for you, Bessie love, not for myself. I had rather have died than kill him for myself. You will marry John now, and you will never, never know what I did for you. I am going to die. I know that. I am dying. Oh, if only I could see his face once more before I die—before I die !'

Slowly the westering moonlight crept down the blackness of the rock. Now at last it peeped into the little cave and played upon John's sleeping face lying within six feet of her. Her prayer had been granted; there was her lover by her side.

With a start and a great sigh of doubt she recognised him. Was it a vision? Was he dead? She dragged herself to him upon her hands and knees and listened for his breathing, if perchance he still breathed and was not a wraith. Then it came, strong and slow, the breath of a man in deep sleep.

So he lived. Should she try to wake him? What for? To tell him she was a murderess and then to let him see her die? For instinct told her that nature was exhausted; and she knew that she was certainly going— going fast. No, a hundred times no !

Only she put her hand into her breast, and drawing out the pass on the back of which she had written her last message to him, she thrust it between his listless fingers. It should speak for her. Then she leant over him, and watched his sleeping face, a very incarnation of infinite, despairing tenderness, and love that is deeper than the grave. And as she watched, gradually her feet and legs grew cold and numb, till at length she could feel nothing below her bosom. She was dead nearly to the heart. Well, it was better so !

The rays of the moon faded slowly from the level of the little cave, and John's face grew dark to her darkening

sight.   She bent down and kissed him once—twice—
thrice.

At last the end came.   There was a great flashing of
light before her eyes, and within her ears the roaring as
of a thousand seas, and her head sank gently on her
lover's breast as on a pillow; and there Jess died and
passed upward towards the wider life and larger liberty,
or, at the least, downward into the depths of rest.

Poor dark-eyed, deep-hearted Jess!   This was the
fruition of her love, and this her bridal bed.

It was done.   She had gone, taking with her the
secret of her self-sacrifice and crime, and the night-winds
moaning amidst the rocks sang their requiem over her.
Here she first had learned her love, and here she closed its
book on earth.

She might have been a great and a good woman.
She might even have been a happy woman.   But fate
had ordained it otherwise.   Women such as Jess are
rarely happy in the world.   It is not worldly wise to
stake all one's fortune on a throw, and lack the craft to
load the dice.   Well, her troubles are done with.   Think
gently of her and let her pass in peace!

The hours grew on towards the morning, but John,
the dead face of the woman he had loved still pillowed on
his breast, neither dreamed nor woke.   There was a
strange and dreadful irony in the situation, an irony
which sometimes finds its counterpart in our waking life,
but still the man slept, and the dead girl lay till the night
turned into the morning and the earth woke up as usual.
The sunbeams slid into the cave, and played indifferently
upon the ashen face and tangled curls, and on the broad
chest of the living man whereon they rested.   An old
baboon peeped round the rocky edge and manifested no

surprise, only indignation, at the intrusion of humanity, dead or alive, into his dominions. Yes, the world woke up as usual, and recked not and troubled not because Jess was dead.

It is so accustomed to such sights.

At last John woke up also. He stretched his arms yawning, and for the first time became aware of the weight upon his breast. He glanced down and saw dimly at first—then more clearly.

There are some things into which it is wisest not to pry, and one of them is the first agony of a strong man's grief.

Happy was it for John that his brain did not give way in that lonely hour of bottomless despair. But he lived through it, as we do live through such things, and was sane and sound after it, though it left its mark upon his life.

Two hours later a gaunt, haggard figure stumbled down the hill-side towards the site of Mooifontein, bearing something in his arms. The whole place was in commotion. Here and there were knots of Boers talking excitedly, who, when they saw the man coming, hurried up to learn who it was and what he carried. But when they knew, they fell back awed and without a word, and John too passed through them without a word. For a moment he hesitated, seeing that the house was burnt down. Then he turned into the waggon-shed, and laid his burden down on the saw-bench where Frank Muller had sat as judge upon the previous day.

Now at last John spoke in a hoarse voice : ' Where is the old man ? '

One of them pointed to the door of the little room.

' Open it ! ' he said, so fiercely that again they fell back and obeyed him without a word.

'John! John!' cried Silas Croft, rising amazed from his seat upon a sack. 'Thank God—you have come back to us from the dead!' and trembling with joy and surprise he would have fallen on his neck.

'Hush!' he answered; 'I have brought the dead with me.'

And he led him to where Jess lay.

During the day all the Boers went away and left them alone. Now that Frank Muller lay dead there was no thought among them of carrying out the sentence upon their old neighbour. Besides, there was no warrant for the execution, even had they desired so to do, for their commandant died leaving it unsigned. So they held an informal inquest upon their leader's body, and buried him in the little graveyard that was walled in on the hill-side at the back of where the house had stood, and planted with the four red gums, one at each corner. Rather than be at the pains of hollowing another grave, they buried him in the very place that he had caused to be dug to receive the body of Silas Croft.

Who had murdered Frank Muller was and remains a mystery among them to this day. The knife was identified by natives about the farm as belonging to the Hottentot Jantjé, and a Hottentot had been seen running from the place of the deed and hunted for some way, but he could not be caught or heard of again. Therefore many of them are of opinion that he is the guilty man. Others, again, believe that the crime rests upon the shoulders of the villainous one-eyed Kafir, Hendrik, Muller's own servant, who had also vanished. But as they have never found either of them, and are not likely to do so, the point remains a moot one. Nor, indeed, did they take any great pains to hunt for them. Frank Muller was not a popular character, and the fact of a man coming to a mysterious end does not produce any great sensation among a rough people and in rough times.

On the following day, old Silas Croft, Bessie, and John Niel also buried their dead in the little graveyard on the hill-side, and there Jess lies, with some ten feet of earth only between her and the man upon whom she was the instrument of vengeance. But they never knew this, or even guessed it. They never knew indeed that she had been near Mooifontein on that awful night. Nobody knew it except Jantjé; and Jantjé, haunted by the foot-fall of the pursuing Boers, was gone from the ken of the white man far into the heart of Central Africa.

'John,' said the old man when they had filled in the grave, 'this is no country for Englishmen. Let us go home to England.' John bowed his head in assent, for he could not speak. Fortunately means were not wanting, although practically they were both ruined. The thousand pounds that John had paid to Silas as the price of a third interest in the farm still lay to the credit of the latter in the Standard Bank at Newcastle, in Natal, together with another two hundred and fifty pounds in cash.

And so in due course they went.

Now what more is there to tell? Jess, to those who read what has been written as it is meant to be read, was the soul of it all, and Jess—is dead. It is useless to set a lifeless thing upon its feet, rather let us strive to follow the soarings of the spirit. Jess is dead and her story at an end.

.   .   .   .

So but one word more.

After some difficulty, John Niel, within three months of his arrival in England, obtained employment as a land agent to a large estate in Rutlandshire, which position he fills to this day, with credit to himself and such advantage to the property as can be expected in these times. Also, in due course he became the beloved husband of sweet Bessie Croft, and on the whole he may be considered a happy man. At times, however, a sorrow overcomes him of which his wife knows nothing, and for a while he is not himself.

He is not a man much addicted to sentiment or speculation, but sometimes when his day's work is done, and he strays to his garden gate and looks out at the dim and peaceful English landscape beyond, and thence to the wide star-strewn heavens above, he wonders if the hour will ever come when once more he will see those dark and passionate eyes, and hear that sweet remembered voice.

For John feels as near to his lost love now that she is dead as he felt while she was yet alive. From time to time indeed he seems to know without possibility of doubt that if, when death is done with, there should prove to be an individual future for us suffering mortals, as he for one believes, certainly he will find Jess waiting to greet him at its gates.

THE END